The Banker's Ex-Wife

Phil Lawder

ISBN: 978-1-9997129-0-7

For Jeannine

P. M. LAWDER

Table of Contents

THE BANKER'S EX-WIFE

'Do bear in mind, we have a very exclusive clientele. Given the range of services on offer at this establishment, things can sometimes become, well, a little competitive. Some people may, to be blunt, rather overestimate their own attractiveness. So, there's a lot of responsibility attached to this job and a need for quiet persuasiveness, when necessary.'

Charles finished his carefully prepared speech and looked across at the short man opposite him. He was seated, ramrod straight, listening with head tilted slightly to one side above a carefully knotted green and red striped tie that nestled in a slightly frayed but perfectly ironed collar. Charles was reminded of a particular prep schoolteacher, about whom he still occasionally dreamed.

Though the man's feet barely touched the floor, there was an air of quiet confidence about him that Charles found reassuring. This was, after all, a business where first impressions mattered. He leaned back behind the glass and chrome desk, placed the tips of his fingers together and waited for a response.

The shorter man's gaze never left Charles' face.

'Ah, yes, Mr Charles,' he said with a slow nod, 'as the inhabitants of Uttar Pradesh are wont to say, whether they make love or they make war, the elephants will always make a dreadful mess of your front lawn.'

'Um, quite. Yes.' Charles' brow furrowed then cleared. He stood, hand outstretched. 'Well, we seem to understand each other. I think. The job's yours.'

He winced at the firmness of the other man's grasp, then quickly changed it to a smile.

'By the way, I don't seem to have your first name down here.'

'Muddle will be quite sufficient, Mr Charles.'

Chapter 1

BEFORE IT ALL WENT WRONG

Kate Bradshaw stood at the top of the steps that lead down from the divorce court. A summer sun glistened on her carefully applied make-up.

She felt very pleased with herself.

It had all gone extremely smoothly, greatly helped by the Bastard Stephen not turning up but just sending in his weasel lawyer. 'My client wishes to ensure that he does the honourable thing, blah blah blah blah.' Ninety-nine per cent of the population might consider bankers little better than pondweed but being married to one had its uses, even if he was well short of being one of the Masters of the Universe, barely, it seemed to her, Master of the Postal District. And being just divorced from one was even better. She had the house, a decent regular payment and use of the Florida apartment for a month each year. Unfortunately, she also had the children.

'A most satisfactory outcome, my dear,' a rotund voice murmured behind her. She turned as George, her barrister, leaned in towards her, bouncing on his toes. 'I think we should, ah, go and celebrate,' he smirked with a waggle of caterpillar eyebrows. Kate looked at the sparse grey hair carefully combed across above a flabby face, the bundle of shirt showing through between waistcoat and trouser band. His aftershave hit her full in the face, even in the open air, a blend of loo cleaner and animal sweat, no doubt very expensive and probably highly flammable.

Of course she had flirted with him during the interminable meetings as they had planned their campaign. But why did men always misunderstand? A hand on their arm, a look from under the lashes were not invitations to bed, they were just a natural way of communicating for a girl like her, even for a, she suppressed a brief shudder, thirty-six-year-old girl like her. She answered his raised-eyebrow anticipation with an apologetic dip of the head.

'Perhaps another time, George, darling, I have to go and meet people for lunch,' she murmured, deflating his ego and increasing his fee. Leaving him standing forlornly, she stepped into a taxi, leaned back and headed for Chelsea. The future that stretched ahead of her was a clear, cloudless sky, a sybaritic swirl of fine perfumes, delicious food and subservient shop assistants.

Looking back on that moment two months later, she could not believe how naïve she had been.

She pulled her phone from the capacious handbag and dialled Jane's number.

'Hi, I'm on my way.'

'Darling, how did it go?'

'Pretty good, got just about everything. Still got the kids but I guess they'll spend time with their father.'

'Yes, lots, if you can arrange it. Make sure they are miserable at home. Worked for me. I got the house, he got the brat. Two nil to me.'

'Well, I don't think I dislike them that much.'

'You will, darling, you will.'

Lunch was long and liquid, all the girls around the table full of stories of the idiocy of men. Kate, aware that she had no stories to add, was happy to sit back and listen. She looked around at the slim-hipped waiters, trying hard to ogle and fantasise with the others. It did not come easily and made her feel slightly foolish. Still, practice would make perfect. She tuned back in as Jane reached the climax of her story.

'Of course, as far as he was concerned, I should fall to my knees in gratitude and do whatever one does on one's knees, just because he'd spent the last ten minutes telling me about how rich he was and what a big, throbbing motor car he had. So, I drew myself up to my full five foot nothing and explained. "Look, whatever your name is" always a good deflator, that one, "why don't you just get back into that little car of yours, which, I notice, has a very small bonnet, and toddle off to the youth club. I'm sure you'll find something more your size there." God, it felt good!'

Laughing with the rest, Kate understood what she had been missing for so long. She decided that this was how it would be from now on. Good times, relaxing with friends. To hell with men.

After lunch Jane suggested a couple of hours of celebratory shopping. By five thirty, Kate was laden with bags and her feet, tucked into tightly fitting Manolos to impress the judge, were starting to complain. After one more skinny latte, she bade a tired but contented farewell to Jane.

'Now, darling, we must get you out in the field again.' Jane looked across at Kate's confused face. 'Into the game, on the market. Manhunting, darling.'

'Oh, right. Yes, but a bit more shopping first, I think.'

'Absolutely. Must bait the trap, darling.'

With a promise to do it all again very soon, Kate eased herself into a cab for the long ride back to Teddington, surrounded by the spoils of the afternoon. If she had judged it right, the au pair would have fed the kids, who would now be glued to their separate screens, one to interminable soap operas, the other destroying enemy hoards at the press of a button and the flick of a skinny wrist.

She opened the panelled front door, staggering slightly under the weight of the shopping and the liquid lunch. As she stepped into the spacious hall, a smile spread across her face. Mine, she thought, all mine. Suppressing a giggle at sounding like one of Disney's more wicked witches, she dropped her bags on and around the glass-topped table in the hall and walked through to the kitchen. From the American double-fronted fridge she took a bottle of Sauvignon and poured herself a large one. Glass in hand, Kate sauntered into the sitting room.

This was her favourite room, the far end dominated by a large plasma screen and a cluster of three white leather sofas arranged around it so as to pick up the best of the cinema quality sound system. On the white walls were four enormous, brightly coloured paintings of beaches and beautiful people that she had persuaded Stephen to buy on holiday in Jamaica. The only thing that spoilt the symmetry was Miranda, fifteen years of concentrated moods and moral outrage, stretched out on one of the sofas facing the screen. Ignoring the other seats, Kate walked over to her.

'Budge up.'

'Oh, God, mum. Why can't you sit over there like any normal person?'

"Cos I want to sit next to my little Mandy-wandy.'

'God, are you pissed, or what?'

'No I am not. Now shut up and move over.' With a sigh and a tut that could have won an Oscar, Miranda swung her legs round and shrank back into the corner of the sofa.

'What you watching?' asked Kate as she settled down.

'What does it look like?'

'It looks like all the other things you watch incessantly all week. Cute American or Australian or whatever girls with old-fashioned hair-dos deciding whether they will let dumb but well hung boys have their wicked ways.'

'Why do you always have to bring everything down to sex?'

'Because, darling child, that's what everything comes down to in the end, as you will find out.' And, feeling this was a good exit line, she left the room, glass in hand, but not before she heard Miranda mutter, 'so how come you're not getting any'.

It was a good question but one that Kate did not wish to explore just at that moment.

Kate climbed the curved staircase. In his bedroom, Tom was hunched over the computer screen. She paused by the door. He'd been such a nice little kid, lively and so cute in his OshKosh dungarees and tiny Reebok trainers. Where had this ghastly, gangly, spotty youth come from? His limbs seemed to sprout out of the skinny body like spider's legs.

'What?'

She was still not used to the gruff voice that had replaced, after a long struggle, the childish treble. 'Nothing, darling.

Haven't you beaten the Germans yet?'

"Macedonians. They didn't have Germans in the tenth century.'

'Oh, but they had computers, did they?'

'Ha, bloody ha.'

'Remember what I was doing today?'

'Spending Dad's money?'

'Well, that too but I also got divorced from your father. Remember?'

Tom sat back for a moment, staring silently at the screen. 'Does this mean we don't see Dad any more?'

Kate started to reach out to put a hand on his shoulder, then thought better of it. 'Of course not. You know he's working away a lot right now but he'll be back and will see you. Of course he will. It's all in the paperwork; he'll see you a couple of times a month and take you both on holidays with him.' My God, I hope he does, she thought. I don't want to be stuck with these two all the time.

Tom put his head in his hands. 'So now it's official. I have been abandoned in a house full of women – you, Miranda, Ingrid or whatever next week's au pair is going to be called. It's so bloody unfair.' His hands returned to the mouse and his eyes to the screen. "Oh," he added rather too nonchalantly, "does this mean we are going to be hard up?"

"Darling boy," Kate replied triumphantly, "Your father is a banker."

"And..?"

"And that means an endless supply of money. People seem to pay him an obscene amount of money for moving bits of paper around, as far as I can see. Not that I'm complaining."

"Hm." Reassured, Tom was now totally refocused on the annihilation of Macedonians.

'Fine," announced Kate to no one in particular. "Since neither of you seem to want a conversation about anything to do with how I might be feeling, I'm off for a long, perfumed soak in the bath and then another look at that Colin Farrell movie up in my room.' But first, Kate headed back downstairs to refuel on the Sauvignon. As she came to the hall the phone rang. Kate peered at the Caller ID. It showed the word 'Gorgon', a code that Stephen, in one of his more jocular moods, had put in to warn that her mother was ringing.

'Don't pick up, anyone,' she called. The ringing stopped abruptly and, from the sitting room, she could hear Miranda, suddenly as sweet as apples. 'Hello, Granny, how are you?' She rushed through the door and signalled to Miranda to say she was not yet home. Her daughter looked up, smiled and she said into the phone, 'Yes, Mum's here. I'll pass you over.' With a curtsey and a smug grin, the phone was handed across. Kate gave Miranda a sour look and took the receiver back out to the hall.

'Hello, Mum,' Kate sighed. Her mother's refined Yorkshire tones, Thora Hird with more than a hint of Rottweiler, surged into her ear.

'Kate, dear, we've been so worried about you today. We did think you might at least have called us. How did it all go? Mrs Dorris, her from next door, came round this afternoon, she said for a cup of sugar but I happen to know she's diabetic and if she isn't she jolly well should be, but I know she was just snooping, wanting to know how you'd got on. Well, of course I couldn't tell her, though mind you I wouldn't have told her even if I had known, which I didn't. Was Stephen there? I thought he looked very thin when he called round last week.'

'Whoa. Just a minute, Mum. Did you say that Stephen, as in my now ex-husband, came to see you last week? What was he doing in Sheffield and what the hell was he wanting?'

'Language, dear. We don't want those London habits rubbing off on you. No, he said he was just in the area on business and wanted a chat. Such a nice lad, really. Such a pity you didn't manage to make a go of it. By the way, your father sends his regards.'

'Wanted a chat about what?'

'Oh, this and that. Nothing important. Now, what about that hoo-ha on *The Archers*. What is the world coming to?'

It was clear to Kate that she was not going to get any more

information out of her mother this night. 'Mum, it's been a long and difficult day. I just want to have a quiet evening with the kids.'

'Well, I'm sure I'm not stopping you, dear. I just phoned to find out about my daughter's difficult day but if it's too much trouble, I've got something in the oven anyway, one of those Delilah Smith recipes. She's so much nicer than that awful sweary man, whatever his name is. You know, I'm sure that you can taste the swearing in his food, not that I would ever cook one of his dishes. By the way, your sister called, her regular mid-week phone call. She's got another promotion, Head of Department now.'

Kate winced. 'Your sister'. She was sure her mother knew how much more of a blunt instrument that phrase was than the softer 'Angela'. For at least thirty years, 'your sister' had been used to explain to Kate how useless she was, in lessons, at sport, with boys, as a wife and mother and general human being. Well, to hell with them all, thought Kate. I like my life and I'm going to enjoy it.

'Mum, got to go. I'll call you soon. Bye.' And the phone was down before the final reproach could be delivered.

What was Stephen up to? Kate had come to view him in the last year or two as a rather irritating pet, underfoot, not very bright and of limited interest, occasionally inconveniently in need of exercise. But he was something in the City, which meant not only that he was a very good source of money but also that he must be quite bright. For the first time in a very long while, she thought back to their early days, the flat in Tooting, holidays in B&Bs in Brittany. She didn't miss those times – having money was much better – but it reminded her that Stephen was a human being, and therefore capable of doing something nasty.

She shrugged and headed for her room, a warm bath, Sauvignon and Colin Farrell. After luxuriating in expensive bubbles, she lay on the bed, half watching the film. Divorced. Now it was official. She had all the freedom she wanted and the money to go with it. She just wished she felt more excited about it.

The next three weeks were a round of coffees, lunches, shopping and, especially, the gym. Kate realised that, with all the meetings with George the greasy lawyer and rushing around getting papers organised, she had not had time to keep up her fitness regime. A couple of unwanted pounds had crept on. The gym became a regular daily session, the frequency not totally unconnected with the muscular torso of David, her personal trainer. She was always slightly disappointed to find that her children were still home whenever she came in but, apart from that, life was good.

Jane was building up the pressure for Kate to relaunch herself onto the mating market. Rather than do an initial run in public, and, frankly, to buy some time, Kate decided that the hunky David should be her first new conquest. In snatches of gasped conversation between stomach crunches and squats, she tried to build a rapport. She worked hard at being interested in his detailed knowledge of the musculo-skeletal structure and was always sure to enquire after his mother, now living in Littlehampton and the subject of frequent visits. She arrived for each session with hair perfectly in place and regular new outfits. She cooed and fluttered but, whenever she suggested that the discussion could continue over a coffee, David had a reason to decline.

Finally, she turned to Jane for sympathy and advice.

'Obviously bats for the other side, darling.'

'Sorry?'

'Walks with a light step, friend of Dorothy.'

'No, I don't…'

'He's gay, for God's sake. Obsessed with his own body, worships his mother. God, Kate, it's written over his head in neon. How did you miss it? I can see I'm going to have to take you under my wing.'

Kate quickly finished her coffee. Now was not the time to discuss her own lack of experience, that Stephen had been only her second serious boyfriend and memory of the first still made her shudder. She viewed the prospect of being taken under Jane's wing with a mixture of relief and terror. But, if this is what had to be done, then lie back and enjoy it, though perhaps that wasn't the best phrase to use. Meanwhile, there was money to be spent; clothes to be bought, drinks to be drunk, meals to be eaten, gossip to be shared and a complaint to be made about David and his incompetence as a trainer.

Muddle checked his reflection in the tall mirror on the back of his bedroom door. Yes, that was better. A few minutes with needle and thread and the buttons now fitted more snugly, the tassels on the lapels hung straight and true, the torn seam was perfectly aligned.

Clearly, the previous wearer had not appreciated the symbolic significance of a uniform, its value as a statement of all that is good and worthy, of belonging to a greater cause. A suit might make a boy into a man but a uniform made a man into an emperor.

Now there was just the task of shortening the arms, the hem and the trouser legs before the evening began.

Then he could get on with what he'd come here for.

Chapter 2
WHEN IT ALL STARTED

On a bright day in early August, Kate went to the cash machine to draw out enough money to fund a day in town. She punched the £250 button. A page came up that she had never seen before. 'Insufficient funds,' she read. She punched the number again. Same message. She withdrew the card, entered it again, put in the code and hit the £250 button. New wording appeared on the screen. 'Your card has been withheld.' With an expletive about bankers' right-handed habits that shocked the elderly lady standing behind her, she marched into the bank.

'I want to see the manager immediately,' she announced to the first window that was free.

'I'm sorry, I'm afraid Mr Jameson is with a client. Could someone else help you?'

'Your stupid machine clearly doesn't know who I am and seems to think that there is no money in my account. It has eaten my card. I want it put right immediately.'

'One minute, please.' The teller disappeared behind the screen, to reappear four minutes later. 'If you would like to take a seat in that cubicle, madam, Miss Davies, our Assistant Manager, will see you very soon.'

'Assistant? No, dear,' Kate tried a smile, 'I don't deal with assistants.'

'Then I'm afraid you will have to wait for about two hours.' Was there a note of triumph in the voice?

Kate sighed. Loudly. 'Very well. Tell her to hurry. I'm already late for meeting my friends.' Ignoring the stares, grins and mutterings of the lumpen masses around her, Kate went into the cubicle. It smelled of dust, stale coffee and desperation. She stared around at the posters advertising mortgage rates, loan rates and insurance and understood none of it. Seizing the reassuring slimness of her mobile phone, she called Jane's number.

'Darling, I'm going to be late. The bloody bank has made a

mess of things and I need to see some minion about getting it sorted out. Yes, I know, bloody typical. Bye.' She looked up to see a young woman in a black suit watching her from the door of the cubicle. 'Ah, you must be Miss Thingy, come to explain why your bank has cocked up.'

'Mary Davies,' replied the young woman, holding out her hand. 'Assistant Manager. And you are?'

Taken aback, Kate shook the hand. 'Well, they certainly start you young these days. I am Kate Bradshaw and your damned machine won't give me any money.'

'Do you know your account number, Mrs Bradshaw?'

'Ms Bradshaw nowadays,' Kate replied with a tight smile. 'And no, I don't know it. It's on my card and my card, as I hope has been explained to you, is in your machine.'

'Just a moment, then,' and Mary Davies moved to a computer in the corner of the cubicle. Kate watched, impressed in spite of herself, as her fingers confidently pressed a sequence of buttons. Droopy Tom had more dexterity, to be fair, but he stayed in the realms of death, destruction and car chases. This was the real world, the world of money. Within a minute Miss Davies looked up.

'May I have your address, please? And date of birth?' Kate thought that she detected a slight smile from the girl as she asked the last question. She chose to ignore it and gave the information.

'No, Ms Bradshaw, it's quite correct. There is no money in your account.'

'But I should have had a major payment, several thousand, last week. You must have lost it.'

'I don't think so. We are a bank; we tend not to lose money.'

'That's not what the papers say.'

Miss Davies ignored her remark. 'Are you able to check whether it has been sent?'

'Too bloody right I am.'

'Good. You know, we are getting a lot of this at the moment, what with the difficult economic times. What industry is your husband in?"

'He's a banker.'

'Ah. Investment or high street?'

'Something in the city. Investment, I suppose. Certainly not high street, God no.'

Miss Davies' eyebrows shot up. 'Right. Well, I suggest you check him out as soon as you can. In the meantime, we can extend overdraft facilities to you. I'll get the forms. I think it's best if we keep your card for now. It has a very high credit limit that seems inappropriate in the circumstances. Just come in with your chequebook any time that you need cash and that way we can keep everything under control until the money turns up. Or whatever. OK?'

Half an hour later, suffering from writer's cramp, Kate left the bank. Mary Davies watched her go from behind the glass. 'Minion, indeed,' she muttered, and returned to her office.

Kate felt dazed and troubled. Why had the Bastard Stephen not sent through the money? She called Jane again, claimed a headache and cancelled their day's shopping. 'Oh, really, darling. What a shame.' Did she detect a rather knowing tone in Jane's drawl?

She settled into the reassuring leather seat of her Mercedes coupé. Last year's Christmas present, a last ditch attempt by Stephen to fend off an expensive divorce. She had accepted with the necessary squeals of delight, while knowing that the appointment with lawyer George was already in her diary. Stephen had tried to explain to her the significance of the model number but she did not care. As far as she was concerned, its sleek lines and obvious cost said all that she wanted to say about herself.

She scrolled to Stephen's mobile number on her phone. A voice, irritatingly calm and condescendingly female, informed her that this number was no longer in use.

Back home, Kate made herself a strong coffee, looked up the number for Stephen's office and punched it into the phone.

'I wish to speak to Stephen Bradshaw, immediately.'

There was a pause. 'I'm sorry, Mr Bradshaw does not

work here any more. Can anyone else help you?'

Kate dredged her mind for the name of any of the associates that Stephen had endlessly droned on about but no name came. 'Do you have any number for him?'

'No, but I can put you through to Personnel.'

'Yes. Do that.'

'Personnel, may I help you?' The voice seemed to belong to a twelve-year-old who was being forced to speak to a particularly irritating great aunt.

'Well, if you can't help me I will be talking to your boss, so do try to concentrate if only for a few seconds. My name is Kate Bradshaw and I was calling for my husband, my ex-husband, Stephen Bradshaw. OK so far? I understand that he has left. It's very important that I reach him. And you are going to give me his number.'

A heavy sigh. 'Just a moment, I'll look up his file.'

Kate waited, spending the time devising tortures for the chronically stupid to suppress her rising anxiety. At last, the voice was back. 'Now then, yes, here we are. Ah. Um, who did you say was calling?'

'Kate Bradshaw. Still.'

'Er, no, sorry, I'm afraid that we don't have a new contact number for him. I'm so sorry, goodbye.'

The line went dead. Kate stood, receiver in hand, blinking. There was no alternative, she would have to call Stephen himself. Taking a deep breath, she called his mobile.

'The number you are calling has been disconnected.' The smug voice seemed to have been expecting her. With a slightly shaking hand, she dialled her lawyer's number.

'I must speak to George.'

'Who is calling?'

'This is Kate Bradshaw.'

'One moment, Mrs Bradshaw.' Kate decided not to correct her.

'Mrs Bradshaw, I'm sorry but Mr Williams is tied up at the moment. May he call you back later?'

'But I need to talk to him now.'

'I'm sorry. He is not available. Now, if you give me your number, I'll ask him to call you back as soon as he can.'

'Please make sure you do. It really is very urgent.' Kate gave her number and rang off.

Five hours later, at four thirty in the afternoon, George Williams rang back. 'Kate, my dear, how are you?' Kate could almost smell the claret through the phone.

'Not good, George. The money has not come through from the Bastard Stephen. What can we do?'

'We? Am I still your lawyer, then?'

'Well, of course you are, George, darling. What makes you ask?'

'It's just that I had heard nothing from you and after we had been so close.'

'Georgy, sweetie, I'm sorry. I've been so busy. Little Katie has lots to do, now she's on her ownsome.'

'Yes, so I hear. Now, this little problem with Stephen. I'm sure it's nothing. You just leave it with good old George for a few days and I'll do some sleuthing for you.'

'Georgy, you're the bestest. I'm so grateful.'

'Yes, well. We'll see.'

For the next few days, Kate stayed home, wandering about the house, picking things up and putting them down, wishing she were somewhere, anywhere else. Her children, in turn, were clearly unhappy with her hanging around all day, especially in holiday time, and the au pair's body language made it plain that Kate was intruding. She even avoided the gym, in spite of having bought three new outfits. She was aware of the secrets that can be gasped out in moments of weakness on the treadmill. Calls to George got a polite 'Mr Williams says that he is working on your case and will get back to you as soon as he has any news.'

On Wednesday, Jane rang.

'Darling, how are you? We thought you'd gone into a monastery or something. No, I mean a nunnery, don't I? Though monastery would be good. All those sex-starved monks.'

'Sorry, Jane. Bit of an upset tum. Need a few days to recover.'

'Of course, darling. How about some shopping therapy on Saturday, then? I've got this hot date to somewhere very naughty that night. I'm sure he can find a hunky friend for you.'

'Actually, I said I'd do something with the kids.' Kate grimaced both at the lie and the prospect of spending a day with the children. There was a stunned silence at the other end of the line.

'Are you sure you're all right, darling? Sounds as if you're getting a bit stir-crazy.'

'Jane, I'm fine. Just need a few days to, you know…'

'Well, OK, whatever, darling. Must dash, got to get to my foot massage.'

Muddle strode through the entrance hall, the tails of his frock coat billowing out behind him. It was still early but he liked to be at his post before the first arrivals, to ensure that everything was in order. Sheep gathered before the storm were coats on the children's backs, as he had explained several times to Mr Charles.

A girl in a maid's uniform approached him.

'Ah, Miss Polly, I trust my advice was of use.'

'Oh, Muddle, you're a lifesaver. My mum is ever so much better now. Who'd have thought that honey and toothpaste could have such an effect?'

'My pleasure, my dear. Do wish her well. Mothers are, after all, the fountain head from which all wisdom and understanding flows.'

'Certainly will and thanks again.'

Muddle moved on, bowing deeply to a Chinese girl who sat at the reception desk at the side of the hall. He spoke a few words of Mandarin with her, causing her to laugh shyly behind her hand, and went off to his now quite familiar post.

'Spread sunshine and you will reap rainbows,' his mother had said and he had no reason to think otherwise.

Chapter 3
THURSDAY

By Thursday, the cash had run out. Kate went into the bank, chequebook in hand, and made out a cheque for £200. The cashier took it and entered the details into her computer. A look of embarrassment flitted across her face. 'Oh, Mrs Bradshaw. Miss Davies would like a word. If you wait in the office over there, I'll ask her to come over.'

'Is that really necessary? I just want some money. That is what you do here, isn't it? Give people money?'

In the office again, Kate waited, ready to explain to the dark-suited one who was working for whom. After a five-minute wait, Mary Davies came in, closed the door behind her and sat at the table.

'Now, Mrs, sorry, Ms Bradshaw, isn't it? Ah, yes, the phantom payment.'

Kate started to protest but could not think of the right words. Anyway, she needed Little Miss Busy on her side.

'Well, Ms Bradshaw, not only has nothing come in, but I'm sorry to say that you have reached your overdraft limit. I am afraid that you and I need a serious chat.'

Why, Kate wondered, did people, as soon as they had a suit and a name badge, start behaving like primary school teachers? She smiled what she hoped was a confident but firm smile, but suspected that it was neither.

'Miss, er, Davies,' Kate made a point of checking the name badge, 'I assume it is Miss; I'm guessing you're not married? Look, I am sure that this will sort itself out very soon. My lawyer is on the case.'

'I find that the words 'lawyer' and 'very soon' rarely go together, Ms Bradshaw. I really think that you must now look at a significant reduction in your spending and, indeed, find a means of generating income.'

'Generating income?'

'Getting a job, Ms Bradshaw, getting a job. It's what

people usually do in these circumstances.'

Kate smiled at the girl's naivety. 'Miss Davies, I am not people. I don't do working. Well, a bit of modelling when I was younger and I worked as a chalet maid in Gstaad for a couple of winters. But that's it. And, besides,' she remembered suddenly, 'I have children to look after.' Kate racked her brains to remember the last time that she had actually cooked or cleaned for her two. Wasn't that why one had au pairs? Dear God, there must be some compensation for having to deal with their dreary homesickness for Ober Klopfenpoff or Woomeroomarooma or wherever.

'Well, Ms Bradshaw, there is the DSS. They have plenty of jobs available, I'm told. I am willing to extend the overdraft by a further £500, as long as you undertake to find some sort of employment. You will find your nearest Job Centre just around the corner, in Station Road. I suggest that we meet again this time next week and you can tell me how you are getting on.'

Mary Davies stood up and extended a hand. The lesson was clearly over. Kate stood, silently shook the hand and made for the door. She needed fresh air. Once outside, she remembered that she had not withdrawn any money. Unwillingly, she returned to the bank, to stand in line and wait. She remembered the pleasure with which she had frequently said, only partly in jest, 'My dear, I don't do queues.' She presented her cheque again to the same teller.

'Your Miss Davies has agreed this,' she said with as much dignity as she could salvage.

'One moment, please,' and the teller disappeared behind a partition. Within a minute she was back.

'Miss Davies suggests that £100 might be more appropriate. In the circumstances, you know.'

Anger rushed through Kate, a red wave that left her breathless. 'Did she really? Well, you can tell Little Miss ...' The wave subsided as Kate realised that she was not in a position to argue. 'Give me the cheque.' It was pushed back under the glass. Kate tore it up, once, twice, three times, then pushed the pieces into her handbag. She wrote a new cheque for £100 and silently passed it back under. The money came back, equally silently. Kate stuffed it into the pocket of her jeans and left, carefully avoiding the stares of those queuing behind her.

She needed a cappuccino. Opposite the bank was a small café that she had frequently used. She went in.

'Ah, good morning, signora. The usual?'

Kate looked at the smiling face of the large, moustachioed man behind the counter, noticing him for the first time. Though she doubted that the smile was genuine, she was nevertheless glad of it.

'Yes, thank you,' and she went to sit at a table in an alcove at the back of the café.

The man brought her coffee. 'You do not want to enjoy the sunshine at the window, signora?'

'No thank you. This will be fine.'

'You are sad, perhaps, signora. That is not right for a pretty lady.'

Kate looked up to see that the two couples who were the only other customers had stopped talking and were studiously not looking her way.

'I'll just have my coffee, thank you,' she said firmly. It really was none of his business, nice though it would be to unburden to someone.

Fifteen minutes later, starting to feel human again, she went to the counter to pay. While waiting for her change, she noticed a small hand-written sign, saying, 'Help Wanted – Part time waitress'.

'Your part-time job. How much does that pay? You see,' she added hastily, 'I have a friend who is looking for some work.'

'£4.50 an hour and all the coffee she can drink. Any friend of yours would be a great asset to the Trattoria, I'm sure, signora.'

'Thank you, I'll, er, I'll let her know.' Kate left the café, amazed that anyone would consider working for half what she paid for an hour's parking in Chelsea.

The wellbeing brought on by the cappuccino quickly faded. The sun had gone in and the first drops of rain were in the air. Even so, she pulled large sunglasses out of her bag and pushed them onto her face.

'Station Road Job Centre,' she thought to herself. 'Well, girl, might as well get it over with, just to keep Little Miss Tightknickers off your back.' She turned resolutely to the right and set off down the road. The town centre was not a pretty sight, narrow pavements full of litter from the endless burger bars and fast food outlets, cars and buses growling past, the smell of fat and stale beer. Kate remembered why she avoided it as much as she could, preferring the more refined atmosphere of South Moulton Street, Chelsea or even, at a stretch, Fulham.

Rounding the corner into Station Road, she found herself directly opposite the Job Centre, its orange and blue fascia presenting a cheery face to the world. She paused at the kerb. A taxi slowed to a halt to let her pass. She stepped back and waved it on, to be thanked with a shout of 'make your bloody mind up, darling'. She made her mind up, turned and walked back the way she had come, paused, made her mind up again and walked back. Checking up and down the road to ensure that there was no one in sight that she knew, Kate crossed over. She peered in through the window. It was clear that the cheeriness of the fascia did not extend inside. No, this was not the place for her. She turned and walked up the road.

Rain started to fall. She stopped. She had a choice. She could wander aimlessly in the rain and face the prospect of no more money or she could get it over with. Telling herself that it could be no worse than the dentist, she turned back, took a deep breath, pushed open the door and walked in.

Immediately she was struck by a smell that she had not experienced since her early schooldays, a mix of stale milk, sweat and dust that took her straight back to Totley Primary School on the outskirts of Sheffield. She was five years old again, queuing for extra milk at break time, Alec Markham pulling at her pigtails, at that time naturally blond.

Forcing herself to breathe through her mouth rather than her nose, she turned to the first desk on her right. At it sat a youth in his early twenties, short sparse hair greased down over a spotty forehead. His neck sprouted from his collar like a banana in a vase. He was staring without interest at a computer screen, his right forefinger pushed firmly up his right nostril. 'My God,' she thought, 'is that what Tom is going to look like in five years?'

Kate walked over. 'Is it you I talk to about arranging a job?'

No reply.

She leaned both hands on the front of the desk. "Oi, service. Is it…'

Without looking up, or indeed extracting his finger, the youth croaked, 'Busy. You have to go and talk to them over there.' He pointed, with his left hand, Kate was relieved to see, towards a row of desks on the other side of the room.

'Thank you so much. You've been a tremendous help. I'll leave you to your excavations, then.' Turning away from the youth's confused grunt, she crossed the room past a line of people and approached one of the desks. Immediately there was a chorus of shouts from behind her.

'Hey, who do you think you are?' 'Where are you going, Lady Muck?' 'We're not standing here for the good of our health, you know.' A woman looked up from her desk. 'Back of the queue, please, dear.' Kate turned to see twenty pairs of eyes glaring at her. Her first impulse was to explain to them all exactly why she should go ahead of them. She suppressed it, and moved with as much dignity as she could to the back.

The man in front of her was a stocky man with a shock of red hair, starting to grey at the edges. He was wearing a blue suit that Kate could see was well cut if a few years out of date. He smelled of Aramis aftershave, a smell that her father had once described as 'very pleasant, but a bit racy for me, I fear' and her mother as 'not for the likes of us'. It made her warm to him, though she took no action, just stood, counting the specks of dandruff on his shoulders. After a few minutes, he turned to her with a smile.

'Would I be right in thinking that that this was your first time in this fine establishment?' The voice had the well-modulated tone of a BBC newsreader behind which Kate detected a soft Irish burr. It was attractive but Kate was not in the mood for conversation. 'I mean, you're not exactly dressed for the part, are you?'

This rankled. Kate had deliberately dressed down that morning to avoid another lecture from Miss Schoolma'am and she was not now going to be lectured by Mr Yesterday's Burton Suits about what she should wear. 'Well, I'm hardly going to wear my best things to come down here, am I?'

'No, my dear, you're not getting my drift. I wouldn't dream of criticising your outfit. I mean, I'm hardly the epitome of contemporary fashion myself now, am I? No, what I mean is,' and his voice took on a conspiratorial whisper, 'you need to dress down to come here, otherwise there's no way you'll get any supplementary.'

'But I have dressed down. Believe me, I don't usually look like this.'

The man's eyes took in the silk shirt, the leather jacket, the designer jeans and the Gucci belt. 'As you wish. I think we're coming at this conversation from two rather different starting points.'

'What's this supplementary thing, anyway?'

'You really are a beginner, aren't you? Supplementary is when you can prove hardship and get more money out of them.'

'Hardship? I know about that. When your ex-husband defaults on payment after one month and the bank takes your credit card so you can't go shopping with your friends. I don't even go to the gym any more in case I meet someone who invites me out to lunch and I can't pay my share. Don't talk to me about hardship, I know all about it.'

'OK. I suggest it's best if you don't go into too much detail with them about that. Look, we're coming to the front, now. After you've had your session why don't you come over at the Station Hotel? I'm meeting up with a few pals to have a couple of snifters and we can give you a run down on how to get the best out of the system.'

Before Kate could refuse, the man was called to one of the desks. He moved forward, greeting the woman behind the desk loudly and cheerfully by her first name. Three minutes later, a voice from the far end called out 'Next' and Kate moved forward. She sat gingerly on the torn and stained chair opposite a middle-aged woman wearing a tweed jacket over a sagging cardigan and gazing at her over half-moon spectacles.

'Well, now. What can we do for you?'

'I understand that you arrange jobs. It seems that I have to get one. What do you have?'

'Yes. It doesn't quite work like that. There is still a recession on after all. Now, let's start with your name.'

'Kate Bradford. Ms.'

'Just a moment, just a moment. I have to get a new record page up on the screen.' She methodically pressed a series of buttons, while muttering, 'no, no, not that' and sighing. Kate found herself longing for Miss Fussy from the bank to be there.

'There. Ready. Now, what was the name?'

'Kate Bradford. Ms.'

'Are you sure, dear?

'Sorry?'

'Are you sure you want to be Ms. I always find it, forgive me, a little mannered.'

'Are you married?'

'Oh, yes dear. Three grandchildren.'

'Well, bully for you. I was. I'm not. So I'm not a Mrs any more and I certainly don't want to be a Miss Left-on-the-Shelf, so, Ms. Please.'

Kate offered up a silent curse to all feminists for creating this absurd, barely pronounceable title. The lady gave her the sort of smile usually reserved for children and small pets.

'As you wish, dear. Now, address and date of birth.'

Kate gave the information.

'So, just National Insurance number and this bit's done.'

'Sorry?'

'National Insurance number.' She observed Kate's bewildered look through the half-moons. 'You know, dear, the number you're issued with when you start working.'

'No, sorry, no idea what you're talking about.'

'You have worked before, haven't you, dear?'

'Well, yes, sort of. Modelling, chalet maid, that sort of thing. Mainly board and keep and a bit of pocket money, a few hundred here and there. All cash, obviously.'

'Yes, obviously. And I assume that this was a long time ago.'

'Well, yes, I suppose. You make it sound like the last century but, gosh, yes, I suppose about eighteen years ago.'

'So, no National Insurance number.' She turned to the screen, muttering quietly to herself, 'And therefore, of course, no payments.' She entered the data and firmly pressed the return key.

'Payments?' Kate brightened up. 'Am I supposed to have received some kind of payments from you?'

'No, dear, you are supposed to pay us. We call it National Insurance.'

'Pay you. Why would I want to do that? I mean, you're supposed to help me out, aren't you.'

'No, you see…. Oh, never mind. We'll get to all that in due course, no doubt.'

'So,' said Kate, feeling the need to move the conversation on. 'What do you have for me?'

'Well, no modelling or chalet maiding. Not much call for that in Teddington and,' again the pause and the half-muttered comment, 'certainly not for a middle-aged woman.'

Kate's eyes widened. She had never been accused of being such a thing before and now was not the time to start. She stood up to leave.

'Oh, before you go, dear, there's a few forms that you need to take away and fill in.' The woman leaned over to the pigeonholes behind her and extracted a handful. 'There's the P273 that will get you a National Insurance number. The P61 which details your work history – that one shouldn't take you long, dear – and the P128 that will get you onto our books so that you can receive payments, so long as you can show that you're looking for work.'

Kate took the thick wedge of papers and sat down again. 'Ah, now. Payment. What would I get?'

'Well, you'd probably get the full income-based Job Seekers Allowance.'

'And how much is that?'

'Well, it's just gone up. It's now £57.45 a week.' The woman seemed astonished that Kate did not know this basic fact of life.

'All this,' said Kate, waving the handful of papers, 'All this for fifty quid a week.'

'£57.45.'

'Whatever. And when can I have this princely sum?'

'As soon as you fill up all these forms and get them back to us, we can set the wheels in motion. We will have to get you the NI number first as nothing happens until that's done. If they accept the form, and they may, of course, want to talk to you about your undeclared earnings but, that aside, we should be able to set something up that would get the first payments to you in about, oh, four to five weeks.'

'Four to five weeks. But I've got a bank breathing down my neck and a stopped credit card. And two children to feed.'

'Better go and see Jobcentre Plus, see if they can help in the meantime. They can do what they call Crisis Payments. They're just upstairs, you could see them now. You'll need a form SF 410; I think I've got one here somewhere. Yes, here you are. And they may, of course, want to have a National…'

'Insurance number,' Kate completed the sentence. 'Yes, I rather guessed that might be coming.' She rose again. 'Well, this has been instructive. Good day.'

'Goodbye, dear. See you again, no doubt.'

Kate could not face the prospect of another session, whatever the benefit might be. She needed to be away from the primary school smell and the forms and the queues. She stepped out onto the street. A watery sun was showing through. Directly opposite her stood the Station Hotel.

'Oh, what the hell,' she thought and crossed the road.

The lunch crowd was thinning out. Muddle opened and closed the door with a raised hat and a small bow, as people headed out to their cars. A few offered him a tip, which he politely declined.

'The sun in the sky and a smile on the face are more than gold and silver worth,' he would explain.

Few replied.

Soon, he would be able to take a break before the evening shift. The Times crossword and one of the barmen's immigration challenges awaited.

CHAPTER 4
STILL THURSDAY

The bar of the Station Hotel had seen better days but was like an oasis to Kate. She crossed the red carpet, its paisley swirls almost obliterated by years of smoke and spillages. The man from the Job Centre queue was standing by the bar with a group of friends, all roaring with laughter. Kate realised that she had not heard laughter, other than the canned variety from the television, for a week.

The man spotted her. 'Ah, the new girl. Come on over. What would you like?'

'A very large vodka.'

'Half of Stella, please, Fred,' he called to the barman. 'That'll do you a lot more good. Now, introductions. I'm Patrick, and this bunch of reprobates are Jimmy, David and Charles.'

'Kate. It's nice to meet you all. Are you all refugees from that dreadful place over the road as well?'

'Good heavens, no,' Patrick laughed. 'I'm the only one playing that game. These gentlemen represent the cream of the local entrepreneurs. Anyway, how did it go over there?'

'I felt like I'd been caught smoking behind the bike sheds.'

'Bad as that, eh.'

Patrick moved aside so that Kate could sit at the bar. She picked up her glass and looked at it.

'I can't remember the last time I drank a lager.' She took a long drink, finding to her surprise that the cool, sharp taste was more pleasant and refreshing than she expected. She could feel it washing away the Job Centre.

'Get used to it, love,' advised Patrick. 'You won't get many large vodkas out of what they give you over there. Mind you, there are ways.'

Kate looked up to see an exchange of grins pass between

the men.

'Oh, yes,' nodded the one who had been introduced as Charles. 'There are ways.'

Kate looked at him more carefully. He was tall, something she always liked; she had never really understood why she had married short-arsed Stephen, other than the money, of course. Charles' hair was well-cut and just touching the velvet collar of his coat. Pale blue eyes stared straight back at her.

'Tell me more.'

Charles smiled, letting Patrick reply. 'Charles runs a private club, very select, and is always looking for help from people who know how to behave and are comfortable around money. Jimmy over here is a wholesaler.'

'Wholesaling what?'

'Oh, anything that needs to be wholesaled. And David is a lawyer, looks after business for us. Very useful chap.'

'And you, Patrick. What do you do?'

''Oh, a bit of this, a bit of that. Whatever keeps the wolf from the door.'

'Well, the wolf is knocking at my door, sure enough. You see…'

'It's OK, Kate. I told them about your current predicament.'

'Did you? Right, so you know about my bastard husband and his disappearing act. David, you're a lawyer. How do I get him to pay up?'

'Not really my department; I'm more in business to business. Much less messy. You could get a private detective to help; I know a few good ones, very discrete. But, of course, they would need paying. That's the problem, really, isn't it? Nothing happens without money. It all rather grinds to a halt.'

'God, how true.' Kate turned back to Charles. 'So, this club of yours. Any vacancies?'

'Actually, yes, since you ask. One of my best girls just had to leave. Some embarrassment about work permits. Mind you, it's hard work.'

Kate had been a guest in many clubs in her time,

entertaining clients with Stephen. She had never been aware of it being particularly hard work. How hard could it be to serve a few drinks and smile at people, after all?

'Not a problem,' she smiled up at Charles. 'I'm ready for a bit of hard work, to be honest. I'm getting bored doing nothing.'

'OK. Why don't you come up and see how it is, see whether you like it?'

'What would you want me to do?'

'Oh, just make sure everything is running smoothly, that everyone is buying enough drinks, that sort of thing.'

'Sort of manageress, then?'

'Well,' Charles hesitated. 'Not quite manageress. I tend to look after the running of it. No, you'd be helping out, but it's responsible work. And it'll give you a chance to wear all those smart outfits that are not getting an airing nowadays.'

Kate could feel a weight lifting off her. 'When do I start?'

Charles handed her a card. It was dark blue and on it, in gold copperplate, were the words 'Starlight Lounge, Private Bar and Restaurant. Nightly floor show.' She turned it over to see an address with a map of the location. Although she did not know the area well, she realised that it was no more than a thirty minute drive from her house.

'I really need someone this Friday.'

'What, tomorrow?'

'Yes, is that a problem?'

'No, I suppose not.'

'Good. Get there about eight thirty in the evening. We'll give you a trial session and see how you get on.'

'Well then,' cut in Patrick, 'Now that's settled, who's for another quick one before we head off?'

'I have to go but I feel that I should pay for this,' volunteered Kate. 'After all, you've made me feel a whole lot better.'

'Fine,' smiled Patrick. 'Double vodkas all round then.' Seeing Kate's startled look, he touched her arm. 'Don't worry, dear; we're old fashioned around here. Wouldn't dream of letting a girl buy the drinks. David, your round, I believe.'

'Oh, that reminds me,' Kate blurted. 'What about the money? How much do I earn with you, Charles?'

'Oh, the money's good, don't worry about that. Some of the team can earn several hundred a week.'

'Sounds great. I'll see you tomorrow, then, eight thirty.'

She gathered up her bag and headed for the door to a chorus of goodbyes from the men. Stepping out into the grey day she felt elated. She had shown Miss Smart Suit from the bank and Grannie Saggy Cardigan from the Job Centre that she was above their petty fussing. She didn't need them. But it was more than that. She had done it herself. For the first time for a long time, she was going to get money for herself, not just an allowance from someone else. Kate had never had much time for what she called the hairy armpits of feminism, a phrase, to be fair, that she had borrowed from the *Daily Mail*. Now, though, she was beginning to see their point. Not that she would want to describe herself as a feminist. That was not the way to get dinner bought for you. She headed off to the only decent dress shop in the area to buy a celebratory dress. Then she remembered the lack of credit card and turned for home.

Back home, she was impatient to give the kids her news, even if they were not impatient to hear it.

'Guess what,' she announced over a lunch of microwaved pizzas at the breakfast bar in the kitchen, it being the au pair's day off. 'I have a job.'

'What?' It pleased her to look across at two astonished pairs of eyes.

'Since when did they employ people to stand around criticising other people's dress sense?' Miranda wanted to know.

'Yeah, or driving really, really badly,' added Tom.

'There's nothing wrong with my driving. At least I can do the real thing, not just some plastic screen version.'

'That's just because you won't let me take that driving course at Brand's Hatch.'

'The one that has a minimum age of twenty-three? I don't think so. Anyway, is no one going to congratulate me for finding a way to keep some food in your mouths?'

'What do you mean?' Miranda raised a quizzical eyebrow

'Haven't you listened to anything I've said in the last week? Your darling father has not paid the money this month.'

'Yeah, we know, you told us that. But that just means that you can't go spending it on lunches with your cronies. What's that to do with us?'

'Facts of life, my little fledglings. To buy food, pay for the heating in the house, buy clothes, have holidays et cetera, et cetera, you need a thing called money. Without it, we starve.'

'Well, der, obviously,' responded Tom. 'But that's not our … Ow.' Kate looked up to see him reach down and rub his shin.

'What?'

'Nothing, Mum, he's just being his usual clumsy self,' cut in Miranda. Tom glared at her and hobbled away from the table.

'I assume you've finished, Tom,' Kate called after him. 'What's up, are your toy Germans getting impatient? Can't wait to invade Greenland or whatever?'

'Bloody Macedonians,' came grunting back down the stairs.

'What's up with your brother?'

'Hormones.'

'Oh, God, say no more.'

'And he doesn't like pizza anyway.'

'Really, since when?'

'Oh, about two years.'

'Oh. But what was the kick about?'

'Forget it, Mum. As if I need a reason to kick him. Anyway, tell us about this job.'

'Oh, so now you're interested. Well, I went down to the Job Centre today. And I met a guy there….'

'Sorry, what? You went to the Job Centre?'

'Yes, that bossy woman at the bank said I had to.

Anyway…'

'But, I mean, the Job Centre. What if someone had seen you? What if one of my friends had been going past? It is holidays, you know. Other people are around.'

'They would probably have thought I was going in to employ someone. Anyway, I looked around before going in.'

'Oh, so that makes it OK, does it, you standing there like a spy in some crap movie peering in a pervy, short-sighted way up and down the road. I suppose you were wearing sunglasses as a disguise.'

'Actually, it was quite bright out today. I needed them.'

'No-one ever needs sunglasses in Teddington.'

'Be that as it may, do you want to hear about the job or not.'

Another theatrical sigh from Miranda. 'OK, then, what did the Job Centre offer you?'

'Well, that's just it. They didn't. You see…'

The guttural sound of Miranda's mobile cut in. 'Emo, mother,' Miranda had informed her the first time she'd heard it. 'Not that I expect that'll mean anything to you. And don't try clicking your fingers to it.' At the phone's first groan, Miranda held up her hand like a traffic policeman and fished the bright pink appliance out of her jeans.

'Hi, Natalie, how was it? You didn't … You did? … You slag.' Miranda jumped up from her seat and left the room, phone glued to her ear. The door slammed behind her. Kate sat surveying the scattered pizza crusts. Her shoulders drooped. The phone beside her on the breakfast bar rang. Without checking, she picked it up.

'Kate?' The stentorian tones of her mother filled her head and most of the room. 'It's your mother,' she added unnecessarily. 'Remember me?'

'Hello, Mum. Look, I've got to go out. I'll call you tonight. OK?'

'Well, all right, though I'm sure I don't know what could be more important than talking to your mother. Be sure you don't call during *The Archers*. Though why I still listen to that filth, I don't know.'

'Ok, Mum, I'll call after that. And I've got some good news for you.'

'Well, good news would be a welcome change.'

'Bye, Mum.'

Ignoring the washing up, Kate went through to the sitting room. Miranda, curled up on the couch giggling into her phone, glared at her. When Kate showed no sign of leaving, she stood up.

'Hold on a minute, Nat. It seems I can't get any privacy here.' Her stalk out of the room was pure catwalk. Kate settled down to a fifty-three year-old afternoon film about brave ranchers.

Muddle surveyed the car park, now weeded, the white lines clearly marked, the posts all standing to attention, and felt pleased. The hard work of the last couple of weeks was showing results. He thought back to when he had completed the water project in the highlands of Thailand and he'd watched the small Karen tribe children gazing at the stream of clean water in amazement and joy. Not quite the same, a certain lack of that essential social benefit here, but certainly the satisfaction of a job well done.

Yes, things were progressing very satisfactorily. He had initially felt ambivalent about taking on the assignment. As it turned out, it had taken his mind off the recent sad events and he felt that, while he was here, he could be of use in so many ways.

Chapter 5
FRIDAY EVENING

The following day, Kate decided that a lie-in was in order. It was going to be a long day and she did not want to flag at the new job. Rising at about eleven, she put on loose clothes. From the sitting room she fetched a particularly forgiving exercise DVD and slotted it into the player in her bedroom. Although there was less room than downstairs, she had no appetite for Tom and Miranda's running commentary. After ten minutes the lure of the cappuccino machine in the kitchen became irresistible.

The day dragged on and by five o'clock she was bathed, made up, dressed and ready. As she was wondering what to do for the next three hours, the phone rang. Gorgon showed on the panel.

'Hello, Mum.'

'Well, I waited all last night.'

'Sorry?'

'You were going to call me. Or have you completely forgotten that you have a mother?'

'Oh, I'm sorry, Mum. I just got swamped with things to do.' Six hours of forgettable television and half a bottle of that Chablis that Steven had been hoarding. Yes, swamped.

'Well, it must have been very important to make you forget your promise. Still, I won't be here for much longer, no doubt, then you'll not have to bother with such things.'

Kate felt it better to say nothing. After a moment's silence and realising that no further response could be wrung out, her mother continued.

'So, I don't suppose you want to hear my news, then.'

This would be a toss-up between a development on her varicose veins, Kate's father's carrots or the immoral goings on in *The Archers*.

'No, of course I want to know, Mum. Tell me, what's going on up in Sheffield.'

'We're not Sheffield, dear, as you well know. We are Dore, altogether a different proposition.'

'Yes, but Dore is a suburb of Sheffield, isn't it?' Kate was puzzled by this new layer of social status. 'On the bus routes, bins emptied by the council, all that sort of stuff?'

'I prefer to think of us as a village that is surrounded by an alien culture.'

'With the same post code as the alien culture?'

'What the Labour government and its communist lackeys on Sheffield council choose to do to reduce us all to the level of the cloth-capped whippet owners is no concern of mine. Someone has to keep up the standards. By the way, your father has been elected head of his lodge, Grand Wizard or whatever.'

'What does that actually mean?'

'Several new dresses and endless dinners of chicken murdered by that dreadful Mrs Cartwright of the socials committee.'

'Well, Mum, that is good news. Now, I've got some news for you.'

'Wait a minute, Miss Me-me. I haven't told you the news yet.'

'But I thought that the news was Dad's appointment.'

'Good Lord, no. You must be leading a very dull life if you think that's interesting. No, you remember I told you that Stephen came to see us?'

Kate started as she heard the name. She realised that, with all the goings-on down here, she still had not quizzed her mother about that visit. Keeping her voice as steady as she could, she replied. 'And has he been back again?'

'No, but he sent us a postcard. Wasn't that nice, keeping in touch like that?' This was not a question that expected an answer. 'So like him.'

'Where was it from?'

'Where was what from?'

'The postcard, where was the postcard from?' Kate could hear her voice rising.

'Don't take that tone with me. I'm not senile, you know.'

'Sorry, Mum. But can you tell me, where did he send it from? It is important.'

'Well, I'm surprised you don't know.'

'We're divorced, Mum. Why should I know?'

'Well, now. You've put me off now. The place has gone right out of my mind. I remember it had a very pretty stamp, birds of paradise, or flowers, I think.'

'Do you still have it, Mum?'

'Oh, yes, it's on the mantelpiece.'

'Could you go and get it for me?'

'Well, you're not going to be able to see it over the telephone, are you, you silly girl?'

'Perhaps you could read it to me.' Kate became aware that her fingernails were digging painfully into the palm of her hand.

Her mother sighed. Kate realised that Miranda had learned her theatricality from the expert.

'Wait a moment.'

Kate sat, waiting, wishing that she had poured a very large glass of wine before the phone had rung.

There was a clatter as the phone was picked up again.' Ah, yes, I was right. Hong Kong.'

'Hong Kong? What on earth is he doing there?'

'Now, he did say something about that. Something about being head-searched.'

'I think you mean headhunted, Mum. What exactly does he say?'

'I don't have my reading specs with me but it was what I said, headhunted.'

'Could you get your reading specs, Mum?'

'Good Lord, it's like a cross-examination. Why is this all so important?'

'It's important because Stephen has disappeared off the face of the earth.'

'No, Katherine, he's in Hong Kong. I just told you. Do try to concentrate.'

'That's not what I mean. He has vanished from my life. He has stopped paying maintenance and done a runner.'

'Oh, I don't think so. Not Stephen. He wouldn't do something like that. You've probably got the paperwork mixed up, or spent it all too quickly. You were never any good at maths.'

Kate had had more than enough. Usually, she would have let these conversations run on for their full twenty minutes but now she felt the need to protect herself. 'Mum, I have to go, there's someone at the door.'

'So, don't you want to hear what he said, then?'

'Of course I do. But you haven't got your reading glasses.'

'Oh, I've found them. They were here on the telephone table all the time.'

'So?'

'So what?'

'So, what does he say, for God's sake?''

'Now, Kate, I've told you before about your language.'

Kate's legs were crossed so hard that her ankles were hurting. 'Sorry, Mum. Would you please tell me what he says?'

'That's better. Now then, let's see. Dear Elizabeth and Ted, that's nice, isn't it? Though I was always taught that you did not put people's names on a postcard. Too public, I suppose. Still, times change. Dear Elizabeth and Ted, just a short note to let you know that I am now working in Hong Kong, having been headhunted from my old company. My office is in the big white building that I've marked. More soon. Love, Stephen. There, wasn't it nice of him to write. We get so few letters nowadays. People don't seem to write any more.'

'Mum, could you send me the postcard, please?'

'Well, I'm not sure about that, dear. After all, it was sent to us and I did want Mrs Cartwright to see it, so that she knows that we have friends in far off lands.'

'Please, Mum. It is important.'

'Well, we'll see. I'll have to ask your father.'

Experience had taught Kate that this was as close as she would get to a yes.

'Thanks, Mum. I have to go now.'

'Yes, is that poor person still standing at your door? You

really should be more hospitable, you know.'

'No, that's OK. Um, Miranda has opened the door.'

'Oh, how is Miranda? It's so long since I spoke to her.'

'She's fine but she's, it was a friend of hers and they've just gone out.' And besides which, Kate thought, she hasn't been in the house since eleven o'clock this morning.

'Well, perhaps I could talk to my grandson.'

'Yes, I think he's in. Just a moment.' Kate took the phone upstairs to where Tom was bent over his computer. 'Tom, it's your grandmother.'

'What is?'

'On the phone. She wants to talk to you.'

Ignoring the gesticulations and glares, she thrust the phone into Tom's hand, just as her mother was starting on the 'your sister' portion, and left the room.

Hong Kong. Wasn't that British? Did that mean that she could get at him? She decided to call George. She ran downstairs, took her mobile out of her handbag and dialled.

'Hello, I'd like to speak to George.'

'Who's calling, please?'

'Kate Bradshaw.'

'One moment, Mrs Bradshaw.'

After a long pause she heard the familiar, well-oiled voice.

'Kate, my dear, you just caught me.'

'George, I think I know where Stephen is.'

There was a pause. 'Really, do tell.'

'He's in Hong Kong. He sent a postcard to my parents.'

'Did he indeed? That's a shame.'

'Why is that a shame? We can get at him there, can't we?'

'Not really. It is China, you know.'

'Yes, I know it's in China. But it's British, isn't it?'

'Not for the last few years, no, it actually belongs to China now. They are not known for being very co-operative.'

'Oh.'

'Oh, indeed. Do we know any more, like who he's working for?'

'Well, yes, at least we know the building.'

'What's the address?'

'Um, that I don't know. We have a postcard with a building marked on it. At least, my mother has.'

'So, we have a mark on a postcard which you don't actually have. It's not really a lot, is it?'

'Well, it's a start. Isn't it?'

'Barely. Look, if and when you get the postcard, bring it in and we'll see what we can do. But I don't hold out much hope, to be honest. Other than that, how are you?'

'Oh, top of the bloody world. Thank you so much for asking.' And Kate pressed the call end button as if it was George's right eye.

It was still only half past five. Kate wandered through to the kitchen to pour herself a glass of wine. She could feel the sharp apple taste of the Sauvignon clearing the irritation from her mother's call and George's unhelpful attitude. This job is not coming a moment too soon, she thought. I'm down to my last case of this stuff.

Tom came stomping into the room, slammed the phone back on its cradle, muttered something about daft old biddies and stomped out again. Kate did not even look up. She took her glass through to the living room, picked up the remote and began to flick through the programmes. Finally, as the Six O'clock News loomed, she settled on a *Simpsons* that she had seen several times before.

She relaxed, letting the images flicker in front of her, and sipped her wine. Forty-five minutes of Springfield anarchy had floated over her and the glass had been replenished each commercial break, when the doorbell rang. With a sigh, she hauled herself out of the armchair and made for the door. Two men were standing there. The taller of the two was in his late forties, Kate judged, with dark hair brushed straight back and shiny with hair oil. His face wore a look of concerned sincerity, rather like an undertaker pitching for business. Behind him stood a stocky man, running to fat, his legs apart and hands behind his back. His only movement was to thrust out his jaw every few seconds. Both wore blue t-shirts with the logo Swift'n'Sure emblazoned across the chest. A Transit Van with the same logo was parked in the road at the end of the drive. Her first thought was that her mother would have sent them round to the side door.

'Yes?'

The taller of the two spoke. 'Oh, good evening, madam.' The well-spoken voice was polite and calm, matching perfectly the facial expression. 'Are you,' he quickly checked the papers that he held in his hand, 'Mrs Katherine Susan Bradshaw?'

'Yes, though it's Ms Bradshaw nowadays.'

'I'm sorry?'

'Never mind. What do you want?'

'And are you the owner of the grey Mercedes SLK, registration HL15ADW that I see parked over there?'

'Yes, why?'

'Well, Mrs Bradshaw, I am afraid we are here to repossess it. It seems that you have not been keeping up the payments.'

Kate stared at him for a moment while the implication of his words sank in. 'Excuse me. What payments? It was a gift from my husband, my ex-husband. If there's any payments to be kept up, that's up to him.'

'Ah, yes. That would be Stephen James Bradshaw.'

'Exactly. So, you'll have to get onto him. And, if you do find him, you can let me know which rock he's hiding under. There's a couple of things I'd like to discuss with him too.' And Kate started to shut the door. To her surprise, a large boot prevented her.

'Would you please remove that? Your business here is done.'

'I'm afraid it's not quite that simple.' The man's voice remained calm, in spite of Kate banging the door against his foot. Behind her Kate could hear Bart Simpson berating his sister. Kate stepped back and the man pushed the door open again, though he stayed outside. 'You see, Mrs Bradshaw, on the 21st of July, Mr Bradshaw transferred the ownership to you. Together with the outstanding debt of…' again he checked his papers… '£19,850. With interest, that is now £21,153. You did confirm to me just now that you were the owner, did you not? So, if you could let us have a cheque for, say, £4,000 and an agreement on a payment schedule for the balance, we need trouble you no further.'

'I know nothing about this. You've obviously got everything completely wrong. Now, I suggest that you toddle off back to whatever Portakabin you call your office and check the paperwork.'

'I can assure you, Mrs Bradshaw, that we do not get these things wrong. I have here all the correspondence. I have a document with your signature confirming that you are taking on responsibility for the debt and I have copies of the letters that the finance company have sent to you, telling you that the payments are outstanding.'

'Show me.'

The man shuffled through the papers in his hand, extracting first a legal-looking document that he handed over. Kate took it. The wording made little sense to her but clearly, at the bottom, was her signature. Beside it, as witness, was the signature of her mother.

'This is fake. I've never seen this before.'

The man took the paper back. 'I see that, where it says 'relationship of witness to signatory, the person has written 'mother'. Is that your mother's signature.'

'Well, yes, it seems so. But…'

'Perhaps we can move on to the reminder letters, Mrs Bradshaw,' and he pulled out a sheaf of five or six letters headed First Finance Corporation. 'Do these ring any bells or are you perhaps suggesting that these might be fakes as well? And, before you answer, I do know that First Finance is a real company, they are based in Basingstoke, that is their letterhead and this is their usual wording.'

From the sitting room came the jaunty tune that marked the end of *The Simpsons* episode. Silently, Kate took the letters. They were addressed to her, but at her parent's address. 'Well, there's your problem. They've been sent to the wrong address.

Look. You do know the difference between Teddington, suburb of London, Thames, Hampton Court et cetera and Sheffield, steel works, Yorkshire, a hundred and forty miles up the M1?'

'Yes, madam, I am aware of the difference. But, if I can refer you back to the paper I just showed you, the transfer of ownership, you did request there that all correspondence be sent to that address.'

'Oh, for God's sake. I requested no such thing.' As Kate's voice rose, the second man took a step forward. The first man held out his arm and he stepped back but the message to Kate was clear. She took a deep breath. Her heartbeat echoed in her head. She reached out her hand to support herself on the door frame. 'Look, I have told you. This is a fake. That's all there is to it. Now, I suggest that you just go back and tell that to First Finance or whatever they are called. I'm sure they will be pleased to have it clarified.'

The man's face evolved a well-practised pained expression that reminded Kate of a particularly sadistic teacher at her primary school in Sheffield. It was the expression that had usually preceded a smack, in the 'this is going to hurt me more than it hurts you' mode. 'Yes, again, you see, Mrs Bradshaw, that's not quite how it works. Perhaps I should have explained earlier. We represent a company called Swift'n'Sure. Our job is to collect items that people have been careless enough not to pay for. So, returning to our earlier part of the conversation, either you can let us have a significant part of the outstanding debt, four thousand, as I suggested, or we can simply take the car off your hands. Either way, from your point of view, problem solved.'

'But I don't have anything like that amount. My husband has defaulted on his alimony payments. I've told you, if you want the money, you will have to see him.'

'I'm afraid he is none of our concern. You, as I have pointed out and you have confirmed, are the owner and therefore, the debtor.'

'But I didn't sign that stuff.'

'I'm afraid we can only go on the evidence as we see it, Mrs Bradshaw. I'm sure that, if the finance company find that there has been a mistake, they will return the car to you.'

Kate stared at them, trying to get her bearings. Such things did not happen to her. She felt dizzy, as if she had been whirled round too fast.

'Just a minute, I have to make a phone call.'

'Well, to be honest, Mrs Bradshaw, we are a bit pushed. We have to get on to another job after this.'

'Two minutes. That's all it will take. Wait here.' And, leaving the door ajar, she ran across the hall to the phone. Quickly she pressed her lawyer's number. It rang three times, then there was an ominous click. A voice came on, 'This is the office of Williams, Matthews and Jones. I'm afraid we are closed now but please leave a message or call back between the hours of…'

Kate slammed the phone down and quickly dialled her mother. Her father answered the phone.

'Oh, hello poppet, what can we do for you?'

'Daddy, I need to speak to Mum. It's very urgent.'

'Sorry, love, she's listening to *The Archers*.'

'Well, surely she can be interrupted. This really is important.'

'More than my life's worth to interrupt the sacred fifteen minutes. Is there anything I can help with?'

'Well, maybe.' Kate could not remember a time when her father had been able to help. She felt a fist of panic start to clench around her stomach. 'Daddy, do you remember when Stephen came to see you a few weeks ago?'

'Oh, yes, though I was out at a committee meeting at the golf club for most of the evening, to be honest. Why?'

'Did he ask you to sign any papers?'

'No. Not that I recall. Shall I get your mother to phone back? She shouldn't be long. It's finished by quarter past.'

'Daddy,' Kate could hear her voice breaking, 'It really is very urgent. There's some people here and they, it's something to do with the car. It seems there's some payments due.'

'Well, I'm sure there are. It's a very expensive toy you've got there. But I'm not sure what this has got to do with your mother.'

'Well, it seems she has signed some papers. I'm not too clear myself, to be honest. But they want to take the car away.'

'Who do?'

'These men. At the door. Here. Now.'

'Now don't go upsetting yourself. I'm sure there's a very good explanation. You've probably just overlooked some paperwork.'

'Daddy, they want four thousand pounds.'

'Well, give it to them, if it's owed. Neither a borrower nor a lender be, as the bard rightly says.'

There was a loud cough from the door.

'Mrs Bradshaw, we really do have to resolve this now.'

'Yes, all right. Just wait a minute. Daddy, listen, can you please tell Mum to call me back right away, the moment *The Archers* is over.'

'Yes, of course, dear. I'm sure that supper can wait for a while. To be honest, given your mother's cooking, an extra few minutes in the oven is no bad thing.'

'Thanks. Bye.'

Kate turned back to the door. 'Now, you're going to have to wait for my mother to call back.'

'I'm sorry, I'm afraid that's not possible, Mrs Bradshaw. We really do need to resolve this now.'

'Five minutes, for God's sake. What difference is that going to make?'

'Well, all right, Mrs Bradshaw. Five minutes. We'll give you until twenty past. But if nothing has happened, I'm afraid we will have to take the car. Perhaps you could have the keys ready. And maybe empty your things out of the car.'

'Thank you, but I'm sure that won't be necessary. Now, I suppose you'd like a cup of tea. You people always seem to.'

'That would be very nice. Milk, no sugar for me, Earl Grey if you have it, and standard builder's tea for my colleague here. Milk and four sugars for him.'

'Yeah, sweet enough already,' guffawed the squat one, proving that he could actually use his vocal cords as well as just stretch them. Kate busied herself in the kitchen as the clock silently ticked away the minutes. She added a couple of chocolate biscuits hoping they would somehow distract the men. They did not. Twenty past came and went. The phone remained silent.

'Well, Mrs Bradshaw, it seems that the clock has beaten you. Now, the keys, if you please.'

'Wait. Wait just one minute,' and she grabbed the phone. She pressed the speed dial and held the phone to her ear. It rang four times before it was picked up.

'Hello.'

'Daddy, it's Kate. Is Mum free?'

'I'm sorry, love, she's just popped out.'

'She's what? Did you give her my message?'

'Oh, yes.'

'And did you tell her how urgent it was?'

'Yes.'

'Well?'

'Well, she said something about "let her see how it feels to be kept waiting" and went out. I'm sure she'll be back soon. There's not that many places to go to in Dore at quarter past seven on a Friday evening, to be honest.'

Kate swallowed hard. 'OK. Thanks anyway, Daddy.' She slowly returned the phone to its base. She turned back to the men.

'I'll get my keys. Wait here for a moment.' Her handbag was in the kitchen. She pulled out the keys and grabbed a plastic bag from the floor. She walked past the men without speaking, clicked the key to unlock the car and reached inside. From the glove compartment she took an array of lipsticks, perfumes and sunglasses. Maps, gloves and papers were tucked into the side pockets. Everything went into the bright orange bag. She checked the boot, which was empty save for a pair of gold high-heeled shoes. 'So that's where those went.'

The two men were hovering behind her. Passing the key

to the older man, she started to walk back to the house.

'Oh, Mrs Bradshaw,' the voice pulled her up. 'There are a couple of other things.'

'What?'

'We do need you to sign these papers confirming that you have willingly handed over the car.'

'Willingly? I don't think so.'

'Yes, silly word, isn't it. I think that they mean without coercion. Without us threatening you.'

Kate paused. She certainly had felt threatened, though she could not put her finger on any specific example.

'Oh, what the hell. Pass it over.'

The man came towards her with his sheaf of papers. 'Just here and here, please. And here. And here. Many thanks. Now, just one more thing. There are usually two sets of keys. I wonder if you could also let us have the other.'

Without a word, Kate walked back into the house, pulled open the drawer under the telephone and took out the spare keys.

'Many thanks, madam. Now, we'll be off out of your way.'

'Yes, I think that would be a very good thing.'

'Don, you take the van and I'll take this. We'll head straight off to the next job. No time to get back to the office now.'

Don nodded, clearly disappointed at not getting the chance to drive the Mercedes. Kate walked back into the house and closed the door. She heard the sound of her car starting up, or rather the car that she thought was hers. It reversed and headed off up the drive. She did not watch it go.

What was Stephen up to? Although theirs could never have been described as high romance, they had been useful to each other. She had born the children, decorated his arm at functions, arranged the holidays and the domestic comfort. He had provided the money. It had been a business-like arrangement and had worked to both their advantage. Clearly not well enough for him in the end, otherwise he would not have strayed. But what had she done to make him act like this?

Try as she may, and to be fair she did not try too hard, she could think of nothing that could justify this underhand behaviour.

She walked into the living room, picked up her glass and took a long drink. Tom came wandering in.

'What was that all about?'

'It seems your dear father, as well as not letting us have any money, also omitted to give the car company any. Result, they want their car back.'

'Wow. Bummer. Can they do that? I mean, just come and, like, take it? Feels a bit fascist if you ask me. Police state and, you know.'

'Short answer, yes. It seems they have all the paperwork and, as I'm quickly finding out, paperwork rules the bloody world. Oh, shit.' Kate suddenly felt overwhelmed and she could feel tears running down her cheeks. Damn, she would have to redo her make-up now.

'Hey, chill, Mum. It's only a lump of metal, you know.'

'Yes, but it was such a lovely lump of metal,' Kate wailed.

'Yeah, that's true. It was pretty cool.'

'Tom, you're not helping. But it's not just that. Everything seems to be falling apart. It was all so perfect and now it's just, oh, I don't know, it's just…' Kate searched for the word… 'it's just totally shitty, Tom, that's what it is.'

'Yeah.' Tom reached out hesitantly and patted his mother's hand.

'Oh, thank you, Tom. That's just what I needed.'

Tom pulled back, embarrassed, not sure whether his mother was being her usual sarcastic self or whether this was a new and scarily human side that he was glimpsing. He decided to push his luck. 'Still, you're looking, er, cool. Except the mascara running down your face, of course, but, you know, nice dress and stuff.' Tom felt he had said enough. This was harder than a French oral exam.

''Thanks, Tom. You're really quite sweet under all that gawkiness, aren't you? Oh, bugger.'

'Sorry?'

'Bugger, bugger. How am I going to get to my new job without the car? I don't have the cash for a taxi.' Kate sank back in the sofa, defeated.

'Yeah, see what you mean. Hey, what about the Toyota?'

'The what?'

'The Toyota. Ingrid's car.'

'Ingrid?'

'The au pair, Mum. Remember?'

Kate did suddenly remember the old car that they had bought some time ago, after the escalation in au pair expectations had forced them to concede. It was kept hidden around the side of the house, out of sight from the road. 'What, that old rust bucket? Forty-seven careless owners including the last six au pairs. Would it even manage get the few miles to the club?'

'Do you have any choice?'

Kate looked at Tom. That was such a male thing to say, matter of fact, straight to the conclusion, no messing about with emotional stuff. She felt quite proud of him.

'You're right, Tom. I have no choice. Can you find, er…'

'Ingrid?'

'Yes, Ingrid, and get the keys off her? I'll go and sort out the make-up. I'll need to be off in about fifteen minutes.'

'Yes, Ma'am. Oh, and Mum.'

'Yes, Tom?'

'Anything for supper?'

'Oh, um, yes. I think there's some of that lasagne from yesterday. You can reheat it with some beans.'

'Sounds good. OK.' And he lolloped off in search of Ingrid.

Kate went quickly back upstairs. She felt the need to change her outfit. This one was somehow contaminated by the confrontation with the two men. She walked into her dressing room, ran her eye along the dresses and drew out a low-cut, loose and flowing one, which always made her feel good by accentuating the good bits and glossing lightly over the less than perfect parts. With an eye on the clock, she quickly reapplied her make-up and was back downstairs within ten minutes, quite surprising herself with how quickly it could be done when necessary.

Ingrid appeared and sulkily handed over the keys. 'I was going out also myself this evening. Is not fair.'

Kate smiled back at her. 'Very little in this world is fair, Ingrid, as I am discovering, and you no doubt will too one day. Thank you for the use of the car. It will be yours again tomorrow. Unless I need it.' She picked up her handbag, swung a coat over her shoulders and turned to the door. 'Wish me luck, dears. Mummy's off to make some money.'

Tom gave a big thumbs up. 'Good luck, Mum. Hope it goes well.' Ingrid grunted and stomped back upstairs.

Kate walked around to the side of the house. There, screened by a row of bamboo, stood the Toyota, its red paint dulled by age and drifting towards rust over the wheel arches. Kate pushed to key into the lock and pulled the door open. It creaked in protest. She was struck by the overpowering smell from the old hamburger wrappers that littered the floor and the back seat.

'Bloody au pairs. No wonder they're all so fat and greasy.' Picking up the wrappers between thumb and forefinger, she dropped them on the ground beside the car. Taking a tissue from her handbag, she wiped the steering wheel. The tissue was added to the pile on the ground. Then, carefully laying her coat on the driver's seat, she eased herself in.

For a moment, she sat, staring through the streaked windscreen, overwhelmed by the events of the day and sudden uncertainty about the evening. She took a deep breath, told herself to pull it together and turned the key in the ignition. The car groaned into life, the engine firing unenthusiastically and unevenly. It was a long time since Kate had driven a car that was not automatic. She pressed down on the clutch and pushed the gear stick forward. As she eased her foot up the car leaped forward and stopped. Silence, apart from Kate's long and explicit curse. She started the engine again. This time, the clutch came up very slowly and the car grumbled forward onto the drive and away. Before turning out towards the main road, Kate felt around in her handbag for the card that Charles had given to her, with its little map on the back. She glanced once at it and drove off.

Chapter 6
FRIDAY NIGHT

Within twenty minutes she was turning off into a factory estate, driving past a seemingly endless row of anonymous metal-clad warehouses with names like 24-7 No-Hassle Delivery Systems, Britalife Kitchens, Bespoke Joinery Services. As the road eventually curved round to the right, trees took the place of bare grass and tarmacked car parks. She came to a gate. High pillars either side told of a grand history now long past. The gates were open. Kate doubted that anyone could ever disentangle them from the creepers and ivy that wound through their bars. Ahead, a short drive led to a wide low house. 1920's, Kate guessed, from the green roof tiles and a wide, porticoed front door. The gateway had promised something much older.

There were no signs to reassure her that she had indeed arrived at the Starlight Lounge. In front of the house, three cars were parked. Each was large and expensive. Kate felt a pang as she pulled up beside them in the Toyota. She climbed out, wrapping her coat around her against the wind that had picked up and headed for the front door.

'Excuse me, madam, may I be able to offer any form of assistance?' The clipped voice that came from behind her made her think of every sergeant major in every British comedy that she had watched during the long afternoons recently, albeit rather better spoken. She turned to see a short man wearing a bright red braided coat. His barrel chest and the top hat that perched on his rather small head made him look like an enthusiastic steam engine.

Suppressing a laugh, Kate asked, 'Where did you spring from?'

'It's my job to, as you put it, spring, madam. I am here to welcome you to the Starlight Lounge. That is the purpose and intent of my springing.'

'Oh, right. That's, um nice. I'm here to see Charles.'

'That would be Mr Mannings, am I right in assuming,

madam?'

'I suppose so. I'm not really sure of his surname, to be honest. I met him yesterday and he offered me a job here, starting tonight.'

'A job, is it, then, madam? May I therefore recommend, with all due respect, that you re-enter the vehicle in which you have recently made your arrival and take it round to the rear of the building, where it will cause less ocular offence to our clientele?'

It took Kate a moment to decipher this instruction. 'Oh. Oh, right. Yes, of course. You see, it's not my car, well, it is, but not my usual. My Mercedes. That was, well, it's off the road. And, I…'

'Fascinating though this conversation is becoming, I suggest that immediate action would be an appropriate response to my suggestion. You follow the drive round to the left and behind the house. You will then see a rear entrance. We refer to it as the staff entrance. On account of it being the entrance for the staff.'

Kate climbed back into the car, aware that the smell of beefburgers still lingered and hoping that it was not lingering on her. She reversed out, stalled, restarted the car and drove round. As she rounded the back of the house she stalled again. But this time with good reason. Parked in front of her, neatly against the back wall of the house, was her Mercedes.

Kate sat staring. Questions tumbled over each other in her mind like excited puppies, all starting with how, who and why. She sat, stunned, for a full minute. Well, she finally thought, eliminating thoughts of a global conspiracy by a malevolent deity with a dislike of everyone called Kate, there's only one way to find out what's really happening here, and I certainly intend to find out.

She parked the Toyota next to her car, as she still wanted to call it. Not bothering to lock the door, who, after all, would want it, she walked over to the Mercedes and looked inside. All was as she had left it. Only the addition of a pair of black leather gloves on the passenger seat spoke of a change of ownership. She sighed, turned and made for the door into the house. It led directly into a narrow corridor, dimly lit and smelling of boiled vegetables and damp. Half way down another door led off to the left. From behind it she could hear the sound of a busy kitchen. Ignoring it, she walked on to the end of the corridor. She pushed open the large, panelled door and was surprised to find herself in an opulent hallway. Wood-panelled, with a thick red carpet, it was hexagonal in shape. Directly opposite, Kate could see the wide front door from which she had been turned away and the red coat of the doorman beyond. In four alternate walls of the hall, a high, elegantly proportioned door was set. All were shut. A staircase curved upwards and, in the centre of the hall, a large sculpture stood of two figures intertwined. Kate approached for a closer look.

'Hello, Mrs Bradshaw. What a pleasant surprise.'

Kate spun round, feeling increasingly irritated at the way people seemed to creep up on her here. Behind her stood the man from Swift'n'Sure who had made off with her car. Now, though, he was wearing a dinner suit.

'Pleasant for you, perhaps, though you'll forgive me if I don't share in your ecstasy. But why the hell are you…? Ah ha, at least I now I'm beginning to understand why my car is sitting outside. Did you enjoy the drive?'

'As I pointed out to you at the house, we were running late because of all the telephone calls that you insisted on making.'

'We? Do you mean that your voluble little friend is here too?'

'Oh, yes. We work as a team, you see. I'm getting a bit old for the heavy stuff now.'

'Work? You mean you actually work here?'

The man bowed slightly.

'And what do you mean, heavy stuff?'

'Oh, when things turn a little unpleasant. That's the bit that Don quite enjoys.'

'Well, I wouldn't think there'd be much cause for that here.'

The man merely smiled back at her.

Kate felt disconcerted and did not like the feeling. 'So, how long are you planning to cruise around in my car, Mr…? Look, I'm sorry, I don't remember your name.'

'That would be because I didn't tell you.' He paused to enjoy the effect of his words. 'Geoffrey Hamilton, at your service,' and he gave a mocking little bow. He allowed an awkward silence to fall.

'And my car?'

'The car that is now owned by my employer will shortly be returned to them.'

Kate remembered that feeling in the playground, when someone snatched away her favourite doll.

'Well,' she cleared her throat. 'Fun though this is, I need to find Charles.'

'Really? A friend of yours, is he?'

'Maybe. Do you know where I can find him?'

'Well, you could take a look at the staircase. I believe that would be him coming down now.'

Kate looked up and caught Charles' eye. 'Ah, Kate. You do look nice.' She smiled back with relief. He ran down the last few steps and took her hand. 'Welcome to my humble abode. Not much but I call it home and all that stuff. Evening, Geoffrey, are you making yourself known to our new colleague?'

Kate saw Geoffrey's eyebrows lift in surprise at the word 'colleague'. 'Well, that's one thing you didn't know about me,' she thought with some satisfaction.

'Yes,' Charles continued, 'I feel she'll be a great asset to the club. You carry on doing whatever it is you do, Geoffrey, and I'll show Ms Bradshaw round the premises.' With a curt nod of the head, Hamilton moved away, opened one of the high doors and slipped through. 'So, Kate, let me show you round.'

'That would be great. Then you can tell me exactly what you want me to do. I have to admit I'm a little hazy on that after our conversation.'

'Plenty of time for that. Come.' He led her over to the door to the left of the wide front door. Pushing it open, he stepped aside to let her through. They were in a long, low room. Curtains were drawn and the lighting was soft, not so dark that you could not see but low enough to make people's faces a blur. The room was divided into alcoves, with a sofa and a low table in each. Two or three of these alcoves were occupied, by the owners, Kate guessed, of the smart cars outside. She noticed with irritation that each couple seemed to consist of an older man and a younger woman. Typical, she thought, men whose sex appeal sits in their wallet, living out their sad fantasies with No 2 wife or partner or whatever. No doubt Stephen was up to something similar on the other side of the world and with her money. Or maybe he was still with what's her name.

'You're frowning, Kate. Do you not approve?'

Kate started. 'Oh, no, no. It's nothing. I was just, you know, miles away for a moment.' She gave him her widest grin. He seemed satisfied. 'Concentrate, girl,' she muttered to herself. 'You need this job.' They moved towards one of the alcoves.

'Good evening, Jack. Everything OK?'

A man in his early sixties was clearly engrossed in conversation with a young woman with an Oriental face. Hand gestures appeared to be a major form of communication. He looked up.

'Hello, Charles. Yes, everything's fine as usual.'

'That your new 7-series outside, Jack? I must say, they seem to be looking after you well.'

The man laughed. 'Yes, and I can still afford your outrageous prices.'

Charles gave a rueful grin. 'Well, we've all got to keep the wolf from the door.'

'Yes, and you know that I ensure our local wolves stay well away.'

'Thank you for that. It is greatly appreciated.'

While this exchange, which meant nothing to Kate, was going on, she checked out the girl, who was sitting looking down at her glass. Her dark hair was piled on top of her head in a way that looked casual but Kate's experienced eye could see that it had been done with care and skill. Her long dress looked like silk but was actually a clever imitation of something Kate had seen that week in *Marie Claire*. She clearly knew what she was doing.

Charles nodded goodbye to the man and led her across to the small bar at the other side of the room. They sat and a girl quickly walked over to them.

'Two glasses of our champagne, please, Amanda.'

'Lovely,' enthused Kate.

'Wait and see.'

'So, what was that all about? '

'Jack? Oh, he's a very useful client. Deputy Chief Constable. Helps with any little local difficulties.'

'First name terms with the Deputy Chief Constable. I am impressed.'

'Everything is first name here. Whatever first name they choose. They don't come here to talk shop.' The drinks arrived. 'Now, see what you think of this.'

Kate took a sip, then another. 'Your girl's made a mistake. This isn't champagne.'

'No mistake. This is what the staff drink. You order champagne and you get this. A subtle blend of herbs and fruit extracts, I think it says on the bottle. This way, you stay sober all evening and we make a nice profit.'

Kate was a little disappointed. She had been looking forward to a good drink. 'Oh, right. Clever.'

'Come on, I'll show you the rest. Bring your *champagne* with you,' he added with a smile.

They crossed the hall and went through the door directly opposite. The room contained ten small tables laid for dinner. At the far end, a dark red curtain was drawn across a stage.

'What's that for?' asked Kate.

'Cabaret. Saturday nights only. You'll probably not see it, as I want you to work next door. But I'm sure you'll hear it.'

They moved through an archway swathed in more red

curtains to the adjacent room. This was laid out for gambling. Kate could see roulette, blackjack and poker tables standing ready, though no clients or staff were visible.

'Doesn't start until ten. I though you could start in here tonight.'

'Sure. Doing what?'

'Moving around, making sure glasses are topped up, chatting to the guests. Don't want anyone to feel lonely or unappreciated, do we?'

'I'm sure I can do that,' Kate replied with a smile that hid some confusion. The job, as Charles, described it, seemed very straight-forward. But work was supposed to be hard and complicated, wasn't it? There must be more to it than she was realising. She realised that Charles was speaking.

'… get on with preparations. I'll take you to the staff room and you can meet some of the others."

Kate's mind spun on as they crossed the hall to the door next to the one that she had used to come in. Inside, the décor was very different from the rest of the house. This room was simply furnished. A few rather tired and stained sofas lined the walls, low tables were piled with old copies of OK and Hello, all of which Kate recognised. A coffee machine stood against the opposite wall, its brightly lit panel promising 'delicious hot beverages'. There was only one person in the room, sitting curled up on one of the sofas, cradling a plastic coffee cup. She did not look up.

'Anastasia, this is Kate. She's starting with us tonight. I'd like you to show her how everything works.' A languid arm waved a silent greeting. 'Right, I'll leave you to it. You'll need to be in the gaming room by nine forty-five. Anastasia works the roulette table so she can show you where everything is.

Charles left the room. Kate realised that she had not asked for more detail about how much she was to be paid. She really had to get better at this work thing.

Anastasia took slowly drained her coffee. The silence continued. Feeling uncomfortable, Kate walked over to the coffee machine.

'How do I make this work?'

'You press buttons. Press any. All tastes horse piss.' The voice was surprisingly deep for such a small frame. Kate could not work out the accent but from the name she guessed Russian.

'OK. So, I'll try horse piss with two sugars then.' Kate pressed a series of buttons hopefully. The machine gurgled and clunked. A cup appeared and, with much hissing, pale brown liquid poured into it. Kate gingerly took it out and tried it.

'Yes, I see what you mean.' More silence. 'So, um, Anastasia. That's a nice name.'

'Is not my name.'

'Oh, did Charles get it wrong. Typical of men. You know, I once…'

'No. Is my name but is not my name.'

'OK.' Kate was starting to feel that silence was the preferred option.

The girl took a deep breath. 'My name is Agneskuva. Mr Charles say make it simple. So, Anastasia.'

'I see. Fair enough.'

'Why you English always say fair enough. Is typical. Nothing is fantastic. Nothing is terrible. Everything is fair enough.'

'Well, that's…' Kate caught herself just before she agreed that the comment was indeed fair enough. 'That's an interesting point of view.'

'God. Always so polite.'

'OK. That's a load of crap and you're an idiot for saying it.'

To her surprise, Anastasia threw her head back and laughed loudly. Kate was astonished that the girl could summon up enough energy to move and laugh at the same time.

'Is much better. You not like white puddings.' Kate felt that something had been lost in translation but decided to let it pass. 'Now we can be friends. You make me more coffee. We talk.'

Kate busied herself with the coffee machine. 'Sugar?'

'Press extra sugar two times.' Kate did as instructed.

'What you do?'

'Oh, I'm a mum. Two kids. Divorced, looking for some cash, you know.'

'No. What you do here?'

'Oh, Charles wants me to just kind of mingle. Make sure everyone is happy. That sort of thing.'

Anastasia's face took on a look of surprise. She paused before taking the coffee; Kate waited with burning fingers. 'You are that kind. I did not expect.'

'That kind?' Kate put the coffee firmly on the table.

'What they call here hospitality.'

Kate felt lost. 'Well. I suppose. But why are you surprised?'

Anastasia shrugged, sipped at her drink. 'Is up to you. I not judge.'

'Sorry. Can we go back a bit? Why would you judge me? I need money and if I can get it by walking around talking to people and filling up glasses that sounds OK to me. What's your problem with that? Is it because I've left the kids at home because don't worry, they are more than able to...'

'Have no interest in your kids. But, Kate, are you sure know where you are?'

'A club for middle-aged men with more money than sense, by the looks of it. Maybe I should be working with orphaned Africans but frankly, there's no money in it.'

Anastasia stared at her then very deliberately put down her coffee. 'Come. I show you.'

She pulled herself off the sofa, took Kate by the hand and opened the door to the hall.

'Good. Is empty. Come,' and she moved quickly across the hall and up the stairs. At the top, corridors led off in two directions. Anastasia pulled Kate to the left. The first door was slightly ajar. She pushed it open and, with a theatrical sweep of her hand, motioned Kate silently in.

Kate looked around. 'So, it's a bedroom. Big deal. They

put people up for the night. What's wrong with…' Her eyes caught sight of the mirrored ceiling and the pictures around the walls. 'Oh. Oh. Oh, bloody hell.'

'Like you say. Oh, bloody hell. This part of job description.'

Kate stood in the centre of the room, feeling very stupid.

'Anastasia, believe me. I had no idea.'

'No, I see you have no idea. You not very bright, Kate.'

Kate could not argue with that. But she could argue with Charles. She spun round and headed for the stairs.

'Kate, wait. This is bad time. People coming in. Hold it till later.'

'I will hold nothing till later. I mean, how dare he think…'

'He dare think because he can. This is his place, his rules. Now, if you want to do something about that, you wait.'

'Do something?' Kate turned back towards Anastasia. 'What do you mean?'

'Not now. We wait, talk later. Is now time for working. But don't worry, tonight he will not ask for extras from you. Be patient. Revenge eats cold, you say.'

'Well, nearly.'

'Come. Follow.' And Anastasia led the way back along the corridor to some back stairs. At the bottom a door led into the staff room.

'I think I need another cup of horse piss,' muttered Kate.

'If you press red button, you get double strength horse piss,' and Kate noticed for the first time a slight smile on Anastasia's scarlet lips. She waited for the machine to go through its usual rumbles and gurgles then took the cup, blew on it and drank deep. Anastasia's dark eyebrows arched. 'You ready to play pussycat now?'

'Oh, yes. It's what I do best, when I'm in the mood. And you know, I think I'm in the mood.'

Feeling reinforced by the hit of caffeine, Kate followed Anastasia into the central hallway. Charles was there, greeting some new guests. He spotted them.

'Ah, Kate. Come and meet David and Peter.'

Kate fixed on her best smile and walked forward, hand outstretched. Each man took her hand and leaned forward to kiss her on both cheeks. From David, she caught expensive aftershave, from Peter just a stubbly cheek and the sour smell of dirty hair. His left hand eased round to the small of her back and headed lower. Remembering techniques from many years ago she moved her body sideways and out of reach.

'Good evening, gentlemen,' Kate purred. She was aware of Charles watching her.

'Kate's just joined us this evening. She will be working in the gaming room.'

Peter gave what he clearly believed was a sexy grin. 'Well, I'll be sure to pop in and throw away some of my hard-earned money later.'

'You do that,' smiled Kate and turned to Charles. 'Anastasia has been very helpful in showing me the ropes.' She thought she saw his smile flicker off for a brief moment. 'I'll just go on in and work out what I should be doing. Don't want to give the wrong impression, do I? Goodbye, gentlemen. Maybe we will meet again later.' Kate turned slowly and undulated towards the gaming room door, aware that three pairs of eyes were watching her go and quite enjoying the feeling.

Anastasia was busy setting up her poker table, piling the chips in their differently coloured stacks and unwrapping a new set of cards. In the corner stood Don, legs apart and hands folded in front of his considerable stomach, the chin still jutting forward every few seconds. He had shed his Swift'n'Sure t-shirt and was now in a bulging dinner suit. It was clear to Kate that Don's body was just not built for formal clothes. Anything other than a t-shirt and jeans looked like newspaper wrapped round a rock. He looked across at Kate and gave a brief nod of recognition. Clearly, Hamilton had briefed him.

Kate crossed to Anastasia. 'So, where do I stand?'

'You not stand. You walk.'

'Sorry?'

'Walk. Around the room, filling glasses, talking to punters.

Make them spend more money. You go to bar, get bottle.'

Kate nodded and walked across the hall to the bar. Several more of the alcoves had filled, some with more men with younger girls, some just with groups of men chatting and laughing together. Kate went to the bar. The girl who had served them earlier came across.

'Hi. I hear you're working the gaming room.'

'That's right. Topping up the drinks. What should I have with me?'

'Hold on.' The girl went to the back of the bar, took a bottle of champagne out of the chiller, filled a bucket with ice and pushed the bottle into it. 'Park that on the side table and go round with the bottle every few minutes. Glasses should already be there, in the cupboard on the right as you go in.'

'This is the real thing this time, is it?'

The girl lowered her voice 'Well, near enough for this lot but don't believe everything you read on a label.'

Kate grinned, picked up the bucket and walked back across the hall. Short-skirted waitresses were moving swiftly between what Kate assumed to be the kitchen and the dining room. She wondered where all these staff had been hiding earlier. The doors to the gaming room were now open wide and people were starting to drift in. She put the ice bucket down on a table next to Don.

The chin jutted in her direction. 'Want me to open that for you, darling?'

Kate looked directly at him. 'No, thank you. I was born to open champagne bottles.' He blinked and resumed his statue-like stance.

Kate found the next three hours quite easy. The men were mainly absorbed with the gambling. A few were happy to chat for a couple of minutes about nothing in particular and were glad to have their glasses filled. One man who had been crouched over Anastasia's table since it opened would click his fingers and hold up his glass every twenty minutes or so while not taking his eyes off the table. Kate satisfied herself with the thought that the more he drank, the more he was likely to lose.

At about one o'clock, she noticed the greasy head of Peter at the roulette table. He looked up and waved to her. She waved back but kept her distance. He held up his empty glass. Reluctantly, but still with the fixed smile, she walked over. As she filled the glass, he reached up with a chip, clearly intent on slipping it between her breasts. Kate swung easily out of reach and took the chip in her free hand. Adopting a Southern American accent, she beamed at Peter.

'Why, honey, you put your little old chip down there you ain't never goin' to see it again.'

After a brief frown of disappointment, Peter put the grin back on. 'Well, maybe I'll have to launch a diving expedition later.'

'Honey, when a Southern lady says never, she don't mean sometimes.' Leaving Peter to get the message, she turned and headed for the other side of the room.

By half past one, Kate's feet were beginning to ache. The smile was starting to hurt too. Charles came in and Kate caught his eye. He came over.

'How's it going?'

'Fine, but it's starting to hurt. And you and I need to talk.'

He looked around the room. 'Look, there's only a few die-hards left. Why don't you slip away? I can get one of the others to cover for you.'

'As I said, we need to talk.'

'Sure, but I'll be on duty here till about three.'

'Tomorrow, then.'

Charles looked steadily at her. 'So, you are coming in again tomorrow, then?'

'We'll see.'

'Eight o'clock here then.' It did not sound to Kate like a request.

She walked over to Anastasia, whispered to her that she was leaving and they would talk tomorrow, then slipped out and down the corridor to the back door. The night was cold but clear. Kate paused for a moment, enjoying the chill freshness after the smoky warmth of the gaming room. A single light shone down dimly from the corner of the house but the stars were clearly visible. It reminded her of nights on the slopes when she had been a chalet maid. The sight of the rusty Toyota brought her back to the present. She started to walk towards it.

'Well, hello again.' She turned to see Peter standing behind her. Even in the shadows she could see that the grin was still in place but the eyes were narrower. He swayed slightly.

She took a deep breath, forcing her voice to stay calm. 'Good night, Peter. I'm off home now.' She walked towards the car. Quickly, he skipped round her, blocking her path.

'I thought we could, ah, develop our relationship.'

'I'm going home.'

'Fine. I mean, I can understand why you might want to be discreet. And, of course, that way you keep all the money.'

'No. I'm going home. Alone.'

He took a step forward. 'Alone? Seems such a waste. No, I don't think we can have that.'

'We?'

'I.' He reached out and grabbed her arms, pushing her against a car.

'Get off me.'

He leaned over, his face inches from hers.

'Just relax. It'll be worth your while. It's a long time since I've done it in the open air.' His body pressed up against her. Kate struggled to free her arms. She could not move. Her voice seemed trapped in her throat.

'Excuse me, sir.' The clipped tones came from behind Peter. He eased his grip slightly and looked round. Just past his shoulder, Kate could see a red braid uniform.

'Sir, I believe that Mr Charles will have acquainted you with the rules of engagement of this establishment. Willing partners et cetera.'

'Fuck off and mind your own business.' Peter turned back towards Kate.

'I don't believe I am making myself clear, sir. Let me rephrase. Would you please be so kind as to release the young lady, who, I surmise, I believe correctly, is not a willing partner. Am I right, miss?' Kate could only nod. 'I will take that as an affirmative. Release, therefore, please, sir. At once would be good.'

Peter swung round, holding on to Kate's left arm. He towered over the doorman by a full foot. 'Or what, short arse?'

The doorman's eyes remained steady and his tone remained polite. 'Or, sir, I will be forced to apply more persuasive methods.'

'Ooh, I am scared. And what might that be?'

'Well, sir,' the tone could have been that of a solicitous grocer informing him of the week's special offers. 'I will be forced to rip off your gonads and stuff them down your throat.'

Peter stared at the man for a full ten seconds. The stare was returned. He released his grip on Kate. 'What the hell. She's too bloody old anyway. I'll go back in and get something fresher.' He turned back to Kate, legs apart and shoulders hunched. 'You don't know what you're missing, woman. At your age, you should take it when you can.'

Without a word in reply, Kate brought her right knee up as quickly as she could. She felt a great sense of pleasure and relief when it made contact exactly where she had intended. Peter gave a loud grunt and bent double.

'No-one calls me old,' she shouted, bending towards him to make sure he got the full impact. Peter turned and waddled back through the door, muttering.

The doorman watched him go. 'Not a gentleman, I fear. Still, a spirited riposte from your good self, if I may say so. Are you feeling able to drive, miss?'

'Thank you so much. You really saved me there.'

'Yes, an inappropriate way to treat a lady, really, miss.'

Kate looked at him, taking in for the first time the upright stance, neat, boyish haircut and wizened face. 'You do have a way with words.'

'Well, thank you, miss. I do pride myself on an extensive vocabulary, acquired from many years of perusing the great English classics. It's amazing what one can pick up if one doesn't watch television. Curse of the masses, that machine.'

'Sorry, can I hold onto your arm for a moment. Feeling a bit wobbly.'

'Of course, miss. Allow me to escort you to your vehicle. The rusty one, as I recall.'

'Yes. Thank you. I'm sorry, I don't know your name.'

'Muddle, miss.'

'Just Muddle?'

'Yes.'

'Well, thank you for everything, Mr Muddle.'

'No, miss, just Muddle.'

'Oh, sorry. Well, thank you anyway. Are you ex-army, er, Muddle? You certainly look it.'

'Sadly no, miss. Didn't have the stature, you see. Same with Her Majesty's police force. However,' he added, brightening, 'I did hold a position of some seniority in the boy scouts.'

'Really. Bravo. I suppose I'll get the sack now, after that.'

'Oh, no, miss. Mr Charles is very particular about such things. Only those who desire such liaisons. Here we are.' They had reached the car.

'Oh, my keys. They were in my bag. I must have dropped it.'

'Never fear, miss.' He produced a large torch from an inside pocket and shone it around. 'Aha.' Carefully propping Kate against the car, he trotted a few steps and stooped to pick up the bag. Kate fumbled inside and found the keys. She opened the door.

'Fond of hamburgers, are we, miss?'

'No, sorry, not my car. Well, not the car I usually use. Long story.'

'Ah, yes, I do remember you saying. Well, duty calls, I must get back to my post. Keep alert and all that.'

'Yes, of course. And, thank you again, Muddle.'

'Any time, miss,' and he gave a smart salute, spun on his heel and disappeared back into the darkness.

Kate climbed in, locking the door behind her. She put her

hands onto the wheel to stop them shaking. After a couple of minutes she took a deep breath, turned the key in the ignition and drove home. It had been quite a day.

Chapter 7
SATURDAY

'Right, you bugger. This is where you get the full force of Hurricane Kate.' Kate locked the Toyota. She felt good about having driven all the way without stalling once and was looking forward to her confrontation with Charles. The evening sun was disappearing behind the trees. The long shadows across the car park made Kate shiver as she remembered the night before. What would have happened if Muddle had not turned up at that moment? She had given him a friendly wave on the way in and made a mental note to see him during the evening to thank him again.

The day had started slowly. Two very large Sauvignons to steady her nerves when she had reached home the night before ensured that Kate had slept in. She had planned to wake up at ten o'clock but the dutiful alarm clock had hit the opposite wall with some velocity and had wisely remained silent after that. Finally up at two, she showered, sent Ingrid off grumbling to do the grocery shopping and spent the afternoon wandering between the kitchen to recharge with tea, sandwiches and cake and the sitting room, where she completely lost track of two consecutive episodes of *Columbo*.

Miranda had left early for her regular prowl around the shops with her friends but Tom briefly abandoned the Goths and Macedonians to fend for themselves and came wandering down into the kitchen. He made straight for the fridge. Disappointed at its emptiness, he turned to his mother.

'Any chance of food?'

'Ingrid's out now. She'll be back in an hour or so. Think you can survive until then?'

Tom clutched his stomach and rolled to the floor. 'Too late, too late. I'll have faded away,' he moaned.

Kate did not look up from her magazine. 'As my mother said all through my childhood, think of the poor starving

Africans and be grateful. And there's crisps in the cupboard.'

'Ooh.' Tom jumped up and grabbed a large bag of beef flavoured. 'How was last night, by the way?'

'Oh, interesting.'

'And?'

'And nothing much, really. It's a club, people drink and eat and gamble and, er, stuff.'

'Sounds great. When can I come?'

'Over 25s only. You'll have to wait,' Kate replied rather more hastily than she intended.

'And what did you have to do for your money?'

'What do you mean? What are you suggesting?'

'Whoa. Chill. Just, like, wanted to know what you, like, had to do.'

'Oh. OK. I had to, well, make people feel at home, chat to them, fill up their glasses, you know, that sort of thing.'

'Sounds cushy.'

'I'll have you know, Tom, it's very hard work being nice to people for that length of time.' She looked puzzled as Tom collapsed on the floor again, this time convulsed with laughter. 'And what's so funny?'

'You,' Tom gasped. 'Just the idea of you having to be nice. It must have been hell for you,' and the laughter burst through again.

'Hm. Well, you might try it some time and you'll see what I mean.' Kate gathered up her cup of tea and the magazine and stalked through to the sitting room. As soon as she settled down, the phone rang. She picked up the remote handset.

'Hello.'

'Kate, dear.'

'Oh, hello, Mother.'

'Your father tells me that you wanted to talk to me about something.'

'Yes, I did. Last night.'

'Well, you know how it is with your father. Never the most reliable conveyor of messages.'

'Really? He said that he did tell you last night and that you wouldn't call me. Something about see how she feels.'

'Oh. Did he? Well, that's as may be. Now, what was it you wanted? I'm in a rush. Got to go to that ghastly Mrs Wainwright's for a planning meeting for the Bridge Club party. Why they don't just leave it all to me, I don't know.'

'Mother. Did you sign some papers for Stephen?'

'What? What papers?' For once, her mother sounded hesitant.

'Papers about the ownership of the car.'

'Oh, no. Well, I don't think so.'

'Let me put it this way. Yesterday some man pushed some papers under my nose before taking my car away. They had your signature on them. Can you explain?' Kate was starting to feel that watching *Columbo* was having a positive effect.

'Don't you cross-examine me, young lady. I've not done anything wrong.'

'Not done anything or not done anything wrong? Which is it, Mother?'

'I will not be spoken to like this.'

'Mother, did you sign anything?'

'Well, he did ask me to sign something, if you must know, but nothing about your precious car. Just some papers he said were to do with his visa.'

'He said?'

'Yes. I hope you're not suggesting that Stephen is a liar. That's just typical of you, always—'

'Mother. Enough. You've told me what I needed to know. Now, off to your meeting and give them hell.'

'Kate. You're in a very funny mood today. I expect you to be a lot more civil next time I call.'

Resisting the urge to shout 'Don't hold your breath' down the phone, Kate settled for a simple 'Goodbye,' and hung up. She felt good. She had information and she had actually won a conversation with her mother. And she hadn't even got to the 'your sister' bit. No doubt there would soon be a major counter attack but she would be ready for it.

And now she stood in the car park, more than ready for

her next confrontation. She checked her watch. Five to eight. She strode towards the door.

The hall was deserted. She looked in the gaming room and the restaurant. Equally empty. She crossed to the bar. The same girl as yesterday was behind the bar. The alcoves were empty.

'Hi, it's, er Lucy, Isn't it? Seen Charles?'

'Amanda. He's around. He was in here a couple of minutes ago. You could try his office.'

'Where's that?'

'Upstairs. First on the right.'

'Thanks.'

Kate made her way up the curved staircase. At the top, before going to the office, she checked to see that the corridor was empty, moved silently to the left and pushed open the door to the first bedroom. She flicked the switch and soft lighting swept through the room. It was as she remembered. Red satin sheets were draped over the bed, a soft carpet underfoot, the pictures around the wall showing illustrations, she guessed, from the Kama Sutra. She looked closer at one, trying to work out where one set of limbs ended and another began. It looked painful. She stood back and surveyed the room.

'Very tasteful,' she muttered.

'Well, thank you. We do try.'

She spun round at the sound of the voice. Leaning on the door jamb, arms folded, was Charles, a smile on his lip and one eyebrow arched.

'I…. I was just making sure of my, er, evidence. Just, you know…..'

'Shall we go into my office?'

Kate followed, feeling rather sheepish and cross with herself for losing the advantage. Charles opened the door and stood back to let her in. The room was quite small, dominated by an incongruously modern glass and chrome desk on which stood a laptop computer. The walls were lined with fake antique shelves full of folders, all carefully labelled. There seemed to be some kind of colour-coding to them. A window looked out onto the staff car park.

'Do sit.'

Kate sat in the only chair available. It was old, with a leather seat and wobbled slightly. Charles moved behind his desk and settled into a high-backed very modern swivel chair. Kate noticed that he was higher than her and had his back to the light.

'Now, Kate, what did you want to discuss?'

Kate grappled for the well-rehearsed words that had sounded so good earlier in the day.

'You brought me here under false pretences. You never told me what kind of a place you were running here.'

Charles' smile did not falter. He said nothing. Kate felt the need to continue.

'I mean, you didn't say anything about the, the bedroom stuff. You just said you wanted someone to help out. God, Charles, how dare you. I mean, how dare you think that I, that I would, might….'

Charles let the silence fall. He leaned forward, rested his elbows on the desk and his head on his interlaced fingers. 'Well, now let's see.' His voice was calm. 'False pretences? Not really. I told you I had a job going. True. I thought you could fill it. True. I said that some of the girls earn a lot of money. True.

Now, the bedroom stuff, as you call it. I think you already know my rule about that; only willing participants. And, by the way, I am very sorry about what happened in the car park last night. That gentleman will not be allowed admittance again.'

Goodness, thought Kate, he is well informed. She responded with a curt nod.

'No, the bedroom stuff,' Charles repeated, the smile widening. 'It's one of many services that we offer here. Many tastes are provided for but I do have to say that I haven't really tested the level of interest in the, how shall I put it, the slightly more mature lady. However, if you are interested, I am sure that we can explore this.'

Kate was on her feet. 'I can give those skinny clothes racks a run for their money any day. But no, no, no.' Her hands flew to her head and she sank back into her seat, which wobbled and squeaked under her. 'No. This is not what I signed up for, Charles.'

'Well, strictly speaking, you haven't signed anything. But look, if you want to stay away from that stuff, fine. There's a job for you to do here. Just don't complain about the pay packet.'

'So, how much will I get if I, you know, stay away from that stuff?'

'Five nights, say three fifty a week. More if I think you're upping the sales and winnings. Look, Kate, I was watching you last night. You're a natural. You can do very well here.'

'Cash?'

'Of course. Do we have a deal?'

Kate paused. She thought about her options; it did not take long.

'OK. But no, you know, stuff.'

'Fine. Let me know if you change your mind. It could be interesting. Now, to work. I'd like you to start in the bar tonight, mixing with the all male tables. We have quite a lot of those on a Saturday. Keep the drinks flowing and so on. Things will quieten down about midnight when we have the floor show but that's when you go to the gaming room until close. OK?' Charles' eyes turned to the screen of his laptop.

It was clear that the conversation was over. Kate stood up and saluted. 'OK, boss.' There was no reaction to the intended irony. She hesitated. Charles looked up with a patient smile.

'Was there anything else, Kate?'

'No. That's um, fine. I'll just get ready and, er…'

'OK. Off you go.'

Kate walked slowly downstairs, not sure whether she had won the conversation or not. She decided to settle for a draw; she still had a job and Charles now knew exactly where she stood. The crack about the slightly more mature lady still smarted a bit. She would look for the chance to prove him wrong. At that moment, a plan started to form in her mind. Her quickest way to becoming a major player in this establishment was not going to be by her wits and talent; Kate was starting to feel that she had a long way to go in that area. But she did understand men and how to make them feel good. She would make herself indispensable to Charles in every sense. A man all on his own in such a large house must feel lonely. Perhaps he was the one who hankered after the slightly more mature woman. So, that's what he was hinting at. She could already see herself striding through the rooms, keeping a watchful eye on the staff, greeting guests, her arm linked proprietarily through Charles'. What would her title be? Manager sounded much too dull and Madame was certainly to be avoided. There was a French word. What was it? She had heard it on a television programme last week and it had struck her as a very classy title. Kate racked her brain as she crossed the hall. Something to do with cats, as far as she could remember. Yes, chatelaine, that was it. 'Hello, I'm Kate, no Katherine would be better, I'm Katherine, chatelaine of this fine establishment. Yes, maybe even a hint of a French accent. She would need to put Operation Charles into action as quickly as possible, in case anyone else had the same idea.

She pushed open the door to the staff room. As before, Anastasia was draped over one of the sofas like a tiger-skin rug. Kate looked with some envy at her slim curves, still defying a diet of coffee and hamburgers. The younger woman looked up in surprise, the dark eyebrows shooting up theatrically.

'Kate. You here again. I not expecting this. I think you are one hit wonderful.'

'Sorry?'

'Come for one night, never see again. Many like this.'

'Oh, did you? Well, you underestimated me. I'm here for the whole game. Now, I think it's horse piss time,' and she crossed to where the coffee machine crouched in the corner.

'I am thinking you will need a lot of this tonight.'

'Why?'

'Is Saturday.'

'Oh, usually busy, is it?'

'Yes, that too.'

'And?'

'Is show time tonight.'

'Oh, cabaret. Nice. What do we get? Song and dance?'

Anastasia smiled and said nothing.

'Sorry, am I missing something?'

'You wait, Kate. Will be a good surprise, I think.'

Feeling irritated, Kate changed the subject.

'I was watching you last night at the card table. Where did you learn to do all that?'

Anastasia shrugged. 'Is not so hard. Is just throwing cards around the table.'

'Well, yes, but it's more than that, isn't it?'

'How you mean?'

Kate busied herself persuading the machine to give up the cup of coffee. 'Well, I noticed that, for example, you dealt an eight of hearts and then, four goes later, from the same pack you dealt an eight of hearts again. I mean, that doesn't happen normally does it?'

Anastasia looked up at her in silence, eyes wide.

'And then I noticed that there was no King of Hearts. And then...'

Anastasia leapt from the sofa. She pinned Kate face first against the machine. The coffee went flying. For the second time in twenty-four hours, Kate could not move.

'Who are you? Are you police? What you want? Speak or I hurt you, Kate.'

'No, No. For God's sake. Police? Me? Come on. I mean, I was just watching you. I meant it as a compliment. Please, Anastasia. Please, let me go.'

Kate felt the grip ease. Anastasia stepped back, allowing Kate to turn to face her.

'Is true. You are too stupid. Even for police person.'

'Thank you, I think.'

'You wait here. Go nowhere.' Anastasia left the room. Kate sat down, shaking. What had she said that had upset her so much? Within a minute, Anastasia was back, a pack of cards in her hand.

'Kate, you come here, sit at table.'

Obediently, Kate moved to the scarred and wobbly table in the centre of the room. Anastasia sat opposite her and held the cards in her hand.

'Kate, you watch cards.' Kate nodded.

Anastasia dealt six cards in quick succession, each one covering the previous one. 'What were these cards?'

Kate shrugged. 'Six of clubs, jack of diamonds, eight of spades, three of spades, five of hearts and the six of diamonds that's on the top there.'

'Ok, again.' This time she dealt ten cards. Again, Kate reeled them off without hesitation. Fifteen cards. Same result.

'How you do this?'

'Do what?'

'Remember cards.'

'I don't know. Is it that unusual?'

Anastasia stared at her. 'Yes, Kate. Is very, very unusual.'

'Oh.'

'As you say, Oh. You are telling me that you never knew.'

'Well, when I was young we didn't have cards in the house. My parents were Methodist, you see. Didn't approve. And we never bothered with them at home with the kids.' Kate smiled. 'Actually, you know, I remember, just after we got married, Stephen was trying to teach me poker and I beat him three times in a row. He got all huffy and never played with me again. I just thought it was a fluke.'

'And you can do this with other things too? With books and things?'

'Oh, God, no. Complete dunce in that area. Now I think about it, it does seems to work with maps. I can look at one once and find my way to wherever I'm going. Is that the same sort of thing, do you think?'

'Maybe. I don't care. The cards are the only interesting thing. Kate, you suddenly very interesting person. We go work now but we talk later.'

'But, I don't understand. What have I done?'

'Is not what you done. Is what you will do. Kate, you can be very rich. We can be very rich. Better than little scams in this place.'

'Really.'

'Yes, really. Now, we go work in this shitty place,' and she swept out of the room. Kate took a deep breath, checked herself in the mirror and, after a few adjustments, stepped out into the hall. From the bar she could hear the soft murmur of male voices, interspersed with the occasional loud laugh. She walked through.

Several of the tables were already taken. Amanda signalled her over from behind the bar. 'Kate, can you give me a hand. They've all arrived at once and Mr Charles doesn't like it when people are kept waiting.

Nor will I, thought Kate, when I am chatelaine. She could see herself directing girls hither and yon to ensure that everyone knew that this was a high-class establishment.

'Kate. Kate. Hello.' She came back to reality.

'Sorry. What can I do?'

'Go and see what they want on table six, that's the one over on the right there.'

Kate made her way across. At the table sat six men, all in their forties or fifties. One of them looked up as she approached.

'Ah, waitress, over here please.'

Kate paused, deciding whether to correct him. Now did not seem like a good time. Perhaps name badges with titles would be good. She would suggest it to Charles.

'What can I get you gentlemen?'

Another of the men looked up. 'Two bottles of champagne for now and we'll see what comes later.' His emphasis on the word 'comes' had his friends guffawing.

'Yeah. And a nice bit of totty to bring it to us.'

A chorus of 'Totty, totty' started up around the table.

Kate gave one of her thinner smiles. 'I'll be right back, gentlemen, if you promise to be good boys.'

'Ooh, domination. Just what a young man needs,' camped a small, bespectacled man on the far side of the table. The laughter quickly stopped as his friends eyed him awkwardly.

Kate returned to the bar. 'Amanda, what champagne do you have that combines outrageously high prices with really poor quality?'

Amanda grinned. 'Most of it, to be honest.'

The bar steadily filled to capacity and Kate worked hard, moving from table to table, ensuring that the punters ordered more expensive drinks than they had planned.

At ten, people started to drift through to the gaming room and she followed, bottle in hand. Although this was only her second night, it already felt easy and familiar. Don was in his usual place at the side of the room, bulging and jutting.

All three tables were soon full, with Anastasia and the other croupiers working swiftly and smoothly to ensure a steady stream of money from the gamblers to the house. Occasionally there would be a whoop as someone won and Kate was swiftly there to suggest champagne all round. Then, at about a quarter to twelve, the room virtually emptied. Only three or four hardened gamblers remained. Kate felt sure that, if the roof had blown off and the London Philharmonic had descended playing the 1812 overture, they would not even have looked up. She noticed that Anastasia had closed her table and slipped away through the curtains at the back of the room. Slightly nonplussed, Kate put her bottle into the ice bucket beside Don, who remained stationery.

'Awright?' The jaw shot in her direction.

'Yes, thank you, Don, and how are you tonight?'

The question seemed to be too much for Don. His brow furrowed and his gaze settled on the far wall of the room. 'Cabaret,' he mumbled.

'Right.' Kate felt an understanding nod was the correct way to finish the conversation and she moved towards the tables. No-one looked up, so she walked on into the hall. The entrances to the two rooms were side by side, so Kate could keep an eye on her charges while satisfying her curiosity.

'Good evening, Ms Bradshaw. Come to enjoy the show?'

Kate turned slowly to see the thin smile, the raised eyebrows and the brylcreemed hair of Geoffrey Hamilton.

'Mr Hamilton. I see that you haven't taken my Mercedes back to your employers yet.'

'Whose Mercedes, Miss Bradshaw?'

'My Mercedes, Mr Hamilton.'

The smile widened. 'Perks of the job. It'll be back with them soon enough. Now, if you'll excuse me, I have to check the bar.'

Without bothering to reply, Kate turned towards the room next door. It was crammed with men. The lights were dim and spotlights lit the small raised stage, reflecting off the red velvet curtains and making it look like a cross between hell and a funeral parlour. But then, reflected Kate, that's probably a fair way of summing up a brothel. She gasped. That was the first time that she had allowed herself to use that word. Up to now, even in her thoughts, it had always been 'the club' or 'the place'.

My God, she thought, I'm working in a brothel. Me, Kate Bradshaw, daughter of Methodists, polite suburban housewife, mother of two, always give money to the Christian Aid lady, well, nearly always, I am actually working in a brothel. Kate giggled. What would my headmistress say now? In that last report, the old bag had written "Kate will no doubt marry well and become an upright member of the community, eventually." Ha, been there, done that. Now look at me. She was surprised to discover that she was actually enjoying herself, more than she had for quite a long time. She looked back into the gaming room; the figures were still slumped over the tables. Just then she heard a woman's voice from across the hall behind her and froze.

'Come on, Charlie, hurry up. We don't want to miss the good bit.' A voice from so many liquid lunches, source of a hundred dirty jokes, most of which Kate had to pretend to understand. The voice that had constantly hectored her to do better at the gym, to spend more in the shop, to drink faster, find a man. Jane. What the hell was she doing here? Head down, Kate slipped furtively over into the gaming room as the two figures rushed by. Very, very slowly she took a few steps backwards until she could peer round into the other room. Jane and her companion, tall and chunky, as usual, were pushing their way into the centre of the crowd with liberal use of elbows. She took a deep breath; she could feel herself shaking. The pleasure of just a moment ago had evaporated and, in its place, reality had forced its way in.

She could picture it, people pointing and whispering in Waitrose, the kids coming back from school with looks of disbelieving shock, she would need to move, start a new life, probably leave the country. It was Spain, wasn't it, where the criminals and low life crawled off to, as her mother put it? Her mother! Think what capital she would make of it. 'Well, at least your sister has made something of herself but you have ended where I always suspected, in a den of iniquity. I can see that I shall have to come down and sort you out, young lady.' Kate shuddered.

Just then all the lights in the room dimmed and music thumped out. A cheer rose from the crowd. Two spotlights speared the stage. Kate's eyebrows shot up to see the stud who was now standing there, gyrating slowly and secured into his costume by so many belts, straps and buckles that Kate's immediate thought was to wonder whether he'd remembered to go to the loo before the performance; this was not a costume to be caught short in.

A rather embarrassed silence fell on the mostly male audience, a silence that was broken by a loud whistle, unmistakably from Jane. Then a roar went up as two obviously feminine arms, clad in elbow-length lace gloves, wound themselves from behind around his chest. The hands started to undo the straps that secured his jacket.

Then two more arms, this time in red leather, reached between his legs and started to undo the straps at his ankles. The big man, still gyrating slowly, licked his lips and waggled his eyebrows. Kate worked hard to suppress her giggles.

She had seen a show like this before. Stephen had taken her on a business trip to Berlin some years ago and the very important client had insisted that dinner be followed by a trip to The Big Love Apple, a club that Stephen had clearly known.

It had done very little for her then, much to Stephen's later disappointment, and this was having a similar lack of effect.

Then something happened that ensured that her attention was unwavering. The two sets of arms started to ease round the body, black lace to the left, red leather to the right. Black lace appeared first, a short, curvaceous blonde whom Kate did not recognise. Then red leather swung out, striking a pose. There, with legs astride, hands on hips, the leather catsuit unzipped to the waist, stood Anastasia, glowering at the audience, lips curled.

Kate gasped and had to bite her own lip to stop shouting out. What was she doing there? Wasn't she a croupier? The music swelled louder and all three started a dance that entailed, as far as Kate could see, wiggling their hips to the point of dislocation while randomly running their hands over each other's bodies. Cheers rose again from the watching crowd. Shouts of 'Sandwich, sandwich' started up. Kate looked around to see if the catering team had arrived before realising that the three dancers had now closed up, the man sandwiched between the two women. Again the man licked his lips and waggled his eyebrows. This time Kate did not feel like giggling. Black lace had started shedding parts of her clothing. Anastasia had eased the catsuit off her shoulder. Several of the man's straps and buckles were now hanging loose.

At first, Kate thought that the flashing blue light that seemed to suddenly bathe the room was part of the show. Then she realised that it was coming from behind her. A shout and a crash made her spin round.

Muddle came flying through the front door, coat tails spinning, locked in the arms of a large policeman. For a moment, their strange waltz, five foot two Muddle and the six foot policeman, seemed part of the equally bizarre act that was happening on the stage behind her. Four more policemen burst through the door. Kate was knocked to one side as Don came galloping out of the gaming room. She glimpsed something close to a smile on his face as he charged at the men in blue.

Heads had turned in the cabaret room, faces changing

quickly from delight to fear. The three performers stood, confused and out of time while the loud music continued to bump and grind, ignorant of the intrusion of the real world. On the floor, where Don's rugby barge had sent her sprawling, Kate reversed quickly on all fours until she was under one of the unoccupied tables in the gaming room; the hardened gamblers did not even look up as she crawled crab-like past them. Although well towards the back of the room, she could see out into the hall. Don was grappling with three of the officers and seemed to be winning. Just then, she saw the long, elegant legs of Charles come down the stairs and heard his voice above the music.

'Gentlemen, gentlemen. We seem to have a bit of a misunderstanding here.'

One of the policemen broke away from the mêlée. 'If you don't chain up your bloody gorilla, here, you will be in even more serious trouble.' He adjusted the helmet that had slipped over one eye. 'Sir.'

Charles did his best. He came down to the floor of the hall and danced around the fight like a boxing referee. 'Don, Don,' he attempted. Then, even louder, 'Donald, do stop, there's a good chap. These people are guests.' It took a few moments for the word 'guests' to filter through to Don's few remaining synapses but gradually he stopped. He stood, three policemen hanging from him, with a look of childish disappointment spreading on his face, as if he had just been refused his favourite chocolates.

Kate glimpsed Hamilton oozing out of the bar opposite and making his way across the back wall towards the staff area. She was delighted to see a blue arm reach out and grab his collar. Guests were starting to move nervously out of the cabaret room, looking for a way out. Charles was in earnest conversation with one of the policemen. Still, the music blared. Transfixed, Kate watched from her hiding place under the gaming table.

A hand suddenly grabbed her shoulder. She screeched, jerked up, banged her head on the underside of the table. A voice whispered in her ear.

'Shut up, Kate, follow.' Head thumping, Kate turned awkwardly round, still on all fours, to see the leather-clad figure of Anastasia crouched beside her. 'Follow, silly person. Is time to go. Now.' And she moved across the room at a crouching run to the back wall. Kate staggering behind, still holding her head. Anastasia pressed against one of the panels, which swung open.

'So that's where you went earlier. How does it work?'

'You want science lesson or you want escape?' hissed Anastasia. 'Follow.'

'Wait, my handbag. It's on the cabinet there.'

Anastasia's eyes widened in exasperation. 'You want apply make-up too, Kate?'

'No, it's got the car keys and my house key and stuff in it.'

'Go, quick.'

Kate dashed across the room, grabbed the bag and returned. She noticed that, although the croupier had now vanished, the three poker players remained crouched over the table.

She ran through the hidden door. They were in a dark corridor. Anastasia led them off to the right, through another door and they were in the passage that led to the back car park. They ran towards the back door and out into a dark, warm night.

Kate ran towards the Toyota, fumbling in her bag for the keys.

'Wait.' Anastasia's imperious voice pulled her up. 'I think we take better car.'

'What?'

'You like your Mercedes, no, Kate?'

'Anastasia, this is no time for a discussion about cars. We have to go, get away.' She found she was starting to shiver, in spite of the warmth.

The other girl held up her right hand. Kate saw something glinting.

'I think these will help.'

'My keys. Anastasia, how..? I mean, what…?'

Anastasia grinned. 'Now you not speak good English. I explain later. Come, we go. You can drive or is head too hurting?'

Kate grinned back. 'Oh, yes. Even a broken skull would not keep me from doing this.'

They ran towards the car. Kate took the keys and pressed the pad to unlock the doors. They plunged into the leather seats. Kate took a moment to breath in the sweet smell of opulence. Then as she reached to close the door, a voice came from the darkness.

'Excuse me, madam. I wonder if I could prevail upon you to provide me with some assistance. In the transportation area, that is.'

The rather bedraggled figure of Muddle emerged from the darkness. One lapel of his red jacket was torn, his usually immaculately combed hair hung loose, he was limping.

'Do excuse the appearance, madam. Not up to my usual standard.'

Kate swung out of the seat and lifted it forward. 'Jump in, Muddle.' The small man fitted easily in to the tiny space in the back of the car.

'Thank you, madam. Most kind.'

'Oh, God,' said Kate suddenly. 'They'll be out front. How the hell are we going to get past them?'

Muddle cleared his voice. 'I believe you will find that that track over there leads to a rear entrance. I strongly recommend its use. It would perhaps be prudent to negotiate it without the use of headlights.'

Kate eased the car down the bumpy track. After about half a mile they came to a gate. Anastasia jumped out, swung it open and they were away. Kate headed for home. And an uncertain future. She had no idea what would happen now but, somehow, she knew it would be interesting.

Chapter 8
LATE SATURDAY NIGHT

'OK, Anastasia, now tell me. How did you get those keys?'

'Mr greasy Hamilton, he likes to, how you say, cop a feel with the girls. He try it with me many times. So, tonight, he tries again and I am thinking, you want from me, I get from you. So, while he is doing the hands thing, I am doing the pockets thing. Is fair exchange, as you English say.'

'Is very fair,' laughed Kate.

'And I have his wallet as well, in case we need. I have feeling he not need for some time.'

A voice came from the back. 'I have to say, Miss Anastasia, that, while I do not usually condone such criminal activity, from my observations, the gentleman in question did, indeed, have it coming to him.'

'You don't miss much, do you, Muddle?' observed Kate. 'Now, where can I drop you off?'

'Actually, madam, I live back at the house. A situation that, on reflection, was perhaps not the wisest course of action.'

'In that case,' Kate replied without hesitation, 'I would be honoured if you would be my guest tonight.'

'Why thank you, madam. The honour would be entirely mine, I assure you. Then, with the breaking of the day, I shall seek more appropriate employment.'

'Well, we can let tomorrow look after itself. That's always worked for me. What about you, Anastasia.'

The dark hair was tossed in a loose shrug. 'I have friends. But tonight, I will stay with you also. We have to talk business in the morning, Kate.'

For a moment, Kate was confused. Then she remembered the trick with the cards. 'Oh, that. Yes, tomorrow.'

The rest of the drive back to her house was taken up with sharing the impressions of an eventful evening. Muddle told of his attempts to keep 'the heathen hordes at bay'. When asked how he had escaped, he replied rather proudly, if enigmatically, 'Once a boy scout, always a boy scout,' and would not be drawn on any further explanation. Anastasia explained how she had slipped away through the back of the stage, leaving the other two performers confused and leaden footed, and Kate worked very hard to stop herself asking what on earth Anastasia thought she was doing, making such an exhibition of herself in the first place.

It was quarter past one by the time they reached Kate's house. They were still in full conversation, laughing with the relief of having escaped, as they burst in through the front door.

As they stood in the hall, deciding whether they needed white wine or gin, Tom appeared, bleary-eyed, at the top of the stairs.

Looking down at his dishevelled mother, flanked by a tall, black-haired girl in a red leather cat suit still unzipped to the waist and a small man dressed as a circus ringmaster, he sank down to sit on the top step.

'Bloody hell, Halloween has come early this year,' and he then fixed his gaze on Anastasia's cleavage, the like of which he had only witnessed so far in his young life in computer games and a couple of borrowed, dog-eared and rather smeared magazines. 'That or Christmas' he murmured and sighed happily.

A rare matriarchal moment came over Kate as she saw her fourteen-year-old drifting rapidly towards the rocks of adulthood. 'Tom, back to bed. And stop drooling.'

'What? Aren't you even going to introduce me, then?'

'In the morning. Go.'

Anastasia stepped forward and undulated up the stairs. 'Good evening, Tom. I am...' she paused, drew in a deep breath as she leant forward, testing the retaining power of leather to its full... 'Anastasia,' she exhaled, holding out her right hand. Tom stared at it for a full five seconds before grasping it in a way a man might grasp a live electricity cable.

His mouth opened and closed like a guppy's. 'Erm ...

Ger,' was all he could manage.

'Anastasia,' said Kate sharply, 'Put him down and come back here immediately.'

Surprised at the firm tone, Anastasia looked down at Kate, one eyebrow dramatically raised. She turned back to Tom. 'Goodbye, Tomasko, for now,' and she glided back down, leaving him enveloped in perfume and confusion.

'Find someone your own size to play with,' Kate hissed. 'Tom, off with you.'

'I think I'll just sit here for a minute, if that's OK, Mum.'

Kate was about to insist, then noticed Tom's anguished face. 'Oh, right. Well, just for a minute, until you're, until, oh, whatever.'

'Muddle,' came a clear, loud voice to her left.

'Sorry?'

'Just introducing myself to the young gentleman. Can't be standing in a stranger's house and remain a stranger. Bad etiquette.' He bowed towards Tom. 'Muddle,' he repeated, 'At your service.'

'OK,' replied Tom with a wide-eyed look towards his mother.

'Now, let's get out of the hall before we wake Miranda up.'

'Oh, no risk of that. She's much too...' Tom's voice petered out as he came up against his mother's icy glare.

'She's much too what?'

Tom suddenly had the look of someone on the edge of a chasm, knowing with absolute certainty that he was on his way down into it.

'She's much too what, Tom.'

'Er, she's, er, she's much too asleep?' Even Tom winced at that one.

Kate stormed up the stairs, pushing past Tom who, now well able to stand, ran up behind her. She swung open the door to Miranda's room and snapped the light on. What she saw; too big a shape in the bed, too many limbs, confirmed her worst suspicions.

'You, whoever you are, out. Now. Eugh, no, OK, no, five,

no two minutes to get dressed, then out.'

She swung back down the stairs and took a deep breath as she faced the two upturned faces. Muddle's wore a look of quiet concern, Anastasia's one of amused detachment.

'Would you excuse us as we sort out a little domestic issue? Please go through into the sitting room. Tom,' she clicked her fingers at her son, 'Tom will bring you a drink.'

Tom eased carefully past her. She grabbed his arm. 'And don't even think of coming out of that room until I tell you.'

As soon as the door closed behind the others Kate collapsed against the wall. What was happening to her life? She had escaped rape and jail thanks to people who, two days ago, she had never met nor imagined to exist, while her own family, her babies, seemed to have morphed into strange aliens with grown-up, Kate shuddered, urges.

A door opened upstairs. A tall figure in a black leather jacket with long dark hair over his face came pounding down the stairs. With a muttered, 'Sorry, Mrs Bradshaw,' he was down and out of the front door.

'It's Ms, actually,' muttered Kate to the gaping door. She turned and headed upstairs to Miranda's room. Her daughter was sitting on her bed, now wearing a T shirt and a frown like a knitting pattern.

'Now, you listen to me,' Kate started.

'No, Mum, you listen to me. How could you be so embarrassing? Are you really so jealous? Do you know what this is going to do to me with my friends?'

Kate fought back from the onslaught. 'Don't even begin to think about your friends. You won't be seeing them for quite a while, I can promise you that. What the hell did you think you were doing?'

'You mean you didn't recognise it,' spat Miranda. 'God, it has been a long time. Poor daddy.'

'How dare you. I am your mother. You don't talk to me like that.' Kate fought down echoes of her mother's voice saying exactly the same words.

'My mother? Now you want to be my mother. Now that

you can't afford to do anything else, you want to be mummy. Well, news flash. It's too late. You can't suddenly come in here with the caring conscience crap and expect me to be your little baby.'

'But, you're only fifteen. You're my responsibility.'

'I'm sixteen in two weeks. Then it's all legal and nice and you can stop fretting. You're just worried that you might get sued because we were doing it in your house. Well, don't be; we'll stay outside for the next two weeks, Darren and I. Or you don't come home until you're supposed to, then you won't have to think about it.'

'Darren? Was that Darren? Linda Johnson's boy? He must be at least nineteen.'

'So?'

'So, he's too old.'

'You mean it's OK if I do it with someone my own age?'

'No. No. I mean, I mean it's not OK with anyone, not at your age.'

'So, it'll be OK in two weeks, then.'

Kate felt real fury rise up in her for the first time in many years. She was angrier even than when she had found out about Stephen. That, at least, had not really been a surprise. Staring at the sulky face opposite her, she shouted at it without restraint, 'It will not be OK. Whatever has gone before, it's obviously time for a few changes around here. First thing tomorrow, we talk. No, I talk, you listen.'

Kate spun round before Miranda could recover, slammed the door and went downstairs.

Taking a deep breath, she opened the door to the sitting room. Anastasia was lying full length on a sofa, glass in hand, staring with little interest at a comedy show on television. Muddle was winding a piece of string round a metal upright lamp.

'And that, young man,' he was saying to a fascinated Tom, 'Is a round turn and two half hitches, such as the Macedonians would have used to tie up their horses.' Tom was nodding as if the secrets of the universe itself were being revealed.

'Tom, bed. And don't talk to your sister.'

Tom was about to object until he saw the expression on his mother's face.

'OK, Mum. See you tomorrow.'

'Now,' said Kate briskly, 'We need to get beds sorted out for you both. Anastasia, you can have the au pair's room. She's out with friends tonight. I'll get you some clean sheets. Muddle, I am afraid that you will need to sleep in the study. There's a fold-down bed in there.'

'Not a problem, madam. It will, I'm sure, be most commodious.' He paused and looked closely at Kate. 'Is there anything in particular that you might like to discuss at this juncture, madam?'

'That's kind of you, Muddle, but not tonight. I really don't think I can tonight.'

'I understand, madam.'

Kate busied herself getting sheets, blankets and towels together, showing where the bathroom was and getting everyone settled. Finally alone, she paused on the landing, looking at the firmly closed doors of her two children. She went into her bedroom and only then allowed herself to weep.

Chapter 9
SUNDAY MORNING

For once Kate woke early. She lay half out of her duvet, which was twisted and crumpled by an unsettled night. It took her about four seconds to remember the various causes for the interrupted sleep. Garish clips of the previous night exploded in her head in quick succession until bouncers, half-naked teenagers, heavy-footed strippers, liveried doormen and police, oh, God, police gavotted together like one of those 1960's Italian movies that Stephen had made her sit through.

Kate groaned. OK, she had a choice. She could stay in bed like a coward or get up and face the world. No contest, pull up the duvet, snuggle down, the world does not exist. So it was with some surprise that Kate found herself, even before the thought had finished, up and on the way to the en-suite bathroom. She turned the shower on full, shed the satin pyjamas and stepped in. She would wash away all that bad feeling; it never really happened. She scrubbed hard but it was not working. 'Right, time for the full works.' A defiant, pioneering spirit surged through her as she reached over and turned the knob to cold. This would get her ready for the day.

The needles of freezing water hit her like shotgun pellets.

'Shit,' she yelled, stumbling back and twisting away. 'Bad idea. Bad idea.' Trapped against the shower door, she fumbled for the handle. The water pounded her back. Her shaking hand finally located the handle, wrenched the door open. She stood, crouched, shivering, dripping water onto her pyjamas.

'Bugger, bugger, bugger,' she moaned, clutching for a towel. She wrapped herself into its warm folds and sank to her knees. She felt tears pushing through again.

'Oh, no you don't. Get up and get on with it, my girl.' Kate barely recognised the inner voice. For so long, she had been listening to the other one, the one that said, 'Oh, poor you, of course you don't have to do it if you don't want to' in that soft, girly, seductive way that had guided her along the lower, easier path through the world. But not this time. The last twelve hours, indeed the last three days had shown Kate very clearly that she could not sit back and wait for someone else to sort things out for her.

She rose to her feet and quickly dried herself off. She marched back into her bedroom, taking care not to look in the bathroom mirror. Recently, Kate had found that her face tended to wake up some thirty minutes after the rest of her body and mirrors were not good friends until after the first cup of coffee. Today, she knew, would need at least two cups.

Quickly pulling on jeans and a sweater, she left the safety of her room. Walking cautiously past her daughter's closed door, she hurried downstairs. From the kitchen came the aroma of fresh coffee. Muddle appeared in the hall.

'Ah, good morning, madam. I took the liberty of preparing some coffee. I always find that a brew of the finest Arabicas does improve one's view of the world. One's Weltanschau, as I believe our Germanic cousins would say.'

'Well, whatever that means, the coffee's certainly very welcome. Thank you, Muddle. And please stop calling me madam. My days as a madam, or even a trainee madam, are well over after last night, I feel.'

'Yes, that was a bit of a palaver, was it not? So, how would you like me to address you?'

'I think Kate would be fine, Muddle.'

'Very good, madam. I shall bear that in mind. Now, if you'll excuse me, it's time for my morning constitutional. I do like to smell the day, so to speak, before I get too deep into it.'

'Oh, er, right. If you go to the end of the avenue, to the right, you'll find there's a small wood just opposite. It's quite nice there, I think.' Kate could not recall having been down there for several years and did wonder if it was now full of beer cans, condoms and needles. She hoped not.

'Sounds perfect. I am very partial to trees.' He pulled his doorman's jacket off the back of one of the chairs. The gold braid flashed as he swung it on.

'Er, Muddle. Would you like something a little less, well, conspicuous?'

'I am what I am, madam,' and he was gone out of the door. Kate noticed as he left that the torn lapel was already sown back.

She took a grateful swig of coffee. She did not usually bother with breakfast but the need for fuel for the morning, coupled with the lack of food last night had her rummaging in the cereal cupboard. Choice was limited but she emerged with a packet of Chocolate-flavoured Honey Pops. Kate glared at the cheery teddy bear on the front of the packet that assured her that they were choco-wocko-licious. She conjured up an image of a teddy bear being spit-roasted over an open fire and felt a little better.

She found a plate, poured in a small amount of cereal and some milk from the jug that Muddle had placed on the table. Taking a spoon from the drawer, she scooped up some of the dark brown mush. 'My God, no wonder those kids are so weird if this is what they eat.' Survival instinct took over and she replaced the spoon, cut herself a slice of bread and dropped it into the toaster. Just as it popped up, she heard the door to Miranda's bedroom slam. She knew it was Miranda's; no other door in the house slammed with quite such an attitude. Taking a deep breath and wishing fervently that she had listened to the other voice and stayed in bed, Kate went to the kitchen door. Miranda was coming down the stairs, a coat pulled tightly around her, her crossed arms holding it in place and the world at bay.

'Good morning, Miranda. We need to talk.'

'I'm going out.'

'What? Where? No, you're staying in.'

'You going to stop me?'

'If I have to, yes.'

Miranda glared at her mother, gave one short, sharp laugh and pushed past to the door.

'Miranda, this is important.'

'To you, maybe, not to me.'

'Are you going to meet…?' Kate's mind went blank.

'See, you don't even remember his bloody name.'

'I've a lot to think about.'

'And I'm well down the list, obviously.'

'No, of course you're not. I mean, you're my daughter.'

'Yeah, right.' Miranda spun round and was gone. The floor shook with the reverberation of the slamming front door.

'Darren,' shouted Kate to the closed door. 'It's Darren.'

'Well,' said the cute little voice in her head, 'That did go well, didn't it?'

'Oh, shut up.'

'I haven't said anything, yet.' The plaintive voice came from behind her. Tom was walking blearily down the stairs.

'No, sorry, Tom. Not you.'

The boy looked around, saw no-one else and decided that an explanation would probably not help. 'Is that coffee I can smell?'

'Yes, Muddle made it. Help yourself.'

Tom poured himself a cup. 'That Muddle guy's pretty cool. Where did you find him?'

'Oh, um, at work.'

'So, what's he doing here?'

'He… well….he is helping me on a project.'

'Cool. Are you going to eat those Honey Pops?'

'No.'

'Great.' He reached over, grabbed the spoon and started shovelling. 'Was that Miranda I heard going out?'

'Yes.'

'Oh.' More shovelling. 'That other person, that woman.' Kate detected a tremor in the voice, even through the Honey Pops. 'I mean, who is she? Is she, like, helping you on your project?'

'She certainly is.'

'So, I mean, is she going to be staying for while too?'

Kate smiled. 'Yes, she probably is. Is that a problem for you?'

'No, no. I mean no, no, not at all. Is it OK if I have a few friends round later?'

'In the interests of Anglo-Russian relations, you mean.'

'What? No. Oh, shut up, Mum.' Kate watched the colour creep over Tom's face, right to the tips of his ears and felt a fondness for him that she had not felt for many years. It was an unexpectedly good feeling.

'Don't worry, Tom, I'll keep Anastasia on a lead,' she assured him, not at all sure that such a thing was possible.

'Hey, don't worry about me. I can handle myself. Do you want that bit of toast?'

'OK, Tom.' Suppressing a laugh, she refilled her coffee mug. Just then, she heard the front door open. She turned to see, coming into the kitchen, Muddle and Miranda.

'The young lady thought she would come back and have a chat with you, madam. Good morning, young Thomas. If you'd like to accompany me to the sitting room, I shall introduce you to the wonders of the Ashley's stopper knot, also known as the Oysterman.'

'Cool,' grinned Tom, jumping from his chair, toast in hand.

'Ladies, if you'll excuse us.' Muddle gave a brief bow and ushered Tom out, closing the door behind him.

Kate and Miranda stared at each other in silence.

'Well?' Kate broke the stand-off.

'Well what?'

'What made you come back?'

'That guy, where did you find him?'

'I work, worked at the same place as him.'

'Worked? You lost your job already?'

'Sort of, I suppose.'

'Typical. He's, well, quite persuasive, isn't he.'

Kate thought back to the altercation with the drunk in the car park two nights before. 'Yes, I guess he is. Why, what did he say?'

'Dunno, really. He just sort of appeared beside me up the road and we started chatting. Funny, he gave a little kind of bow when he introduced himself. 'Pardon me for intruding,

Miss Miranda,' he goes. I mean, Miss Miranda, where is he from? 'But we didn't have the opportunity to make acquaintance last evening' or something like that. Weird.' Miranda gave a short, embarrassed laugh.

'Ah, yes, last evening.'

'Yeah.'

'Look, I…'

'Mum, you're not going for the big heart to heart, are you. I mean, I came back but that doesn't mean it's all roses and luvvy, you know. I meant what I said, you can't just step back into the mummy role just because you've nothing else to do.'

'I know, and, by the way, I have plenty else to do, like earning some money to get you food, for a start.'

'Well, and how much did you earn so far?'

For the first time, Kate realised that she had not received any money for the last two days. And almost certainly never would.

'Never you mind.'

'It's nothing, isn't it? You've lost the only job you've ever had after two days. Nice going, Mum.'

'Well, it wasn't suitable.'

'Hm.' An unconvinced grunt was Miranda's only reply.

'Anyway,' Kate struggled to get back to the topic that she wanted to cover, 'That's beside the point. Something else will come up, already has, actually.'

'Like what?'

'Never you mind.'

'Yeah, right.'

'Listen, Miranda, you're fifteen. That's the point of this conversation. You're fifteen and you shouldn't, well, shouldn't be doing what you were doing last night.'

'So, what was I doing last night?'

'Do you really want me to say it?'

'Yeah, go on.'

'You were in bed with a boy, well a man, frankly.'

'Yes, and..?'

'What do you mean, yes, and. And, well, and that's illegal,

for one thing.'

'What is, being in a bed with someone?'

'Yes, I mean no, not just being in a bed, of course not, but doing what you were, well, you know.'

'Yes, I do know, actually, Mum, but do you? What was I doing, then?'

'Well, you were, I mean, weren't you?'

'Do you mean, was I screwing him, Mum? Is that what you want to know? Whether Darren and I were fucking?'

'Miranda!'

'Well, for God's sake. You can think it but you can't say it.'

Kate fumbled for the kettle, walked to the sink to fill it and switched it on. Refocused, she swung round. 'Right, you listen to me. Whatever you think of me, I am your mother and you are in my house.'

'Dad's house, you mean.'

'No, my house. Legally, my house. Not your father's, mine. And that means that I have a responsibility for you whether you like it or not. And, frankly, whether I like it or not. Do you wonder that I wanted to spend as little time with you as I could, I mean, listen to yourself. You're really not nice to be around.'

To Kate's astonishment, her daughter's eyes began to fill with tears.

'Oh, Miranda, I'm sorry, I didn't mean...'

'Yes you did. You've never liked me, 'cos I got on so well with Dad and you were jealous.'

'What?'

'Don't deny it, I could see it, we both could, we were even having a laugh about it last....'

'Last? Last what? Last what, Miranda? When?'

The door flew open and Anastasia stood, clad only in one of Miranda's old tee shirts and a pair of pants. Miranda gazed at the intruder, astonishment transforming her face from a scowl to a wide-eyed stare.

'I need coffee,' announced Anastasia. 'I do not wait

longer.'

'Not now, Anastasia.'

'Now. Coffee. Then you can shout at each other like butcher's wives some more.'

Miranda found her voice, or at least part of it. 'Mother, who... why... what... is this? Another person you used to work with?'

'Anastasia, Miranda. Miranda, Anastasia.' Anastasia paused, looked Miranda up and down. 'Is very young for sex.'

'Thank you, Anastasia. Just what I've been trying to tell her. Fifteen is really...'

'Is fifteen? Oh, that not so bad. In my country...'

'Anastasia. Enough. You're not helping.'

'We need to get rid of car. I can do.'

'Get rid of my Mercedes. I don't think so.'

'Man with busy hands, Hamilton, he know where you live, yes?'

'Well, yes, but he's in jail.'

'Is ten o'clock,' Anastasia said slowly, as if explaining to a primary school class. 'He will have bail by eleven and will come looking.'

'You seem very well informed.'

Anastasia shrugged. 'Anyway, is too small.'

'Too small for what?'

'For you, me and Muddle. And her.'

'Her? Miranda? You're not thinking of involving her, are you?'

'Involving me in what?'

'And you are not thinking of leaving her here on her own, are you,' Anastasia mimicked.

Kate was confused. 'But where are we going?'

'To make money, Kate. Is for what we are here. Now, do you make me coffee or do I make myself?'

Without thinking, Kate took a mug down from the cupboard, spooned in some instant coffee and poured on milk from the jug.

'I not get real coffee?'

'Oh, sorry, it's gone cold. I'll make some more later.'

'OK. I take horse piss.'

Miranda stared as both women burst out laughing.

'Here,' Kate spluttered. 'Here is your instant gold freeze-dried horse piss.'

Anastasia gave a bow, confirming in the process that she wasn't wearing a bra. 'Thank you.'

'And whatever you do, Anastasia, do not go into the sitting room before you're dressed. I might at least be able to save one of my children.'

'I go shower,' and she swept out of the room.

Miranda remained rooted to the spot.' I am never going to wear that tee shirt again. You know, Mum, you're starting to get interesting.'

'Last what, Miranda. When did you talk to your father?'

'What? Oh, that was nothing. Slip of the tongue, you know. Anyway, I'd better go and, er change, or something.'

'No. you're staying right here until you tell me what's going on.'

'Mum, it's nothing. I mean, he is my dad. Why can't I talk to him if I want to?'

'Where is he?'

'What? I don't know. It's a mobile number, OK? He calls me, whatever. OK? He does the same with Tom, you know. It's not just me.'

'Is it a UK number?'

'Why?'

'Well, I want to know whether your father, the person, by the way, who has defaulted on paying what he owes me, owes us, whether he's in this country or Hong Kong, as he claims or wherever.

'Der. What does it matter? He could be anywhere and still have a UK number. You don't really know much about the modern world, do you, Mum?'

'Get me that number, now.'

Miranda turned and stalked out of the kitchen. Kate took a deep breath.

'Tom,' she shouted at the top of her voice. 'Get in here.'

Tom came bouncing into the kitchen. 'That man is so cool, I mean weird but really cool too. He's just been….' Tom caught sight of the expression on his mother's face. His own face took on the default teenage boy look of 'I know I've done something wrong, I'm not sure what it is but I'll just stand here and see if I can bluff my way out.'

'What's up, Mum?' His attempt to sound nonchalant was wide of the mark.

'Have you been talking to your father?'

'Ah.'

'I take that as yes, then. How could you, Tom? How could you go behind my back like that?'

'What? It wasn't behind your back. I mean, not really. Not like that. It was just, you know, he called, on Mirry's phone and I was around and she's, like, come on, you've got to talk to Dad and he's there asking me how I am and what I'm up to and that and, I mean, am I supposed to ignore him or what?' Tom paused for breath, hoping for a reply. None came. He ploughed on. 'It's only happened a few times.'

'When was the last time?

'Last week, I think. Yeah, no, earlier this week. Monday? Tuesday? Not sure. Probably. Yeah, probably.'

'Well, I'm glad we've cleared that up. Where was he calling from?'

'His mobile.'

'Yes, I know he was calling from his mobile. But where from. Where was he when he called you?'

'Don't know. Didn't use the camera phone. The Bat Cave, maybe.'

'Don't try and get smart, Tom. Smart is way beyond your reach. How good was the connection? Did he say what time it was? Did he say what the weather was like? Did you hear anything in the background?' Thank you, *Columbo*, Kate thought.

'Wow, good questions, Mum, real detective stuff. But no, no and no. Background, could have been waves but was probably just static.'

'So, a long way off then.'

'No, sorry, Mum, but you can get static from just round the corner. Or he could have been sitting in a tub of snakes.'

Kate allowed herself a brief moment with that image, then pulled herself back. 'Tom, this is very serious. This man, your father, is cheating us.'

'Yes, well, maybe, but he's still Dad, isn't he? I mean, he's not going to do us any harm, is he?'

'Tom, listen to me. Your father…'

The door flew open and Anastasia appeared, a very small bath towel draped around her. 'I need knickers, Kate. Do you have? But not those balloon bags you English women wear. I need small, not like my grandmother wore in Siberian winter.' She spotted Tom's open-mouthed gaze. 'Ah, good morning, Thomas,' she purred. 'And did you sleep well? Nice dreams?' Tom's mouth opened and shut but no noise emerged.

'In my room, Anastasia. Top drawer on the left. Help yourself. Since I have not yet experienced a Siberian winter, I'm sure you will find what you want,' Kate said firmly, fervently hoping she was right. Anastasia swung out, closely followed by her towel and Tom's eyes.

'Now, where were we?"

'Huh?'

'Tom, hello. Earth to Mars. Sorry to disturb your fantasies but we were just having the most important conversation of your life. May I drag you back to it?'

Reluctantly, Tom's eyes came back into focus. 'Not much more I can say, Mum, really. Told you all I can.'

Miranda came back into the kitchen. 'I've checked, Mum, and no help I'm afraid. It comes up as Private Number.'

'What do you mean?'

Miranda sighed. 'If someone does not want you to know the number they're calling from, they can have private number come up on your screen. You can't call them back.'

'But you said just now, you said 'why can't I talk to him whenever I like?' That means you were calling him.'

'No it doesn't.'

'It does.'

'It doesn't, Mum. God, don't you believe me, then? That's typical. And I suppose you believed everything geek-face here told you. It's just how it always is. Your precious little boy can't do a thing wrong.'

Tom turned on her. 'Oh, shut up, Mirry. It's not my fault if you're such a bad-tempered cow.'

'Right,' Kate intervened. 'Miranda, back to your room and Tom, back to yours.'

'Oh, Mum, that's really unfair,' they chorused.

'Now.' The two scowled at her and, to her astonishment, trooped out. Kate reached for her coffee, now tepid but still welcome and needed. The phone rang. She sighed and put down her cup. Muddle's head appeared round the door. 'Shall I get that, Madam?'

'Oh, would you, Muddle? Thanks.'

She heard him pick up the receiver in the hall. 'Mrs Bradshaw's residence. Whom shall I say is calling? Her mother? One moment, please, madam, I shall enquire.' Kate rushed to the kitchen door and gesticulated wildly. Without hesitation, Muddle raised the receiver to his mouth again. 'I am so sorry, madam, but Mrs Bradshaw is otherwise engaged at this moment. May I take a message to ameliorate the inconvenience? I, madam? I am an acquaintance currently temporarily residing on her kind hospitality. My name is Muddle. No, madam, Muddle. Yes, that is correct. No, just Muddle. So, what may I convey to the lady in question? Is that so? Oh, yes, I do sympathise. Though I have to say, as one only recently acquainted with your family, I would observe that the blessings that progeny bring do appear to far outweigh any minor discomfitures. Well, yes, that may be, madam, but I have personally found Mrs Bradshaw nothing but a supportive colleague and a true friend in need. Yes, Mrs Katherine Bradshaw. That is the one of whom I speak. Certainly, madam. I will pass on your message at the first opportunity. Yes, and to you, madam. Goodbye.'

He carefully replaced the phone on its cradle. 'Would you please call your mother at the first opportunity? A lady of opinions of considerable strength though rather less substance, if I may be so bold.'

'You may and she is. I think you have summed her up very well.'

Anastasia appeared on the stairs. 'I am ready to go.' Kate looked up, recognising her own leather jeans and Armani sweater. 'I borrow from you. Is a bit big but will do for now.' Kate swallowed hard.

'I'm sorry, Anastasia, I meant to say, if you needed a bra, I have…'

'I no use. My breasts still facing upwards.' Kate was sure she heard Tom moan through the closed bedroom door. 'Now, I go change car. Keys.'

'Look, are you sure about this? I mean, it's a very expensive car.'

'Is unpaid car. Is known car. Is no good car. We change, no-one find us.'

'Well, OK. Perhaps I should come with you.'

Anastasia looked at Kate, eyebrows arched. 'Is my world, Kate. I do, you stay.'

Kate meekly handed over the keys. 'I come back later, then we make money, casino money' and she swept out of the door.

Kate felt as if she was seeing a fraction of a picture and being asked to describe the rest of it. Discomforted, she looked around for something that would take her mind off whatever Anastasia was up to. She had a vague feeling that, whatever it was, it would be illegal. But then, what was one more bit of illegality amongst so much? She sighed and turned her attention to Muddle, who was waiting beside her, poised on the balls of his feet, eyebrows raised, looking very like a Jack Russell waiting for a biscuit.

'Was there something, Muddle?'

'Well, madam, I was just thinking again about your comment concerning my apparel. I do confess that, during my brief sojourn this morning, I did encounter a modicum of rather startled glances and one comment along the lines of, and I will omit the profanities, madam, 'Oi, mate, where's the rest of your circus?' or words to that effect. Given the need to lie doggo, as it were, I do now see the validity of your recommendation for more apposite garments.'

'Oh, good. What do you suggest?'

'Well, madam, if I may be so bold, young Master Thomas does seem to be of broadly similar build to myself. A strapping young lad, does you proud, yes, indeed.'

'Well, yes, I suppose he is, does, I mean.'

'Do you think there might be something in his wardrobe that might not be too inappropriate for someone of greater years?'

'Let's go and check. Tom,' she called out, then remembered that he had been banished to his room. 'Come on, we'll go up and have a look.' She knocked on Tom's door and was greeted by a grunted 'What?' Going in, she explained the situation. 'It's only until we can get to the shops and buy something more permanent.'

'Sure. Why not. Help yourself.' Tom tore himself away from the computer screen and opened the wardrobe doors. 'Don't take any of the t-shirts. I need those.'

'Worry not, Master Thomas,' Muddle replied. 'I do not covet the t-shirts. I find the concept of being a walking advertisement for nihilistic musical bands and the consumption of illegal substances inappropriate for a former scoutmaster.'

Tom's eyebrows furrowed as he tried to work out whether this was a compliment or not.

'No, I believe a shirt of more classic cut, a tie and possibly a suit would fit the bill most satisfactorily.'

'Well, there's that suit you made me wear for Cousin Lucy's wedding last year, Mum. I can't see me wearing that again in a hurry.'

'Hey, steady, we're not talking about giving it away forever. Just until we get to the shops. You don't get rid of it that easily. That was an expensive suit.'

'Fear not, madam. I shall take great care of it.'

'OK, let's give it a go.' She took the suit down from the wardrobe. 'Now, shirt and tie.' Tom rummaged in the drawers and came out with a purple shirt covered in blue butterflies.

'Most decorative but not, I fear, my thing, as you young people say.'

'Oh, OK. I'm sure there's a plain one here somewhere.' He rummaged deeper and eventually came up with a plain white one. 'My school shirt, before they changed the rules,' he announced triumphantly.

'Oh, so white, oh so soft, oh, so sweet is she,' proclaimed Muddle.

'I beg your pardon?'

'Ben Johnson, madam.'

'What, the chap who used to blacken up his face and sing 'Mammy'?'

'No, madam. I believe that was a Mr Al Jolson, an American, though one cannot blame him for that. I was quoting Ben Johnson, a fine English poet. 1573 to 1637, I believe.'

'Oh.'

Muddle cleared his throat. 'Be that as it may, I think that a white shirt would be the bee's knees.'

'Is that another quote from this Ben Johnson guy,' enquired Tom, feeling that things were slipping away from him.

'Quite possibly, young Thomas, though I am not aware of the derivation of that particular phrase. There are, however, many literary references to our apian friends...'

'I think we need to get back to the matter in hand.' Kate was feeling the need for more coffee.

'Quite right, madam. I am letting my attention wander. A dangerous thing when you are out on reconnaissance.'

'Are we out on...? Never mind. Will the shirt fit?'

'Ah, madam. Thereby hangs the rub. I fear that Master Thomas' neck and mine are of considerably different circumference.'

'Oh, yes. Good point.' Kate pondered for a moment. 'I

know. When Stephen went, he left behind a couple of shirts, said they were too ordinary for his new life, the bastard. Sorry, Tom. I've got them in the back of a cupboard somewhere.'

'Sounds ideal, madam.'

Kate went through to her bedroom and pulled down three shirts that were hanging at the back of her wardrobe. She had often looked at them but had been unable to throw them away. She did not know why. It was not as if Stephen meant anything to her now. Fifteen years of marriage seemed distant, another person. Now she was glad about her hesitation. She went to the chest of drawers, opened the bottom drawer and pulled out two silk ties. Returning to Tom's room, she offered them to Muddle with a flourish.

'Excellent, madam. I shall try them on immediately.' Muddle withdrew to the bathroom. Kate went back downstairs and refilled the kettle. Tom wandered down after her.

'Can I come out now?'

'Sorry?'

'You sent me up to my room. Remember?'

'Oh, yes. Right, I suppose so, but you haven't heard the end of this matter of phoning your father.'

'We didn't phone him. We told you. He phoned us.'

'Whatever.'

'No, not whatever, Mum. Us phoning him would be like going behind your back, you know? Him phoning us, well, that's just him phoning us.'

'Yes, I suppose. OK, Tom, but tell me when it happens again. And find out where he is.'

'Well, if we can.'

The kettle boiled. Kate decided that the morning warranted a raid on the last of the ground coffee, a luxury that could not be replaced at the moment. As she was plunging the cafetiere, Muddle appeared at the doorway. Kate was astonished. By just changing his clothes, Muddle had transformed from a strangely comical figure into a smart man about town. Quite at home in the dark grey suit, he would have fitted in round any board table.

'Muddle, you look, well, tremendous.'

'Well, thank you, madam. I must say, I do feel rather fine, if that is not too boastful. As they say, clothes maketh the man.'

'Is that from your…'

'No, madam. Ancient Greeks, I believe, though there is some similar remark in Shakespeare's Hamlet, though I do not recall the exact wording.'

'Coffee?'

'That would be most pleasant.'

Chapter 10
SUNDAY EVENING

The afternoon passed slowly, punctuated only by Miranda appearing silently in the kitchen every half hour to extract a yoghurt from the fridge, make a drink or just glare at whoever happened to be sitting nearby.

Kate began to get anxious. She should have asked Anastasia more questions. She had no idea where she had gone, nor when she would be back. If, indeed, she was coming back. Kate began to feel rather foolish. She did not want to discuss it with Muddle, knowing how it would sound. And he had done nothing to stop her going. Was there some kind of conspiracy going on? Was she being fleeced by the two people who, she believed, were her friends? She shook her head, trying to rid it of thoughts that she could not cope with. These were good people. Hadn't they both rescued her from potentially disastrous situations? She turned on the television to distract herself. *Columbo*. Again. Kate was sure she had seen this episode before, at least once, but watched anyway. Sensing Muddle looking at her, she turned towards him with an enquiring look.

'I was just wondering, madam, when you might be returning your mother's call of ten twenty-five a.m. this morning.'

'Oh, God. Yes. I suppose I should. I'll just make myself a cup of tea first. I find that lessens the pain.'

'As you wish, madam.'

Tea cup in hand and unable to delay it any longer, Kate pressed the speed dial for her mother's number. It was her father's voice that answered.

'Hi, Dad.'

'Oh, hello, Angela.'

Kate sighed. 'No, Dad, it's the other daughter. It's Kate.'

'Oh, sorry, poppet, you both sound the same to me. Hold on, I'll get your mother.' Kate waited, wondering if she would ever have a proper conversation with her father again. Again? Had she ever actually had one in her life? Certainly, she could remember plenty of joshing and rather absent-minded, meandering half-finished sentences from him. But nothing she could really call a conversation. She determined to put that right as soon as possible.

'So, you are still alive, then.' Her mother's sharp tone brought her back. 'I was wondering if that strange man I spoke to had done away with you.'

'Muddle? No, he's great. A, um, work colleague and he's being very helpful around the house while he's here.'

'So, managing to get over your failed marriage, then?'

Bitch, thought Kate, but just managed to resist saying it.

'No, no, nothing like that. Just a friend.'

'Hm. Anyway, I hope you are in a better mood than you were yesterday.'

'Yesterday?'

'Yes. All that rubbish about papers and things. I don't know what had got into you.'

God, thought Kate, was that only yesterday?

'Was there anything in particular you wanted, Mum?'

'You sound like my doctor. People never have time for anyone nowadays.'

'So…?'

'Well, not really. Does there have to be a reason for ringing one's eldest daughter? Your sister's coming over tomorrow, by the way, and bringing the family.' Which, roughly translated, thought Kate, equals, 'so why have I not seen you for so long?'

'Really? Do give her my love.'

'You could give it yourself. When did you last speak to her? She says she never hears from you.'

'No, well, she knows how to dial a number as well, you know.'

'Don't be childish, Kate, it doesn't suit a middle-aged woman.' Kate gritted her teeth.

'Was there anything else, Mum?'

'No. No, not especially. I have to go anyway. They have just opened a casino here in Sheffield and the Townswomen's Guild, of which, as I hope you know, I am past president, are organising a picket.'

'A casino?' Anastasia's words echoed in her head. Though she did not understand the whole story, she felt there was what her more hippy-dippy friends would call a cosmic connection happening. 'You know, Mum, it is a long time since I was up with you. Maybe it's time we paid a visit.'

'Well, it would be nice to see you one more time before I die, I suppose.'

'Are you about to die, Mum?'

'That's not the point, Kate. Mind you, we do have a busy couple of weeks ahead. Well, I do. I suppose your father will just potter around and get in the way, as usual. Still, I'm sure we can fit you in, at a stretch. You'll be bringing the children.' It did not sound like a question.

'What? Oh, yes, I suppose so. They may be busy. I'll see.'

'Too busy to see their grandparents? What is the world coming to?'

'And I may bring a couple of friends.'

'We are not a boarding house, Kate.'

'No, I know, Mum, but they are no trouble. You'd hardly notice they were there.' Kate crossed her fingers very hard.

'Is one of them that strange person I spoke to this morning, your friend?'

How could one word carry such cynicism?

'Well, maybe.'

'Hm. Well at least he sounded more interesting than most of your empty-headed crowd.'

'Well, anyway, Mum. Better let you get off to your meeting or picket line or whatever.'

'All right, but be sure to give me some warning if you are coming up.'

'OK, I will. Bye.'

Kate put the receiver down. She sat back and smiled. A casino and free board; an ideal place to start the experiment with the cards. All she needed now was the car to get them up to Sheffield. She looked anxiously at the door.

The key turning in the lock made her jump. At last. The door swung open but instead of the slim undulating form of Anastasia, there stood the significantly larger and more shapeless Ingrid, the au pair, she of the empty hamburger cartons in the car.

'Good evening, Ms Bradshaw,' she muttered. Despite the thick Austrian accent, the voice made Kate think immediately of her school days and being sent to the headmistress's study.

'Oh, hello, Ingrid. I had forgotten about you.'

Ingrid stared at her through lank hair. 'Ja. Everyone forget about me. In this house I am not a person. I am just hands and feet.'

Kate felt that this must be some Austrian expression that had clearly lost quite a lot in translation.

'So,' Ingrid continued, 'I am leaving now. I have come to collect my clothes and I will go now. I will use the Toyota to take my things and bring it back tomorrow.'

'Well, bit of a problem there. The Toyota is, er, otherwise engaged at the moment.'

'Where is it?'

'Oh, elsewhere.'

'Then you pay for taxi.'

'Where are you going?'

'I stay with a friend. In Twickenham.'

'Well, OK but I'm a bit short of cash. I'll have to give you a cheque.'

'No. No cheque. The last one bumped.'

'Sorry?'

'Bumped. Not paid by the bank.'

'Oh, bounced, you mean. Well, sorry. It's that or nothing.'

Ingrid's voice rose. 'You must pay me my money. Is not fair that you do this to me.'

'Look. If I had it I would but I don't, so tough. It's cheque or nothing.'

'No. I get the police.'

'Police? Oh, I don't think… Look, er, Ingrid, I promise I can get you the money in a couple of days, if you will just hold on.' Kate could think of no way of sticking to this promise but the prospect of the police arriving did not thrill her.

'This is what you always say and then bumping. No. Money now or police.'

Kate heard a throat being cleared behind her.

'May I be of assistance, madam?'

'Oh, Muddle. This stupid girl is being a pain about money. I mean, I've no problem with her going but she has to be reasonable.'

'May I enquire as to the sum involved in this altercation?'

'Oh, a couple of hundred, I suppose, not much, but I just don't have it at the moment.'

'Two hundred and eighty-seven pounds, plus twelve pounds for the taxi,' Ingrid hissed.

'Whatever, two hundred and whatever she said.'

'May I be allowed, madam, to render you an advance to cover this particular eventuality?'

'What? Oh, Muddle, thank you but that's not necessary. She can wait.'

'No, I do not wait. Money now.'

'Please wait one moment, young lady, I shall return forthwith.' Muddle trotted to the study, reappearing almost immediately with a wallet in his hand.

'So, young lady, you are requiring two hundred and ninety-nine pounds, if I am not mistaken in my calculations. Here is three hundred. Feel free to keep the change or perhaps donate it to a worthy cause.'

Ingrid took the money, sniffed meaningfully and marched upstairs.

'A rather unhappy young lady, I feel.'

'Oh, they all are, these au pairs. Muddle, thank you for bailing me out there. I will, of course, pay you back.'

'Oh, as and when, madam, as and when.'

'It was lucky you had that much cash on you.'

'Be prepared, madam. The scout's watchword. Now,

would you like me to prepare something for dinner for one and all?'

Kate realised that she had eaten nothing since breakfast.

'That would be fantastic, though I don't know that we have much in the fridge. I usually go to the butcher today and it hasn't happened, what with one thing and another.'

'I'm sure I will find the wherewithal for a repast, madam,' and he disappeared into the kitchen.

Kate settled herself in the sitting room, flicking through the television channels. She heard Ingrid call the taxi and say goodbye to Miranda and Tom. Eventually, there was the sound of a horn outside. Ingrid appeared at the doorway.

'I go now. Goodbye, Mrs Bradshaw.'

'Goodbye, Ingrid.' An awkward silence fell. 'Oh, and thanks for your help.' With a final sniff and a curt nod, Ingrid turned and left. 'Well,' muttered Kate, 'That should reduce the biscuit and bread bill considerably,' and she turned back to the television screen. After about half an hour, Muddle put his head round the door.

'Soon be ready, madam. Would you be so kind as to lay the table? By the way, do you have oregano?'

'I, well, I'm really not sure. I doubt it, to be honest. Salt and pepper is as much as I can usually rise to. There may be some kind of general seasoning mix in the cupboard on the left but I don't know how old it is.'

'Never fear, madam, I shall improvise,' and the head disappeared.

Kate turned the television off and went through to lay the table. Mostly, they ate on their laps or round the kitchen table. The dining room felt lifeless and unused. After a moment's thought, she decided to use the best cutlery and glassware. She laid a place for Anastasia, more in hope than expectation. After five minutes careful work, she stood back to admire a table set for a dinner party. Muddle's head loomed into view again.

'Would you like to call the young people down, madam? I believe we are within a gnat's whisker of being ready to serve. Oh, and a very fine table, if I may say so.'

Kate went to the bottom of the stairs and called up. 'Supper.' Tom came bounding down the stairs immediately. No reply from Miranda. Hesitantly, Kate mounted the stairs. She tapped on her daughter's bedroom door.

'Miranda, supper's ready.'

'Not hungry.'

'Muddle's gone to a lot of effort. I think you should come down.'

Silence, then, 'OK then.' The sigh was audible even through the closed door. 'But I'm eating it in my room.'

The two children followed Kate into the dining room. They surveyed the table.

'Wow, what's this?' exclaimed Tom. 'We expecting the Queen or what?'

Miranda tutted.

'No, I just thought how nice it would be to have us all together round a table. I mean, we don't eat together very much.'

'As in never,' interjected Miranda.

'Well, OK, but since Muddle is preparing a meal for us I just thought, well…' Kate's voice trailed off, defeated by the uncomprehending looks from her children. To her surprise, it was Miranda who came to her rescue.

'Well, I suppose, since you have gone to all this bother, we might as well sit down. I just hope Muddle knows what he's doing. I mean, he does know I'm vegetarian; you did tell him.'

Vegetarian, thought Kate, since when? Just at that moment, Muddle swung in, bearing a bowl of steaming rice in one hand and a covered dish in the other.

'Ah, Miss Miranda, Master Tom. I hope my humble offering will suffice. And yes, it is vegetarian, a fact not unconnected to the lack of meat in the refrigerator.' He placed the two bowls on the table and lifted the lid from the dish with a theatrical flourish. A profusion of roasted vegetables, carrots, peppers, courgettes, aubergine and tomatoes gave off a deliciously rich Mediterranean smell.

'Cool,' murmured Tom.

'Not bad,' conceded Miranda.

'Wine,' announced Kate and leapt up to get one of the few remaining bottles.

'Shall I serve?' enquired Muddle.

'Oh, please do.'

'Yes,' confirmed Tom. 'Don't wait for her. Let's get stuck in.' He noticed the extra place setting. 'Oh,' he added, trying but failing to sound casual, 'Is Anastasia joining us?'

'Maybe later,' confirmed Kate.

The meal progressed with much muttered approval. Kate poured small glasses of wine for Miranda and Tom and large ones for herself and Muddle. Occasionally she looked across at Anastasia's empty chair and her heart lurched. But she let this be no more than a small blemish on the pleasure of an evening being a family, an unfamiliar sensation but a surprisingly comforting one.

By ten, they had cleared away the dishes, congratulated Muddle once again and Kate was encouraging her children to get ready for bed. She had given up all hope of seeing Anastasia again or the money for her car and was working on a way of retrieving the Toyota from the club. So far, no ideas had come.

'Muddle,' she asked, 'what do you actually know about Anastasia.'

'Not enough to elucidate, I'm afraid. An interested and high-spirited young lady, as is apparent to anyone within a second or two but as to background, family and such accoutrements, sadly nothing of use or value.'

'Shame. I could do with a bit of info on her accoutrements just now. Goodnight.'

'Goodnight, madam. Sleep well.'

'I doubt it.'

And Kate resignedly climbed the stairs.

She was half asleep in bed shortly after eleven when she heard the sound of a car pulling into the drive. She sat upright, straining her ears. She could hear voices. Throwing on a dressing gown, she crept downstairs. As she reached the hall, the bell rang loudly and insistently. She jumped, then moved quickly forward. Keeping the door on the chain, she eased it open.

'At last. Is cold out here. Hurry. Open up.'

Kate fumbled the chain free and Anastasia push in through the door. She was followed by one of the largest men that Kate had ever seen, ducking as he came through the door. He stood shyly back, shifting from one foot to the other, an awkward smile on his face. Although he seemed to be trying to squeeze himself into a corner, he still filled the hall, making Kate step back towards the kitchen.

'We have car. Now we ready for making money,' announced Anastasia. 'You have food? I have not eaten all day.'

'Anastasia, aren't you going to introduce me to your friend?'

'Him? Oh, he is Boris.'

A hand the size of a grizzly bear's was extended towards her. 'Boris,' the voice rumbled as if from a deep cave.

Kate took the outstretched paw, watching nervously as her hand disappeared up to the wrist.

'How do you do, Boris?'

'I do well thank you. And I hope you do too.' The voice carried barely a trace of Russian accent.

'Well, I… I'm not too sure if I do or not at the moment, but thank you for asking.'

'My pleasure.'

Kate looked quizzically at Anastasia, who was examining her nails, adorned, Kate noticed, with new varnish inset with small glittering jewels. It was clear that Anastasia had had a productive day out. It was also clear that Kate was not going to learn anything more about Boris from her. She turned back to the friendly giant.

'So, Boris, what brings you here? And so late?'

'Anastasia thought I might be useful to you. I know a little about cards.'

Anastasia looked up from her nails. 'The man is too, how do you say, not strong about himself. He knows everything about poker. He is one of the best. A mathematics genius.'

Boris coughed apologetically. Kate looked up to see the chandelier above her head quiver. 'Anastasia is too kind. I do know something about mathematics, I taught it for a while in the US. And I have applied some of my learning to the game of poker. I would not say that I have a system but I seem to do quite well.'

'He has system. He very rich. Genius, teach you everything.' interrupted Anastasia. 'Now we eat,' and she marched into the kitchen.

'I'm not sure what we have left,' Kate worriedly followed.

'Do not worry about me,' assured Boris. 'I ate earlier.'

One wolf or two, Kate wondered.

Anastasia was already peering in the fridge. 'Kate, did you not do shopping today?'

'No. It's been quite busy.'

'I will call takeaway. Give me your credit card.'

'Oh, I'm sorry. I don't have one.'

'You London woman. Of course you have credit card.'

'No, you see, the bank took it away. Because the money from Stephen, you know, wasn't…'

'Here, Anastasia. Take mine.' The big hand pulled a soft leather wallet from the inside of what Kate now saw was a very well-cut suit. He flipped open the wallet to show five or six credit cards. He passed a black one across.

'Dobra.' Anastasia took the card. 'Kate, do you have list of takeaways?'

'I think there's one by the phone.'

As Anastasia left the kitchen, Muddle appeared, swathed in one of Tom's dressing gowns. 'Ah, I thought I heard voices. Forgive me for not appearing sooner, I was performing my ablutions up aloft. Muddle.' He held his hand out towards Boris.

'Boris Kratin.' The big man bowed, though Muddle still only came up to his chest.

'Ah, you must be an acquaintance of Miss Anastasia?'

'Boris is here to help me learn about poker.' Kate explained.

'Ah, the game of millionaires and paupers. I wonder which you will be, madam.'

'Well, we shall see. Now, I suggest that we leave everyone to their own devices and get a good night's sleep. Boris, were you planning to stay the night?'

'If I may, then we could start early tomorrow with the training.'

'Fine. Um, I'm not sure where I will put you.'

'Oh, that's not a problem. I can share a room with Anastasia.'

'Oh. Right.'

'Do not worry. It's not what you think. Anastasia is my sister.'

'Oh, really. Goodness.' Kate was finding it impossible to imagine the two of them coming out of the same womb. 'Oh, I forgot the most important thing. The car. Did Anastasia manage to get a car for us?'

'Oh, yes. No problem. I think you will like it. Would you like to see?'

'Love to.'

They went out to the hall, passing Anastasia shouting down the telephone, 'Why you people not understand good-speaking English?' Boris opened the front door with a flourish. There on the drive was a long black Rolls Royce.

'You have to be joking,' Kate exclaimed.

'No. It's really very practical. Anastasia said that you needed room for six people. We could have got you one of those dull little vans with windows but this seemed a more suitable car for touring the casinos. And they are very cheap. No-one wants the old ones nowadays and they roll on for ever. I believe this one belonged to the Mayor of Birmingham.'

'The pride of Great Britain, madam.' Muddle's head peered round Boris's waist. 'Most suitable, I would say, for the enterprise in hand.'

'Gosh. Well, all right. Sorry, did you say 'tour of casinos'?'

'Yes. That is what Anastasia is planning.'

'Is she?'

'Ah, she is not the best communicator, sometimes. Anyway, we can discuss that in the morning.'

'Yes, I think we'd better.' Kate felt suddenly very tired. 'I'll say goodnight.'

'Good night, Kate. Sleep well.'

'Oh, I shall, I shall.'

Chapter 11
MONDAY

Kate awoke the next morning to the smell of bacon and the sound of voices, Muddle's clipped tones and Boris's soft rumble. She threw on a dressing gown and went down to the kitchen.

'Ah, good morning, madam. Mr Boris and I were just having a most interesting discussion about Einstein's Theory of Relativity. Do you know, madam –'

'Not until after the second coffee, please, Muddle. Good morning, Boris. Did you sleep well?'

'Thank you, yes. And you, Kate? Are you ready for your lessons?'

'I think so. Coffee first, though. Where did you find the bacon?'

'Supermarket, Madam. Fortunately, Mr Boris is, like me, an early riser, up with the proverbial. We took the liberty of obtaining some provisions for the next few days.'

'Are supermarkets open this early?'

'Oh, yes, madam. From seven a.m.'

'Goodness me.'

'Bacon sandwich, madam?'

'Not just yet, thank you.'

Kate took her coffee and quickly showered and dressed. When she came back down, she was astonished to find Tom sitting at the kitchen table.

'Tom, up before ten in the holidays? Are you ill?'

'Just the smell of bacon, Mum. It lured me downstairs like the call of a dusky maiden.'

'I must remember that trick. So, Boris, a quick slice of toast and we can get started.'

'Good.'

'If you will excuse me, madam, I will today endeavour to retrieve some of my accoutrements from my previous abode.'

'Sorry?'

'I will return to the Starlight Lounge, madam.'

'Isn't that a bit dangerous?'

'In my experience, the police tend to lose interest after the first day or two. And I do have my Woodcraft badge. If you would like to give me the keys to the Toyota, madam, I will see if I can retrieve it also.'

'OK, but won't they trace it back to us here?'

'I believe only I and Miss Anastasia were aware that the car belonged to your good self. The management were only interested in the larger, more expensive motors.'

'Well. Good luck. We shall see you later.'

She sat at the dining table with Boris.

'Now, Kate, let's start. First, show me your memory trick.'

He pulled a pack of cards out of his jacket pocket and dealt them face up on the table. Kate marvelled at how delicately those enormous hands manipulated the cards. When he had a pile of twenty, he stopped. Kate recalled them all without hesitation.

'Interesting. Quite impressive. Now, what do you know about the game of poker?'

'Not much, to be honest. It's five cards, isn't it and you have to get pairs and flushes and things.'

'Kate, we have work to do.'

The morning passed quickly. Kate had not concentrated so hard for so long since her school days, in fact not even then. Her mind was a swirl of patterns and numbers as she struggled to remember the different ways that a hand could be formed. By half past eleven, she needed a break.

'I have to call my mother. Tell her when we will be arriving to stay.'

'Your mother?'

'Yes. Oh, I forgot to tell you. They've opened a casino in Sheffield. It's where my parents live. We can stay with them, or at least some of us can. Keep the cost down.'

'Oh. Good idea. OK, we take a ten-minute break.'

'When will I be ready? To play for real, I mean.'

'Today is Monday. I would say Friday, at the earliest.'

Kate staggered to the kitchen to refuel her cup and then picked up the phone. It was a rare experience to be glad to be calling her mother.

'Hello. Elizabeth Bostock speaking.' Always the same greeting, even though the whole world, or at least those permitted to use her first name, called her Betty.

'Hello, Mum, it's Kate.'

'Oh, good morning, Kate.'

'How was the picket line last night?'

'Well, not as satisfactory as I had hoped. There were only four of us; it seems that people find watching so-called celebrities dancing and otherwise making fools of themselves more important than saving the morality of our nation. And after I had gone to the trouble of informing the press as well. Well, they'll be sorry when their children are in rags and they're living off scraps.'

'Yes, I'm sure they will. Now, Mum, about us coming up.'

'Yes, next week would be quite convenient. I've things on, of course, but not too onerous.'

'I was wondering whether we could come up this Friday.'

'Friday's awkward. We have the McDonalds coming for dinner.'

'Oh, that's OK. We'll go out in the evening.'

'Oh, will you? Just using us as a hotel, are you? Well, all right, I suppose we know our place. How many of you are coming? I hope you're bringing the children.'

'Oh, yes, they are longing to see you both again.' And, with no au pair, there's no way I'm leaving them here, Kate thought.

'And are you bringing that strange man?'

'Yes, Muddle will be coming too. At least, I hope so, I haven't checked.'

'Kate. You really must get yourself organised. I can't be expected to be a proper hostess if I don't know who's coming, now, can I?'

'Sorry, Mum. I'll let you know this evening.'

'Any more waifs and strays coming, while we are about it?'

'Um, no. Probably not.' Kate felt this was not a good time to introduce Anastasia and Boris into the conversation.

'And how long are you planning to stay?'

'Oh, a long weekend, if that's all right.'

'Well, I shall expect you for tea on Friday. And you'll let me know this evening for certain how many of you are coming. And bring towels. I don't want to spend all next week washing.'

'Thanks, Mum. I'll talk to you later. Bye.'

'Goodbye, Kate.'

She returned to the dining table. 'Boris, about going to Sheffield. I'm not sure that my mother will be able to put up you and Anastasia.'

'Not a problem. We will stay in a hotel near the casino. Do you know of somewhere nice?'

'Yes, I'm sure I can give you some names. Boris, can I ask you something?'

'Yes. Of course.'

'If you have made so much money and are so clever and everything, how come Anastasia was working in a place like that?'

'Like what?'

'Like smart gambling club.' Anastasia's voice came from the doorway. She was glaring at Kate over Boris's mighty shoulder.

'Um, yes, like a smart gambling club.'

Boris laughed. 'My sister, as you will have seen, has her own agenda. She is not a person to depend on anyone, not even her brother. Especially her brother.'

Anastasia grunted her agreement and went to the kitchen. 'Don't worry, Kate,' Boris's voice dropped to a whisper like a distantly rumbling volcano, 'I keep an eye on her. I know more than she thinks I know.' He winked at her. 'Now, we continue the lesson. What is the difference between a Royal Flush and a straight?'

'Um, the Royal Flush is a run of cards of the same suit that starts with the ace and goes king, queen, jack, ten and a straight is when you, um… Sorry, Boris, I can't remember.'

'It's a run of five cards that follow on from each other, but not in the same suit. There are 10,200 possible straights but only four Royal Flushes, of course.

'Right. OK. I think I've got that.'

The rest of the morning was spent playing hands to see what happened each time. By one o'clock, Kate felt exhausted. Her eyes ached, her legs ached and she felt that her head had been turned inside out.

'Lunch, I think.'

'Yes, let's ask your children to prepare something. Meanwhile you, Kate, will take ten minutes outside to clear your head. Then we can return to the lesson.'

'Do we have to keep at it? Can't we take the afternoon off?'

'Kate, there are 2,598,960 different hands that you can get from one pack alone.'

'But I can never learn all of that.'

'You don't have to. The odds drop very fast as the pack is dealt. And this is where your memory of cards becomes so important. If you know what has been dealt, you can be more sure of what is to come. And poker is a game of stamina, Kate. You may have to be at a table for four hours or more. That is also why we keep working.'

Kate nodded, although she still did not quite grasp how this trick of hers would make such a lot of money. But she knew that, somehow, she had to make money and there was no Plan B.

Tom and Miranda put together a bowl of salad and some sandwiches. Kate had no idea that they were so domesticated but welcomed the food, choosing to overlook the large thumbprint in her cheese sandwich. After the short break, she sat down again with a sigh and concentrated on an afternoon of trying to remember the difference between a flush, a straight and a straight flush, playing hand after hand, all the time working on memorising what cards had gone before. She watched the bright sunshine fade outside. So often, she had felt no need to be outside, happy to watch TV and let the day pass. Now, she regretted those lost opportunities.

At five thirty, Boris stood up. 'Right, Kate. It is time to exercise. Do you have a track suit?'

'Yes, well, I have gym outfit, if that's what you mean.'

'Go get it. We are going for a run.'

'I'm sorry.'

'A run. You have to be fit for this work. You cannot concentrate if the body is not working well. OK?'

'Well, yes. I suppose so.'

'Good, see you down here in five minutes.'

Kate went upstairs. Tom was at his computer, his spine curved over the keyboard.

'Tom, you need exercise. Boris and I are going for a run. You should come too.'

Tom looked up astonished. He took a moment to consider this proposal. Until the last few days, he had been clear that his mother did not really want to be seen with him in public. He had been quite comfortable with this, as the feeling had been mutual. Too much was changing too fast. Still, might as well go along with it.

'OK, I'll be right there.'

Kate called across the landing. 'Miranda, how about you?'

Miranda, wired to her iPod, removed an earpiece from one ear.

'Er, no. It will be quite embarrassing enough to have the rest of you pounding around the streets.'

Kate changed, choosing from four options the outfit that she felt most flattered her; you could never be sure whom you might meet.

Boris was already waiting downstairs, Tom standing beside him. Both had changed into t-shirt and shorts. Kate looked at their legs. It was like two oak trees growing next to two raspberry canes.

Kate slapped her hands together with all of the enthusiasm she could muster. 'Right, let's be off.'

'Wait. I come too.' Anastasia descended the stairs in a

sleeveless t-shirt and satin shorts, very short satin shorts. 'Well, that should wake up the neighbours,' muttered Kate, as she worked hard not to look at Tom, who was suddenly bending down adjusting the laces on his trainers.

They set off, Boris taking the lead and Tom following behind. Kate had to admit, as they settled into a brisk pace, that it was good to be outside. She missed the gym and the satisfying feeling of physical tiredness that it brought. She looked across at Boris, surprised to see that the paving stones were not shattering under his feet. Indeed, he seemed to tread very lightly.

After half a mile, Kate's sense of wellbeing was fading fast. She was feeling the effect of every slice of pizza that she had consumed in the last two weeks, every coffee, every hour in front of the television. Ahead of her, Boris ploughed along like an ocean liner, Anastasia moved with infuriatingly effortless grace with Tom bouncing beside her like a small enthusiastic terrier. She was passing a low brick wall that seemed to be beckoning her. Accepting the beckoning, she slumped down.

'Wait,' she gasped. No response; the others ploughed on, unaware of her imminent demise. Her chest heaved, her legs shook, her face burned. She started counting to one hundred; she had no idea why. Gradually, her blurred vision started to clear. She could see Boris galloping back towards her. She got unsteadily to her feet.

'I … we … I, um, I feel we've probably gone far enough for one day, don't you?'

'Come, Kate. You have not even warmed up yet.'

Kate felt her red face become even redder. 'Right. Enough. I have spent the last three days being bossed around by your sister and now by you. Enough. Really. I'm a grown woman. I know what I can and can't do.'

'Kate, I don't think you even begin to know what you can do.' Boris's voice was soft. 'Come, I take you back to the house, but only if you run alongside me.'

Kate resisted the urge to ask him to carry her. 'OK. What about the others?'

'They will be OK. Tom knows the way home.' Kate hesitated. 'Don't worry, my sister's not as dangerous as she looks.'

That still leaves far too many levels of dangerous, thought Kate. Still, they were outside. In the open air. In full view of the world. Oh, God, she thought, don't even go there. She smiled brightly.

'Off we go then. But take it easy.'

Kate puffed along beside Boris, needing two steps for every one of his. He kept up a continual conversation all the way back, to which she responded with the sort of incoherent noises normally reserved for the dentist's chair.

As they turned into her drive, she was surprised and relieved to see the Toyota parked neatly in front of the garage beside the Rolls.

She collapsed into the front door to find Muddle standing amid three suitcases and assorted carrier bags.

'Ah,' cried Muddle, looking up, 'Home is the sailor home from the sea…'

Kate racked her brains. She knew this one, somewhere deep inside, buried in a compartment called Form 4a. Something about …

'… And the hunter home from the hill.' That was it. But the voice was not hers. Miranda stood by the kitchen door, two mugs of tea in her hand.

'I knew that, I knew that,' cried Kate.

'Sorry, Mum. Didn't know it was your turn. We did it in class last term, Robert Louis Stevenson, isn't it? Here's your tea, Muddle.'

'Why, thank you miss and yes, it is indeed the great RLS.'

'How about tea for us too? Or gin,' pleaded Kate.

'OK. I'll see what I can do, but it'll have to be tea. No gin left. How do you take yours, Boris?'

'Black, please.'

Miranda disappeared. Kate surveyed Muddle's collection of packages. 'So, Muddle, you seem to have managed to retrieve quite a lot. How did it go?'

'Most satisfactory, madam, though I have to say that I found the levels of awareness and observation among the boys in blue most unsatisfactory. It gives one pause for thought, it really does. A symbol of the demise of our nation.'

He paused, sipped his tea with a sad shake of the head.

'So,' he continued, 'though it is strange, is it not, this habit of starting every sentence with 'so', I must guard against it.'

'Muddle, please,' sighed Kate, 'the story. We are on tenterhooks.'

'Tenterhooks. Interesting word, comes from the making of linen, I believe. Sorry,' he added, seeing Kate's expression, 'I will continue my tale. There seemed very little activity around the building at all when I arrived, having traversed the fields making full use of available cover. Just a couple of members of Her Majesty's rooting around in the bar. I am glad to say that they were so taken up with their task, which appeared to include considerable imbibation at a most inappropriate time of day, that I was able to ascend unheeded.

There were more of the boys in blue in the office, though these, being in plain clothes, were not actually in blue. Though one was wearing a blue jumper, as I recall. Anyway, judging by their expressions of dissatisfaction, it appears that Mr Charles kept quite a discreet set of accounts. Time will tell.

Suffice to say, I was able to pack my belongings without impediment, remove them down the back stairs and return via our previous escape route to the main road.'

'Well done, Muddle. It's good to have you back.'

'Thank you, madam. Now, with your agreement, I will clean out the car, unless you feel that the odour of old grease and stale bread somehow enhances its value.'

'No, that's fine, you go for it. It was used by the au pairs, you see…'

'Yes, madam, I remember you explaining that to me on our first acquaintance.'

'Oh, yes, so I did. Right, I need to get into a bath before my muscles seize up.' Kate made for the stairs. 'Ouch, too late,' she gasped as she forced her legs to bend with each step. She paused half way up, turned and ascended the last flight backwards. It seemed to help. 'Miranda," she called out, "You seem to know how to cook. Can you see what you can do about supper?'

Miranda appeared at the door of her room. 'I suppose so. I was planning to go out.'

Kate stopped and, with difficulty, turned round. 'I don't think so.'

'What?'

'Where were you planning to go?'

'Just round to see some friends. God, it's like I'm a prisoner here.'

Kate felt a storm brewing. It was time for compromise.

'I think tomorrow would be better. I won't need you to help tomorrow. Tom can take a turn.'

Another theatrical sigh. 'I suppose so.'

'Check with Muddle what he bought this morning.'

At that moment, Tom came bursting in through the front door, closely followed by Anastasia. His voice carried triumphantly up the stairs.

'I win!'

'Only because I let you. I know how men always unhappy if they do not win.'

'You want to go round once more?'

'Tomorrow maybe.'

Kate continued her weary way upstairs, determined to get first call on the hot water.

Chapter 12
TUESDAY

The next morning, Kate awoke with a start, aware that somehow her body was not her own any more. She checked the clock. It was already half past eight. She swung out of bed and stopped, crouched, as every muscle objected in outrage to the idea of movement.

Gently, she eased herself up. Her bathroom door seemed a mile away. With great concentration, she pushed one foot forward. Then another. Holding onto furniture she finally reached it.

After a shower and a few slow circuits round her bedroom, she felt able to face the stairs. Boris was at the bottom to greet her. He bowed.

'Good morning, Kate. Please note that I am not bossing you around, but I am just reminding you that we have a lot to do today.'

'Toast, coffee, aspirin and possible amputation and I will be with you,' muttered Kate, feeling her way into the kitchen.

The morning was an endless round of hands, counting the cards, memorising combinations and learning about the rules of betting, when to call, when to raise and when to fold. Kate's legs still felt like stone; the only reason she was glad to stay playing was that it meant that she did not have to move them.

By lunchtime she had had enough.

'Right. No more. This afternoon I need to switch off, take a break.'

To her surprise, Boris nodded. 'Good idea. I agree.'

'You do?'

'Yes, we will take a break until two thirty, then we will run.'

'Oh, no, not that.'

'Yes, Kate. It is essential that you are fit.'

'But it hurts. Everywhere.'

'We must get you fit, Kate. Otherwise it is not worth doing. And to make up for the time, we will then train at the cards again this evening, but only until about midnight.'

'Well, whoopido. That's really kind and generous.'

'That's OK.' The irony slipped past Boris. 'I know that it is hard work for you. But if I tell you that you can get at least two thousand pounds a week if you get this right, does this change your mind?'

Kate considered this for the briefest of moments then sat back down at the table. 'Deal those cards, Boris.'

Boris laughed, a rich, deep sound that seem to come up from below the earth. 'Not yet, Kate. I mean it, take a break, you deserve it.'

Feeling that it really was time for her to provide some kind of meal, she went to the kitchen. As she stood surveying the contents of the fridge, Miranda came in, dressed up, made-up and clearly ready to head out.

'Hello, you look, um, nice. What's the plan?'

'It's like I said, I'm going out.'

'Where to?'

'Lay off the inquisition, Mum, all right? I'm going to meet my friends, those I have left after everyone's heard, no doubt, about your vigilante act on Saturday.'

'Miranda, I'm not going over that again and I'm certainly not going to change my position. I'm your mother and that's that.'

'Whatever. I'll see you later.' She spun away through the kitchen door.

'When?' called Kate after her.

'Later. I don't know.'

'Well, are you in for dinner?'

The slamming front door was her only answer.

Kate stood staring at the fridge, trying to remember what she was looking for. The outrage built up in her. If she had spoken to her own mother like that, a sharp slap around the head and no supper would have been the quick and indisputable answer. God, she sounded old.

With a sigh she returned to the matter of lunch. Here, at least, was something she could control. She pulled some fresh pasta and a tub of sauce from the fridge and set to preparing the meal.

Boris allowed half an hour after lunch to let the food settle before they went running. Kate sank gratefully into an armchair. She reached for the remote control then changed her mind; television just seemed like an unwelcome distraction now.

After a few minutes, Muddle came to sit with her, bringing her a cup of coffee.

'Ah, thank you, Muddle. You're a life saver.'

'My pleasure, madam, and my thanks for an excellent repast.'

'Muddle,' Kate started, hesitantly, 'Can I ask you what your plans are? I mean, you are very welcome here, don't get me wrong, and a great help, but I don't want to seem to be taking you for granted. I don't, you know, want to hold you back if you've got something…. So, well, er what…?' she petered out.

'Well, madam, I have considered, as you might expect, the various options that present themselves to me at this unusual juncture and I believe, though feel free to correct me, that I have between seven and eleven alternatives, depending on how you divide them up. Allow me to enumerate.'

'That's OK, Muddle. Just the conclusions will be fine.'

'As you wish, madam. My conclusion is that I have at this time two choices. Either I can seek gainful employment, accommodation included, as a doorman or similar in a central London location, thus allowing me access to the cultural treasures of our fine capital city, or I can stay for an agreed length of time with your good self, as long as I can be of use and with, of course, your permission and agreement.'

Kate considered for a moment the prospect of continuing without Muddle. It frightened her.

'Muddle, I would be delighted if you could stay on with us, at least until after the trip to Sheffield. Indeed, my mother would be very disappointed not to meet you.'

'To be honest with you madam, that would be my preferred option at this time.'

'I'm afraid that Teddington does not offer the cultural splendours of London.'

'On the contrary, you have many gems round here.'

'We do?'

'The fine houses of Marble Hill and St Margaret's, the television studios if one requires mindless entertainment and, of course, the mighty River Thames in all its summer glory.'

'Well, yes, I suppose so. You do understand that I cannot pay you anything. Maybe later.'

Muddle held up a hand. 'Madam, never fear. It is of no consequence. I have savings that will more than suffice, indeed I insist on paying my way. Give me neither poverty nor riches; feed me with food convenient for me, as I always say. Book of Proverbs, madam,' he added in response to Kate's puzzled expression.

'Then it's settled. But we do need to do something about your sleeping arrangements. I think I should ask Tom to give you his room for the next couple of nights and he can sleep in the study.'

'No need, madam. He's a young lad, needs his sleep. I have slept in many a mossy dell and dank cave in my time. The put-you-up in the study is luxury compared.'

'Well, if that's OK with you.'

'Absolutely, madam.'

'Then,' Kate hauled herself wearily from the soft chair, 'I had better get ready for the dreaded run.'

'Would it be acceptable if I accompanied you today?'

'If you want to.'

'Mens sana, in corpore sano.'

'Absolutely,' agreed Kate, pleased for once that she recognised the quotation.

Ten minutes later, she had changed and was waiting in the hall. Tom had decided that the computerised Macedonians held more interest than 'hammering round the block with a bunch of oldies', mainly because Anastasia was washing her hair, an undertaking that seemed to require several hours. Boris appeared. Kate noticed that, for all his size, he did not seem to carry an ounce of extra fat.

'OK, Kate, are we ready?'

'You might be but I am seriously unsure about this. It's going to hurt, isn't it?'

'Only for the first hundred metres or so. After that, the muscles will remember what they are supposed to do and it will be fine, better than yesterday, at least.' The rumbling laugh seemed almost to reassure Kate. Almost.

She gave him her bravest smile. 'Well, given that yesterday felt like being churned round in a cement mixer, that can't be difficult.'

Boris's eyebrows shot up and Kate turned to see Muddle emerging from the study. He was wearing a faded red singlet which revealed arms that were freckled, lean to the point of skinniness but wiry. His navy blue shorts reached down below the knees and nearly met white socks coming the other way, pulled up to their maximum height. On his feet were white shoes, the like of which Kate had not seen since her mother gave up playing tennis twenty years ago after an altercation with Mrs Pembury during the mixed doubles semi-final. Atop his head perched a baseball cap bearing the slogan Free Burma. Kate stared.

'Ah, I see that you have noticed my cap, madam. A worthy cause, don't you think, and one deserving of publicity. Still so much to do.' He reached up to adjust the cap and Kate noticed a long, curved scar on the inside of his arm.

'Goodness me, Muddle, where on earth did you get a scar like that?'

'Shark bite, madam.'

Kate waited for more detail. None came.

'Right then,' she declared, realising that it could be put off no longer, 'Let's go.'

Boris was right. The first couple of hundred metres were agony but then, to Kate's astonishment, it became easier, though it still fell short of anything that she could describe as enjoyable. Boris glided along to her left and Muddle bounced to her right, elbows tight in to his sides, chin forward and feet slightly splayed, a look of great determination on his face. Her neighbour, to whom she had not spoken since he had attempted a grope at their Christmas party, was working in his front garden. Kate enjoyed his astonished stare and greeted him cheerily.

'Just taking my bodyguards for a run, Mr Simmons. You can never be too careful who you might meet nowadays,' and she was on round the corner before he could think of a reply.

They ran for a full twenty minutes before Kate decided that there was a lot to be said for walking or indeed being driven. By then, they had nearly completed the circuit and the house was in sight.

'That's it. If you want me to survive long enough to make all this money, I'm going in.'

'OK, that's fair,' Boris replied. 'You have done well, Kate.'

'If I may, madam,' Muddler announced, 'I will indulge in a couple more circuits while you avail yourself of the ablutions.'

Kate nodded. 'Boris, what about you?'

'No, I think that is enough for one day.'

They walked back to the house, watching Muddle disappear down the road, bouncing along like a kite in a high wind.

'You know, Boris, I hate to admit that you might be right, but I haven't felt this good for a long time.'

'Even though the feet hurt and the lungs are collapsing?'

'Even though all that. To be honest, it feels good to have something to do. I mean, I've enjoyed doing nothing for a long time but it, you know, it was a bit, well, nothingy.'

'Kate, you can do much.'

'You keep saying things like that. What do you mean? How do you know?'

'Kate, I know people. Was my job as professor, to see who had potential. So, believe me.'

They had reached the front door. Kate turned away,

unsettled at the way the conversation was going. Her eyes fell on the Rolls.

'We really must take that car for a spin. It has been sitting here for two days now.'

'We will, tomorrow, after lessons.'

Kate opened the door. "Always work first with you, isn't it, Boris?"

He spread his arms wide. 'I am Russian. I can't help it. We take guilty conscience in with our borscht as children.'

'Go and shower,' Kate laughed, 'see if you can wash off some of that work ethic.'

She went into the kitchen for a glass of water. Anastasia was there, her hair wrapped in a towel turban. She looked up as Kate poured herself water from the tap.

'So, Kate, you like my brother.'

'He's a nice guy.'

'Yes, and has penis like cucumber.'

Kate coughed, sending water spraying across the room.

'Anastasia,' she spluttered, 'You can like a man without wanting to go to bed with him, you know.'

Anastasia shrugged. 'Why?'

'Well, it's not all about sex.'

'With you, is not ever about sex. Why, Kate? You not so bad looking, considering.'

'I'm not having this conversation.' Kate headed for the door.

'Is not all you not having,' muttered Anastasia.

Kate ran up to her room and closed the door. Sitting on the bed, she felt her cheeks burning; she knew it was not from the exertion of running. How dare Anastasia tell her how to behave? Why did everyone go on about sex all the time? Even her own daughter had told her, in her own words, that she needed to get a life.

But, if Kate was honest with herself, she had never really found sex that interesting or, indeed necessary. By the time she was old enough to experiment, she was surrounded by advertisements telling her that everyone who had sex would die of AIDS. It seemed safer to continue to fantasise about David Cassidy and George Michael. An overweight teenager in an era when thin was everything, she had never had boys beating a path to her door and those that did were usually frightened away quite quickly by her mother's questioning of their lineage and intentions.

So, a few fumbles in the backs of cars that smelled of engine oil and old rugby kit and some hurried groping at the end of parties, as the cider kicked in and standards were lowered, left Kate with low expectations which Stephen had barely lived up to. He had seemed to consider sex a race, the winner being allowed to go and watch the cricket on television. Indeed there had been the memorable time when he had tried both sex and watching the cricket at the same time, resulting in a wrenched back that had, to Kate's satisfaction, caused him problems ever since.

She sighed deeply and finished her water. Setting the glass on the bedside table, she went to run her bath.

After a rather subdued dinner, for which Miranda did not return, Kate and Boris settled down to another card session.

'Tonight, Kate, we will just play some poker so you can practice your bets.'

Kate was relieved. No more learning. Banishing all thoughts of cucumbers and, indeed, a range of root vegetables from her mind, she concentrated as hard as she could.

After five hands, though, she was puzzled. Her pile of Monopoly money had virtually gone and she could not understand why. When her cards were good, Boris just folded immediately. When they were bad, she relied on her memory to anticipate the cards but still Boris seemed to know when to push her and when to fold.

She knew about the poker face and kept hers as impassive as possible but still he beat her every time.

Finally, after two more hands had depleted her funds, she sat back in her chair. 'Well, it looks as if the cards don't love me tonight.'

Boris looked up. 'Cards are cards, Kate, just bits of

laminated paper. They don't love you or hate you.'

'So, what happened? Is it just the luck of the draw?'

Boris smiled. 'A reporter once said to a famous golfer that he seemed to have had a lucky day. The reply was 'Yes, the more I practice, the luckier I get.' It's the same with poker.'

'So, what am I doing wrong?' wailed Kate.

'Kate, I knew exactly when you had a good hand.'

'How? I made sure I kept a straight face.'

'Well, you only kept the straight face when you had a good hand. And you always put down a big bet when you had a good hand. And you tapped the table four times with your right index finger when you had a good hand.'

'I did?'

'You did. You see, Kate, all poker players look out for what we call the tell; the little ways that players give themselves away. And you have lots. Here's what we will do, and I should have thought of this before, so my apologies. When we go to the casino in Sheffield, you will start by playing blackjack and we will watch the poker players.'

'Blackjack? What's that?'

'It's what you may have called pontoon or vingt-et-un.'

'Oh, right, when the numbers have to add up to twenty-one. I remember playing it with my grandparents. It was considered rather wicked but less likely to condemn you to eternal hell and damnation than poker.'

'That's the one. I think we will switch tomorrow.'

'Oh, but hold on. What about all the work…' She heard the phone ring. 'Excuse me a moment.'

She walked into the hall and picked up the receiver. 'Hello.'

'Mum?' the voice was faint and cracking, almost drowned by the sound of music, but unmistakable.

'Miranda?

'Mum, I need your help.'

'Where are you?'

'I don't know.'

'You don't know?'

Kate was aware that Muddle had materialised at her side, while Boris watched anxiously from the living room doorway.

'Mum,' Miranda's voice whispered in her ear, 'I'm in a flat and something's happened. I think they've given me something.'

'Miranda, can you get out?

'I don't think so. We're quite high up. I'm in the bathroom at the moment.'

'Ask her what she can see, madam.' Muddle's voice was urgent at her side.

'Miranda, go to the window. What do you see.'

'Just a minute. There's shops.'

'What shops?'

'There's a Sketchleys and next to it a MacDonald's.'

'Sketchleys and MacDonald's,' whispered Kate to Muddle. He immediately took out his phone and started tapping. 'Miranda, what else?'

'I don't know. My eyes are a bit fuzzy.'

'Try, Miranda. What else.'

'Um, a restaurant, I think. Looks like Oriental something. The second word begins with a T, I think, but the neon has bust and I can't read it.'

'Oriental something beginning with T,' Kate whispered. Muddle nodded. Kate heard a loud knocking and voices. 'Mum, I've got to go.'

'Miranda, listen, we are coming to get you. Keep your phone on.'

'My battery's almost gone. Please hurry, mum.' And the line went dead.

Kate stared at Muddle as he rifled through screens, flipping from one page to another. After a wait that had Kate close to screaming, he raised his thumb in triumph. 'Got it, madam. Oriental Temple in Raynes Park, two doors down from a Sketchley's. Just the other side of Kingston, as I recall.'

Kate looked around.

'Boris, we are going to bring forward that trip in the Rolls. We have to go and get Miranda.'

Boris ran upstairs for the keys. Muddle looked across at her.

'Never fear, madam. Good will prevail.'

'God, I do hope so, Muddle.' Boris came back, waving the keys and Tom, too, had appeared at the turn of the stairs. 'Right, let's go. Tom, you stay here with Anastasia. No, no, on second thoughts, get in the car.'

'Cool.' Tom bounded outside.

'I come too.' Anastasia appeared from the living room. 'Is nothing good on television.'

'OK, but come on. Go, go, go. Muddle, you're the scoutmaster, get us there.'

Muddle jumped into the front of the car next to Boris; the others piled into the back. Kate resisted the urge to sink back into the comfort of the leather seats and sat forward as far as her seat belt permitted as the car purred out of the drive and headed for Kingston Bridge. She found herself muttering a prayer to a God who had been a stranger for many years.

As always, the traffic over the bridge and around the one way system in Kingston crawled and meandered. Late night shoppers crossed slowly with heavy bags and drivers searched for empty car parks. Kate drummed her fingers on the window sill, Anastasia leaned back onto the soft seats as if she had been travelling in such cars all her life, Tom pressed every button he could find.

At last they were free from the traffic. Boris sped along the road, Muddle quietly giving directions. Rain started to fall steadily. They came into Raynes Park, a rather bedraggled no-man's-land between Kingston and Wimbledon, just a street of nondescript shops.

'There, to the right,' came Muddle's triumphant cry, 'Our journey's end.' Gold letters on a cracked and worn red background spelled out Oriental Temple. Boris swung the car in to the kerb. They all piled out. Muddle paced the pavement, standing first in front of the restaurant, then Sketchley's, then MacDonald's. He returned to the group, waiting in the rain.

'By a process known as triangulation, I can fairly

confidently surmise that Miss Miranda is incarcerated in that block there.' He pointed to a 1930's block, painted a dirty cream with rusting metal windows. 'The frosted windows will be the bathrooms and I notice that the one on the third floor to the right is ajar.'

'Kate,' Boris leaned in to her and put his hand on her shoulder, 'I suggest that Muddle and I deal with this. You wait here.'

'No way. That's my daughter in there. I'm coming too.'

Boris nodded. 'As you wish. Come. Anastasia and Tom, you wait in the car.'

'Oh.' Tom's complaining cry was ignored by all.

The three of them splashed across the road to the door of the flats. It had a security lock. 'Now what do we do?' wailed Kate. It was always simpler in the movies, she thought. Someone always comes out at the right moment. Muddle stepped back looking up and then pressed hard on one of the buttons. Nothing happened. He pressed again. This time there was a click and the door buzzed. He pushed it open.

'How did you do that?'

'In my experience, madam, young people are most lax about security,' he replied heading for the stairs and taking them two at a time. 'There was the sound of music in the background to Miss Miranda's call, implying some form of social event. In such circumstances, it is not uncommon for this generation to have an open house policy. A most unwise approach but highly convenient from our perspective.'

Kate followed him and Boris up the stairs. As they came to the third floor, they heard the music coming from one of the flats. Muddle pounded on the door. It was opened by a young man with a can of beer in his hand. He wore a beany hat and a t-shirt that read *Kill the Rich*. Wisps of beard hung at his chin. Muddle's right arm swept up and pinned him to the wall. Boris stepped forward. The door opened straight into the living room. About ten people, boys and girls, were sitting around on the battered sofa and the encrusted carpet. Smoke hung in the air. The music boomed.

They looked up in astonishment as the two men stared down at them, Boris from his great height, Muddle from a significantly lower angle.

'Bloody hell,' muttered one, 'It's Shrek and Donkey.'

'Just shut up,' Boris's accent had become markedly more Russian, his voice if anything, deeper, 'Or it might be more like Pulp Fiction. Turn off the music.'

Silence fell immediately. Kate pushed through into the room. 'Miranda,' she called. 'Miranda.'

One of the boys stood up. 'Are you looking for Miranda? You her mum or something?'

'Yes. What have you done with her?'

'She's in the bedroom. With Darren.' He pointed behind him. Seeing Kate's expression, he added hastily, 'Asleep. She's asleep. Overdid it on the vodka. Darren's like, keeping an eye on her.'

Kate ran across the room and threw the door open. The smell of the bedroom hit her hard. Damp and dirty clothes blended with rancid butter and burnt toast. Miranda was sprawled on the bed, Darren sitting beside her. Kate was relieved to see that this time they were both fully dressed.

'What have you done to her?'

Darren jumped up from the bed. 'Nothing, Mrs Bradshaw. Nothing. She just, well, drank rather a lot rather quickly and I guess she's not used to it.'

'You bet your life she's not used to it. She's fifteen, Darren.'

'She's what? She told me she was sixteen. I mean, I'd never have, you know...' Kate's glare stopped his voice.

'Why didn't you stop her? You are her boyfriend, after all. You're supposed to look after her, aren't you or am I just being old fashioned?'

'Well, that's it. You see, I'm not her boyfriend.'

'I see, you just sleep with her, is that it?'

'No, I mean, I was her boyfriend, well until today, actually, but I, well, kind of dropped her. I think that's what made her drink that much.'

'You kind of dropped her. Why?'

'Well, to be honest, I … Sorry, Mrs Bradshaw, this is really awkward.'

'Get over it. Why?'

'Well,' he took a deep breath and the words tumbled out, 'She's a bit of pain. I mean, she just complains all the time. Nothing I do seems to be right. It was just doing my head in.'

Kate stared at him, not knowing whether to smack him over the head for hurting her daughter or to make him a cup of tea and sympathise. She decided on neither, took a deep breath and moved over to her daughter, who had managed to sleep through this altercation.

'Miranda,' she bent down and called softly to her. 'Miranda, it's mummy.'

Miranda opened one eye. 'Mum? I want to go home,' she croaked. The smell of alcohol wafted over Kate, who jerked back.

'Wait here, not that you can go anywhere.'

Kate went back in to the silent sitting room. All eyes turned towards her. Boris and Muddle had not moved, indeed Muddle still had the boy pinned against the wall.

'Put him down, Muddle. I think we have solved the mystery. Boris, could you give me a hand, please?'

Boris crossed into the bedroom with Kate.

'Would you be kind enough to carry my drunken daughter downstairs?' Kate said quietly. Without a word, Boris picked up Miranda and slung her over his shoulder.

'Goodbye, Darren.'

'Um, goodbye, Mrs Bradshaw.'

The three of them left, Muddle last, reversing out of the room like a cowboy leaving the saloon.

Outside on the pavement Kate instructed Boris to put Miranda down. The girl stood unsteadily. Kate leaned in towards her.

'Miranda, listen to me. If you are sick in that car, you are cleaning it yourself. Understood?'

The girl nodded, face turned down to the ground. Then, as

if on cue, she staggered over to the nearby lamppost and, holding it tightly, threw up noisily in the gutter.

The others stood waiting, the steady drizzle easing down their necks.

'Better an empty house than a bad tenant, I always say.'

'Thank you, Muddle. I knew I could count on you to find the right words.'

The journey back was silent. Miranda lay slumped in the corner of the back seat, hair falling in damp rat's tails across her face. Kate sat beside her, hands clenched in her lap and staring straight ahead. Even Anastasia was silent.

Eventually, the car purred into the drive and all disembarked.

Miranda was sent straight upstairs to bath and bed. Tom retreated to re-join his Macedonians. The others hovered awkwardly in the hall.

'Miss Anastasia, would you be kind enough to help me to finish tidying the kitchen?' Muddle asked. 'The job is not fine till the surfaces shine.'

'Yes, and I need coffee,' Anastasia replied. 'Anyone else?'

Kate and Boris nodded and watched the two of them disappear through the kitchen door. Kate moved through to the dining room and slumped into a chair.

'Well, we had better get on with the training programme.'

Boris followed her in and remained standing awkwardly. 'I think, Kate, that you have done enough for one day.'

'No! I have to do this. I have to think of something other than that stupid bloody child. God, Boris, how did I bring up such a disaster?'

Kate could feel the tears start to run down her cheeks. She wiped at them furiously with the back of her hand. 'Look at me. I must look like some giant panda. If I have to carry on living with her under the same roof, I'm really going to have to get some waterproof mascara.'

Boris moved behind her chair and started to massage her shoulders. 'Kate, I am not an expert on children but I have seen enough to know that no-one gets it completely right.'

'I seem to have got it completely wrong.'

'Kate, what were you like at fifteen?'

'Oh, God, dreadful. Lots of door slamming, as I recall.' She leaned back in the chair as she felt the tension disappear from her shoulders.

'Well, it is a difficult time. Anastasia was, well, you can imagine. She had to be sent away to a very strict school in the middle of the country with no men within thirty kilometres. I don't think it did anything for her but it stopped my mother murdering her. Miranda has a lot of anger. It will pass.'

'Yes, but when? I can't take much more of this.'

There was a knock at the open door and Muddle stood with the coffees. Boris stepped back from Kate's chair.

'Refreshments, madam.' He cleared his throat as he came in. 'I could not help but overhear the end of your conversation, there. I hope I am not intruding or speaking out of turn if I say that I agree with Mr Boris's analysis. In my experience, and, in all modesty I have to say that I have extensive experience on three continents with children of this age, a regime of healthy training and good food does the trick. Expends the energy on the right things and adds positive fuel for positive deeds.'

'I don't see Miranda taking to that.'

'Oh, there are ways, madam, there are ways.'

'Well, good luck to you. Feel free to try anything as of tomorrow morning. With the hangover she's going to have, it will be an interesting challenge for you.'

'I took the liberty of placing a large glass of water by her bed with a written instruction to drink it all. With that and the fact that she has, ah, disposed of a large amount of the iniquitous substances, she should not be too fragile to start training.'

Kate could see Muddle's eyes lighting up at the prospect.

'You like to have a project, don't you, Muddle?'

'Yes, indeed madam. Never saw the point of that poem about the benefits of standing and staring. Seemed like a bit of a waste of time in my book.'

'What did you mean about experience on three continents?'

'Long story, madam, and not for this late hour. Another time.'

Kate looked at her watch. It was ten fifteen. It felt much later.

'Well, madam, Mr Boris, I will wish you good night.'

'Night, Muddle,' Kate replied.

He left, closing the door quietly behind him. An awkward silence fell. Kate picked up her coffee and took a long draft. Boris moved to sit opposite her, rather to Kate's disappointment.

'Thanks for the massage, Boris, and for the good advice.'

Boris shrugged his mighty shoulders. 'Is OK. I don't know much about these things to be honest, Kate. My world is more about casinos and hotel rooms.'

Picking up a note of sadness in his voice, Kate looked across at this great bear of a man.

'Is that what you want? I mean, is that a good life for you?'

Another shrug. 'It's not what I planned but life happens. It's a living.'

'How did you get from being a university professor to being a card player?'

'As Muddle said, it's a long story.'

Kate put her cup down. 'I've got time.'

Boris hesitated. 'Perhaps we should be practicing the blackjack.'

Up to last week, Kate would have nodded demurely and allowed the other person to have his way. But not now. 'Tomorrow. There's plenty of time to practice tomorrow.'

Boris allowed a small smile. 'You are determined, Kate. I am impressed. You need that to play the casinos.'

'Don't change the subject.'

'It's what men do best, haven't you found? OK, I see there is no escape.' From the living room came the sound of the television as Anastasia settled down to watch a rock concert.

'Do you need to ask her to turn it down?'

With a smile, Kate shook her head.

Boris took a deep breath. 'Well, how far back should I go?'

'As far as you want. I'd like to know.'

'OK. Well, I was always good at math, a star pupil at my school in Moscow. It was a school especially for the children of senior party members; my father was something important at the Ministry of Labour, or so I thought at the time. When I was twelve, they wanted me to train to be a chess grand master but I just could not get excited about staring at a chess board for the rest of my life. So they got a bit cross with me – they don't like people not doing what they are told over there.

Before I know it, they were talking about dropping me from the school. Big fuss, as you can imagine. My father comes down to talk to the headmaster. I remember the day. He goes into the office with the guy and I'm left sitting on the bench outside. No more than ten minutes later he's coming out again. He smiles at the Head, shakes his hand and says something like 'I knew you would understand my point of view,' and that's it. I'm staying at the school, no question. Except that every time the Head sees me after that he looks at me as if he wants to stamp on my face.

Anyway, I keep working away at my maths and then the whole glasnost thing gets going. A couple of years into it, when I'm about fourteen, I come home from school one day and there's my father. I mean, he was never home before about eight at night. He's sitting at the dining table, smoking one of his cigars, as usual. He looks up at me across the room. 'Pack your bags, Boris. We are going on an adventure."

Kate saw that Boris was staring at the wall behind her head. His body was motionless.

'What did he mean?'

'Twenty minutes later a car comes to the door. We head straight for the airport and onto a plane to Washington. No time to say goodbye to anyone, just him and me. I ask him about my mother. 'She will follow,' he says.'

'And did she?'

'No.'

'What about Anastasia?'

'Not yet born.'

'So, what had happened?'

'Kate, Russia is a strange place. You never really get answers to questions, things just gradually fall into place and sometimes, years later, you realise what was going on.

All I know is that, ten hours later, I'm getting off a plane and it's snowing and people are speaking a language I have never heard before. I'm fourteen years old with just a suitcase and my father, who is busy talking to some other people and I have no idea who they are. There is a strange smell in the air, a kind of sweet bread smell and everywhere I look there are brightly coloured advertisements for things that mean nothing to me. Imagine. Until that time I had hardly ever left Moscow, let alone Russia. I walk over to my father and try to hold his hand. He tells me to go and sit on a bench at the other side of the room.'

Kate stood up and walked round to the other side of the table. She leaned over Boris, took his head in her hands and kissed him on his cheek. He reached up and put his hand on her face. The phone rang.

'Bugger.'

'You had better answer it.'

'No, it can go to answerphone.'

They heard the ringing stop but, instead of silence, Muddle's clipped tones wafted through the door.

'Mrs Bradshaw's residence. How can I help you?'

'Double bugger,' muttered Kate.

'Ah, Mrs Bostock. Yes, it is indeed. How clever of you to recall my name. Yes, your daughter is here. One moment, I shall get her for you.'

'And treble bugger.'

Kate went through to the hall and took the receiver from Muddle.

'Your mother, madam,' Muddle announced rather superfluously, before disappearing back to the study.

'Hello, mother,' Kate sighed into the phone.

'Well, I think I could reasonably expect a bit more enthusiasm in your response when I go to the trouble, not to mention expense, of calling you.'

'Sorry, mum, it's been a busy day.'

'Well, I'm glad to hear it. You've had far too many idle ones, if you ask me.'

'Was there anything in particular, mum. It's a bit late and I'm just getting ready for bed.'

'Yes, I've just got back from a Road Action Committee meeting and your father hasn't washed up properly; I'll have to do it all again.'

'And that's why you called me? To tell me that?'

'Don't be smart, Kate, it doesn't suit you. I just wondered if you might be kind enough to tell me when you are arriving and how many of you I will have to accommodate.'

'I thought I'd told you.'

'Well, if you think all those ifs and maybes were a clear message I'm glad you're not doing anything important like running the country. Mind you, that lot that are don't seem to have the first idea. There's been no-one with half a clue since Margaret Thatcher. Biggest mistake they ever made, getting rid of her.'

'Friday, mum, we're coming on Friday. Late afternoon.'

'It will have to be Thursday.'

'Thursday? Why?'

'I told you, the McDonalds are coming for dinner on Friday and I can't have everyone milling around and littering the hall with their luggage while I'm preparing boeuf en croute.'

'Well…'

'And you'll have to be gone by Sunday evening. I've got the bridge club coming round at seven.'

'OK, mum, we'll be with you at five on Thursday.'

'We usually have tea at four.'

'We'll try to make four then.'

'And are you going to tell me how many of you are coming?'

'We will be four, mum, myself, Miranda, Tom and

Muddle. There will be a couple of others with us when we arrive but they won't be staying.'

'I should think not, though no doubt I will have to give them a cup of tea. And is this Muddle still just a friend?'

'He's a friend, mum. Nothing more but a friend and a very good one.'

'I'm relieved to hear it, even though it means I will have to make up yet another bed.'

'Don't worry, we'll bring a sleeping bag for Tom. He can sleep in the lounge.'

'Not when the McDonalds are here.'

'We'll work it out, mum. Now, I must go. We'll see you on Thursday.'

'Yes, well, I've got plenty to get on with too, you know.'

'Night, mum.' And Kate returned the receiver firmly to its cradle.

She walked slowly back into the dining room.

'My mother. Always had an exquisite sense of timing,' she smiled ruefully.

Boris stood up. 'Kate, I think we are all tired now. It is time to sleep.'

'Oh, OK.'

Boris picked up the two cups and carried them to the kitchen.

'Good night, then,' called Kate.

'Good night, Kate, sleep well.'

Kate passed Muddle coming down the stairs from the bathroom.

'And how was the dear lady?'

'Like the tarantula from hell,' replied Kate without stopping.

Later, as she settled into bed, she looked around the room. Since Stephen's departure she had relished the space of this room dedicated solely to her needs and comforts. Now, it felt too big and the bed felt, for the first time, too empty. She pulled up the covers, thumped her pillow hard five times and tried to sleep.

Chapter 13
WEDNESDAY

Kate did not sleep well, waking frequently with confused, broken bits of dreams hanging in her head. She was running, had to run but did not know who from. Scruffy teenagers laughed at her from broken down sofas; Russian bears crushed her; phalanxes of cucumbers danced around her; her mother, shaking her head and saying, 'I told you no good would come from it'.

Finally there was light around the edge of the curtains. She pulled herself out of the crumpled bed and showered.

Downstairs, all was quiet. She checked the kitchen clock. Six fifteen. Bugger. No point in going back to bed now, though. Kettle on, kick start the system. As she was spooning coffee into her mug, she was surprised to hear a grunting noise.

Cautiously, she eased herself out into the hall. The door to the study was open. There, in the centre of the room, was Muddle, clad only in his underpants, standing on his head, his legs straight up in the air. He was breathing in deeply, then expelling the air in a grunting whoosh.

Hoping that the day would never come when Muddle stopped surprising her, Kate went silently back to the kitchen, made her coffee and carried it out to the back garden. She felt a slight chill in the morning air, a reminder of the previous night's rain. She looked around. Gardening had never really inspired her; she had always seen her role as sitting on the terrace with a cold white wine, accepting the compliments of friends for the work that the Portuguese gardener had put in. But Portuguese gardeners need money and the garden was now looking neglected. Suddenly determined, Kate put down her coffee and went back into the house. She rummaged in the cupboard under the stairs and found an old pair of secateurs.

In her mind she was a child again, watching her father at one of his favourite occupations. 'Just popping out into the garden for a spot of deadheading, dear,' he would announce and Kate would be on her feet. 'Can I come, daddy? Can I help you?' and the two of them would prowl the garden seeking out fading blooms. 'There's one,' he would cry and swoop with the secateurs. Kate was allowed to cut the plants that did not have thorns. 'That's it, just below that bulging bit,' her father would whisper as if the plant might overhear.

Out in her garden, Kate set to. She gathered up a bucket from the terrace and, with a long swig of her coffee, headed for the roses. Ten minutes later she stood back and surveyed her work. The bucket was three quarters full of browned petals and the roses stood trim, the new buds clear and free to grow. There were scratches on her hand and dirt under her fingernails. Several threads were pulled on her Gap top. She did not care.

Feeling hungry, she headed back to the kitchen. Muddle, now dressed, was standing by the sink, looking out through the window.

'Ah, madam, il faut cultiver son jardin, wouldn't you say?'

'Would I? Not sure.'

'The satisfaction of cultivating one's garden, madam. Rarely surpassed in my experience, though I have not had the pleasure of having my own little God's acre in this country for some years now.'

'Where were you brought up, Muddle?'

'Oh, here and there, madam, here and there. Father was a military man, you see, lots of travel, lots of up sticks and on the road, as I recall.'

'That must have been hard for a young child.'

'One gets used to it. Good training for life, in a way. Having to be adaptable, settle in, make new friends.'

'Still…'

'No, madam, I am not one to bewail my lot. Carpe diem. Life is good and I glean what I can from it. May I mow your lawn?'

'What? Oh, yes, certainly. You'll find the mower in the shed down there. Key's here, on the rack.'

'Thank you, madam. That will give great satisfaction. One must not allow unruliness to take control. That way lies anarchy and chaos.'

Boris appeared at the doorway. 'Anarchy and chaos? You must be talking about Russia. Good morning, everybody.' Kate noticed that he avoided her eyes.

'Good morning, Boris. You're up early. '

'Lots to do, Kate. I thought we could do our practice this morning, run this afternoon and then maybe rest a while before going to a casino this evening, so you can get a feeling for what they are like.'

'OK.' Kate decided to reflect his business-like manner, hiding her anxiety at the suggestion of the casino. 'That sounds like a good plan. Let's have some breakfast first.'

Breakfast soon over, Kate and Boris settled down at the table. 'Now, Kate, blackjack. It's just a matter of counting. What have you done to your hands?'

'Oh, just a bit of early morning deadheading.'

'The English are never happy unless they are trying to controlling nature, make it stand in straight lines.'

'And the Russians? I think they are never happy, full stop.'

'Touché.' He looked up and smiled briefly. 'Anyway, let's talk about counting. As you will have worked out, the more high cards there are left in the pack, the better the chance for the player.' Kate nodded to pretend that she had, indeed, worked this out. 'There are many people who count, using simple methods of ascribing values to different cards. And, to be honest, they are quite easy for the casino to spot. You, Kate, can take it to a more sophisticated level. I will explain how later. First, let's practice the basic counting. It works like this. All twos, threes, fours, fives and sixes you count as plus one. Ten, jack, queen, king, ace are minus one. Everything else is a zero. OK so far?'

'I think so. You're saying that I count as each card comes out.'

'That's right. The more smaller cards are played, the better your chance of winning. So you're always looking for a score that's positive.'

'Sorry, why?'

'Well, that means that it's more likely that you will be dealt good cards. If you have more chance of getting two cards worth ten, you are more likely to score twenty. And that's good,' he added.

'Oh, yes. I see. Sorry.' Kate felt embarrassed at the simplicity of his answer.

'That's OK. It can be a bit puzzling to start with. It also means that the banker is more likely to go bust. Also a good thing.' He smiled across at her.

'OK, let's give it a go.'

Boris dealt the cards one by one, stopping regularly to ask Kate what the count was. After a few false starts she was soon getting it right.

'Well done, Kate,' Boris said as he continued to deal. 'By the way, there was something I wanted to tell you.'

'Really? What's that?'

'You know I was telling you yesterday about when I was a kid, how I ended up in Washington airport with my dad?'

Kate looked up at him. His eyes seemed distant again.

'Yes, of course I remember.'

'Well, what I didn't tell you was… By the way, what's the count?'

'Five, no six, four. Oh, I don't know.'

'Exactly. Kate, they are clever in these casinos. If they think you are counting, they will distract you with drinks, questions, some sort of commotion. You will have to learn to count while you are holding a conversation and hardly looking at the table.'

Kate gave a thin smile. 'Thank you. I shall bear that in mind.'

She concentrated harder and soon was able to count and talk at the same time. They paused for a coffee.

'Well, that wasn't too hard.' Kate smiled confidently.

'There is one more thing you should know. The casinos usually deal the cards from a thing called a shoe; it stops the croupier cheating. Each shoe contains at least three decks, one hundred and fifty-six cards, all shuffled together. So the counting gets to be a little more difficult.'

'Ah.'

'Some now have shoes that automatically shuffle the cards, though I've not seen these in Britain yet so we should be OK.'

Kate looked across at the serious face opposite, at how his hair curled over his ears, a small scar just above his right eyebrow. She wanted to know more about this private man.

'Kate. Kate? Do you agree?'

Kate jumped. 'I'm sorry, Boris. I was miles away. What did you say?'

'You seemed to be somewhere very nice in your head. Where was that?' he smiled.

Kate blinked. She heard the spluttering roar as Muddle marched up and down with the lawnmower. 'Oh, just thinking about my garden and how nice it is at this time of year.'

Boris looked closely at her, seemed about to say something then clearly changed his mind. 'I was saying that we should try a few hands. We'll use two packs for now.'

'Oh, OK. Let's go then. Right.'

Boris dealt rapidly, pushing Kate for decisions. After ten hands, he paused.

'Right, Kate. So far, with an average £20 bet per hand, you would be down £160. You might play two hundred hands in one session, so if it carries on like this, that would leave you £3,200 down.'

'Oh, hell. Not good, then.'

'Actually, not bad. Because it's not going to carry on like this. Tell me, how many tens and face cards have already been dealt?'

'Thirteen, two tens, four jacks, two queens and five kings.'

'So, how many left?'

'Um, seventeen?'

'How many aces?'

'Three. Five left.'

'That's right, so what's your count?

'Plus seven.'

'So, have your chances of winning gone up or down?'

'Oh, I see. This is when I start betting more.'

'That's right.'

Kate sighed. 'Boris, am I ever going to understand all this? I mean, it's not just a matter of remembering cards, is it? There's all this other stuff.'

'Honest answer, Kate, I don't know. But I know you will have a better chance if you concentrate.'

'Yes, professor.'

Boris laughed. 'Sorry, Kate, am I getting bossy again? Let's play some more and then we will have deserved our lunch. This time I will deal the cards face up so we can discuss tactics.'

By lunchtime, Kate was feeling thoroughly demoralised. Even Muddle displaying an immaculately cut lawn failed to lift her spirits.

'Is something troubling you, madam? It is rare that someone does not feel joy at the creation of order out of chaos.'

'Sorry, Muddle. It's all a bit much, all these techniques and strategies.'

'I understand, madam. I believe the Australians felt the same way about cricket when they first encountered it and now they seem to wallop us every time.'

'Thank you, Muddle, most reassuring, though I don't feel I have the resources of a whole sub-continent behind me.'

'No, madam. A point well made.'

As Kate was preparing lunch, Miranda appeared.

'Well, good morning, or rather good afternoon, Miranda.'

'Oh, God, don't start, Mum, please.'

'Have you anything to say?'

'Yes, actually. I'm, well, look, I'm sorry about yesterday. It's just that, you know...'

'Yes, I do know, your boyfriend dumped you so you got drunk. It's happened to a few other people before but, for heaven's sake, Miranda, why you? Haven't you learnt anything about self-preservation?'

'Yeah, mum, yeah I know. It's easy to be wise and sensible about it now but at the time I felt so, you know, really shitty.'

Kate decided to let the word pass. She had bigger matters in her sights.

'Did Darren say why he dumped you?'

'So now you remember his name.'

'Well, did he?'

Miranda looked awkward. 'Sort of, yeah.'

'And?'

'Well…' The girl hesitated. Kate waited, appearing to busy herself with preparing a salad. Miranda picked up a piece of bread and twirled it in her fingers. 'Well, he was a bit vague. He said, like, I was too intense or something. Wanted too much from him.'

'Is that what he said?'

'Yeah.'

'And?'

'OK, he said I was being a pain. There, satisfied? He said I just complained about everything.'

'Did you?'

'I suppose I did, a bit. But it was him who was the pain. I mean, he did such stupid things all the time. Really childish.'

'Like Tom, you mean.'

'Yeah, just like Tom, actually. Oh, I see, you mean … you mean all boys are like that?'

'They think it's impressive. Somehow they think that being able to burp the National Anthem is going to make you love them.'

'Yeah, that was one of Darren's. Though it wasn't burping in his case. Thank God he never got past the first line. Gross.' Kate looked at Miranda's screwed up face and started to laugh. After a moment's confusion, Miranda joined in until the two of them were holding on to each other in helpless giggles. Finally, Kate stopped and pulled back.

'So, do you think you did give him a bit of a hard time?'

'Yeah, I probably did. I mean, he can't help being a boy, can he?'

'You seem to be giving a lot of us a hard time at the moment.' Kate stood back and waited for the explosion. None came. She turned back to the salad. 'So, how's the head?'

'Not as bad as I expected. I guess the episode in the gutter helped and someone put a glass of water by my bed with a note to drink it all.'

'That would have been Muddle.'

'Thought it must have been. Anyway, I did and then a couple of paracetamol that I found in the bathroom and I'm almost human.'

'Cold meat and salad for lunch. That OK?'

'Sounds good. Look, thanks for coming to get me yesterday, Mum. Apparently you were, you know, really cool, what with the Roller and the heavies and all that. One of the girls texted me this morning, well impressed.'

'Well, don't make a habit of it.'

The phone rang. 'Go and see who that is, would you.'

Miranda was soon back in the kitchen, her hand over the cordless phone. 'Someone called George Williams wants to speak to you.'

'George? He was my lawyer in the divorce. I wonder what he wants.'

'Better ask him, then,' and she handed the phone to her mother.

'George, sweety, it's been a long time. Do you have news for me?'

'Not exactly, Kate my dear.' The voice was, if anything, even fruitier. 'First of all, how are you? Are you bearing up?'

'Oh, I think I'm bearing up, George.'

'Good, good. The suburbs can be so cruel, I've found, when you're on your uppers.'

'Really. I have to say I've found the opposite.'

'Have you? Marvellous.' Kate had the strong impression that this was not what George wanted to hear.

'So, what can I do for you, George?'

'Um, I just wondered if you had heard from Stephen.'

'Not a whisper, though I gather the kids are occasionally in touch.'

'Really? Really? Well, that's, er… No, it's just that I've had this letter, someone wanting to reach him.'

'Why have they contacted you?'

'I suppose they knew I was involved in the case.'

'But wouldn't they have gone to his lawyers?'

'Yes, you'd have thought so, wouldn't you. Anyway,' he continued hastily, 'Seems like a bit of a dead end for them. I'll write accordingly.'

'OK.'

'So, everything else tickety boo with you?'

'Yes, thanks, George. And you?'

'Oh, fine, fine. Look, must go, someone on the other line.'

'OK, Bye.'

'Bye.'

Kate put the phone down and frowned. Even for George, that had not sounded believable. She found herself wondering what the real reason for his call had been.

Chapter 14
WEDNESDAY NIGHT

After a bit more practice and the obligatory run, Boris announced rest time at four thirty. They would go out at nine, to get to the casino by ten, when the action, he explained, would be starting to warm up. After an early supper, prepared by Muddle with Miranda's help, Kate had a long soak in the bath, then dressed in the outfit she had worn the previous Friday to Charles' club. She was pleased to feel that already it was less tight around the waist and hips.

She came back down to find Boris explaining to Tom and Miranda for the third time why an Over 21's ruling at the casino was not negotiable. He looked up.

'Kate, you look very fine.'

'Yeah,' Tom butted in, 'You've scrubbed up well, mum.'

Not as good as "Darling you look wonderful," thought Kate but the best I'm going to get. She smiled regally around. 'Thank you both for those well chosen words.'

'Muddle is in the sitting room and as soon as Anastasia is ready, which, with my sister, will be any time between now and two o'clock tomorrow morning, we can go.'

'Fine, how about a glass of wine before we go?'

Boris shook his head. 'Not for me, thank you and I would suggest not for you either. It will be a long night and we will have to concentrate.'

'Well, I find I concentrate better after a glass or two,' Kate replied defiantly and pushed through to the kitchen. She pulled a bottle from the fridge, muttering to herself about domineering males, filled a glass, took a sip. She sighed, carefully poured the rest back into the bottle and pushed it back in to the fridge.

'God, being conscientious is a real drag,' she muttered, before rejoining the others in time to see Tom's mouth drop open like a small fledgling bird's.

A voice came from the stairs. 'So, are we to stand here all night or are we to go have fun?' Kate looked up to see Anastasia. She was wearing a purple satin dress, slashed down to the waist and up the side of the leg. She did not seem to be wearing much else.

Anastasia struck a pose. 'Will this do? I have so few clothes.'

'So I see,' responded Kate tartly.

Anastasia's eyebrows shot up and her mouth set in a firm line.

'Perhaps I should explain, Kate,' Boris cut in quickly. 'Anastasia has a particular job to do this evening. That is to take the attention away from me. It will be her job to sit at a table placing regular small bets until the time is right for me to join her.'

'And that will be when the cards are working the right way?'

'That's right. Anastasia is a counter, like you. Unlike you, she has had to learn the technique from scratch.'

'Hey, don't make me sound like girl from farm. A grade in Math, I remind you.'

'True,' nodded Boris.

'And A grade in imaginative card shuffling, if I remember from our last employer,' added Kate.

Anastasia looked straight at Kate as she descended the stairs. 'Kate, some of us have not been able to get rich husband to pay for everything. We have to learn other tricks.'

Kate felt her cheeks redden. 'Well, in case you haven't noticed, a rich husband has not done me a lot of good in the last few weeks. And don't you think for a minute that mine has been an easy life, Anastasia. Double glazing and a wide-screen TV aren't the be all and end all of a happy life, you know.' She glared across the hall.

Anastasia held her stare in silence for a full five seconds. Then she looked across to Boris. 'Be all and end all. Ha, what a stupid bloody language.'

'Well, if you don't like it, you don't have to stay.'

A dismissive grunt was Anastasia's only reply.

Boris laughed awkwardly. 'Maybe, but it's the language we all have to use, so let's put up with it.'

Kate pushed through the assembled group and stomped out to the car, calling good night to her children over her shoulder. The others followed quietly. Kate heard Anastasia muttering to her brother in Russian. She was clearly not talking about the weather.

'Would you like to sit up front this evening, madam?' Muddle's head bent solicitously towards her.

Kate considered the prospect of sharing the back seat for the next hour with Anastasia.

'Thank you, Muddle, you're very kind.'

A gentle rain started to fall as they drove into London. She watched the wipers drift languidly across the wide windscreen and listened to the sound of the tyres swishing along the damp road.

'Would you like music, Kate?' Boris asked.

'If you want.'

He turned on the radio and gentle violin music wafted into the car.

'I know this,' said Kate. 'What is it?'

'Johann Sebastian Bach, madam,' came a voice from the back seat. 'Sonata No 1 in G minor, if I'm not mistaken.'

'Oh, right, thank you Muddle. But I've heard it somewhere else.'

'That would be as the signature tune to that television detective series set in a pleasant Cotswold village where life expectancy seems to be remarkably low, madam.'

'I thought that you didn't watch television.'

'One must keep abreast of cultural trends, madam.'

Kate thought back to long afternoons frittered away in front of television programmes half watched and never fully understood. She felt suddenly sad.

'Kate.' Boris' deep voice interrupted her thoughts. 'You look Russian. What is the matter?'

'Oh, nothing. Just, I don't know, it seems to have taken

me a long time to get the point of life, I suppose.'

Boris grinned. 'You have the secret of life? I'm impressed. Are you going to share it with me?'

Kate stared through the skittering raindrops on the side window. 'Boris, I think you
know more about these things than I will ever learn.'

Boris shrugged and, reaching across, patted her hand.

They drove on in silence, Kate still feeling the imprint of his hand on hers. She put her other hand over the place he had touched, as if to capture the sensation.

Within half an hour they were in West End traffic, stopping and starting. Boris turned to Kate.

'Now, Kate, I want you to watch carefully tonight.' He reached into his pocket and passed her an envelope. 'When you feel ready, sit at a table and play with this.' Kate looked into the envelope, which was stuffed with ten pound notes.

'Boris, there's a fortune here.'

'Only four hundred pounds. Try not to lose it all, Kate.'

'But, what do I do?'

'You count, Kate, like we have been doing for the last two days. When you think there's more tens in there, you raise the bets. Not too much, or you'll get them suspicious.'

'Suspicious? Is this illegal?'

'Absolutely not. Counting is not illegal but, on the other hand, our friends in the casinos are not very interested in what's legal anyway. Let's say they are not too happy about someone taking their money away. And on that subject, if you see Anastasia and me walking away from the tables at the same time, head for the car.'

Kate swallowed.

Muddle's head leaned forward. 'In what way may I be of assistance, Mr Boris?'

'Well, just make sure that Kate is not being bothered. Other than that, I think you can relax and enjoy yourself.'

'Not a problem. I will blend into the environment like a tiger under a banjan tree.'

Boris swung the car into a side street. 'That sounds very

effective, Muddle. Thank you.' He pulled up by the kerb.

'Where are we?' asked Kate.

'Mayfair. The casino is just around the corner.'

'Oh, I thought we would just swish up to the front door and flunkeys would spring forward to open the doors for us, then drive the car off. You know, like in the films.'

'No, Kate, they only do that when you regularly lose a lot of money. This way, we can be away fast if we need to be. This road leads straight onto Park Lane round the back of the Hilton.'

Kate took a deep breath. She unbuckled her seat belt and, though the car was stationary, felt immediately vulnerable. 'Well,' she breathed out, 'Let's go then.'

The rain had stopped and the streets smelled fresh, the summer dust settled. They walked back round the corner into the wider road, the girls' heels clacking on the surface, the men's steps silent. The canopy of the casino reached out over the pavement a hundred yards further up. A discreet sign and two square men in dark suits announced its business. Each man had a telephone earpiece, the wire curling round behind their heads making them look disturbingly robotic.

They swung in up the steps. The plate glass doors glided open and they stepped into the foyer.

'Good evening, ladies and gentlemen.' The quiet voice came from behind them, making Kate jump. They turned. A man in a very well cut dinner suit stood, hands clasped in front of him, a cold smile on his lips.

Boris stepped forward. 'Good evening.' The Russian accent came strongly. 'A friend tells me that this is a good place to spend a pleasant evening.'

'And who would that friend be, sir?'

'David Cavendish.'

'Ah, yes, Mr Cavendish. One of our regulars. Well, you are welcome, gentlemen, and ladies. Just a few formalities. Perhaps you could sign in over there.'

Boris leaned over the desk to sign the book. 'I assume that one signature will be enough.'

'If you wish, sir, but I will need a contact address.'

Boris looked up at the man. 'The Russian Embassy.'

The other man's eyebrows moved up a centimetre. 'I quite understand, sir. Please, go through.'

A red curtain was held aside and they moved through into a passageway. 'What was that all about?' Kate asked when they were out of earshot.

'This is a private club, so they have to go through the motions of membership, just to keep the licensing authorities happy. Luckily, my compatriots have a reputation for spending a lot of money and not worrying about it. The embassy staff are under orders not to visit casinos, which is bad news for the casinos. This way, I can be sure that they will be discreet.'

At the end of the corridor stood another square man, also fitted with the robotic earpiece. He held the door open. They moved through into the gaming room.

In front of them was a crescent of tables, each with a croupier and five chairs. To the left were slot machines, glittering and sparkling. To the right, a bar and two roulette tables. The soft lights, thick carpet and murmur of conversation oozed wealth. Kate felt the excitement bubble up inside her.

'Ah, but 'tis pretty to see what money will do,' murmured Muddle. 'Browning, madam.'

'And that's the way the money goes, pop goes the weasel. Nursery rhyme, Muddle,' responded Kate.

'Very good, madam, very good. Now, I think I shall avail myself of a small beverage.'

'I'll just take a look around.'

As Muddle headed for the bar, Kate wandered over to the slot machines, feeling like a child in a fun fair. Their flashing lights were mesmerising but gave no clue as to how any of them worked. She looked around until she spotted one that displayed the familiar fruit and bells. Fishing a pound coin from her bag, she pushed it in and pulled the lever. The reels spun and, one by one, clunked into place. A bar appeared. Then a second. Then a cherry dropped into the third window. So close. She could see the third bar, just above the cherry. Lights flashed on the machine. Kate shrugged and turned to walk away.

'Nudge.' A voice came from behind her.

'Sorry.'

'Nudge. Like this.' A hand reached past her and punched a button below the first window. The third bar dropped obediently into place. Coins poured out into the metal tray below.

'Wow, money,' gasped Kate. She clapped her hands and bent down to scoop up her winnings. 'How did that happened?' She turned to look at the man standing behind her. He seemed familiar.

'Well, hello again,' he grinned.

Kate focused on his face. 'I remember you, you were that chap in the queue at the job centre. The one who introduced me to Charles.'

'Patrick Hagan, at your service.' He gave a little bow.

'Well, Patrick, it's great to see you, especially as you've just won me some money. I think I owe you a drink.'

'Well, I've never been known to refuse a drink from a beautiful woman.'

They headed for the bar. 'You certainly started me on an interesting road.'

'Yes, and I heard that our friend had a little local difficulty.'

'Do you know how he is? Have you heard anything?'

Muddle stood as they approached.

'Patrick, this is a good friend of mine, Muddle. Muddle, this is Patrick, who first introduced me to Charles at the, er, club.

'Good to meet you, Muddle.' Kate was impressed that Patrick had not shown the usual confusion at the name.

'My pleasure. Any friend of Miss Kate's is a friend of mine. What will you have?'

'No, no, Muddle, this is my round. Patrick here just helped me win a fortune on a machine.'

Patrick shrugged. 'Hardly a fortune. I think you'll find that there's only twenty-five pounds there.'

'Only?' Kate bubbled. 'That could feed my family for, oh, two days, probably, not sure really. Or it could buy three glasses of champagne.' Kate looked up to attract the eye of the barman, who nodded to show that he had heard. She turned back to Patrick.

'So, what have you heard about Charles?'

'Well, he's out on bail, thanks, it seems, to having friends in high places and a clientele who are, themselves, in high places. A lot of red faces and a major bollocking for a junior police inspector, who's likely to stay junior for a very long time. Seems the lad was a bit over-enthusiastic. Never a good career move to raid an establishment where your boss is a regular customer. Charles reckons that he'll get his knuckles rapped for some minor licensing offence and that will be that.'

'So he'll be back in business.'

'I doubt it. After an episode like that it's a bit difficult to persuade your clientele that it's a safe place to relax, if you follow my drift. And Charles was saying that most of his best girls have disappeared into thin air anyway. He's thinking of selling the place. Apparently a girls' school is looking for new premises in the area.'

Kate giggled. 'They're going to have to do some major redecorating pretty fast.'

The champagne arrived.

'Cheers,' announced Kate. 'Here's to fresh starts.'

The three of them raised their glasses. Kate and Patrick drank appreciatively. Kate felt as if the champagne was lifting her almost physically. Muddle took a sip and placed the glass by the Coca Cola that he already had on the bar.

'So, Kate, what brings you here? A bit different from the public bar at the Station Hotel, I'd say.'

'Certainly is. God, you know, that was only about ten days ago. Such a lot has happened.'

'So tell me.'

'Well, to cut a long story short, I managed to get away from the raid with the help of a friend. Actually,' Kate looked around, 'She's ....'

'The fact is, Patrick,' Muddle cut in, 'We are indulging ourselves in something of a celebration tonight. We had a most enjoyable repast in the close proximity and someone informed us of this august establishment. So, rather than return to the leafy suburbs, we thought we might have a minor flutter.'

Patrick grinned. 'Your man here has quite a way with words, does he not? What are you celebrating, then?'

Kate looked at him blankly.

Muddle cut in. 'The successful outcome of the Battle of Britain.'

'Fine if you don't want to tell me.'

'No, indeed, I do assure you. I am a keen student of the history of aviation.'

'Fair enough.' Patrick stood and drained his glass. 'Well, I'll take a wander round. Probably see you again later.'

They watched him walk over to the tables. 'Muddle, what was that all about?'

'How much do you know about that man, madam?'

'Well, I met him, like I said, at the job centre.'

'And?'

'And what?'

'What does he do? Who does he work for? Is he working here tonight?'

'Oh, I see. Gosh, I didn't ask him anything, did I? Bit of a one-way conversation.'

'Precisely. Given the purpose of our visit, namely to relieve this establishment of some of its operating capital, I would submit that caution in communication should be our watchword.'

Kate felt chastened. 'You know, Muddle, I'm really not cut out for all this subterfuge.'

'Perhaps we should try our luck at the tables, madam. Not that luck should have much to do with it.'

'That's what we're here for, I suppose. Well done, making up all that stuff on the spur of the moment, by the way. Battle of Britain and all that. Very imaginative.'

Muddle looked shocked. 'Imaginative, madam. Are you suggesting I told an untruth?'

'You mean…?'

'This very day, a great and decisive victory, madam. You should know by now that I am not one to utter falsehoods.'

'I apologise, Muddle. You are indeed the most upright of men. Shall we?'

She could see Anastasia crouched over a table at the far end. Boris was walking round, looking on at different tables in a rather distracted way. She walked over an empty table, glass in hand. The croupier was just setting up. Kate sat down, Muddle beside her.

'Good evening sir, good evening madam.'

'We'd, er, like to play, please. '

'Certainly, madam. How much would you like?'

'Sorry?'

'Chips. How many chips would you like?'

'Oh.' Kate rummaged in her handbag and drew out the envelope. She pulled out a handful of notes and carefully counted out two hundred pounds. 'That will do to start, I think.' She noticed a slight smile twitch across the face of the croupier. 'And you, sir?'

'The night is young. I'll just sit it out for now, thank you.'

'As you wish.'

Two other players joined them as the croupier started to deal. Before Kate knew it, five hands had passed. She had won just one, with a ten and an eight, after everyone else bust. But she was counting and the score was going up. When she reached plus seven, she increased her bet.

Over the next ten hands, she won six times, once with a straight blackjack. She looked at her chips and calculated that she was about one hundred and fifty pounds up. She couldn't believe that it was so easy. All she had to do was count and the money just rolled in. She imagined herself a millionaire, striding through the stable yard to choose a horse for the day's exercise. She tried hard to remember the name of the best label for riding gear.

'Hello, there, you seem to be doing well.' Patrick's modulated tones with the soft Irish burr came from beside her, making her jump. She felt Muddle tense on her other side.

'Yes, I've been lucky.'

'And I thought it was only us Irish who believed in luck. Leprechauns and all that rubbish, you know.'

The cards for the next hand were being dealt.

'No. we're all entitled to our share, I'd say.'

'So, tell me, Kate, we got interrupted earlier on. You clearly got away from the raid at Charlie's. How did that happen?'

'Oh, well, luck again I suppose. Excuse me a second, I just have to play this round.' Kate stared at the table. Eleven before, plus two, no three minus two. This was still heading the right way. She checked her first card, a queen, and bet high. At that moment she saw that Boris had slipped into a seat at the other end of the table. She gave him a nod.

'Friend of yours, is he?'

'Yes, he's, um, he's with the Russian embassy. I met him through a mutual friend and he invited us down here tonight.'

'That would be at the restaurant earlier.'

'Sorry?'

'No matter.' Patrick nodded slowly. 'You are moving in high circles. So, no more need for the Job Centre?'

'Oh, I really hope so. Not a nice place, that. I'll be very glad if I never go back.'

The second card was dealt. Kate took a look. A seven. The dealer face-up card was an eight. She thought back. Five aces had gone, three twos and six three but only two fours. If the dealer had a ten or a face card she would be beaten anyway. She would go for it. She placed her bet. She saw Boris bet high as well.

The two other players folded. Kate asked for one more card. A four. Twenty one. Trying hard to keep a straight face, she looked up at the croupier. 'Stand.' He turned to Boris, who shook his head.

The dealer turned over his other card, a five. He dealt

himself another card. Jack of spades. Bust.

Kate laid her cards down and collected her winnings. Boris laid down a blackjack.

'Time for me to have another drink, I think.' She turned to Muddle. 'Shall we?'

'Certainly.' The usual 'madam' seemed to hang in the air. She collected up her chips.

'I'll just stay and try my hand a couple of times,' said Patrick. He signalled for some chips and took a seat next to Boris. As Kate moved away, he heard him say, 'So, how do you know our friend Kate, then?' She hoped that Boris would remember the Russian embassy story.

They sat at the bar and Kate breathed a heavy sigh.

'Tired, madam?'

'Exhausted, Muddle. I haven't concentrated so hard for years. Still, I seemed to do OK, didn't I?'

'A most commendable debut, I would say, madam. Comparable in its way to Lewis Hamilton's on the grand prix circuit or, indeed, the young Mozart astonishing the Saltzburg court.'

'A bit over the top, even for you, Muddle.'

'I say as I find, madam, I say as I find.'

'Have you ever been to university, Muddle? I mean, you seem to know a lot about a lot of different things.'

'I am blessed with a retentive memory, madam.'

'And the university?'

'Yes, madam. I had the honour of studying in three fine establishments.'

'Three?'

'I feel it is a waste to overspecialise.'

'So, if you don't mind me asking, why did you end up working as a doorman?'

'Well, firstly, madam, I did not, as you say, end up. We none of us end up until we are called.'

'I stand corrected.'

'And as for being a doorman, as my mother, rest her soul, used to say, it's not what you are, it's who you are.'

'Your mother was a very wise woman.'

'That she was, madam.' Kate thought she detected the hint of a tear in Muddle's eye.'

'I think we need another glass of that excellent champagne. What do you think?'

'Something soft for me, if I may.'

Kate looked at the cocktail list. 'They have a rather interesting alcohol-free cocktail. How about that?'

'Celebratory yet secure. An excellent choice.'

Kate called the barman over. When the drinks came she reached for her pile of chips.

'That's all right, miss. On the house.'

'Really? Who do I have to thank for that? '

'The management, miss. Enjoy,' and he moved away to serve some men on the other side of the bar.

'Well, madam, I feel that confirms our suspicion that yonder Patrick is on the home team.'

'Yes, I think you're right.'

Kate checked her watch. Midnight. No wonder she was feeling tired. She knew that she should be heading back to the tables but decided to sit for a while. The barman discretely refilled her glass.

After half an hour and feeling a pleasant buzz from the champagne, she felt it was time to make some more money and walked back to the tables. They had filled up but she found herself a place on Anastasia's table. She settled in, Muddle standing beside her, and looked across at Anastasia. Without looking up, the other woman shook her head slightly, while counting her small pile of chips. She rearranged them so that a pile four high were nearest to Kate.

'Fine then,' thought Kate, 'Ignore me. See if I care.' She carefully arranged her own chips, making sure that Anastasia could see how much she had won. Her first card was a ten. Kate bet high. Her second was a three. A nine followed and she was bust.

Within fifteen minutes her pile of chips had dwindled. Anastasia had left the table after the second hand with a glare at

Kate that she chose to put down to jealousy. She was now standing by Boris. Muddle leaned forward.

'The cards do not seem to be falling our way. May I suggest a pause?'

Kate gritted her teeth. 'Muddle, let me do the playing. I've a feeling it's going to come my way now.'

Muddle said nothing and moved back. After four more hands, Kate had not only lost all her winnings and her original stake, she had also lost another hundred pounds of the stake money. Chastened, she stood up rather unsteadily from the table and walked slowly and carefully back to the bar.

Boris appeared beside her. 'Kate, I think it's time we took you home.'

Kate hung her head, unable to look at him. 'Boris, I'm so sorry. It just all seemed to go haywire and after I was doing so well.'

Patrick Hagen walked across to them.

'Well, Kate, it's been most interesting to see you again. I hope you've enjoyed your evening.'

Kate gave a thin smile. 'In parts, I would say.'

'Well, I don't expect we will be seeing you again here.'

'Oh, I don't know. Never say die.' Kate tried to sound jaunty, aware that she was wide of the mark.

'No. You misunderstand me, Kate. We will not be seeing you here again. That is not up for debate. If any of you try to come in here again you will be unlikely to leave by the front door. We don't like to be taken advantage of. And as for you,' he turned to Boris, 'I suggest you find yourself some less amateur partners who can at least get their story right. You're just lucky that her losses compensated for at least most of your gains tonight.'

Boris said nothing but stepped towards Patrick, towering over him.

'Oh, yes, I can see how big you are. I assure you, we are well staffed here to deal with all sizes. I've noticed that people find it difficult to hold their cards with broken fingers.' He stepped back and gave them all a beaming smile. 'Well, good night one and all. Have a safe journey home.'

Kate felt an acid sickness surge through her throat. She fought hard to keep it down as she walked unsteadily towards the door. She was certain that she was going to faint. Boris put his arm through hers to steady her.

'Keep walking, Kate. We'll be out in the fresh air in a moment.'

'I don't understand. What's happened?'

They passed the doormen who scowled at them, flexing their shoulders. Kate was reminded of Don, the solid bouncer with the jutting chin at Charles' club. She suddenly felt like giggling.

They were outside and the fresh air hit her, making her reel. She held on to Boris.

Anastasia stepped past her and spun round, confronting her.

'You stupid bloody amateur person,' she shouted into Kate's face. 'You come to table like Paris Hilton on wet Tuesday. I give you clear signal that the table is minus four and still you sit and loose all that money like is chewing gum wrappers. Boris, man is right. Why we waste time with amateurs? She good only for watching television and drinking with her friends.'

'That was a clear signal? I've seen clearer from a... from a dead mole.' Kate paused, her fury set aside for an instant as she tried to work out how that image had found its way into her head. The fury quickly returned. 'You're just a jealous little girl, Anastasia. I can do what you can't and you can't stand it. You always have to be queen bee, don't you, flashing your bits at everyone. Well, I've news for you, you're just decoration. Boris and I are the experts here.'

'Decoration? And you as decoration as a cow on harvest night.'

Boris spoke sharply to Anastasia in Russian.

'Oh, you shut up. Just because she flashes her false eye hairs at you, you like thirsty dog.'

An awkward silence fell. Muddle cleared his throat. 'As I

recall, the car is down that side street. Shall we?'

The silence continued as they walked to the car. Kate still felt unsteady but detached herself from Boris. Muddle quickly stepped forward and took her arm. Boris and Anastasia walked ahead, muttering at each other.

'I don't get it, Muddle,' she whispered to him. 'Just three glasses of champagne. That's nothing usually.'

'I suspect dirty work at the crossroads, madam.'

'What?'

'I believe there is a high likelihood that your drink was not the pure grape that it appeared to be.'

'Oh, you mean, Patrick had it tampered with?'

'Exactly, madam. As Mr Boris put it earlier, they don't like to lose.'

They had reached the car. Kate climbed carefully into the front seat next to Boris and put on her seat belt.

'Muddle thinks my drink may have been spiked.'

Boris nodded. 'I'm sure it was. That man Patrick was asking me a lot of questions. It was clear that he was on to you from the start. We should have left earlier. It was my fault.'

'Why didn't you just come and pull me off the table?'

'I had to let you lose. Otherwise it would have been nasty.'

'And that wasn't nasty?'

'Oh, that was nothing. I've had a lot worse. The only downside is that our pictures will be circulated to the other casinos in central London.'

'What pictures? No-one took our pictures.'

'There was a camera above the door at the end of that passageway and at least two over each table.'

'Wow. Look, this just makes me think I'm not right for this stuff. Anastasia's right. I am an amateur.'

She heard a snort from the back seat.

'Yes,' relied Boris calmly. 'You are an amateur. So was Anastasia when she started. One day I'll tell you how much she lost before she got it right.'

'Hey, you tell nothing to silly woman. I make lots of money for you.'

'And for you, I remind you. Now, be quiet or I tell everyone what happened to you in Vegas, in Caesar's.'

Kate sensed Anastasia slump back into her seat and determined that, come what may, she would find out about Vegas.

Kate dozed on the way home, waking only when the car swung into the driveway. Her head hurt and her vision seemed slightly blurred. She got out of the car and steadied herself against its door. Muddle stepped quickly forward to take her arm.

'Come, madam, let's get you into the house.'

Silently, they all trooped in. Anastasia peeled off up the stairs without another word. Muddle gently placed Kate on a sofa and disappeared into the kitchen. Within a minute, Kate could hear the sound of the blender whirring busily.

Boris sat beside her on the sofa.

'How are you feeling, Kate?'

'I'm feeling like a kid in water wings who's just been told to swim the channel.' Tears came to her eyes. ' Boris, I can't do this. It's one thing to be able to remember cards, it's quite something else to be able to deal with threats to my life.'

'Well, I think that's a bit extreme. That was just a warning shot.'

'Well, it's bloody well worked. I'm feeling sick, dizzy and frightened. And pathetic. Pretty good for a night out, wouldn't you say?'

'Let's sleep on it. We will talk about it in the morning.'

'No, we will not sleep on it. We will talk about it now. I'm not doing it any more and that's that.'

Boris nodded slowly. 'OK. If that's what you want.'

'Look, I'm sorry. I know you've put a lot of effort into teaching me and I appreciate everything you've done but I just can't. Boris, this stuff is second nature to you; you virtually live in those places. But, you know, I'm just Kate Bradshaw, a girl from Sheffield. I hate saying this but I'm just a housewife. This is not my world.'

'Firstly, Kate, you are much, much more than a housewife. Do you think I would be investing my time in you if I thought that was all you were?'

'Investing? You make me sound like a building site.'

'Sorry. I didn't mean it like that. Look, this is not the time, when you're feeling so bad but there is something special about you, Kate. I, look, as I say, not now, but, what I mean is…'

The door opened and Muddle came in carrying a large glass of a murky orange liquid. It was fizzing busily.

'Try this, madam. I think it will help.'

Kate looked suspiciously at the glass.

'What is it?'

'A concoction that I learned about in Zambia some years ago. The natives of the region use it mainly for recovering from snake bites and the like but I've found it an admirable cure of a certain amount of over-indulgence, intended or, as in your case, not intended.'

Kate did not reach out for the glass.

'What's in it?' she asked cautiously.

'It's quite a complex recipe, but ingredients you would recognise would include banana, orange juice, milk, vitamins C and B, crème fraiche and a courgette. I have, of course, adapted the original due to the lack of certain ingredients, the bark of the pooyang tree being particularly hard to come by in Teddington. It has, however, lost little of its efficacy.'

Muddle held the glass forward. Kate tentatively took it and sniffed. Reassured by the familiarity of the orange smell, she took a sip. The bubbles burst in her mouth and it was as if someone had switched her brain back on. She drank deeply then put the glass down. She gave a small belch.

'Oh, I do beg your pardon.'

'All part of the process, madam.'

'Thank you, Muddle,' Kate said between hiccoughs. 'As usual, you come to the rescue. You know, I really don't know how to thank you for everything you're doing for us.'

'Your thanks is thanks enough, madam. Now, I wish you good night.'

'No,' interjected Boris quickly, 'Sit with us for a while, Muddle.'

'Well, if I'm not intruding.'

'Not at all.'

Kate felt inclined to disagree but said nothing.

'We were talking about the evening. Kate feels that she can't really take that level of excitement.'

'I've been drugged and threatened. A bit beyond excitement, I'd say.'

Muddle perched on the edge of the chair opposite them. He leaned forward, putting his two hands together, fingertips touching.

'If I may say so, Mr Boris, Miss Kate did seem rather like, as the Malays put it, a frog in a motor boat. Out of place,' he added, seeing their rather confused stares. 'However, that is not surprising. This has not been her milieu, after all. The issues that appear to be at the heart of the matter are two-fold. Firstly, can she do this task? And, secondly, does she wish to do this task? Based on observations this evening, the answer to the former is an emphatic yes, to the latter a hesitant probably not.'

'Thank you Muddle' nodded Boris, 'A good summary.'

'In that instance,' continued Muddle, 'Is it possible to find what our politicians liked to call the third way? By this I mean to allow the good lady to use her skills in non-threatening environs.'

Boris thought for a moment. 'Well, there are the on-line sites but they use a random electronic shuffle so counting gets you nowhere. No, I think the best idea would be to start Kate in the casinos with the lower stake tables. They don't care too much about those as they don't stand to lose so much. And they don't expect experts there.'

'So, that seems to be the solution.' Muddle made to rise from his chair. 'We can set that in motion in Sheffield tomorrow.' He looked at his watch. 'Or indeed later today. It is time I retired for the night.'

'Excuse me,' Kate interrupted. 'I'm glad you've come to such a satisfactory decision but would either of you like to know at all what my view of this is? I am, after all, the one who is supposed to be making money for everyone.'

Muddle sat back down. The two men looked at her expectantly.

'Well,' Kate hesitated. Now that she had their attention she was not at all sure what her view of their proposal was. 'I will let you know in the morning. This needs to be slept on.' A small snort of laughter from Boris was met with a raised eyebrow. 'Boris, a girl is allowed to change her mind.' Another hiccough undermined the firmness of the voice.

'Of course, Kate.'

Muddle stood up. 'Well, good night to one and all.'

'Night, Muddle,' they choroused.

'How do you feel now, Kate?' Boris asked after Muddle had left the room.

'Remarkably better. That man is a genius.'

'Yes, and an enigma. I would like to know more.'

'Me too. And by the way, talking of enigmas, what's this about Anastasia and Las Vegas?'

Boris smiled. 'Another time. Let me just say that if she ever gives you any trouble again, ask her about Curly Manciatti.'

'Boris, you can't just leave me with that. I want more.'

'Not now. Anastasia deserves to have some secrets too, you know.'

'Seems everyone in this house has secrets except me. Maybe I will have to be a little more inscrutable in future.'

Boris threw back his head and laughed loudly, quite startling Kate.

'Oh, Kate, I'm sorry but when it comes to inscrutability, you're up against experts here.'

'But why? Why is everyone so secretive? I don't even know what my children are thinking.'

'Oh, you'll never know that. It's the only power they have over their parents. But as for the rest of us, it's not that we are secretive, at least I don't think so. There just hasn't been the time to talk.'

'OK, then. Tell me something, Boris. Tell me three secrets

about the life of Boris Kratin. I mean, I'd really like to know you better.'

Boris looked straight at her, a concentrated stare, like a man about to take a penalty kick. Kate's words hung in the air, gathering importance. She felt the red rise to her cheeks and looked down. After ten seconds of silence he shifted on the sofa, turning to face her directly.

'OK. This is what you want, so here you are. I will give you three facts. One, I can probably never go back to Russia. Two, I have a kid there aged eight whom I have never seen. And three, I have killed two men. There, Kate. Does that make you feel better?'

Kate looked at him in silence, mouth slightly open. The big man got up and headed for the door. Before leaving, he looked back at her.

'You see, Kate. Sometimes it is better not to know everything.' And he turned and left the room.

Kate hiccoughed.

Chapter 15
THURSDAY MORNING

The slow drizzle that had lurked the previous evening had settled into a steady rain. Kate looked out of her bedroom window and felt almost reassured that the weather matched her mood so well. The moment that she had woken, the memory of Boris's words flew into her head. The first two facts that she had demanded had been shocking enough but the third... She found it hard to equate this big, gentle man with - could she use the word? - murder. Maybe it wasn't murder, maybe self-defence. Yes, that was it. Boris could not be that nasty; she would have sensed it by now. Though all those years with Stephen rather undermined that assumption of her perceptive nature. She was even more shocked to realise that, if anything, it made him even more attractive.

She took her time to dress, delaying the moment when she had to see the others. She pulled together some clothes for the next few days; some demure outfits to keep her mother's eyebrows level with her ears and, after some thought, a smarter outfit for the casino.

Shortly after nine she made her way downstairs. Muddle was busy washing up his breakfast things.

'No-one else up yet?'

'On the contrary, madam. Mr Boris was up at sparrow fart, if you'll excuse the expression, one of my father's more military idioms. I believe he's taking a constitutional in the garden.'

'In this weather?'

'He said it reminded him of a Russian summer's day.'

Kate quickly poured herself a coffee. She grabbed an umbrella from the hall and went out through the back door. At the far end of the garden, past the now well-trimmed roses, was a small copse of trees. Boris was standing among them, looking up at the rain. She walked cautiously down the path, taking care not to slip on the wet stones, and stopped a few feet away from him.

'Mind if I join you?'

Boris did not look down. 'It is your garden. Of course you can join me.'

Neither spoke. The rain ran off Boris' face. Finally, he turned to her.

'It is good to feel the rain on your face. It seems to wash things away.'

'And do you have a lot to wash away?'

'Kate, you're fishing.'

'It is better to weave a net than to pray for fish.'

'You're sounding like Muddle.'

Kate gave a wry grin. 'I read it in a *Reader's Digest* at the dentist. Not completely sure what it means but it felt like the right thing to say.'

Boris looked at her. 'It's from a Russian expression. It means you have to make things happen rather than sitting hoping they will.'

Again silence. Kate took a deep breath, walked quickly over to him, reached up on tiptoes to take his face in her hands and kissed him.

'Like that, you mean?'

Boris blinked. 'Yes, I suppose. Just like that. Um, or like this,' and he reached down and returned the kiss.

'Kate,' Boris murmured.

'Yes,' she whispered, nuzzling into his chest.

'I wonder if you could move the umbrella. It keeps hitting me in the face.'

'Oh, sorry. I don't think I can hold it high enough to clear you. We'll just have to get wet.'

'I think you'll find the rain has stopped.'

'Oh, OK. Boris, look, I meant that, just then. I mean…'

'I know. I could tell. I did too, you know.'

'Yes. Listen, about last night, what you said, I mean, you don't have to tell me. Not if you don't want to.'

'Kate, let's see. I think you deserve to know more. Why don't we go in; I think it's going to rain again very soon anyway.'

Rather reluctantly, Kate turned back to the house, a grin having replaced the frown lines of five minutes before.

In the kitchen, Muddle had finished drying up and was putting the cups away.

'Kettle's just boiling, madam. What will it be?'

'Do we have any of that ground coffee left?'

'I believe there is a smidgeon. I think I can coax a cafetiere-full out of it.'

'Sounds good. Let's do that.'

'Consider it done. And, if I may be so bold, high time too.'

'Sorry? Oh, I see. Not much gets past you, does it, Muddle.'

'Scout's training, madam. Look out for the signs of change. You two have gone from carrying the weight of the world on your shoulders to floating like helium balloons, and, in the case of Mr Boris, that's quite an achievement. Something over and above the laws of physics at play, I sense. Go and sit down. I will bring the coffee. By the way, what time do we have to depart?'

'Depart?'

'Sheffield, madam.'

'Oh, God. For one glorious moment there, I had forgotten about that. Well, we have to be there at four so about twelve thirty, I guess, to be safe.'

'I shall be ready, standing by my bed. Metaphorically speaking, of course.'

Kate walked through to the living room, where Boris was waiting.

She stood awkwardly at the door.

'Muddle is, er, bringing coffee.'

'Good. Good. Come and sit, Kate.'

She moved thankfully forward and sat by him on the sofa. He took her hand. It disappeared into his.

'Kate, look. I - I'm sorry I was a bit, how do you say, melodramatic last night. Is that the right word?'

'Yes, I think you could say that's the right word. But, as I

P. M. LAWDER

said, you don't need to tell me anything if you don't want to.'

'Well, let's try a bit and see how it goes. I think it's best if I start where I got to last time. I had just arrived in America with my father?'

Kate nodded.

'Well, as you can imagine, it was all very strange to start with. My father, you remember I said how he was talking to those men at the airport, well, he was involved in some, let's say, some very complicated stuff.

We were quite hard up for the first few years and then, suddenly, he made a hell of a lot of money very quickly. Whatever it was, and even today I don't know all of it, it seemed that almost overnight we were moving into a swanky new apartment. You may remember, that was the time in the early nineties when Yeltsin was selling off all he could, just to keep the country going. I guess my dad made sure he was in the right place at the right time.'

'But why did he have to leave Russia so quickly?'

'His story was that the Ministry of Labour needed a representative at the embassy in Washington. I don't really buy that. Sure, he went off to work every day but I'm not sure it was to the embassy. I think, and later events seem to support this, he was involved in something in Russia that went wrong. At that time, during perestroika, power was shifting every day and you could easily find yourself suddenly on the wrong side. It's much simpler again now; there's only one right side, like the good old days.' Boris gave a slight grin.

Kate leaned over and kissed him. 'Just thought it was time I did that again. In case you forgot.'

He grinned back. 'Don't worry. I won't forget. Anyway, I was enrolled in a local high school, took a crash course in English – at that time I was at the 'my bicycle is bigger than your apple' stage – and I just kind of got on with life.

Right from the start it seemed every night there were guys round at our small apartment, sitting with my father, planning stuff. One night it would be all Russians, drinking vodka, the next night Americans and the bourbon came out. Sometimes it was both, so vodka and bourbon in equal quantities. I realised that one of the main secrets of my father's success was his ability to drink and keep standing longer than anyone else. My job was to make sure that everyone had a drink, that there were chips, crisps, you call them, on the table and then, as my father would put it, always in English, to bugger off to my room.

American sitcoms became a major part of my education. Trying to work out why something is funny in another language is hard work. And, in the case of most of those sitcoms, not very rewarding.'

'Oh, Boris, I've got this terrible picture of you sitting on your own night after night in a strange country. You must have been so lonely.'

'For a while, yes. But, you know, America is really good at absorbing people. I was pretty big for my age, still am, I suppose.'

'Well, yes.'

'So, I was on the basketball team within a few weeks – hell of a lot better than playing chess. And then, of course…' Boris looked down shyly… 'then there were the girls.'

'Sorry?'

'Well, being Russian was kind of exotic at that time. We had been the great enemy for so long that I was seen as exciting, even a little dangerous. I learned,' Boris grinned, 'to take advantage of that.'

'I think there's still a bit of that lurking around you.' Kate moved across and sat astride Boris' vast legs to give him a hug.

'Oh, God. Is all I need, the genius and the idiot sharing germs.' Anastasia stood in the doorway, hands on hips.

Boris sighed heavily and leaned back. Kate determinedly stayed where she was.

'Anastasia,' said Boris sharply. 'Go get yourself some coffee and, while you are there, get some manners as well.'

'Manners no use. Is easier to say what I think. And I think everyone go crazy in this stupid English house. I think…'

'The trouble is, excuse me, Kate,' and Boris lifted Kate easily to one side and rose to his feet. 'The trouble is you don't think. You just walk around telling everyone else what to do. It's time you took a look at yourself, Anastasia.'

'Yes,' chipped in Kate from the corner of the sofa where she was now tucked. 'We don't want another Curly Manciatti episode, do we?'

She watched with pleasure as Anastasia's mouth fell open, her face went first quite pale and then bright red. The girl gasped for breath. She spun on Boris.

'You tell her about that? You betray your own family to this English moon-face?' and she burst into a stream of Russian that was clearly not complementary. Boris waited quietly for her to run out of breath. It was a long wait. When Anastasia finally paused he seized the moment.

'Anastasia, you have a choice. You come to Sheffield with us today and you behave or you go stay in London, with Irena.'

Anastasia's eyes widened. Kate waited, muttering, 'Stay in London, stay in London'

'Irena? You would not…. I could not…..'

Muddle appeared at her side. "Ah, Miss Anastasia. I believe I might be able to coax out one last cup of this fine coffee. Care to join me for a spot of Arabica?'

Anastasia spun on her heel and marched into the kitchen. Boris sat back down. He took two long slow breaths.

'Well, Kate, I'm not sure that was the best time to release your secret weapon.'

'It was worth it. Who's Irena?'

'Our great aunt. Lives in Kensington. One of the old school. Discipline, regular meals and early nights.'

'So, do you think your sister will come with us to Sheffield?'

'I'm sure of it. Anything is better than Irena.'

Kate frowned with disappointment. 'Why are you so keen to have her with you?'

'Experience has shown me that it is better to know where she is and what she is doing.'

'Has she always been like this?'

Boris shrugged. 'I don't know. I've only known her for the

last two years.'

Kate jerked up. 'What do you mean?'

'You remember me saying that I was promised my mother would follow soon after we went to America?'

'And she never came.'

'She, Anastasia, she's the reason why.'

'You mean, she was…, your mother was pregnant with Anastasia when you left for America?'

'That's right. Though I don't think they knew at the time.'

'So what stopped her coming out later?'

'It was not that simple.'

'That seems to be the answer to any question about Russia.'

Boris smiled. 'You're learning.'

Kate felt an urge to be away for the house, to be able to get her bearings on the gentle but, apparently violent man. She jumped up and kissed him. 'Listen. Let's get out of here. Take a walk. We're going to be cooped up in the car for several hours, then under the searchlights of Stalag Sheffield.'

Boris checked his watch. 'Sure. There's time. That would be nice.'

They walked out into the hall.

'Mum,' Tom appeared at the turn of the stairs. He was dressed in a t-shirt that proclaimed 'Oi be a West Country yokel' and deliberately torn jeans. 'Have you got a minute?'

'Not really and, by the way, you'll have to change before we go to Granny and Grandpa's.'

'Yeah, sure, but I really want to show you something. On my computer.'

'Can't it wait? To be honest, Tom, I'm really not that excited by ancient Greek wars or whatever.'

'Macedonians. But it's not that. Something I was looking up. It'll only take a minute. Please.'

Kate sensed an urgency in Tom's voice. She sighed. 'OK,' and climbed the stairs.

'Boris,' called Tom. 'You come too. I think it will really interest you.'

Tom's room was, as usual, in chaos. Clothes were on the floor, on the chair, on the bed. On one wall, a Teletubbies poster had been drawn over in felt tip, the cuddly creatures transformed into punks and Goths. Lala's look of surprise was explained by the real safety pin that had been pushed through his nose. His handbag was replaced by a machine gun. Under the bed, Kate glimpsed the ragged corner of a magazine. She decided, as she had several times before, not to investigate its subject matter. She did, however, open a window.

Tom swung himself into position in front of the computer. He pressed some keys.

'I've been googling.'

'You've what? Oh, googling. For a moment there, I thought … never mind.'

After a short and awkward silence, Tom drew a breath. 'Anyway,' he said, in that voice that children reserve for when they want to explain to their parents that the world has moved on. 'You know you told me that Muddle's dad had been in the army? So, I googled Muddle and army and this is what I've found.'

He triumphantly pressed the return key. Kate leaned forward. A detailed list appeared on the screen. She wondered, not for the first time, how long she could put off a trip to the optician.

'What's this?'

'Army lists from 1970. Look at this,' and he pointed to a line near the top.

'Sorry, can't make out the words from here.'

'There's no Muddle, but I have found a Major General Thomas Muddle-Alderton, Royal Sussex Regiment,' said Tom, triumphantly. 'And there's more.'

Kate felt uneasy, her curiosity overtaken by a respect for Muddle's privacy. 'Look, I really don't think we should be looking at this.'

'But, Mum, this is the good bit.'

A voice came from behind them. 'I think that Master Thomas wishes to convey that my father was killed in action the following year in Northern Ireland.'

They swung round, guiltily.

'Muddle, I am sorry,' stumbled Kate.

'Madam, I understand, indeed appreciate the curiosity of the young, unwelcome though it may sometimes be. In my day, it was pouring over books about the flora and fauna of this world. I have particularly fond memories of a book of my father's entitled *The Boy's Wonder Book of Why and What.* Full of fascinating facts, as I recall. This is just the new version.'

'That's very kind of you, Muddle, and I assure you we will pry no further.'

'Thank you, madam. That would be appreciated. I do hold the view that people are rather too free nowadays about matters that are best kept private.'

He gave a slight bow and left the room.

'But, Mum,' Tom whispered urgently. 'There's stuff about Muddle himself as well. You wouldn't believe what I've found. He's really not what he seems.'

Kate looked across to Boris and raised an eyebrow. 'Very few of us are, Tom. I'm beginning to find that out.'

Boris grinned broadly back at her. 'What about that walk, while there's still time.'

'Sounds good.'

'But Mum, this stuff's dynamite, I mean, nothing horrible but fantastic, you know.'

'Then keep it safe. You heard what I said to Muddle. That's the end of it. Close it down and leave it alone.'

Tom sighed theatrically. 'I bet MI5 don't have this problem.'

Boris seemed about to answer, then stopped.

They let themselves out of the front door and walked up towards the woods. The rain had cleared. An awkward silence fell between them.

Boris cleared his throat. 'I was very impressed at your self-control.'

'What do you mean?'

'Well, I thought women always needed to know

everything. It was good that you did not want to know more about our friend Muddle.'

Kate stared at Boris. 'Of course I wanted to know. I was bursting to know. If I was a good mother, I'd be making sure I knew everything about you and Muddle that I could possibly find, rather than letting two strange, and I do mean strange, men, not to mention one psychotic woman in to my house. But I have to go on gut instinct. And Muddle's friendship means a lot to me.'

'Yes.'

'And yours as well, of course,' Kate added quickly. She slipped her hand into his.

'I'm not an expert on mothers, but, as far as I can see, you're doing pretty well. Tom's a bright boy. You must be very proud of him.'

'Yes, yes, I suppose he is. To be honest, I'm really only just getting to know him. As a person, I mean. You have them, obviously, as babies and toddlers and all that but they're not really formed, if you know what I mean. I mean, they're very cute and you can dress them up and all that but they're not really people. You know?'

Boris did not reply for a few seconds. Eventually he said quietly, 'No, not really.'

'Oh, Boris, I'm so sorry, I forgot about, you know, what you told me. Last night. About your child. Did you want to talk about it?'

'I think we've done enough of the history of Boris Kratin, if you don't mind, Kate. Maybe another instalment later, or tomorrow.'

'OK.'

Another long pause as they walked into the woods, though this time less awkward, more companionable. For a brief moment, Kate wondered if it was altogether wise to be walking in the woods with a self-confessed killer, but this was Boris and something about him just made everything feel safe and right. She held his hand tightly. The smell of the woods, rich and warm, hung in the air. A slight breeze shook raindrops off the trees around them. Leaves underfoot softened each step. Kate felt a great sense of peace. They climbed through the woods to the top of the hill, which opened up into a clearing. In the distance they could see the curve of the Thames and, beyond, the traffic pounding up and down the M3.

'Can't we just stay here?' Kate asked wistfully. 'Do we really have to go to Sheffield?'

'Well, you haven't said whether you will try the casino there. And what about your mother? I have the feeling that she would not be very pleased if you did not turn up.'

'She's not very pleased, whatever I do. It's always been like that. According to an article I read somewhere, it's because I'm the first-born and a girl. Something to do with lionesses. Can't remember the details now.'

'Then she should look again. She has a lot to be pleased with. And I will tell her so.'

Kate leaned in against him. 'Thanks, Boris, you're a real boost. But I think you should meet her before making any promises. She has reduced many strong men to silence.'

'I have dealt with the FSB, Kate.'

'Who?'

'The new version of the KGB. I think I'm prepared for your mother.'

'I think she could probably teach even them a thing or two. Anyway,' she sighed, 'we'd better be getting back.'

He kissed her neck. 'This is a nice place. Perhaps we come back here soon.'

Kate smiled. 'Yes, I'm sure we will. And, by the way, I will try the casino one more time. But keep an eye on me.'

'That won't be difficult.'

By one o'clock the suitcases were in the hall. One each for Kate, Boris, Tom and Miranda, a small backpack for Muddle and three large suitcases for Anastasia.

'How did she fit all that into the guest room wardrobe?' Kate muttered to Boris.

'Easy. All my stuff was put on the floor.'

The men packed the car; the Rolls' capacious boot took it all. Kate walked around the house to check everything. As she was in the kitchen, Anastasia walked in. Kate stiffened.

'Look, Kate,' Anastasia started, 'I think we have been walking on one leg today.'

'What?'

'You know, starting wrong step.'

'Oh, getting off on the wrong foot, you mean. Well, yes.'

'I think I am a little jealous. Of you and my brother.'

'Oh. Right. Well, yes, I suppose you have been used to having him to yourself a lot.'

'Yes.' The Russian girl paused. 'Did he tell you how that all happened?'

'No, just that he has only known you for a couple of years.'

'And he tell you about Manciatti?'

'Yes, some of it, anyway,' Kate replied vaguely. She was not yet ready to let her advantage go.

'It has been difficult time.'

'I'm sure.'

Silence.

'Anyway,' Kate said with forced brightness, 'we had better get up to Sheffield. Being late for my mother is not an option.'

'She sounds like my Aunt Irena.'

'I guess every family has one. I just wish this one was my aunt, not my mother, to be honest.'

'We will help you, Kate.'

OK, thought Kate. That's as close as I'm going to get to an apology. Time to call a truce, at least for now.

'Thank you, Anastasia. That's good to know. Now, the others will be waiting. Let's go.'

Chapter 16
THURSDAY AFTERNOON

The journey up the motorway to Sheffield was the usual combination of heavy traffic and road works. Boris drove smoothly and by three they were twenty miles away.

'Come off at this next junction,' Kate advised him.

'Are you sure? It does not say Sheffield.'

'That's OK, it's the pretty way in. Anyway, being early for my mother is almost as bad as being late.'

Kate guided them through Chesterfield and then out across the stark moorland, past rocky outcrops and heather-covered hills, through grey stone villages huddled in the dips in the road. To many, this land looked rough and inhospitable but for Kate it still held the magic of her childhood, when every rock hid an elf, every dry stone wall was waiting to be climbed. She felt herself relax.

Eventually they came to the brow of a hill and looked down on Sheffield, lying in front of them in the valley.

Kate took a deep breath. 'OK, let's go. It's down that way. And remember, kids,' she added, turning to the back seat, 'not a word to your grandmother about gambling.'

As they drove down, the houses appeared more frequently. Street lights, roundabouts and traffic lights announced the city. Kate directed Boris up a road to the left, which led into the centre of Dore, her parents' suburb. The local residents liked to call this area The Village, a practice encouraged by the estate agents, who seemed to occupy most of the shops, those not already converted to tasteful, bijou restaurants.

'Turn right here,' Kate instructed. They pulled into a road of large Edwardian villas, all in the grey local stone, gardens immaculate, conservatories visible to the side of each, splendid with their plastic-covered crenulations. Jaguars and Volvos sat complacently in the driveways.

'Number 26, over there on the right.'

Boris pulled up outside the house and switched off the engine. They sat in silence.

Kate checked her watch. 'Five to four. That should be within tolerance levels. Let's go.'

Everyone piled out of the car and stood, letting Kate lead the way up the flagstone path to the gleaming white wood of the mock-Tudor front door.

She rang the bell, heard footsteps crossing the parquet floor of the hall. The door swung open.

'Hello, mother, here we all are.'

'Hello, Kate, dear, nice and early.' A perfunctory peck on the cheek. 'Your father's somewhere in the garden, doing things. Tom, you have grown.'

'Well, Gran, I'm hardly going to shrink, am I.'

'Well, you have become a cheeky fellow.' She looked Tom up and down, taking in his torn jeans and bright orange shirt, the best that Kate could persuade him to wear. 'And such an eccentric taste in clothes. I do hope you're not going to go into fashion. Dreadful business and no place for a red-blooded young man. That's the risk of bringing them up in London, as I've told you, Kate. And Miranda, gosh, make-up already. Such a young lady. I'm sure I didn't allow your mother to have make-up until she was at least seventeen. Still, the world moves on, I suppose. Now then, Kate, are you going to introduce me to your friends, or just leave them standing there?'

'Of course, mother. This is Muddle. You spoke on the phone a couple of times.'

'A great pleasure, Mrs Bostock, to finally make your acquaintance.'

Kate's mother looked down from the front step to the diminutive Muddle. 'How do you do. Voices can be so deceptive, can't they? You're not what I expected at all.'

'The ear doth deceive the eye, madam.'

Mrs Bostock clearly liked being called madam.

'And who is this?'

'Mum, this is my good friend Boris Kratin and his sister Anastasia. Also my friend,' Kate added hastily.

Boris bowed slightly as he took her hand. 'I can see where Kate gets her good looks from, Mrs Bostock.'

'Now, soft soap like that does not work in this part of the world,' she simpered. She turned to Anastasia, her eyebrows arched and she gave the briefest of nods. 'Well, Kate, don't keep our guests hanging about on the doorstep. Take everyone through to the conservatory; it's just too close in the lounge for afternoon tea. We'll have to be quick. The MacDonalds are now coming tonight instead of tomorrow, something about a sick relative. Inconsiderate, if you ask me but I suppose one must be seen to be flexible in the circumstances. And see if you can lure your father indoors.'

She turned and vanished into the kitchen. Boris gave Kate's hand a supportive squeeze, as she watched her mother's retreating form and wondered, not for the first time, how so much power and venom could be packed into such a diminutive form. Each hair on her head was tightly constrained in the hairstyle that had not changed for twenty years. 'If it's good enough for the Queen, it's good enough for me' was the firm instruction to Anton at Salon Dorea, whenever he suggested a change. Kate knew exactly how that hair felt.

They all trooped through to the back of the house. Wicker chairs and occasional tables had been arranged in the conservatory, Fresh flowers were pinioned into formal displays at either side and the blue and white tea service was neatly stacked and ready for action.

The lawn stretched away from the house, every blade of grass standing to attention. 'Hi, grandpa,' Tom called out to the figure stooped over the vegetable garden at the back. The figure straightened and waved, making its way slowly back to the house. Kate watched, sadly aware that in the seven or eight months since she had seen him, he had aged, the once agile body that had so easily carried her on his shoulders as a child now awkward in its movements.

'Hello, poppet,' he peeled off his gloves as he came in and

gave her a slightly formal hug. 'Damned carrot fly are having a field day up there. And Tom, good to see you. Don't think much of Yorkshire's performance so far this season, do you? Hello, Miranda, dear. You're looking very pretty. Sorry, are you allowed to say that nowadays, or am I being a male chauvinist?'

'That's OK, grandpa. I can cope with people telling me I'm pretty.'

'Oh, good.' He leaned over to whisper to Kate. 'Never really know what to say to young girls, you know.'

'No dad, you never did.' She gave his arm a squeeze.

'Now, who do we have here?'

'Dad, this is Muddle.'

'Ah, yes, Betty mentioned Muddle. I think you quite impressed her.'

'Well, I feel we may have established a certain rapport. I think we connect because we are both people who like to get to the point, and are not hesitant in expressing a view.'

'Yes, I know what you mean,' replied Kate's father with a touch of weariness. 'Now, who's this fine fellow?'

Kate introduced Boris and Anastasia.

'Russian, I'm guessing, from the names.'

'That's right, though I've been in America for many years,' Boris replied. 'Anastasia here has only recently come from Russia.'

'Though I too have been to America,' Anastasia added. 'To New York and Las Vegas.'

'Las Vegas? An interesting place to start.'

'My brother is professional gambler. I go with him as fluff.'

Kate's eyes widened at Anastasia's deliberate flouting of her instructions.

Her father's eyebrows had shot upwards. 'Fluff?'

'Is what they call pretty girl who takes attention away.'

'I see. Goodness. Well, better not tell Kate's mother you're a gambler. It's her latest campaign, to close down the new casino here.'

'Actually, to be fair...,' cut in Kate. Just then the door

opened and Kate's mother entered, bearing a large silver teapot. 'Kate, there's scones and sandwiches on the Welsh dresser in the kitchen.'

Muddle leapt forward. 'Allow me,' and was gone before Kate could reply.

'Do sit down, everyone. Now, do you all take it with milk? What about our continental friends? I know you do things rather differently over there.'

'Milk is fine for me, thank you,' replied Boris as he squeezed his frame into the wicker chair.

'For me black,' Anastasia said. 'I never understand idea of putting cow milk into tea.'

Mrs Bostock gave a tight smile. 'Well, dear, it's a tradition. Like democracy.'

Anastasia glowered and an awkward silence fell. Muddle reappeared with the food and set to, helping pass round tea, plates, napkins and food. Kate helped where she could. Finally, all were settled. Everyone complimented Kate's mother on each element of the tea. She received each morsel of praise with a slight incline of the head.

'Cucumbers from our own garden,' proclaimed Kate's father.

'Oh, Jack, you and your garden. He never thinks of anything else. But yes, we have done well this year for produce. I've bottled some gooseberries just last week.'

'Did you grow the cucumbers under glass, Mr Bostock?' Boris enquired.

'Yes, to start them off, then I gradually expose them as the summer warms up.'

'I have always lived in the city so these things are a mystery to me.'

'In Kenya,' Muddle joined in, 'we used to grow many and varied fine vegetables, corn, avocados, peas, beans. I remember when I was a child going out with the servants in the late afternoon to pick for the evening meal.'

Kate's mother sat forward. 'You lived in Africa? With servants?'

'In many places, madam. My father was in the army.'

'He was a general,' Tom cut in.

'Tom,' Kate glared. 'That is not for discussion.'

'Nonsense, Kate,' admonished her mother then turned to beam at Muddle. 'I could tell you were a man of breeding. Such good manners.'

'Well, Mrs Bostock, a man's a man for all that, as Robert Burns so well expressed it. One cannot rely on other's glory.'

'No indeed. Just what I was telling Mrs Grayston last week at the WI meeting. The silly woman insists that, because her mother ran the produce fair for so many years that she should now take it over, when there are such obviously better candidates. Well, one, at least. But tell me, what are your plans for this evening?'

'Well,' Kate replied hesitantly, 'I thought I would show everyone a bit of Sheffield, maybe. Just give them a feel for the place. Find somewhere nice to eat.'

'Well, Kate, that sounds like another of your rather vague plans, if I may say so. I suppose I could rustle up something for you all here.'

'That's OK, Mrs Bostock,' Boris quickly replied. 'The hotel that Anastasia and I are staying at could only do half board, so we are committed to eating there tonight. I was planning to invite Kate and Muddle to join us so you could have some time with your grandchildren.'

'Oh, really? Where are you staying?'

'The Royal.'

'Oh, very nice. We went to a dinner dance there last year, didn't we, Jack? Though I seem to remember their crab soufflés were a little doubtful. I'd advise you to avoid them. Another slice of Victoria Sponge, anyone?'

Kate's father stood up. 'I think that's all a jolly good idea. I'd love to have time to catch up with Tom and Miranda. Now, I can hear those carrot flies munching from here so, if you'll excuse me…'

Boris stood as well, easing himself with difficulty from the tight chair. 'May I come to see what you are growing? As I said, this is all an unknown world to me and I would be very interested.'

'Of course, delighted. No-one usually shows much interest. Yes, come along, er, Boris.'

'I don't know what he finds to do out there,' muttered Kate's mother as soon as the men were gone. 'Whenever I need him to help me on my committee work, there's always some crisis or another in the garden. Still, it gets him out from under my feet.'

'Mum, have you had any more communication from Stephen?'

Her mother looked sharply at her. 'I hope you are not going to start interrogating me again. That was most inappropriate before.'

'Well, have you?'

'Children,' Mrs Bostock swivelled her gaze, 'why don't you bring your cases in? Miranda, you're in the blue room, front left and Tom, you're up in the attic room.' The children gladly went off. Muddle stood up.

'With your permission, Mrs Bostock, I will clear away the tea things. Miss Anastasia, perhaps you will help.'

Anastasia would clearly have preferred to listen to the conversation. However, she rose reluctantly to her feet, picked up a plate and a teacup and went slowly out to the kitchen.

'Your Mr Muddle's a gem, I must say. How did you say he found you?'

'We were working together. Now, don't change the subject. Have you heard from Stephen?'

'As it happens, we did receive another postcard from him just a couple of days ago. He says he is now travelling on business in China and sent the card from somewhere, oh, I can't remember the name.'

'May I see it?'

'Why? I've told you what's in it.'

'I'm interested. I'd like to know where he is.'

'Are you still claiming that he's not paying you? I'm sure that's most unlikely.'

'Never mind that. Where is the postcard? On the mantelpiece in the lounge?'

'Probably, I suppose.'

Kate walked through. The thick carpet and heavy furniture in the lounge made the room oppressive, bringing back memories of straight backs and only speaking when spoken to when visitors came to call. On the coffee table were piles of papers headed WI and Ban the Casino. Over on the mantelpiece stood two official-looking invitations and a gaudy postcard. Kate picked it up and turned it over. She recognised Stephen's neat handwriting. Holding it in both hands, she willed it to give up its secrets.

Finding that telepathy was not working, she sighed and read the text.

Dear Elizabeth and Ted

Just been sent up country to sort some things out with a subsidiary. Very hot and muggy and getting really tired of rice!! Still, should be back in HK by the weekend. Thanks for all your help.

Love S.

Kate was puzzled. Why send a postcard to your ex's parents, people whom you had to be dragged to see for the minimum time each Christmas? And why send such a dull, no news card? And what help? What are you playing at, Stephen?

Her eyes drifted across to the papers on the table. The minutes of recent WI meetings, with their hidden intrigues and rivalries, were often worth a look but this afternoon they did not catch her interest.

Lying next to them was a pile of leaflets with a bright red headline, 'Sodom and Gomorrah come to Sheffield', followed by three exclamation marks. She picked up a leaflet.

Family life and the wellbeing of our young people are under great threat. Collusion between our government and American big business has foisted on the people of the city of Sheffield an undesired haven for gamblers and other low lifes, which will suck in our young people, husbands and fathers, bringing poverty, misery and destitution to many.

Join us in telling them that we, the people of this proud city, say **NO** *to this den of iniquity. We say that Christian family values matter and the* *place of a husband is at his hearth, not caught in the thrall of flashing lights and cheap women in a vortex of evil.*

Sign our petition today, join us on the picket line and turn the devil away from our doorstep.

Women's Institute, Dore and Totley
Evangelical Church of Christ, Savour and Redeemer, Broomhill
British Democracy League, Yorkshire Chapter

The printing of this leaflet has been sponsored by Harry's Hardware Shop, the place for all your bits and pieces.

Kate slipped a leaflet into the pocket of her jeans. She could not remember ever having been in league with the devil before but felt she did not need to let it bother her unduly.

She walked out into the kitchen. Muddle had his hands in the sink, carefully washing the tea things. Her mother was drying up, Anastasia standing to one side, tea towel in hand, finding something very interesting to look at out of the window.

'Can I help?'

'No thank you, dear, you carry on with your private eye work. Mr Muddle here is giving me all the help that I need, thank you.'

Fighting down a reply that would have done justice to a thirteen-year-old, Kate walked away. There was something about being in this house that always made her a stroppy child again. In earlier days, she would have taken it out on Stephen without hesitation, finding fault wherever she chose. Now she did not have that outlet and could feel building up inside her the almost pleasurable desire to scream at her mother and slam doors. She took a deep breath and headed out into the garden to get some air. Leaning against the wall of the house she raised her face to the sun and let its heat seep in. She pushed aside the doubts of the last two days, deciding that she would go to the casino tonight. It did not matter that this was mainly for the satisfaction of doing something that her mother disapproved of; that was such a long list that the pleasure had dissipated years ago. Anyway, the decision was taken. One less uncertainty in this very bewildering world that she now found herself in.

With some relief at a decision made, she crossed the well-trimmed lawn towards the two men. They were both bending down looking at the ground as her father explained something at length to Boris, who was nodding vigorously. Boris. Another major uncertainty. What did she really feel about him? He was nice enough and certainly cute in his own bear-like way. But there was so much that she did not know. All that stuff about his child and why he could no longer go back to Russia. And the killing. Kate shuddered. Could she trust him? And why was she asking herself that question? Trust him to do what?

The two men looked up at her as she approached. She stood awkwardly, still overtaken by her own thoughts.

'Hello, poppet. I'm just explaining to Boris here the difficulties of growing veg that's edible, especially to your mother's standards, which, as you know, would make M&S look sloppy.'

'You'd have been proud of me the other day, Daddy. I was deadheading the roses in my garden, just like you showed me.'

'Well done. I didn't think you were interested.'

'I wasn't, but times have changed.'

Boris stood back from the others. 'Kate, I had better get your things in from the car. We will need to go and check in soon.'

And get Anastasia away from the Mother, thought Kate, before either says something really outrageous.

'Oh, right. Thanks. Mum will tell you where to put them.'

An awkward silence fell between Kate and her father as Boris went off.

'So.' Her father cleared his throat. 'He seems a nice chap. How did you meet him again?'

'I was working with his sister. She introduced us.'

'Oh, yes. The dark and sultry one. Not sure your mother approves of that one.'

'Not sure I do either, to be honest, but they have both been really helpful just when I needed friends.'

'I thought you had lots of friends.'

'So did I, Daddy. But it was a bit like a club. And money and wanting to spend it were the entry tickets.'

'Well, I thought you were always quite good at that. Sorry, I didn't mean…'

'No, that's OK. You're right. That's what I did. But it's interesting what being without it does for you. Money, I mean.'

'Do you miss it?'

'Of course I do. Well, some of the time. I don't think I'd like to go back to my previous life full time but there's nothing wrong with a bit of mindless fun occasionally, you know.'

Her father nodded and said nothing, leaving Kate to wonder about what she had just said. Yes, damn it, she did miss her former life. It had all been so easy.

Her father broke the silence. 'So, Stephen, I mean, I don't want to pry, but it does seem that he's rather let you down.'

'Well, yes. He's done a runner, as they say, and the money's run with him.'

'Never really liked the chap, to be honest. Your mother thought he was the bee's knees, still does, what with him being a banker or whatever, but I never really took to him. And it was odd those two times he came round after, you know, you were divorced. But I kept my own counsel. Thought it best, you know. Don't interfere. Hope you don't mind my saying that now.'

'Well, you were right. Sorry, two times? Did you say two times?'

'Yes, I'm sure of it. Don't know what for, to be honest. I gave him rather a wide berth.'

Kate decided to file that one away for a future confrontation with her mother. 'What do you think of Boris, then?'

'As I said, he seems a very nice chap. Why, is it important?'

'It's always important to know what you think, Daddy. I wish you'd tell me more often, to be honest.'

'Sorry, love. You know me, Mr Discretion.'

Mr Keep Your Head Down, more like, thought Kate.

'No, to be honest, I don't know yet whether Boris is important or not.' She squeezed his hand. 'But you'll be the first to know.'

'Well, I am a bit worried about what his sister said, about him being a gambler. That can't be a good thing. I mean, a fellow of his obvious intelligence should be doing something more worthwhile, wouldn't you say?'

'I think it's only a temporary thing. He was a college lecturer. And anyway, he wouldn't call it gambling. He's doing it to make money, not lose it.'

'So, why is he not a college lecturer at the moment?'

'I really don't know. That's the problem in a nutshell. There's so much I don't know. He seems a really nice guy but there's stuff there. Bits of his past that don't seem to add up. Weird stuff.'

'Well, perhaps you'd better ask him.'

'Yes, perhaps I should.'

'Look, if you need money, you know, to tide you over, you only have to ask.'

'Thanks, Daddy.' Kate felt her voice catch. 'I'm fine at the moment, I've got really good friends and we are fine. Let's see how it goes.'

Her father cleared his throat and turned away. 'Well, better be getting back to my killing spree here.'

'OK, Daddy. See you later. And thanks.'

He nodded and muttered something about family that Kate did not catch. She headed back to the house aware that they had just had the longest conversation of her adult life. Her feelings about the house and its effect on her had evaporated.

Her mother appeared at the French windows.

'I know, Mum, you'd like us to get out of your way so that you can get ready for the McDonalds.'

'So, you're adding mind reader to your list of talents. Mind you, you can leave that Muddle as long as you like.'

Kate smiled in a way that she knew would irritate her mother and went upstairs to her room. Boris was just putting her case down.

'Thanks for that. My mother would like us out of the way.'

'No problem. Your father's a nice man.'

Kate put her arms around Boris. 'And so are you.'

He smiled down at her and held her close. Kate was very aware of her bed just behind her. She was also aware of her threadbare teddy bear that sat primly on it.

'Can we see a bit more of each other tonight?'

Boris raised an eyebrow.

'I mean, there's so much I still want to know.'

'Oh, I see. Well, let's see how the evening goes.'

'You thought I meant something else, didn't you?' she giggled.

Boris flushed up through his enormous face. 'Well, as one of your poets says, hope springs eternal.'

'I think Muddle must be catching. But listen, I mean, if you want to…'

A thundering on the attic stairs heralded Tom's imminent arrival. They pulled apart.

'The joys of children,' Kate murmured.

'Shall we meet at seven thirty at the Royal? There are a couple of things we will need to do before we go on.'

'Sounds good,' she nodded.

'Are you two out on the town again tonight?' Tom asked as he entered the room. 'And we have to stay in with Gran being told what we are doing wrong. It's so unfair.'

'Get used to it. And don't you dare mention anything about casinos or gambling tonight. And remind your sister.'

'What's it worth?'

'Not being hung up by the fingernails and having slugs put down your trousers.'

Tom considered this. 'Sounds fair.' He nodded and charged off down the stairs. His grandmother's voice rose sharply up to greet him.

'Thomas. You didn't tell me you had brought a herd of elephants in your luggage.'

'Sorry, Gran,' came the automatic reply.

Kate kissed Boris on the cheek. 'Well, another dangling conversation. What's one more among so many?'

'Perhaps we can drive off somewhere tomorrow.'

'Sounds good. Now, off you go. And tread softly on the stairs.' She followed him down.

Her mother came to the door to see the two Russians off. As she walked down the path, she saw the Rolls for the first time.

'Goodness me. Rather ostentatious, isn't it?' She craned her neck to see if any of the neighbours were in their gardens and was clearly disappointed that there was no one to be seen. 'Is this yours, Boris?'

'As a matter of fact…' Boris started.

Kate jumped in. 'Yes, it's Boris's. Rather fine, isn't it, and very practical for moving all of us around the country.'

'Well,' conceded her mother, 'it's certainly more useful that that little runabout thing that you drive, Kate.'

'If you remember, Mother,' Kate seized the moment, 'that was taken away because Stephen hadn't paid for it.'

'Oh, not all that nonsense again. Let's say goodbye to our guests, shall we?'

Boris and Anastasia quickly got into the car and it purred off. As soon as they were out of sight, Elizabeth Bostock turned on her daughter. 'Kate, you really must not wash your dirty linen in front of guests. It's very bad manners. I have brought you up better than that.'

'They are not guests, they are my friends, who are very aware, much more aware than you, quite honestly, of what I have been through recently.'

'This is my house and, as far as I am concerned, they are guests. And as for your friends, that young madam is certainly not the sort to put into polite company. That kind of behaviour may be all right in the more louche parts of London that you hover around but not in the real world. And I thought that big chap was going to break my furniture.'

'Well, I'm sorry that nothing I do and no-one I know is ever good enough for you but this is me and this is what you get. This is what you brought up. You'll just have to bloody well learn to put up with it.' Kate turned and stormed back into the house.

Muddle was in the hall. 'May I be of assistance, madam?'

'Yes, you can strangle my mother.'

'Interestingly, madam, I did learn five different ways to strangle when I was working in the Kalahari. Though that was on chickens rather than fully grown humans.'

Kate laughed loudly. 'Thank you, Muddle. You do have a way of putting things into perspective. Shall we go into the garden for a while?'

'With pleasure, madam. Always happy, as you know, to commune with the great Gaia. Though I did promise your mother that I would show her my special recipe for Potatoes Dauphinoise for her guests tonight.'

'She can wait. Come on.' They moved through the house; she heard her mother march into the kitchen behind her. The door slammed.

So not just me with the doors, then, thought Kate with some satisfaction.

Chapter 17
THURSDAY EVENING

By seven, Kate was ready to leave and waiting for a taxi. The rest of the afternoon had been awkward as she and her mother avoided each other.

Leaving Muddle to create a distraction with potato recipes and table setting, Kate took a long bath to pass the time. As she undressed, the anti-casino leaflet fell from her jeans pocket. She realised that she had not shared it with Boris. Never mind, it would be something to laugh about tomorrow. She dressed slowly and with care; she wanted to look good tonight. When she finally emerged, she was greeted with, 'You look nice, poppet,' from her father, 'Not bad for an oldie' from the kids and a grunt from her mother. She noticed Muddle hovering awkwardly by the French windows. She went over to him and he took her outside to confess shamefacedly, that he had been invited, indeed forced to stay for dinner.

'I really don't know how it came to be, madam. Your mother has a better ambushing technique than a full pride of lionesses in the rainy season. One minute we were discussing the regrettable decline in the correct use of soup spoons and the next it appears that I had agreed to stay for dinner. Do you have any suggestions of how one might extricate oneself in a gentlemanly manner?'

'Muddle, you are in the tarantula's web and the more you struggle, the more trapped you will be. But don't beat yourself up, you have been defeated by one of the Grand Masters of the game.'

'But I am concerned, madam, that you will be out there unprotected tonight.'

'Oh, I'm a big girl, Muddle, and Boris will be there. Don't worry. Just enjoy the company of the McDonalds. They usually go to Scarborough for their holidays and I am sure they will have brought lots of photos of their caravan for you to admire.'

Kate looked with amusement at Muddle's appalled face. She patted him on the arm. 'Don't worry. This too shall pass.'

Now, waiting in the hallway, she felt a strange mix of nervousness with a sense of freedom. She realised that this short taxi ride was the first time that she had been anywhere on her own for a week. It was exciting, and exciting was good and bad. After all, she reassured herself, this was not her first visit to a casino and she had learned so much from the previous one. It had been a hard lesson but really valuable. What could possibly go wrong this time?

She heard the sound of a car horn and gathered up her coat. Her mother emerged from the kitchen.

'We do not answer to car horns. You must wait until he rings the bell like he should. One must keep up standards.'

Kate sighed and stood waiting in silence. Eventually the bell rang.

'Off you go then. Don't keep everyone waiting. And remember what I said about the crab soufflé at the Royal.'

Within twenty minutes she was at the hotel. She crossed the lobby slowly, enjoying the feel of the soft carpet under her feet and the admiring glances that followed her. She knew that she looked good. This is where I belong, she thought. It reminded her of her one and only employment at the club, and a smile crossed her face at the memory.

The receptionist looked up.

'I'd like you to call Mr Kratin's room and tell him Kate Bradshaw is here.'

'Would that be Kratin with a K or a C?'

'Why don't you look at your little computer screen and see what's there?'

'Certainly, madam.'

The receptionist checked and lifted a phone.

'There's a Mrs Bradford to see you, sir.'

'Bradshaw, for heaven's sake. And it's Ms.'

'Sorry, Bradshaw. Ms Bradshaw.' Kate felt the emphasis unnecessarily strong.

'Mr Kratin asks you to wait in the bar and he will be right

down. It's just over there on the right.'

In the bar, Kate ordered a glass of white wine and sat up on one of the high stools ready to impress Boris. Two minutes later he was walking over to her.

'Kate, you look lovely.' She held up her face to be kissed. He obliged. 'Now, I thought we would have a quick bite to eat here and then we have to prepare ourselves.'

Disappointed at his rather matter-of-fact tone, Kate pulled back. 'Prepare? You're not going to make me practice again, I hope.'

'No, but I've been checking things out on the web and this casino belongs to the same group as the one we went to in London. They will have photos of us on file.'

'Does this mean we can't go?' Kate asked hopefully.

'No, it means we have to be someone else.'

'Sorry?'

'A little disguise. Nothing too dramatic.'

'And where do we get disguises at half past seven on a Thursday night in Sheffield?'

'Don't worry. I've got what we need. Part of the regular kit in my way of life. Luckily they don't have voice recognition or fingerprinting, so this should be easy. A wig should be enough.'

Kate thought of the care she had taken with her hair that evening and was not well pleased. 'Or we could just stay here and have a leisurely romantic dinner, a deux.'

'Well, it would be a trois, so rather less leisurely and a lot less romantic.'

'Oh, yes. Where is Anastasia?'

'Watching *The Simpsons Movie* on the TV.'

'Well, let's enjoy a drink, at least, while we are here.'

Boris hesitated then relented. 'Why not. One quick one.' He ordered a tonic water from the barman. They sat in silence for a couple of minutes; Kate felt no desire to break it. Finally, she had to speak.

'Boris, listen. This is all getting a bit weird.' He looked at her, surprised and waiting. 'I mean, what's going on?'

'How do you mean?'

'Well, you give me cryptic hints of a mysterious past life. In spite of all that, I practically throw myself at you and nothing seems to be happening. It's like I'm wading through jelly here. Are you ever going to do something, take the initiative, tell me how you feel, kiss me, even?'

Boris sighed. 'Kate, what do you want?'

'Not to be asked what I want, for a start. For God's sake, I want you to do something, anything that might not be carefully planned and business-like.'

Boris sat silent for a long time. Then he reached over and took Kate's hand. 'Kate, I am what I am and, yes, the other night I gave you some idea of what I have had to deal with.' Kate started to ask him about that but he held up his hand, making her feel like she was back in school. 'I will tell you more when it is right. For now, I will say that things have not been easy recently. If it helps, I think you are a really nice person and I hope that we can get together in some way. But you must be patient.'

'God, you make it sound like a business deal.'

Boris shrugged and drained his glass. 'Shall we go?' Kate felt the anger surge up in her. How dare he treat her this way? Feeling an overwhelming desire to batter her fists against his chest, she leaned forward and raised her arms, her stool teetering on two legs. He ducked away, easily evading her. The stool skidded from under her. She crashed to the floor, landing on her bottom. He looked down at her, then leaned in, offering her his hand.

'Don't you laugh, don't you dare laugh.' She felt tears at the corner of her eyes. She scrambled back up, ignoring his hand and the eyes of everyone in the bar.

Boris signalled to the barman, signed the bill for the drinks and they walked into the lobby towards the lifts, staring ahead, several feet apart. He punched the button. Doors slid silently open. They stepped in and stood next to each other facing out. Number eighteen was pressed, the doors closed, he turned to her. Without a word he took her into his arms and kissed her, hard and for a long time. Eventually, as the indicator flashed past five, ten, fifteen, he let her go.

'Like that, do you mean?'

Kate struggled for breath. 'Well, I, um, yes, I suppose… Hey, do you think they have cameras in these lifts?'

'Why?'

'Well, I just thought we could stay here for a while.'

To her disappointment, the doors slid open. Kate stepped out, rather unsteadily. She leaned against the wall as she watched Boris slip the key into the first door on the right and pushed it open. The sound of the Simpson family in full chaotic turmoil smashed into them. Kate took a deep breath, pushed herself upright and marched in.

Anastasia glanced up. 'Kate, you look like you been having nooky.'

'What?'

'Mussed up, red face. Always sign of nooky.'

'Oh, I slipped over downstairs.'

Anastasia's eyebrows arched as she looked from Kate to her brother. She shrugged and turned back to the screen. Kate, avoiding Boris's eyes, looked around the room. It was enormous, a sitting room with two bedrooms leading off it. Even when she had been living well with Stephen at company functions, she had not seen anything like this.

She realised that Boris was speaking to her. 'I will call room service. What will you like to eat?'

'Oh, anything. What are you having?'

'Smoked salmon sandwiches and a salad.'

'Fine.'

'Anastasia, I suppose you want the usual burger.'

'Yes. No food for rabbits for me.'

Boris ordered. 'Right, time to try on the disguises.' He disappeared into one of the bedrooms, emerging a minute later with a handful of wigs. 'Kate, what do you see yourself as tonight? Redhead?'

'No,' interrupted Anastasia. 'I am redhead. I have green dress.'

'OK. I can offer brunette or black?'

Kate was finding it very hard to concentrate. 'Um, brunctte, I suppose. It's my natural colour anyway, to be honest.'

'All English women are mouse,' declared Anastasia. 'Mouse hair, mouse people.'

The others turned on her simultaneously. 'Don't start,' they shouted with one voice, then looked at each other in pleasant surprise. Anastasia sniffed and turned away.

'Two minds, one thought,' muttered Kate.

'It's hard to have any other thought with her,' Boris grinned back at her.

Kate took the wig. 'Where's the bathroom? I'll see what I can do with this.'

'There's one off each bedroom,' Boris answered. 'Use mine. Through there.'

In the bathroom, Kate breathed in the smell of Boris, his aftershave and cologne and that indefinable male scent. She really had no idea how she felt about this man. One minute infuriatingly distant, another lovable and supportive, and always the mystery. But she knew she had to know more. She waited, hoping he would burst in through the door and declare his adoration. The door remained closed.

A plan was needed. She had to start thinking like Anastasia. Well, maybe not that bad but she needed to reel this man in, to crack the shell and find out who he really was. This was all new territory to her. Her mind came up with nothing. Well, park it in the brain cells and something will come up.

Grimacing into the mirror, she pushed her own hair back then dragged the wig over her head. It sat up high on the crown of her head. Strands fell either side of her face. God, she thought, I look like a spaniel after a rainstorm. She struggled for a minute, pulling this way and that, until it started to look at least a little natural. She emerged with an optimistic 'How do I look?'

'Fine,' Boris replied unconvincingly.

'Like person wearing wig,' came the disdainful voice from the sofa. 'I fix when film is finished.'

The dinner arrived and was swiftly consumed. Kate found the smell of Anastasia's hamburger enticing and wished, as she nibbled the lettuce, that she had given more thought to ordering. She also wished that she had ordered another glass of wine, having left half of the previous one. Somehow, although she was sure that there would be a well-stocked mini-bar in the room, she felt that she should not ask.

As soon as the food was finished, Boris jumped up and went to his room. No more than five minutes later, he emerged with a full beard, moustache and thick-rimmed spectacles.

Kate laughed out loud. 'Thank Goodness you gave up the academic life. You might have ended up looking like that.'

Boris shrugged. 'I haven't and I did, though I soon got over it. Anastasia said she would not be seen out with me looking like this. Tempting though it was to therefore stay the same…' he ducked as a cushion came flying across from the sofa, '…I could see her point. Anastasia, we have to go. Get yourself ready.'

'Film is finished in two minutes.'

'You've seen it five times.'

'Is good for my understanding America.'

'God help America,' muttered Kate.

Anastasia flicked off the big screen. 'OK, let's see if we can make money tonight, in spite of having Miss I Can Count Up to Ten Aren't I Clever.'

She swept up the red wig and undulated into her room. Kate turned to Boris.

'Listen, it's been a funny day, what with my mother and everything. I'm sorry about that thing in the bar. I have no right…'

'No, Kate, I want to tell you more. You do have a right to know.'

'I could, you know, come back after the casino. We could talk and whatever…' Was this my plan, thought Kate, not daring to look at Boris. I don't remember thinking this was a good idea. She glanced quickly across at him. He was smiling. She did not know if this was good or bad.

'Some conversation after the casino would be good. And some whatever as well, if you like.'

Kate grinned. 'You are about to get another cushion thrown at you.'

Anastasia appeared. Her white face shone out from under a flame red fringe. 'I think I keep new hair colour. Makes me outstanding. Come, Kate, I fix yours so you not look like cheap Barbie.'

Kate obediently crossed the room.

'Sit.'

She sat.

Anastasia pulled off the wig and roughly brushed back Kate's hair till it was flat against her head. Kate clenched her teeth. Anastasia would not have the satisfaction of hearing her yelp.

After a lot of pulling and pushing, she had to concede that the wig now looked much more natural.

'Thank you, Anastasia. Right, now I'm ready for the evening. Shall we go?'

Boris stood up. 'OK. The plan is this. You two will go first. The casino is open to the public so you will just have to sign the register and go straight in. Anastasia will sign for both of you; I don't want you using your real name, Kate. I will follow in five minutes. Once inside, you do not know me. We will leave at one thirty or earlier if things get difficult.'

Kate suddenly felt a cold shiver. 'What sort of difficult?'

'Don't worry. It should be fine. Now, here's £400 each.' Boris handed out the envelopes. 'Off you go. The casino is just around the corner to the right. You should be there in five minutes.'

The two women picked up their coats and headed off. In silence they descended in the lift, crossed the lobby and walked out onto the street. It was a cool clear evening; Kate welcomed the few moments of fresh air.

They turned the corner into the street that held the casino. Immediately they could see ahead of them a huddle of people with placards. As they came closer, Kate made out the slogans.

'Close Satan's Den'. 'Go back to Las Vegas'. 'Keep Sheffield Free of Sin'. There were about fifteen people, a mixture of older women in sensible anoraks and rather scraggy-necked, earnest-looking young men. As they approached, the group turned towards them.

'Look, Jezebels!' cried one, a heavily set woman with a voice that could slice bread. The group spread out on the pavement, blocking the path to the casino. A chant started, 'Jezebels, they will not pass.' After a moment half of them moved on to, 'Thwart the Devil' while the others stayed with the Jezebel thing and it all became rather ragged.

Anastasia turned to Kate. 'What badly dressed people say?'

'They think we are agents of the Devil and will corrupt their men,' answered Kate matter-of-factly.

Anastasia's eyes lit up. 'Oh, no,' said Kate hastily. 'This is where we turn round and head back to the hotel. Come on.'

She began walking back the way they had come. It took only some five paces to realise that Anastasia was not with her. She spun round. Anastasia was advancing on the group. The women were chanting louder, the men edging backwards.

'Anastasia, no,' she cried in desperation as she ran back. Anastasia had stopped, legs akimbo, hands on hips, right in front of the group.

'Why you ugly people stop us have fun? Just because you never get nooky is not reason why pretty ones can't enjoy. Go back to knitting and Women's bloody Own.'

The heavily set woman stepped forward. 'You go back, back to the fleshpots of...' she hesitated... 'Wherever you came from. We don't want your sort in Sheffield.'

'Why? You want Sheffield stay boring and ugly?'

A small crowd was forming. Kate had got to Anastasia and pulled her by the arm. The younger woman shook her off.

The anorak advanced. 'How dare you, you hussy.' Chins wobbled indignantly. 'Keep Sheffield free from sin,' she announced, turning to her colleagues to encourage them to pick up the chant. A ragged response came nervously back.

'Anastasia,' Kate hissed. 'Enough. Let's go.'

'Is free country. I want casino. I get casino.' And she stepped forward, pushing past the large woman who grabbed her coat, spinning her round. Anastasia stared at her. 'You break button, you big fat doofus. Is Harvey Nicks,' and she swung a fist at the woman, connecting with her chin.

The woman sank to the ground like a small marquee amid gasps and muttered 'Oh, I say's' from her colleagues, most of whom were backing away even more rapidly. A brave few stepped forward. One of the women pinned Anastasia's arms from behind, shouting 'Come on, girls, I've got her'. Several more pushed in on her. Not really knowing why, Kate sprang forward and started to pull people off, trying to get Anastasia as far away as possible. A large placard carrying the statement, 'The wages of sins come in gambling chips' swung down on her head and she was sent sprawling on top of the felled woman. She ended with her face some two inches from the other's. Feeling she should say something, she smiled as politely as she could in the circumstances.

'I'm sorry about my friend. She's Russian. Rather highly strung.'

The other woman's eyes gradually focussed on Kate's face. She pushed her away.

'I know you. I never forget a face.'

'No, I'm sure, I've never...'

Kate felt a firm hand on her shoulder. She looked round to see a young policeman pulling her to her feet. 'Now, young lady. Leave her alone. No need for violence.'

'Oh, no, I wasn't... you see, I was knocked down. I was just....'

'Yes, yes. Save it for the station.'

'No, but...'

'Bostock. That's who you are,' came the voice from the ground. 'Always a complete dunce in Geography. Bostock, Charlotte, no Katherine Bostock. Never forget a face, even under all that paint,' she concluded triumphantly. 'Just you wait till your poor mother hears about this.'

Kate stared at the woman. Years peeled back to boring

summers in a hot classroom as the teacher droned on about oxbow lakes and sedimentary deposits.

The woman turned to the young policeman, who was still holding Kate firmly by the arm. 'Her name's Katherine Bostock. Her mother lives in Dore.'

'Bradshaw, actually,' said Kate weakly as she was led away. 'Ms.'

Chapter 18
THURSDAY NIGHT

There are better places to be at half past one on a Friday morning than Sheffield Central Police Station. Kate sat slumped on the hard bench, leaned against the unyielding wall.

'You know when everything seems to be going really, really well, at least pretty good, some bumpy patches but generally looking up,' she said to the sleeping drunk next to her. 'That sort of day ought to come with some kind of health warning. That, at least, is something I've learned today.' The drunk snored his reply.

She stared across the waiting area, taking in its plastic seats and litter-strewn benches, up to where the blank night sky pressed against the high, barred windows. She tried and failed to block out the smell of summer sweat and stale coffee.

She longed for bed. Images of a suite with champagne in the minibar, not a mile from here, tantalised her. Her wig, which had become seriously dislodged in the fracas, was stuffed into her handbag. She was aware that, with her hair brushed back and make-up smeared, she looked no better than most of the other flotsam and jetsam that were scattered around the large room. In the corner, a coffee machine winked tantalisingly. Even if Kate had dared to take the envelope full of money out of her bag, she was sure that no-one here would have been able to change a fifty pound note to give her the thirty pence that she needed for a hot drink. She smiled grimly as she remembered her friend, ex-friend Jane's contemptuous 'I don't do small change' whenever she was approached in the street by a tramp.

On arrival, she had been dumped in the waiting area by the young constable and told to wait until she was called. She had chosen a seat next to the sleeping drunk, one of the least threatening people she could find. After a wait of about half an hour, she had been taken into a small white-painted cell for the interview. It had not been a comfortable experience.

The only time that Kate had been in a police station before this night had been when she had complained about a parking ticket, issued when she had left the Mercedes near a zebra crossing as she dashed in to get her cleaning, a matter of two minutes. Granted, she had bumped into a friend who just had to tell her about a budding liaison down at the gym between an instructor and one of the pillars of the community and, as she had explained to the policeman on that occasion, one cannot be impolite. This had been a very different conversation. A middle-aged sergeant with an 'I've seen it all' expression and weary tone of voice had entered the room ahead of the young policeman who had brought them in. He had switched on a tape recorder and given the date, time and their names, which Kate was too distracted to catch.

'Name?'

'I beg your pardon.'

'What is your name?'

'Kate Bradshaw.' It seemed superfluous to add the Ms.

'Address.'

'The Dells, Sudbury Avenue, Teddington, Middlesex.'

The young policeman leaned over and whispered to the sergeant, who frowned and looked up.

'I understand that you were reported to be living in Dore.'

'No, that's my parents' address. I'm just visiting.'

'I see,' in a tone that meant 'you may or may not be telling the truth'.

'And where were you heading when the incident occurred?'

'Look, I feel I should have a lawyer here.'

'Up to you. We can arrange for someone if you do not have your own. Mind you, I don't see us getting anyone for a few hours. You would have to stay here overnight.'

'No, I'd rather avoid that. Let's carry on. Look,' she glanced enviously at the hot coffees that they were both holding, 'Any chance of a hot drink?'

The sergeant looked up from his note pad and stared at her. 'Cappuccino or latte?'

'Well, a skinny latte would be great if you... Oh, I see. That's a police joke, isn't it?'

'Shall we continue? As I recall, you were about to tell me where you were going.'

'To the casino.'

'And where were you coming from?'

'The Royal. I met up with friends staying there.'

'All right for some. Friends?'

'Um, yes.'

'You were only with one friend when the incident occurred.'

Kate felt her mouth go dry. Where was Boris? Did they even know about him?

'Yes, only one wanted to go to the casino.'

'I see.' Another 'you may be lying' moment. 'And, tell me, how did you come to be rolling around on the pavement with a respected member of our community?'

'Well, I ... look, it wasn't like that. They blocked our path, started shouting rude things at us. Then one of them grabbed Anastasia and they seemed to be attacking her. So I went to help. I'd wanted to turn back. I mean, if only... But, anyway, someone knocked me over and I fell on top of this lady, Miss Ferguson.'

'You know her?'

'She was my geography teacher. When I was at school.'

'Did you enjoy geography?'

'Not really, to be honest. I was bored stiff. She was a really bad teacher.' Kate allowed herself a tentative smile and was heartened to see it returned.

'So, this was the perfect opportunity for you to get your revenge.' The sergeant was still smiling. Kate was not.

'No. No. It wasn't like that. I didn't hit anyone.'

'So, who did?'

'I ... I don't know. I didn't see.' Kate could hear the lie in her voice. She was convinced that the others could too.

Silence.

'Your friend.'

'Anastasia, yes.'

The sergeant wrote the name down, hesitated.

'How do you spell that?'

Kate told him.

'And her surname?'

'Kratin, with a K. Though don't the Russians add an A if they're female?' And whatever Anastasia was, she was certainly female.

'Thank you. The young lady has been rather uncommunicative.'

Shit, thought Kate. She could imagine Anastasia's reaction to her indiscretion.

'So, you are saying that you were walking along, minding your own business and this group of people blocked your path and then attacked you without provocation.'

'Yes, exactly,' Kate was relieved that the conversation was taking a more positive turn.

'And the fact that your friend, Miss,' he consulted his notes, 'Kratin was verbally abusive and physically attacked one of the group was something that you just felt was not worth mentioning?'

'No, I mean, yes, I…' Kate could now feel tears starting to run down her face. She wondered what she must look like. 'Look, I said, I didn't see what happened.'

'Yes, so you said.' He turned to the constable. 'She did say that, didn't she?'

'Yes, sir. I do believe she did.'

The sergeant closed his notebook and switched off the tape machine.

'Well, Miss Bradshaw. That will do for now.'

'Can I go?'

'Go?'

'Yes, I'd like to get home, I mean, to my parents'.'

'No, I'm afraid that will not be possible yet.'

'But why not? I've told you everything I know.'

'Have you, Mrs Bradshaw?'

'Yes, I … yes. So, why can't I go?'

'Because we have to decide whether we are going to charge you with assault, common affray, or any other crime. Please wait out there.'

'How long for?'

'We will call you when we need you.'

Kate staggered out, straight into the Ladies. The soles of her glittery shoes stuck to the floor with each step. Trying very hard to ignore the smell, she stood in front of the mirror, doing what she could to repair her make-up. In the end, she scrubbed as much off as she could. Another woman came in and stood beside her. She was younger than Kate but looked as if she had lived much longer.

'What they got you for?'

Kate ignored her.

'First timer, eh? You'll get used to it. Just smile and say nothing, that's my advice.'

Kate turned on her. 'When I need advice from a hardened criminal, I shall ask for it.'

The woman shrugged, muttered something about 'stuck-up fucking old bitch' and disappeared into one of the cubicles.

Kate looked at the face in the mirror. Yes, she had to concede, old was a fair description of how she looked.

Now she sat in the large, grubby waiting room, the drunk still snoring peacefully beside her. She stared at the poster on the wall opposite, warning her of the dangers of casual sex. Chance would be a fine thing. The great plan had been to be with Boris in the comfort of the suite at the Royal, maybe a glass or two of champagne and then who knows? Not this.

For the first time since Stephen and his money disappeared, Kate could see the chasm that opened in front of her. She looked around the room and realised just how easy it would be to end up like this. Something had buoyed her along over the last two weeks. Lack of experience, optimism, stupidity, she didn't know which but suspected stupidity. Now she was realising with a clarity that her surroundings forced onto her, just what no money meant.

She could hear her mother's friends gossiping. 'Of course,

I always thought she was a bit flighty. No sooner had that rich husband disappeared, and who could blame him, than she turned to a life of crime. Ended up in the gutter. Her poor children. I blame her mother, I really do.' Only the last sentence brought any comfort. She saw a future made up of unpaid bills, eviction, long queues in faceless offices, trying to get help that was never forthcoming, the kids taken out of school and forced to take menial jobs. She herself taking a menial job. Kate shuddered.

And then there was Boris. Or was there? Where the hell was he? Why hadn't he come to her rescue? She looked around the room again, as if his great bulk would suddenly emerge from behind the coffee machine. Nothing. Even Anastasia's company would have been welcome. Well, maybe. But she was nowhere to be seen. No doubt being given the third degree in one of the rooms. And no doubt giving it back.

Kate felt very alone, wishing even that she had not been so rude to the girl in the Ladies. She could see her, sitting slumped on a chair in the middle of the room, chewing a fingernail. Should she go over and start a conversation?

Kate eased herself off the chair, glad to move a little and get some circulation back. Gathering up her handbag and holding it close to her chest, she walked cautiously across the room. The girl looked up suspiciously as she approached.

'What d'you want, then?'

'Look, I just wanted to, you know, apologise for being rude earlier. I was a bit upset.'

The girl shrugged and looked away.

Kate struggled on. 'Yes, I was out of order. I'd just been questioned and was feeling a bit beaten up, you know. They have a way of twisting your words, don't they?'

The girl slowly looked her up and down.

'Anyway, just wanted to say sorry,' muttered Kate and turned away.

'What they get you for, then?' The girl's voice called her back.

'Oh, it was all a misunderstanding, really.'

'Yeah, the prisons are full misunderstandings.'

'Prisons? Do you think...?'

'Don't know. Depends what you've done.'

'Well, nothing, really. I, we, my friend and I, we were just heading for the casino, you know, the new one.'

'Oh, yeah. Bit of a gambler are you?'

'No, not really. Just a way to make some money.'

The girl looked at Kate's dress, which, although crumpled, still showed its quality.

'Don't look as if you need any money.'

'Don't judge by appearances.'

'Why not? You did.'

'Ouch, I deserved that. Look, do you mind if I sit down?'

The girl shrugged again. Kate took that as a yes and tentatively sat.

'No, you see, I was just heading for the casino and these people with placards blocked the way. And the next thing I know, there's people being hit over the head and I'm on the ground on top of my old geography teacher.'

The girl leaned in towards Kate. 'You decked your teacher? Nice one. I done that a couple of times myself. Feels good, dunnit?'

'Well, no, it wasn't me, I mean, well, actually, yes, there was a certain pleasure, you know, after all these years, well, not that many years, but...'

'Excuse me, madam. I believe I may be of some assistance.'

Kate swung round. She looked up to see Muddle standing politely, hands folded in front of him, head slightly to one side. A strong wall light behind him seemed to give him a most appropriate halo. She leapt to her feet.

'Muddle. I could hug you. I fact, I will,' and she flung her arms around him. The girl looked on, open-mouthed.

'Oh, Muddle, this is, er, I'm sorry, we didn't do names.'

'Sarah,' stammered the girl.

Muddle leaned over and took the girl's hand in both of his. 'Delighted to make your acquaintance, Miss Sarah.' He straightened up slowly, slipped one hand into his jacket pocket in a way that instantly made Kate think of the Duke of Edinburgh and turned back to her.

'Shall we, madam?'

'Shall we what?'

'I think it is time that we wended our way homewards, or at least back to your mother's.'

'No, I'm afraid that's not possible, Muddle. You see, I have to wait here. The sergeant told me to.'

'All taken care of, madam.'

'What?'

'Most accommodating, he was, when acquainted with the facts of the case.'

'Are you serious?'

'Am I ever anything but, madam? So, shall we?'

He stood to one side and waved Kate past. He bowed briefly to the girl. 'Goodbye, Miss Sarah, and good luck. I do hope you find a pursuit that you can do well and legally.'

The girl stared back, shaking her head slightly from side to side. Muddle took Kate's arm and escorted her out of the room. The sergeant looked up as they passed, giving them a wave. Kate nodded back.

'Muddle,' she whispered as soon as they were walking down the long corridor. 'What about Anastasia?'

'In the car, waiting for you, madam. We will drop her off at the hotel on the way.'

Kate gazed at her rescuer with admiration. 'I am so grateful. But you have a lot of explaining to do. How did you manage it?'

'As soon as we are in the car, madam.'

'Of course.'

'In the meantime, would you like me to look after this?' He withdrew from his pocket a bulky envelope. Kate immediately realised it was the money that Boris had given her earlier in the evening.

'But, how…?'

'I took the liberty of removing it from the young lady's

pocket, having observed her dipping into your handbag while you were talking.'

'Muddle, is there no end to your ability?'

'I'm really not sure, madam. I do hope not, for where else does heaven reside, save in the space beyond your fingertips?'

'Right,' said Kate hesitantly, feeling as ever that she was glimpsing brief and tantalising flashes of significant truth in Muddle's pronouncements.

At the front of the station stood the Rolls. Kate could see Anastasia slumped in the back seat. She climbed in the front. Muddle slipped in behind the wheel and the car purred off. No-one spoke for the ten minutes that it took to reach the hotel. As the car pulled up a doorman leapt forward and opened Anastasia's door. She stepped out and disappeared through the swing doors, head held high and heels clacking.

'Well, that was interesting,' muttered Kate. 'I don't think I've ever seen her stay so silent for so long.'

'I fear that she might have been anticipating the discussion that she will now be having with Mr Boris. He is not well pleased with the situation.'

'I'm sure he's not,' responded Kate, thinking once more with a twinge of sadness of the discussions and more that she had planned with Boris at just this time. 'Now, tell me. I really have to know how you sprung me, if that's the right expression.'

'I believe that is the common vernacular, madam. Well, I was just finishing the starter that your mother had prepared, a rather voluminous and liquid prawn cocktail, as I recall, when the phone rang. Your father answered it then called me through into the hall. It was Mr Boris informing me of the fracas that you had, inadvertently in your case, I believe, become involved in.'

'How did he know about it?'

'It appears that he was only a short distance behind you.'

'Then why the hell didn't the silly man do anything?' Kate felt her throat tighten and tears form.

'He has reasons to stay away from the police, as I

understand it. Something to do with business deals he has been involved in. I have not probed; didn't feel it was within my bailiwick to do so.'

'Well, I'm bloody well going to probe. Fancy him just walking away and leaving me, us to that horrible experience. Business deal or no business deal. What a sod.'

'To be fair to him, he did instigate actions to resolve the situation, namely calling my good self.'

'Maybe.' Kate was not to be mollified that easily but there was more to find out. 'How did you get away from the clutches of the tarantula?'

'I told your parents that something had arisen that I could not fully explain at that moment but that I would elucidate in the morning. Your mother said something about me being a man of mystery but I had the impression that this was not a bad thing from her point of view.'

'Clever, gives you time to think up something. Was it hard to drag yourself away?'

'Frankly, madam, I had by that time seen fourteen photographs of Alan and Hilda McDonald's sunrise cream Avondale Rialto four berth caravan, inside and out – do you realise that it takes just twenty-three seconds to convert the banquette into a double bed? - and the Sapphire Blue Vauxhall Vectra 2.3 diesel cdi that towed it, a car that is, I am several times reliably informed, a good little runner, managing some thirty-eight miles to the gallon. My appetite was somewhat diminished.'

Kate laughed in spite of herself, wiping away the tears with the back of her hand. 'You have my undying sympathy. But get to the point. What happened at the police station?'

'Well, Mr Boris had apprised me of how the events unrolled. I simply spoke to the sergeant on duty, explaining the situation. It seems that there is close circuit television overlooking the area that bears out my version.'

'So, why the third degree on me, then?'

'I believe that they were ensuring that you did not feel inclined to indulge in such practices again. That and a long and rather boring night shift.'

'The buggers. You mean they were just playing with me?'

'So it would appear. A not uncommon occurrence, I believe. Still, I assured them that you were a sober and upright citizen.'

'I thought you always told the truth.'

'Ah, madam, if you could but see the rest. You would know that you are a true paragon of virtue by comparison.'

'Well, I started to get a feeling for that tonight. But, hold on. What about Anastasia? I mean, if those cameras were watching, they would have known that she started it.'

'Well, yes, that was a little trickier. But I explained that she was Russian. What is more, if they insisted on pressing charges, they were going to get into a considerable quantity of paperwork and tie their bosses up in some rather complex conversations. The Home Office are not very pleased, I imagine, with junior-ranking officers who instigate matters that create diplomatic incidents.'

'Not sure that the words Anastasia and diplomatic belong in the same sentence but, whatever, it seems to be sorted and you have been an absolute star, yet again. I really am more grateful than I can say.'

'Well, all's well that ends well, madam, and here we are.' They were pulling up outside the house. 'And it appears that the McDonalds are gone. Safe to enter, then.'

Quietly, they eased open the front door and went in.

'The third and the seventh stair creak, Kate whispered. 'Try to avoid them.'

On the landing, Kate thanked Muddle again, gave him a peck on the cheek and headed for her room. Quickly undressing, she did her best to comb her hair, washed her face and cleaned her teeth at the basin in the corner of the room and fell into bed. She checked her watch. Twenty to three. No doubt she would be expected at breakfast by eight. And she would have to deal with Boris, not, it seems, the answer to everything that he might have seemed. She sighed and put out the light, thankful that the day was over.

P. M. LAWDER

Chapter 19
FRIDAY

'Kate, you look as if you've been dragged through the hedge backwards.'

'And good morning to you too, mother. Yes, I had a very nice evening, thank you for asking.'

'Well, I was about to clear the breakfast things away but, since you have deigned to make an appearance, I will have to leave them for a while. There's still coffee in the cafetiere though it's probably cold.'

'It's only nine o'clock for heaven's sake.'

'Allow me, madam.' Muddle leaned across from the other side of the table, picked up the cafetiere and disappeared towards the kitchen. Kate slowly poured herself a bowl of cereal.

'Have the kids come down yet?' she called.

Muddle's head reappeared. 'In the garden with your father, madam.'

'Any calls yet?' she whispered to him.

'Nothing so far.'

As if on cue, the phone rang. Kate leapt up but was only in time to see her mother pick up the receiver.

'Elizabeth Bostock speaking.' Kate hung back, appearing to take great interest in a picture that had hung on the hall wall for at least thirty years. Her mother appeared to be greeting the news with some pleasure, judging by the string of 'Really', 'Well, indeed', 'Serve them right, I say' and 'I would jolly well think so' and then a rather more concerned 'How is she?' that made Kate's heart stop for a moment, followed by a rather dismissive 'Typical of her'.

The phone was eventually replaced.

'Sounded like good news,' Kate offered, tentatively.

'Report from the front line.'

'Sorry?'

'That dreadful casino. Do keep up, girl. Our team were down there last night and they managed to stop two painted hussies getting in and had them carted off by the police. Very satisfactory.'

'Good for them,' Kate managed weakly.

'It seems they laid about one of our number who had to be taken to hospital for observation. Only Edith Ferguson who, quite honestly, is no loss, rather tiresome woman. But really, is there no end to the depravity that these people will stoop to in order to feed their addiction? I suppose as Organising Secretary, I will have to go and see the Ferguson woman. She's being let out this morning. I'll pop round later. What a bore.'

'Oh, but, I mean, no, that is…' Kate's mind was racing but the words were not. Her mother stared at her as if she had just dropped her porridge on the floor. Inspiration came at the last possible moment. 'I mean, I thought it would be nice if we all took a ride in the Rolls today. Go out for a spin, to Hathersage or somewhere. Maybe take a picnic.'

'Well, you might have said. Where am I supposed to conjure up a picnic from, may I ask?'

A voice came from the kitchen. 'Never fear, madam, I have it all in hand. It can be ready in less than an hour.'

'Well, at least there's someone here I can rely on. That will just give me time to pop round to old Miss Ferguson and it gives me a reason for not staying too long.'

Muddle appeared in the hall. 'No, madam. When I say less than an hour, I do mean considerably less than an hour. Some thirty minutes, in fact.'

'Well, I suppose it can wait. But I must fulfil my obligation as Organising Secretary at some point today.'

'That's settled then,' said Kate with a tremendous sense of relief. 'I'll tell the kids.'

'Yes, though I doubt you can drag your father away from his beloved garden. Well, I shall go and find something suitable to wear.'

Kate watched her mother march upstairs.

'Fresh coffee, madam?'

'Oh, God yes. But how are we going to get a picnic together in half an hour?'

'All hands to the pump, madam. If you would be kind enough to summon the children and let me know where the nearest corner shop is, I will get things moving.'

'Dore doesn't have corner shops, Muddle. But it does have a delicatessen just round the corner.'

'Perfect. Now, the children, if you please.'

The next half an hour had the four of them rushing to and fro. When Mrs Bostock appeared at the kitchen door attired in sensible tweeds and looking pointedly at her watch, she was assured by Muddle that all was in hand, given a coffee and steered towards the conservatory.

Kate was amazed as a feast of breads, cold meats and salads took shape, wine was wrapped in damp cloths to stay chilled and plates and cutlery assembled.

When the children had been despatched to the conservatory to keep granny calm, Muddle leaned in towards Kate. 'You do realise, madam, that we are only postponing the fateful hour as regards this lady, Miss Ferguson.'

'Oh, I do. But, frankly, at times like this, there's a lot to be said for total denial. Let's cross one bridge at a time. It may sound cowardly, but…'

'Pragmatic, madam. Sufficient unto the day and so on. I quite understand. Would you pass the aubergine pickle?'

Glad that the subject was closed for now, Kate busied herself with the preparations. But clearing one problem from her mind only made room for another one. Boris. Where the hell was he? And why had she heard nothing from him? Damn him, how could he do this to her? Not being sure exactly what it was that he was doing to her only made her anxiety worse.

Finally everything was ready. Kate took the car keys and carried the first bags down the path. As she was loading everything into the boot, a taxi drew up. She looked up to see Boris ease his massive frame out of the back door.

'Where the hell have you been?' she hissed, aware from long experience that the neighbours had exceptional hearing when there was something juicy to hear.

Boris spread his arms wide. Kate stood her ground. 'Kate, I'm so sorry. You have to understand.'

'Understand? Understand?' She forgot the neighbours and her voice rose to considerably more than a hiss. 'Boris, I was attacked, arrested, spent several hours in the company of people that I didn't even know existed, let alone ever wanted to meet, I'm half way to having a criminal record and my mother will know all about it before the end of the day.'

'Your mother? How?'

'Because the woman that your stupid bloody sister assaulted was, is my old geography teacher. And she knows my mother.'

'Oh, god, I see.'

'Good. I'm glad you see, Boris. I'm glad you just begin to understand what you've done to me. Now I'd be really glad if you and your silly sodding sister get right out of my life.'

Boris took a step back. 'You don't have to worry about Anastasia. I have already sent her to Aunt Irena. But do you mean it? Do you really want me to go?'

'Boris, I just can't take all this. I need supper in front of the tele, shopping at Sainsbury's, drinks with the girls, you know. I don't need to be drugged in casinos and end up rolling around on the pavement with my ex-geography teacher. And I don't need someone who vanishes just when I need him.'

'I'm sorry. Kate, there are reasons why I can't be in the same place as the police, it's all very…'

'Oh, God. You see what I mean? Suddenly it's all Russian mystery again. No, Boris, no. I've had enough. I mean, thanks for everything and all that but no. No more.'

Boris bowed slightly. 'As you wish,' and he turned back to the taxi. He paused. 'By the way, what is the name of the geography teacher?'

'What?'

'Her name.'

'Why?'

He shrugged. 'I suppose I just want to get the whole

story.'

'You want to get the whole story? You, who tells me nothing about anything. That's really rich, Boris.' Kate spun on her heel and walk back to the house. 'Ferguson,' she called over her shoulder. 'Edith Ferguson. There, does it feel good to know the whole fucking story?' And she walked into the house without a backward glance, slamming the door behind her.

In the kitchen Muddle was assembling the last of the bags of food. 'The blue bag is salad, the red bread and butter and the yellow…' He stopped when he saw Kate's face. 'Ah, do I gather that Mr Boris has put in an appearance?'

'You do,' Kate gulped. The tears ran down her cheeks. 'Oh, Muddle, what have I done? I said all that stuff. It just came out. I didn't even know I thought it. I don't think I'll ever see him again.'

A look of intense concern flashed across Muddle's face. 'Where is he now, do you think?'

'In a taxi. Heading back to the hotel, I would imagine. After that, who knows? We've got the car. I suppose he'll take a train somewhere or hire a car or whatever.'

A voice came from the doorway. 'Well, I make it forty-three minutes. I could have fitted in Edith Ferguson after all.'

Kate stared out of the window, keeping her back to her mother. Muddle stepped forward to shield her. 'Mrs Bostock, I assure you that we are ready and raring to go. Time for everyone to powder their noses, so to speak and we can be off. Would you ask Miranda and Tom to give me a hand?'

Kate's mother went back to the conservatory. They heard her commands. 'Now, no more lazing about. Go and help your mother otherwise we'll never get away. And be sure you've spent your last penny before we go. I don't want us to be stopping every two miles and public conveniences are so unsavoury.'

Muddle put his arm round Kate. She leaned into the comfort of his shoulder, so much lower than Boris's.

'Oh, Muddle, what am I going to do?'

'As you said, madam, there's a lot to be said for denial.

245

The sun is shining and we are surrounded by beautiful countryside. This will resolve itself as all things do. Now, it's time to go. If you will excuse me, I must just get something from my room.' Muddle disappeared, leaving Kate rather bewildered by his brusque departure.

She ran a tap and splashed some water onto her face. Miranda came in.

'Grandpa's coming. Says he needs a bigger horizon than his garden, whatever that means. Anything to take?'

'Um, yes. These bags.'

'You OK, Mum?'

'Oh, yes, I'll be fine. Just a bit of man trouble, you know.'

'Tell me about it.' Miranda looked shyly towards her mother. 'Look, if there's anything you want to talk about…'

Kate gave a watery smile. 'Thanks, Mirry. Maybe a good girly chat is exactly what I need. Let's see if we can get some time later.'

'Sure, any time. I'll take these out. Is the car open?'

'Should be. Thanks.'

Miranda gave her a conspiratorial grin, picked up the bags and went off.

The countryside was indeed beautiful, the stark hills softened by thick heathers and gorse, their blue and yellow flowers stringing patterns around the rocks. The sunlight bounced off the sharp angles of the dry stone walls that ran up and over the hills in a vain attempt to impose order on this vigorous wilderness. But it all did little to raise Kate's mood. She had allowed her mother to sit in the front with Muddle, to whom she was explaining the political intricacies of the Dore and Totley Women's Institute as he nodded in wise assent to her conclusions. In the back, Kate sat next to her father, while Tom and Miranda were opposite on bucket seats, facing backwards. Kate stared out of the window, very aware of the missing bulk of Boris.

'Anything the matter, poppet?' ventured her father.

'Oh, you know. Stuff. I'll tell you later.'

'Oh, OK.' Her father seemed relieved to let the silence fall between them. Tom happily filled the void with a full and lengthy description of the battles between the Macedonians and the Goths that occupied so many of his waking hours. His grandfather, whose only acquaintance with computers was adding a postscript to occasional emails, struggled hard to ask the right questions. Fortunately, his ignorance only encouraged Tom to go into even more detail. Kate let the talk of phalanxes, superpowers and war machines wash over her. She was struggling to get a grip on her own world. Here she was, sitting in the back of a Rolls Royce, which, as far as she knew, she owned, but with barely a penny to her name.

She had a comfortable house with no means of maintaining it, two children going back to school in ten days with no way of buying uniform or equipment. She could not even afford food beyond next week. How had she ever thought that somehow things would be all right? Where had she expected money to come from? Somehow, this stupid casino thing was going to be the answer. But all that had got her was a night in a police station. She realised with a start that she still had Boris's four hundred pounds from last night. She would have to find a way to get it back to him.

She looked at the back of Muddle's head as he drove. He was now her only means of support and she had no idea how long he would stay. Why should he? A line about kindness of strangers came into her head. Where was that from? She somehow heard it in a Southern belle accent but could not place it. She gave up the search.

Perhaps she would, after all, have to ask her father for money. She shuddered at the prospect of her mother's triumphant reaction. Deciding to rescue her father from Tom's onslaught, she turned to him.

'Daddy, do you know that quote about the kindness of strangers? Where does it come from?'

A faraway look came into her father's eyes. 'Ah, Vivien Leigh. Such a beautiful creature. Blanche Dubois in *Streetcar Named Desire* with Marlon Brando, 1958, I think. The sexiest film I ever saw.' The two children stared open-mouthed at their grandfather, realising for the first time that he was also a human being. He attempted a Southern accent. 'I have always relied on the kindness of strangers,' he oozed.

'Jack, really,' came a firm voice from the front seat. 'Not in front of the children.' His eyes focused back on to the people around him. He cleared his throat. 'Very good for quotes, Miss Leigh.' Again the accent. 'After all, tomorrow is another day. *Gone with the Wind.* Final lines.' He turned towards his daughter with a twinkle in his eye. 'That's one you'd do well to remember, poppet.'

Kate said nothing, could say nothing. She slipped her hand into his. The world, for a moment, felt marginally less threatening and uncertain.

They picnicked on the hill above Hathersage, looking down on the small market town that scattered along the valley. Muddle adopted the role of butler, with Tom and Miranda as willing footmen. Soon everyone was sitting on folding chairs with plates overflowing with delicious food and glasses of wine or juice. As Kate looked across the sweep of hills she could not help but feel better. Yes, tomorrow and the day after were going to be a problem, possibly horrendous, but right now all was well with the world.

After lunch, Muddle suggested a trip to the Blue John Caves. 'I have always been fascinated by minerals and the stories they can tell us about this great planet of ours. And it may be both entertaining and instructive for the younger ones.' Everyone readily agreed. Muddle quickly and expertly packed the picnic away and they set off.

The cool dark silence of the caves seemed to calm Kate even further. She wondered whether Muddle had known that they would have this effect on her. She immediately dismissed the idea; why would he be concerned for her wellbeing? He was probably just wanting to do something that interested him. You really are going to have to remember, she told herself, that you are not the centre of the universe.

They came back out into the shop. Her father took the

children off to choose a souvenir piece of rock, while her mother went off to check the menu of the café. Muddle came over to her.

'How goes it, madam?'

'Oh, you know. Working hard on the denial. I should just about last until we get back to the house, when it will all come crashing in again. But, to be honest, dealing with my mother's cavalry charge will be nothing compared with how I'm going to manage when we get home.'

'Oh, I'm sure something will turn up, madam. In my experience, it usually does. You just have to be open to it. Do excuse me now, I must just see that exhibition over there.'

Kate watched him walk away. So, that's him gone too, she thought. You're on your own, girl. She was surprised that the prospect did not now fill her totally with despair. Not totally. Ninety per cent, maybe, but there was a glimmer of something. Hope? Probably not, no reason for it. Determination, perhaps. An unfamiliar feeling for Kate, who had never really needed determination before. But not a bad feeling. Must work on it, she told herself firmly and went off to join her mother in the queue for teas.

The journey home was quiet, other than her mother's long explanation about the inadequacies of the café and the iniquities of the Brussels bureaucracy for preventing the WI from selling far superior cakes. Everyone else relaxed into the warm afterglow of a day spent out in the open air.

As soon as they were back at the house, Kate's mother became business-like.

'Now, I'm just going to call on the Ferguson woman and see how she is. No doubt Marjorie Pearson will have stuck her nose in already but as the head of the committee I must care for my troops.'

Kate bowed to the inevitable. 'OK, Mum. We'll just get the things in from the car and wash up. Is there anything we can do to get supper ready?'

She struggled to think of anything else that could earn some compensatory Brownie points but it did feel, as Stephen used to say, that she was farting against thunder. As she watched her mother head off down the road, Kate allowed herself a quick prayer, though the chance of her mother being abducted by aliens before she could reach Miss Ferguson's flat some quarter of a mile away was, she conceded, slim.

Under Muddle's direction, everyone was busy unloading and washing up. Kate threw herself into the activity with such gusto that, within five minutes, she had broken two glasses and a plate and had been gently but firmly removed to the garden, where her father, a stranger to the kitchen, was already digging in the vegetable patch. He looked up at her.

'So, poppet, what were you going to tell me?'

Kate was startled. How could he already know?

'Sorry?'

'In the car. Stuff. You said things were worrying you.'

'Oh, that.' Relief that the greater sin had not yet been discovered made Kate more than willing to talk about other problems.

'Boris came round this morning.'

'Oh, I didn't see him.'

'No, I'm afraid I didn't even let him get to the front door.'

'Ah. Bit of a wobble?'

'No, actually, more like a major cataclysmic landslide into oblivion, horror and the depths of hell.'

'Right.' Her father studied the end of his spade.

'Sorry, daddy. I know this is not your thing. It's just that I need to let off steam.'

'OK. That's fine. I used to find that good run worked well for me. You know, if I was a bit het up.'

'Didn't bring my running kit, sadly. Though that would have been a good idea. I have been running a bit recently.'

'Good for you. Mens sana, thingumy watsit.'

'Exactly. Anyway, can't do that so…'

'Yes.' Another pause. 'Tell you what, why don't you just tell me what happened? Can't guarantee that I'll say anything useful in reply but, who knows? Miracles can happen.'

'Well,' Kate began cautiously, 'He rather let me down last

night. Wasn't there when I really needed him.'

'Was this something to do with the casino, by any chance?"

'Casino? How did you know about that?'

'Kate, I may seem like an old duffer to you but I can put two and two together. You go out for, inverted commas, dinner with a gambler, dressed to the nines and don't come back until three in the morning, and, no, your mother didn't hear you. Well, there's not many places in Sheffield you could have been. And Muddle disappearing half way through dinner, lucky chap, with some cock-eyed excuse. It's obvious something had gone wrong.'

Kate looked at her father with new respect. He was looking straight back at her, no longer fiddling with anything.

'Well, you'll probably find out soon enough but I'll just say for now we got split up and I ended up somewhere where I really needed him.'

'Like a police station?'

'God, Dad. Do you already know?'

'No, lucky guess, but I do now.'

'It really wasn't my fault, Daddy. Honestly, things just got out of hand, thanks to that stupid Anastasia.'

'Yes, I thought she might be in there somewhere. And your Boris did a vanishing act?'

'Well, not my Boris any more, if he ever was.'

'So, when he turned up this morning…'

'He got very short shrift, I'm afraid. I was really horrid to him.'

'And now you're wondering whether you've, how do your generation put it, whether you've blown it?'

Kate smiled at her father. 'You're really quite good at this.'

'I was a lawyer for forty years, you know. Just never really found out how to get a word in edgeways in this house, what with your mother and you two girls. The only other man in the house was dear old Max, but there's a limit to how much male camaraderie you can build up with a Labrador. Anyway, back to Boris.'

'Oh, Daddy, I don't know. It's all so complicated, what with his mysterious Russian stuff and my rather precarious situation. I mean, I'm not sure whether I was just looking at him as a meal ticket, to be honest.'

'Well, that's never a good reason. You know that, you've done it once. Oh, here's your mother back.'

'Oh shit.'

'Kate!'

'Sorry, daddy, but I think you're about to find out that was really justified.'

'Stand firm, poppet, stand firm.' He too straightened his back.

Her mother was crossing the lawn, head down, elbows out, as if she were fighting her way through the January sales. She was quite breathless as she reached them.

'Well,' she gasped, 'Would you believe it?'

'Believe what, dear?' her father asked as innocently as possible.

'I have just found out the most extraordinary thing.' She turned to Kate. 'And you, young lady, have some explaining to do.'

Kate's father leaned on his spade. 'Are you going to share it with us or are we to guess?'

'Jack, don't try to be funny; it doesn't suit you. Well, you know I've just been round to Edith Ferguson's flat.'

'Yes,' they chorused, Kate now wishing for the truth to be out so at least the agony of waiting would be over, replaced no doubt by yet more agony.

'Well, she wasn't there. I spoke to her companion, that woman who used to teach you Science, Kate, fat lot of good that did.'

'Miss Trenchard?'

'Well, I say companion,' Kate's mother ploughed on like a battleship in high seas, 'But I'm sure that one time when I was round there for a committee meeting, dreadful tea she makes, I took a wrong turning and noticed a double bed. Still, I suppose it takes all sorts but really…'

'Mother, what did Miss Trenchard say?'

'Yes, I'm coming to that. Dear me, the impatience of the young. Where has the art of conversation gone?'

'Elizabeth, it's not just the young who are getting impatient.'

'Jack, what has got into you this afternoon? We will have to have words later. Anyway, she, this Trenchard creature, was there all aflutter, the way these people are, and she tells me that Edith Ferguson has gone away.'

'Gone away?'

'Yes. It seems she had a visitor this morning, just before lunch. A large man, she said. They were together for about twenty minutes and then Ferguson comes out to say that she's off to Bournemouth, would you believe. This man is driving her down there even as we speak and the Trenchard woman is due to join them tomorrow. Seems she had to give some private lessons or something first. So, what do you think of that?' she finished triumphantly.

'But mother, why did you say I had some explaining to do? How does this have anything to do with me?'

'She described the man as very large with, and I quote, a bit of a funny East European sort of accent. How such people can be teaching our young, I fail to understand. But, Kate, we know someone who fits the bill for that description, don't we?'

'Yes.'

'Yes. That Boris who nearly wrecked my Lloyd Loom chair in the conservatory yesterday. I've heard no mention of him today, though Mrs Williams from No 21, who made sure I happened to bump in to her on the way home, did say that she saw you having a stand-up row with a large man in a smart suit this morning. Is there something you'd like to tell us about? Now?'

Kate looked her mother steadily in the eye. 'No. There's nothing I'd like to tell you. I am not responsible for Boris Kratin's actions, if it was him, and there are plenty of big people in the world.'

'Of course it was him. And he is clearly something to do

with the attack on poor Miss Ferguson and is trying to cover up. And you know about this, young lady, don't try and tell me you don't.'

'I'm not trying to tell you anything, Mother. I don't have anything I wish to tell.'

Her mother glared back. 'Kate, this is not a game. She may be in great danger. She may be sold into white slavery by now.'

A laugh burst from Kate's lips. 'She's seventy if she's a day. I really don't think it's likely, do you?'

Her father intervened. 'Elizabeth, it's quite easy. Did you get the name of the hotel in Bournemouth from Miss Trenchard?

'Yes. Royal Spa or something like that.'

'Well, why not just call and find out if a Miss Ferguson is booked in.'

'She may be under an alias.'

'Yes, and she may be in a harem of a sheik with very odd tastes but it's a start.'

'Well, maybe.' She started to walk back to the house then turned back on Kate, waving a pointing finger in her face. 'And don't think I've finished with you, young lady.' She stomped off in a swirl of tweed.

Kate's father turned to her, one eyebrow raised.

'Well?'

Kate took a deep breath. 'You've probably guessed it already. I was, er, nearby when Miss Ferguson was knocked down last night.'

'And that's why you ended up in the police station?'

'Yes, but I didn't do anything, I promise you, Daddy.'

'I'm sure you didn't. But do you think Boris is trying to protect you?'

'Yes, without a doubt. You see, Miss Ferguson recognised me last night.'

'Ah.'

'Boris asked me her name this morning. I thought it was strange at the time.'

'Well, mystery solved. Seems he is doing you a favour, in

spite of what you said to him.'

'Mm.'

'I'm sure he's looking after Miss Thingummy very well.'

'God, I hope so.' Kate thought again of killer conversation then, with a shudder, dismissed it.

Her father squeezed her shoulder. 'Complicated stuff, affairs of the heart.'

Kate grimaced and rubbed her cheek. 'You're telling me.'

'Oh, good, here comes your mother again.'

Kate giggled and nudged him in the ribs.

'Well, I've phoned the hotel and there is a room booked for her there,' Kate's mother announced. 'It seems she has safely arrived, so at least he hasn't done away with her yet. So we shall see. Now, Kate, I want to know what's going on.'

'So do I, to be honest, mother.'

'Don't you play the innocent with me, young lady. Miss Ferguson gets knocked down in a brawl with two women and your friend Boris turns up to whisk her away. As far as I'm concerned….' Elizabeth Bostock stopped dead. She stared at Kate, eyes widening. 'Two women. You. You and that trollop you brought into my house yesterday. It was you, wasn't it?'

'Yes, mother,' Kate replied, very calm now the moment had come. 'I was there, though I did not lay a finger on anyone. In fact, I was beaten about the head by your rabble.'

'Rabble? How dare you describe people who are upholding standards of decency as rabble.'

Kate shrugged. 'You weren't there. I was.'

'To think that a daughter of mine could, could stoop…'

'Mother, enough. I did nothing. There was a misunderstanding. End of story. I'm sorry there's not more for you to get your fangs into but that's it.'

'And I suppose you went to that den of iniquity, that casino.' She spat the word out like a sour prune.

'No, actually, we didn't, which just shows how out of line your vigilantes were.'

Her mother's face was bright red. For a moment she wagged her finger at Kate, her mouth moved but no words emerged. Finally her voice rasped out, firm, determined and very loud. 'Out. I want you out of this house. Today.'

'Elizabeth, I really don't think that's…'

'Jack,' she glared at her husband, hands on her hips. 'Don't be so damned lily-livered. I can see how you've been trying to cuddle up to her in your usual wishy-washy way, don't think I've missed it. I've got eyes, you know. A bit more discipline from you over the years and she wouldn't have turned out bad. Thank God I've got one daughter who still knows how to behave.'

'Now, come on. She hasn't turned out bad. That's not fair.'

'Don't you tell me what's fair.' She spun back onto Kate. 'One hour. I want you out in one hour. I shall be in my room. Don't feel you have to say goodbye.' And she was gone across the lawn and into the house.

The two stood in silence for a full minute.

'Well.'

'Well, indeed.'

'Looks like your Boris's good turn has rather backfired, though, to be fair, it could only ever have been a stay of execution.'

Kate winced at the word. 'You know, Daddy, I'm rather glad it has backfired. I mean, at least this way mum and I aren't having this endless sniping at each other round corners. Now, we know it's full scale, eyeball to eyeball war.'

Her father nodded sadly and they walked back to the house in silence.

'That sounded loud,' commented Tom.

'Yes,' smiled Kate. 'Don't let me catch you talking to your mother like that.' She looked round. 'Where's Muddle?'

'After we heard the story about Bournemouth from Gran, he went up to his room. I think he's on the phone.'

'On the phone? Who on earth would he be calling.'

'Like I keep trying to tell you, Mum. There's a lot you don't know about Muddle.'

'Yes,' Miranda chipped in. 'You really should hear what

Tom has found out.'

Kate turned to Tom. 'So, this is how you keep secrets to yourself, is it Tom?'

Tom squirmed. 'Mirry doesn't count,' he muttered.

'Excuse me.' Miranda's eyebrows shot up.

'Anyway, look, I'm sure this is all fascinating stuff and the time will come, probably soon, when I will need to know but right now I have to respect Muddle's privacy. Anyway, there's no time for all this now. Go and pack. We're off back to Teddington.'

'What? I thought we were staying till Sunday.'

'No, change of plan. Go. Pack.'

'Must be something juicy,' chimed Tom.

Miranda smacked him on the head. 'Tom, shut up. Just do it, OK?' Tom shrugged and sauntered into the hall with a 'see if I care' expression. Miranda smiled at her mother. 'Sorry about my brother. He's a boy, you know.'

Kate followed her children up the stairs. She walked into her room and saw the teddy bear still lying slightly disapprovingly on the bed. She thought back to her conversation with Boris just one day before. With a sigh, she dragged her case out from under the bed and started to fill it. Her father brought her a cup of tea. He hovered in the doorway. Kate turned to him.

'I'm not going to let her do this to you, you know,' he said hesitantly. 'She can't just throw you out like this. I'll… I'll talk to her. When she's calmed down. Make her see sense, or, or whatever.'

Kate nodded, feeling that silence was the best response.

Her father gave a sad smile. 'Gosh, I wish I was going with you.'

Kate crossed the room and hugged him. 'Why don't you? Why not have a break and come down with us.'

He shrugged. 'And admit defeat to the carrot fly?'

'Oh, bugger the carrot fly. Just come down for a few days. It'll do you good.'

'Well, we'll see.' He turned away and went slowly down

the stairs. Kate bit her lip and returned to her packing.

When Kate came down, the kids were waiting in the hall with Muddle, bags by their side.

'OK, you two,' Kate said briskly, 'Go and say goodbye to your grandmother.'

'Do we have to?'

'Yes,' Kate replied firmly. 'Her quarrel's with me, not you.'

The two children slouched upstairs.

'A most generous gesture, if I may say so, Madam.'

'You may, Muddle, though I doubt I'll be credited for it.'

'Well, the Good Lord knows and you'll have a tick in the celestial register.'

'That's good to know; I need all the help I can get at the moment.'

When everyone was ready, Kate's father walked with them to the car. Muddle reached out his hand. 'It's been a great pleasure, sir, and many thanks for your kind hospitality.' After a firm handshake he went round to the driver's door and climbed in. Tom and Miranda gave their grandfather a big hug and jumped into the back.

Kate and her father stood facing each other.

'Well, poppet, keep in touch. Oh, you might want to call me on this.' He reached across a scrap of paper with a mobile phone number on it. He gave a soft smile. 'Your mother insisted I got one, so she can call and give me instructions when I'm out.'

Kate nodded and pushed the paper into her pocket. She put her arms round his shoulders and gave him a tight hug. After a moment's hesitation he hugged her back. They stayed like that for a long time then, without another word, she broke away and climbed into the car. She looked up at the house and thought she saw a net curtain move in the bay window upstairs. Muddle started the car and they drove off. Her father stood in the road waving until they were out of sight.

Chapter 20
SATURDAY MORNING

Kate woke early. She swung herself out of bed and drew her curtains. Morning sun slanted across the room, highlighting the print of Klimt's The Kiss on the far wall. Kate looked at the golden, intertwined couple.

'Thank you, morning. Like your sense of irony,' she muttered and headed for the shower.

The journey back had been long, the M1 jammed with Friday evening traffic. Tom and Miranda had alternated between sleep and complaining and she and Muddle had sat listening to the radio. There was a lot that Kate would have liked to discuss, to shine Muddle's wisdom onto the problems but it all seemed so overwhelming that she just did not know where to start. And Muddle had not forced the conversation.

A pile of post had awaited them. Kate had separated off the free offers to see if there was anything worth having, leaving the official looking envelopes to be tackled in the full light of day.

Muddle had gone off to collect a takeaway which had been consumed with relish around the television, after which Tom had gone back to the Macedonians, Miranda had spent a couple of hours on the phone to friends and everything took on a semblance of normality.

This morning, Kate felt little trace of that normality. She dressed quickly and went downstairs.

'Good morning, madam.' Muddle was busy in the kitchen preparing coffee.

'Morning, Muddle. You know, this madam business really does have to stop now. I am just a hard-up, well, actually broke, divorcee living on borrowed time in a semi-smart London suburb. I hardly think I can lay claim to being called madam any more, if I ever could.'

'By what nomenclature would you like me to address you?'

'The same way as the rest of the world, please. Just Kate would be fine.'

'As you wish. So, Kate,' he seemed to be allowing his mouth to get the feel of the word, as if he were learning a foreign language, 'I have to go into town today about a matter of business that I need to settle. I am due at Fenchurch Street at ten, after which I am renewing acquaintance with a cousin from Wiltshire who will join me for lunch. I do trust that my absence does not incommode you in any way.'

And so, thought Kate, this is how a decent man gradually pulls himself away.

'No, of course not, Muddle. You must do whatever you want.'

'Thank you, mad- I mean Kate. Forgive me, it will take a while to adjust.'

'For me too, but don't worry about it.'

'Coffee?'

'Lovely.'

They drank for a while in silence, both preoccupied. Kate eventually spoke.

'How did you get on with your parents, Muddle?'

'Well, as you already know through Master Tom's assiduous researches, my father was an army man. I was only eight when he was killed in Londonderry. He had joined a patrol to get a feel for the frontline and it was ambushed. He went to help a child who had been caught in the crossfire.'

'Oh, how horrible. I'm so sorry.'

'I do remember a lot about him, though. I think he was where I got my enthusiasm for all things outdoors. He was always taking us off on hikes and building tree houses.'

'Us?'

'I have two older sisters.'

'Really? Is that how you learned to cook so well?'

Muddle laughed. 'No, self-taught. We always had staff, you see.'

'Do you still see your sisters?'

'One is running a hospital in Kenya, the other an ashram

on Iona, so not as often as I might wish. But to return to your original question, yes, I got on very well with my parents. My mother, who passed quite recently, endowed me with a well-developed sense of right and wrong which has, I hope, guided me for many years and will continue so to do.'

'I'm sure it will.'

'Do I surmise that your question may have been prompted by your somewhat acrimonious relationship of late with Mrs Bostock?'

'You do. I think I've burnt my bridges there. Twice in one day, come to think of it, her and Boris.'

'Well, Boris is another matter. But as regards the lady in question, you will forgive me, I hope, if I suggest that she would have St Francis himself strangling budgerigars.'

Kate looked at him with surprise. 'Do you know, I think that's the first time I've ever heard you speak ill of anyone.'

'If you do not see God in the face of everyone you meet, you will never see God, as the great Mahatma reminds us. It's a good philosophy and one that I do try to follow. However, in the case of your mother, well, let's say I've had a good peer around and I'm still seeking.'

'I suppose she does a lot of good work.' Kate felt the need to defend her mother in the face of such condemnation. It was puzzling to be in such a position.

'On the subject of work, I must get myself ready for the City.' Muddle jumped up, gathered the empty coffee cups, rinsed them briskly and was gone upstairs.

Kate looked at the post piled on the kitchen table. It glared back at her, daring her to open it. She gathered it up, seized a knife from the drawer and slit the first one open. Gas Bill. Second one, Council Tax. Third, final reminder for the unpaid gym membership. That one went straight into the bin. Finally, her hand rested on an envelope marked with the name of her bank. Time for more coffee.

Suitably reinforced, she opened the letter.

Dear Mrs Bradshaw

With reference to your current account, details above, we note that this account has now remained overdrawn for some considerable time and has now exceeded the agreed credit limit.

We therefore request that you contact us as soon as possible to arrange a discussion with Miss Davies, our Assistant Manager.

Yours sincerely

Why is it, thought Kate, that 'yours sincerely' so often means the very opposite. Seeing that the letter was dated Tuesday, four days earlier, she sighed, reached for the phone and dialled the number on the top of the page.

'Our offices are open from eight until six weekdays and nine to twelve thirty Saturdays. Please try later. Our offices are open from eight till…..'

Kate hung up and checked her watch. Half an hour to wait.

Muddle came downstairs and put his head round the door. 'Just off, er Kate. I'll be back at about six. Should I pick up something for dinner?'

'No, that's OK. I'll put something together.'

'Well, I go, I go, see how I go,' and the door closed firmly behind him.

Kate looked at the letter again. '…exceeded the agreed credit limit…' But she had taken nothing out of the bank for the past week. So how could it now be going up or down or whatever was happening? She suddenly felt very alone. She walked out into the back garden and focused on the roses, examining them for aphids and snapping off any blooms that had faded. It didn't really help.

Finally it was nine o'clock. She dialled again.

'If you want to open an account, please press one, if you have a query about a current account, please press two, for all other questions please press three.' The voice had clearly been selected through market research to be friendly but authoritative but to Kate it sounded like an elder sister telling her how to behave at the dinner table. She pressed two.

'If you wish to make a deposit, please press one, if you

wish to check your balance, please press two,' Kate could feel her concentration slipping and forced herself to listen. She did not want to have to go through it all again. Finally the suggestion came, 'If you wish to speak to one of our client service team, please press six.' Kate triumphantly and emphatically pressed six.

'Unfortunately all our client service team are busy at the moment....' 'Or too hung over to come in,' muttered Kate. 'Your call is important to us. Please hang on and someone will be with you in...' brief pause, then an automated voice announced 'four minutes'.

She reached for the coffee cup but found it empty, so she busied herself in the kitchen tidying up one handed, listening to a tinny rendition of Vivaldi's Four Seasons. Finally a human voice came on.

'Sorry to keep you. Graham speaking. How can I help?' The voice clearly had no desire to help but Kate persisted.

'I need to make an appointment with Miss Davies in...'

'What branch?'

'Yes, I am about to tell you that. Teddington, Middlesex, Station Rd.'

'What is the branch number?'

'Sorry?'

'The branch number? The six digit number in the top right hand corner of your cheque book.'

'I've no idea.'

'Well, it's on your debit card too.'

'Miss Davies has got my debit card and, before you ask, my credit card too.'

'No, it's not on the credit card. They are centrally issued.'

'Look, this may disappoint you but I don't give a toss where credit cards come from. They can come from under a gooseberry bush for all I care.'

'No, it's Newport Pagnell, at least I think....'

'Listen.' Kate realised that she was shouting and drew a deep breath. 'I need to speak to someone at your branch in Station Road, Teddington. Now, surely it's not beyond human intelligence, or even yours, to put me through to that branch.'

'Putting you through.'

The line went dead. Kate held on for another minute in the hope that someone would appear out of the void. Then, bowing to the inevitable, she hung up.

It was time for direct action. Grabbing a coat from the hall rack, she called upstairs 'I'm going into Teddington. See you later.' No reply.

The Rolls stood sedately in the drive. Kate picked up the keys from the hall table then paused. Saturday traffic in Teddington was always horrendous. And, in the circumstances, it would not be the best car to step out of to discuss an overdraft.

She walked briskly and was in the centre by ten. The queue at the bank was even longer than usual. She stood until her turn came.

'I've been asked to arrange a meeting with your Miss Davies.' She slid the letter discretely under the window.

'Just a moment. Miss Davies is, in fact, in this morning. I'll check with her.'

Kate waited, studying the advertisements around the walls for savings accounts, ISAs, student accounts. None of it made any more sense than last time.

The cashier returned. 'As it happens, Miss Davies has a slot at eleven fifteen. She usually only sees commuters who can't come in during the week on a Saturday but says that she can fit you in as it's urgent.'

'Well, it's not that urgent.'

'Miss Davies says it is.'

'Does she indeed? Well, I shall return at eleven thirty.'

'Fifteen.'

'Sorry?'

'Eleven fifteen. That's the time of the meeting.'

'Whatever.'

Kate stood on the pavement wondering how to fill an hour. She checked in her handbag to see how much money she had with her. Tucked into the bottom was Boris's envelope with four hundred pounds in it.

'Sorry, Boris,' she muttered. 'I think our need is greater than yours.'

Her eyes drifted across to the shoe shop opposite, which was advertising a sale. Sadly, she averted her gaze and marched to the Tesco down the road. Forty minutes later she emerged with two bags of groceries that would last the family for a couple of days. With or without Muddle. She wondered if he would return that evening.

She deserved a treat. Swinging into the Italian coffee bar, she was greeted with enthusiasm by the owner.

'Ah, Signora. Is a long time, no see. Table at the back like before?'

'No, I think in the window, if you can fit me in.'

'Of course.'

Kate sat back, sipping her skinny latte, and did her best to plan the meeting at the bank. Other than trying to find out why money was still coming out of her account when she was not withdrawing any, she really had no plan; getting just enough money to live on just did not seem to qualify under the heading of Plan.

As she pondered these issues, she gradually realised that a familiar figure was waving to her through the window. Oh, God, Jane. Forcing a smile onto her face she waved back. To her consternation, Jane pushed open the door and came in.

Fighting down the desire to greet her with, 'Darling, the last time I saw you, you were crawling on hands and knees out of a brothel to avoid a police raid,' Kate stood and returned the air kiss.

'Darling, we thought you'd died. Or been whisked off to the South of France by some ardent young stud. Do say it was the latter. Give us all hope. But no, vanished without trace. Where have you been?'

'Nowhere very exciting,' lied Kate. 'Up to see my parents in Yorkshire, that sort of thing.'

'God, dullsville. Well, we must get you out and about again soon. Do the town. Check out the talent.' She leaned back.

'Antonio, the usual double please.'

'Si Signora.'

'Actually, I've got people staying with me at the moment. I'll have to take a rain check on that. I'll call you.'

'Kate, darling, it almost seems like you're brushing me off and I've so much to tell you. I've got this dishy guy at the moment. Loaded, in every sense of the word, if you know what I mean, and I think you do. He keeps taking me to some very naughty places. My dear, you would not believe what goes on within a couple of miles of here.'

Kate pushed up her eyebrows to express shock. 'Really? Goodness.'

'Dear Kate, so innocent about the world. Well, let your Aunty Jane tell you all about it.'

'I'd love to but I really have to go. A meeting at the bank over there in five minutes.'

'Bank? Got problems, darling?'

'No, no, just some financial stuff they're sorting out for me.'

To prove her point, Kate pulled the envelope out of her bag, drew out a twenty pound note in a way that ensured that Jane saw the full contents and paid Antonio.

'Take for my friend's as well, if you would, please, Antonio. Well, must rush. Bye Jane.'

'Bye darling, a bientot, I hope.'

With another round of air kisses, Kate escaped to the open air, breathed deeply and walked into the bank.

Miss Davies was waiting in the side room and beckoned her over.

'Mrs Bradshaw, sorry, Ms Bradshaw, do sit down.'

'Mrs is fine, Miss Davies.'

'Now, we seem to have a bit of a problem, don't we, Mrs Bradshaw?'

Kate smiled at her gently. 'Well, I do, not sure about you.'

Miss Davies looked up in surprise. 'Yes, well, can you tell me if you have managed to find a source of income?'

Kate's loud laughter surprised her even more.

'My first job I never got paid for, you really don't want to know why. The second, I managed to lose about two hundred pounds, luckily not my money. Again, you don't want to know.'

Miss Davies shifted awkwardly in her chair, aware that somehow this discussion was slipping away from her.

'Mrs Bradshaw, this really is not a laughing matter. You are seriously overdrawn.'

'Yes, let's talk about that. Why exactly has my overdraft gone up when I haven't been spending any money?'

Miss Davies looked rather non-plussed. 'Well, let's have a look.'

She hammered out a tattoo on the keyboard and peered at the screen.

'Ah, yes. I see. That will be the bank charges that are added at the end of each month.'

'Bank charges?'

'Yes. You initially had an unauthorised overdraft, now authorised. We have standard charges for that. It's all in the documentation that I gave you before.

'That'll be the stuff in tiny writing that goes straight into the bin.'

Miss Davies smiled wryly. 'A lot of people do say that. To be honest, I have told them it's pretty user unfriendly.'

'So let me get this clear. I am in trouble because you have taken money out of my account without telling me.'

'Oh, no, we will have told you. You will have had an email and a letter warning you that we are about to take the charges from your account.'

'About as useful as the dentist telling you that this is going to hurt.'

The only reply was the briefest of shrugs, which could have been tacit agreement or just as likely, dismissal.

Kate had a choice. She could indulge in a five minute torrent of abuse about banking and all who worked in it – indeed she already had some choice phrases lined up involving rhyming slang – or she could stay calm and try to get some kind of deal. The first way would feel good, no, it would feel great;

the second would be gut-wrenching. It only took a moment. Gut-wrenching it would have to be.

'Right.' Kate leaned forward. Miss Davies seemed to flinch. 'You're the expert. What do I do?'

A look of relief flashed across Miss Davies' face. Once again she fixed on her serious face and nodded in a way that signalled wisdom beyond her years. Bet you learned that on a course, thought Kate.

'Well. You will need to find a source of income. Clearly the job thing has not got off to a good start but you will have to persevere. Do you have any assets that you could borrow against?'

'Well, I have the house, of course.'

'You have a house? How big?'

'Five beds. It's on the Stillwater estate, near the river.'

'I'm fairly new here so I don't really know my way around. I take it that's a smart area.'

'I'd say so.'

'What's the house worth?'

'No idea. About one and a half million, I suppose, even now.'

'Mortgage?'

'No, my ex-husband was able to pay it off with obscenely large bonuses over the last couple of years.'

'And do you have sole ownership?'

'I think so. I got it in the divorce case.'

'We'd have to check that. Can you ask your lawyer?'

'Sure. I'll call him today.'

'Mrs Bradshaw, it's Saturday. I doubt very much he'll be working today.'

'Oh, yes. To be honest, it's unusual for him to be working after lunch most days as far as I can tell.'

'If the house is yours, you will be able to borrow against it. Money is tight, as you know, but you would only be borrowing a small proportion of the total value, at least initially. You will, of course, be reducing a capital asset, but it would certainly get you out of trouble and enable you to keep the house.'

'Keep the house?' Kate gulped.

'Well, yes, how else were you going to pay the bills?'

'I, well, that's why I'm here, I suppose.'

'Mrs Bradshaw, I'll put you in touch with one of our financial advisors. In the meantime, I do strongly advise you to get a job.'

Kate looked directly at the bright young thing opposite. 'Do you know of any jobs for a woman in her mid-, OK late thirties with no experience?'

'I take your point, but there must be, I don't know, receptionist jobs, sales assistants, things that would value your being so well, er, turned out.'

'That's the first compliment I've had today. Thank you for that.'

Miss Davies grinned.

Goodness me, thought Kate, she may be human after all.

'Now, in the meantime, you need something to live off.'

Kate picked up her handbag. 'Well, I can probably manage for this week.'

'Really, How?'

Kate knew a precipice when she saw one. She stepped back. 'Oh, a friend kindly leant me some money. But he will want it back pretty soon, so, no, you're right, I probably do need something straight away.' The handbag slipped discretely back to the floor.

'How many of you at home at the moment.'

'Myself and two children and one friend who's staying, but he pays his way. And may not be there for long.'

'Well, you're going to need a good £500 a week, I'd say, but an advisor could give you a better fix on that.'

'£500. That's a lot of money.'

'Add it up. Gas, electricity, council tax, repairs and that's before you've fed and clothed everyone.' Kate watched her assess the outfit she was wearing, start to say something and then think better of it. I would jolly well think so, thought Kate. This stuff must be at least three months old.

She spread her arms. 'I suppose so.' She could not think at

that moment of anything more constructive to say.

'By the way, you mentioned someone staying with you. So, do you rent out rooms?'

'No, not exactly. It's, well, it's complicated.'

'No, I only ask because I'm looking for somewhere. I've been in a sort of B&B since I was transferred here and, to be honest, I'm pretty sick of it and have to get out anyway, because the bank won't pay that much any more. And everywhere else I've looked has been just as bad or too expensive. I just thought, maybe, we could kill two birds with one stone.'

Kate thought for a moment. Perhaps, having a serious young woman in the house would be a good thing. An example for Miranda, and someone who could give her free advice about money as well.

'How much would you be willing to pay?'

Miss Davies grinned again. 'Good question. You're definitely learning, Mrs Bradshaw. The bank will still stump up £100 a week, at least for a while, though that would have to included breakfast and an evening meal. I often go home at the weekend,' she added hastily, 'Or go to see my boyfriend.' Kate saw a blush start to spread. So, not Little Miss Tightknickers after all.

She broke the silence. 'Why don't you come over this evening and take a look. 9 Stillwater Crescent. But you know that already, of course.'

'Thanks. I'd really like that. Would six thirty be OK? I can bring some papers for you to sign at the same time, to extend the overdraft.'

'Fine.' Kate stood up and held out her hand. 'It's been a pleasure doing business with you.'

Back outside, she balanced her Tesco's bags in each hand and set off for home.

By the time she reached the house she felt better about the world. She knew she was not yet out of trouble but for the first time she had a sense of direction. And that direction was not just down. Even the idea of a job did not sound so bad. As she opened the door, she was congratulating herself on how far she had come in a week.

She pushed the front door closed with her bottom. It did not strike her immediately that something was wrong. She was carrying her shopping to the kitchen, got half way across the hall, then stopped. She called out.

'Miranda, Tom, I'm home.'

No reply.

Kate felt her scalp tingle. She shook her head, told herself not to be so silly, pushed the door open into the kitchen.

She screamed.

Dropped the shopping.

The stocky man standing on the other side of the kitchen remained totally still. After a few seconds, he spoke.

'Do come in, Mrs Bradshaw. We have been waiting for you.' The accent was foreign, the tone polite.

Kate turned and ran. She cannoned into a second person, standing right behind her.

'Whoops a-daisy.' This voice was Cockney, equally calm. The figure was very tall. It took Kate a moment to realise that it was a woman. She was gently turned round and pushed back into the kitchen.

Kate felt her legs giving way under her. She grabbed at the work surface.

'Do sit down,' said the tall woman, guiding her firmly by the arm. 'This does not need to take very long.'

She moved behind Kate, out of her line of sight.

Kate sank onto a stool. She grasped her hands together to try to stop them shaking. They still shook.

'Where are my children? What have you done to them?'

The voice came from behind her, light and friendly like an encouraging chat show host. 'Your daughter went out at ten forty-two, your son at eleven thirty. You should have firm words with him about setting the burglar alarm. Not that it would have made any difference.'

'Who … who are you?'

'Mrs Bradshaw,' again from behind. 'What do you know

about a man called Anatole Krimovski?'

'Sorry. I've never heard of him.'

'Yuri Andrev?'

'No. Look, I promise you I would tell you if I knew.'

The voice remained calm, almost chatty. 'I know you would. Because I know you are a sensible person, Mrs Bradshaw and a loving mother.'

Kate spun round. 'What do you mean? What have you done to my children? Where are they?'

'Mrs Bradshaw, I'm sure your children are quite safe. You have given no reason for them not to be. Not yet.'

'I haven't heard of either of these men,' Kate wailed. 'I promise you.'

'Nicolas Rysotskin?'

'Will you stop pushing names at me? I haven't heard of any of them.'

The one with the foreign accent spoke again, making Kate spin back round. 'Mrs Bradshaw, they are all one person.'

'What?' Kate looked from one to the other, totally confused. She took in the fact that both of them were very well dressed. And both were wearing black leather gloves. She shuddered. 'I'm sorry,' she wailed, staring at the stocky man, 'I don't understand.'

'I think you do.'

'No.'

'Mrs Bradshaw,' the woman's voice behind her asked, 'how many Russians do you know?'

The quietly asked question made Kate jump.

'Ah, at least one then.'

'Well, yes, sort of.'

'Sort of?'

'Well, there was a guy I thought I knew. But he has gone.'

'Tell me more.'

Kate took a deep breath. 'He's none of these people you have said to me. His name is Boris, Boris something.'

'Boris something? That wouldn't by any chance be the Boris Kratin you asked for when you visited the Royal Hotel in

Sheffield.'

'What? But if you knew that, why did you…?'

Another silent smile. 'Tell me how you met this Boris Kratin?'

'Well, you seem to know everything already. Why don't you tell me?'

'My dear Mrs Bradshaw, please don't try to be clever,' purred the woman. ' That would not be helpful to us, to you nor to anyone else involved with you.' Her meaning was not lost on Kate, who hung her head. 'Now, let's just get quickly to the end of this discussion and we can be on our way.'

The idea of being rid of them spurred Kate on.

'I met him through his sister. She and I were working together and she introduced us. They stayed here for a while.'

'Are they still here?'

'No.'

'Where are they?'

'I don't know.'

'Do you have a contact number?'

'No.'

'You have an affair with this man and you don't know have his number? I find that hard to believe.'

'An affair? I didn't have an affair with Boris. At least not in that sense.'

'You meet him in a hotel. You have a discussion during which you try to hit him. You then go to his room and are not seen to leave.'

The faintest glimmer of hope came into Kate's mind. They had not seen them leave. The wigs had done their job. Perhaps these people were not as all-knowing as they seemed.

'I, no, I mean. Look, OK, a bit of kissing and cuddling but that was all. I mean, his sister was around.'

'Ah, yes, his sister.'

The tall Englishwoman leaned in towards her. 'Where are they, Mrs Bradshaw?'

'I really, really don't know. Anastasia is with a great aunt called Irena.' The two intruders exchanged the briefest of glances. 'But I've no idea where she lives. And Boris is somewhere on the South Coast.'

'Why?'

'It's complicated. His sister was involved in a fight on the street and Boris took the key witness off to get her out of the way.'

'Where to?'

'I don't know. Somewhere on the South Coast. That's all I know, I promise.'

The two stared at Kate. She desperately tried to remember what Boris had told her about giving away when she was bluffing. The silence continued. Kate stared at the counter top in front of her.

The foreign man suddenly banged his hand down on the counter top right in front of Kate, making her jump back with a squeak, nearly losing her balance off the stool. He leaned right in so that his face was just inches from Kate's. She could smell the sharp, sour smell of stale tobacco. Long seconds passed. Finally, he spoke.

'Mrs Bradshaw, I am sure you don't want to see us again. The best chance that you have of that is to tell us everything you know. Now.' The last word was shouted into her face. Kate felt as if she would faint. She longed to tell them more but, at the same time, something assured her that they felt they had all they could get. She just silently shook her head.

The Englishwoman carefully placed a card in front of her. Kate tried to focus on it but couldn't.

'My number. If there's anything else you remember or if he turns up, please call me.'

'Who should I ask for?'

She smiled, gave no reply.

'What do you want him for, anyway?'

'You don't need to know. Let's just say that he has something that does not belong to him. But I would advise you that it would be healthier to stay well clear of him.'

The two moved towards the door to the garden.

'Oh, and Mrs Bradshaw,' the tall woman turned casually

back. 'What made you think that this Anastasia was his sister?'

'What? Well, she told me.'

'She told you? Well, not always wise to believe everything people say to you. Goodbye. For now.'

As they slipped out through the door, Kate slid to the floor.

Chapter 21
SATURDAY AFTERNOON

Barely five minutes later, when Tom returned to the house, burger in hand, he found his mother crouched in the corner of the kitchen sobbing uncontrollably.

'Mum, mum, what's up? What's happened?'

'Where's your sister?'

'I dunno. Why?'

'Call her.'

'What?'

'Call her. Call her. Just bloody call her.'

'OK!' He grabbed the phone and waved it at his mother. 'Look, I'm calling her. OK? Now, are you going to tell me what's happened?'

Kate gasped out the word 'burgled'.

Tom stared at her, then pressed the speed dial for Miranda's mobile.

'Mirry? It's Tom. Listen, you'd better come home. Well, tough, look, listen to me, there's a problem. Look's like we've had a break-in. Anyway, Mum's in a really bad way. No, not hurt, at least I don't think so, just, well, all weepy and a bit shocked, I think. Not sure yet. Yes. Yes, OK, see you soon.'

Tom put down the phone and knelt down beside his mother. 'She's on her way.'

'Thank God. Thank God you're both OK.' She threw her arms around Tom and clung to him.

'Of course we're OK, why shouldn't we be. I've just been into town for a burger, that's all. Now, come on, let's get you up.'

He eased his mother off the floor and towards the stool that she had been sitting on when the man and woman were there.

Kate pulled herself away from him. 'No, not that one. I'll sit over there.'

Tom knew he should not ask why. Instead, he busied himself with making coffee for his mother, taking quick, furtive bites from the abandoned burger when his back was turned to her. He waited for Kate to be ready to speak, half of him longing to know, half not wanting to.

Eventually she started to talk. She decided to tell him the whole story, partly because she really didn't know which parts to leave out. He listened, hamburger forgotten, leaning on the oven, arms folded. Finally, she was finished and slumped, exhausted. Telling someone else, finding the words to describe what had happened, how abused she had felt, somehow made her feel if not better, then at least human. It had started to put some kind of reality onto the event and reality, however dreadful, was better than the sense of an almost nightmare-like unreality that had overwhelmed her before.

Tom walked over and put his arms round her, searching his mind for appropriate words of comfort but settling in the end for what he hoped was silent, manly support. Kate straightened up.

'And how dare you not set the alarm? How many times have I told you? What do you think we have these things for?'

'Whoa.' He stepped back. 'I set the alarm. I know that for certain because I went out then remembered half way up the drive and came back in to do it.'

'But they said you hadn't.'

'And you believe them over me?'

'No, I mean, of course not. But they got in.'

Tom went into the hall. The display panel on the alarm control box flashed ERROR. 'They got round it somehow,' he called back. 'Better get onto the people to get it reset.'

Kate sat silently thinking. If they had lied about that, what else had they lied about? About Boris, about Anastasia, about the whole thing? But they were clever; they would have known that she would find out about the alarm. Were they trying to tell her something? If so, she hadn't the faintest idea what.

Her mind was spinning. She stood, one hand on the worktop to steady herself and went out into the garden, looking cautiously around as if they might still be there. Tom watched her anxiously from the kitchen window, longing for his sister to be home. Kate gazed around at the flowers, at the lawn that had now outgrown Muddle's painstaking mowing. Everything seemed to have taken on a different mood. She felt like a stranger in her own garden.

Suddenly an idea occurred to her and she rushed back into the house.

'Tom, you remember when you looked up Muddle on your computer.'

'Yes,' he relied cautiously.

'Can you do that with any name?'

'Well, yes, within reason. I mean, if you look up Smith or something you're going to get a few hundred million replies but generally, yes. Hey, are you saying that you can remember the names they said to you?'

'Well, sort of. Just the first one. After that it all gets a bit blurred. But it was something like Anatole Krimoski or Krimolski or something like that.'

'Well, it's a start. Come on, let's see what we can find.'

They headed upstairs. Kate paused.

'Why is Miranda not back yet? Shouldn't she be here?'

'It's OK,' Tom adopted a casual air. 'She was some way off.'

'Where, exactly?'

Tom realised this was not a day for more mystery. 'Raynes Park, I think.'

'Oh, Lord, not that dreadful Darren again.'

'Maybe, or maybe one of his mates. Mirry wasn't too sure herself. She was just going to see how it went.'

'Well, that will have to keep.' Kate put the image of that sordid flat out of her mind. 'Now, let's see what we can find out.'

Tom crouched over the computer. 'How do you spell this name?'

'Oh, for God's sake, Tom,' Kate burst out. 'How the bloody hell should I know? Silly of me not to ask those bastards how to spell it?' She looked up to see his shocked face. She put her hand on his arm. 'Oh, hell, I'm sorry, love. Just try something.'

Tom nodded silently and started to carefully type.

A series of references to a 1930's Hungarian biologist filled the screen.

'No, this does not look right.' Tom flicked through the pages but nothing jumped out.

'Let's try another spelling.'

At the fourth attempt, after they had learned more than they needed to know about Latvian actors, Canadian wheat farmers, the inventor of the Cramotski Principle of Plastic Inversion and a rather unsuccessful Borscht Belt comic from the 1950's, the screen finally asked in rather condescending italics, *Do you mean Anatole Krimovski?*

'Try it,' Kate muttered.

The page filled with references to Russian privatisation. Tom clicked on an extract from the Daily Mail, hoping it would be more intelligible than the FT pages that made up most of the list.

They read together.

Russian billionaire goes missing.

Police are fearful for the wellbeing of the young Russian billionaire, Anatole Krimovski, who is missing after a shoot-out at the home that he shared with his father, former Politburo member Yuri Krimovski.

Mr Krimovski senior was found dead when police were called to his home in fashionable Hyannis Port last Sunday by neighbours who heard shots. Two other men, as yet unidentified, were also found dead at the scene.

It is thought that the deaths are the result of Russian mafia battles to gain control of the highly lucrative Russian industries that were privatised in the 1980's. The Daily Mail has also discovered that the Russian government has been going to great lengths in recent months to persuade some of the ex-pat billionaires to share their good fortune with the Russian state or to face the consequences. Two former billionaires already languish in gaols in Moscow.

Yuri Krimovski, who had moved with his son to the United States some years ago, had done well out of speculation and contacts that had given him a controlling interest in the burgeoning Russian electronics industry. His son, Anatole, had turned his back on such matters, preferring an academic career as a lecturer and researcher at New England's Yale University.

He had not, however, turned his back on the wealth and was known to live well, though privately. His name was linked last year with rising starlet, Amanda-May McCormick, known in this country for her role as Scarlett in the Channel 5 soap The Living and The Loving. She was reported to have ended the romance because 'he never takes me anywhere. All he wants to do is sit at home and talk to people.'

American police believe that Anatole may have gone into hiding or even left the country. Equally, he may have been kidnapped or killed.

Forces in other countries, including Britain, have been put on alert.

The piece was dated some three weeks ago. At the time, it had passed Kate by, just another foreign story with no apparent relevance. She looked at the screen again as Tom scrolled. A photo gradually came into view of Amanda-May McCormick, looking sultry, her hair over one eye. A second one scrolled up. It was of Anatole in his university baseball team of 1992, grinning as he sat cross-legged with his fellow team members.

It was Boris.

Kate sat back. With a gasp she remembered Boris's voice 'I have also killed two men'. It all fell into place. She felt a sense of relief that at least some of what he had told her was true. She also felt great guilt at having sent him away at such a terrible time. She longed to be able to call him up and tell him everything was OK and he should come back. But everything was far from OK and coming back was the last thing he should do.

Tom was scanning more press items but Kate had seen enough. She stood up and went back downstairs. Just then, Miranda came into the house. She took one look at her mother's face and flung her arms around her.

'Mum, you look terrible,' she muttered into Kate's

shoulder.

'Gee, thanks. You know how to make a girl feel good.'

She took Miranda into the kitchen and told her the whole tale, finishing with their discovery of the story on Tom's computer. The girl sat open-mouthed until Kate had finished.

'Wow, it must have been really awful for you, Mum. Is there anything I can do, make you a coffee, pour you a gin, whatever?' Kate shook her head. Miranda adopted the tone that mothers use to reassure a child who has just come last in the egg and spoon race. 'But I have to say, if it helps, my friends already find you pretty cool and this whole story is really going to put you into the stratosphere with them.'

Kate looked at Miranda, horrified. 'No, no. Miranda, you are not to talk to anyone about this. Understand? No one. This is dangerous stuff. It's real.'

'Oh, yeah. I suppose you are right. I see.' She paused then asked in a small voice, 'Mum, does this mean we are in danger, do you think, here?'

'No, I don't think so,' Kate replied firmly, trying to convince herself as much as her daughter. 'I mean, I told them everything I knew. Well, nearly everything.'

'Nearly?'

'Well, actually, I do know where Boris is. He's at a hotel in Bournemouth, or at least he was yesterday.'

'Why on earth didn't you tell them? Get them off our backs.'

'Well, because, well, it's Boris. I mean, I can't set those awful people on him and especially now that we know what happened in America.'

Miranda looked gently at her mother. 'We never did have that girly chat, did we? Is now a good time?'

'You know, that's a good idea. Anything to take my mind off what happened here today. As it is, I don't think I'm going to sleep soundly ever again.'

'So, what about Boris? What was the problem? Or is that a dumb question?'

'Oh, it all seems so petty now. There was a bit of a

contretemps on Thursday evening. Anastasia picked a fight with some of your grandmother's vigilantes outside the new casino in Sheffield. We ended up in the police station and Boris was nowhere to be seen.'

Miranda looked in amazement at her mother. 'You know, you get cooler by the minute. I mean street fights, police stations, Russian billionaires, gun fights. Where's it going to end?'

Kate looked steadily at her daughter, as realisation of what she had said spread a blush across her startled face. Miranda gave a small gasp and put a hand to her mouth. 'Sorry, just an expression. What I meant was not where's it going to end end. Not in that sense, just, you know, in a wow, that's my mum kind of, you know…'

Kate decided to rescue her. 'Miranda,' she said gently, 'When you find you've got yourself in a hole, stop digging.'

'Sorry, mum. Anyway, back to Boris. Why did you dump him?'

'Did I dump him? Yes, I suppose I did. Well, he just vanished, didn't turn up to sort us out or talk to the police or anything. Of course, I understand why now but at the time, I was livid. I mean, you've never been in a police station at two o'clock in the morning. It's not a nice place.'

'But, to be fair, it wasn't really his fault you were in there.'

'Well, it was his sister's fault and he carries some responsibility for her. Someone has to.'

'So, did he do nothing?'

'Would you believe he phones Muddle in the middle of a dinner party and sends him down to sort out his mess.'

'Mum, I have to say, knowing what we know now, that was probably the best answer.'

Kate stared out of the window. 'I've blown it, haven't I?'

'Well, yes. But actually no. I mean, think what would have happened today if Boris had come back here with us.'

Kate thought and did not at all like the images that came to her mind. She shuddered. 'I suppose so. Maybe I did him a favour.'

'I'm sure you did. Quite by accident, to be honest, but whatever. Is there any way you can contact him?'

'No. They asked that too but I don't have a number for him and I'm pretty sure he's not going to be in directory enquiries.'

'Rule One, Mum, always get their number.'

'Yes, Miranda.'

'What about the spare room? Their stuff will still be in there. Let's take a look.'

Kate had not wanted to go into the room since their return from Sheffield. It was as if she did not have to acknowledge that they had gone if she did not see the empty room. She now stood up, gripping the worktop firmly. 'Good idea.'

The two hesitated briefly outside the bedroom door then Miranda pushed it open. They both gasped at what they saw.

'Oh, my God,' muttered Miranda.

The room was strewn with clothes and papers. Two suitcases that Boris and Anastasia had left had been up-ended. Papers were splayed across the floor. But this was nothing. What truly shocked them were three letters, sprayed across the Laura Ashley wallpaper at least three foot high. IDG.

'What does it mean,' whispered Miranda.

Tom, realising that he was missing something momentous, ran along the landing and peered round the other two.

'Wow. Serious graffiti,' he exclaimed, awestruck.

Kate threw open the door to her own room. At first sight all was as it should be. She tentatively opened the top drawer of her chest. It was immediately clear that every bra, every pair of pants had been moved. In the next drawer, her t-shirts and jumpers were re-arranged.

She felt a tremendous nausea well up in her, rushed into her bathroom and was violently sick. Afterwards, she reached up and fumbled for the flush, then lay on the floor, her head against the cool of the toilet bowl, breathing heavily. After a couple of minutes there was a timid knock at the door.

'Mum,' came Miranda's shaky voice, 'Is there anything we

can do?'

Kate cleared her throat and forced a jolly tone into her voice. 'What everyone always does in an emergency. Put on the kettle.'

'OK.' She heard the two of them thunder downstairs. Hauling herself up, she washed her face in the basin. She gargled with water and then scrubbed her teeth. Looking in the mirror, she was forced to agree with Miranda; she did look terrible.

She waited until her limbs stopped shaking and then slowly left the bathroom and headed down to the others. In the kitchen, she was greeted by two white faces looking up at her.

'Black tea for me, I think, with two sugars. They do say that sugar is a good thing for shock, don't they. Mind you, I don't know who they are, who say such wise things but...'

Kate realised that she was prattling and stopped. Miranda spoke first.

'Mum, what was it? What did you find in your drawers?'

'They had been through them, moved everything just to let me know they'd been there. Bastards.'

'Wow,' Tom sounded relieved. 'Is that all? We thought there must be a severed arm, at least, in there.'

Miranda nudged Tom so hard with her elbow, he fell off the stool. 'Well,' he complained from the floor, 'You did too. Don't pretend you didn't.'

Miranda looked across at her mother and shrugged her shoulders, on her face a look that combined admission that she had indeed feared something gruesome with resignation at having to have a brother.

'It's OK,' Kate replied, forcing a calm tone into her voice. 'It's just that, you know, when someone has been through your private stuff, like underwear and so on, it feels really creepy.'

'OK. I can see that. How are you now?'

'Well, there are very few things to be said for throwing up but I think, in this case, it was exactly what I needed. I actually feel a bit better. I mean, I've been scared out of my wits in my own kitchen, had my drawers ransacked and something weird sprayed on my guest room wall, so I'm not going to be a hundred per cent, but, all things considered…' She paused. 'Where's that tea?'

'Coming up.' Miranda busied herself, glad to have something to do.

Kate's mind jumped back to the letters on the guest room wall. 'Tom, you know what you were doing earlier with Boris's names, could you try that with those initials, IDG or whatever it was?'

'I can have a go.'

'Thanks.' Tom went bounding back up the stairs.

Kate took her tea through to the living room, mainly so that Miranda could not see her hand shaking. She turned on the television. The credits for *Murder She Wrote* emerged onto the screen. She quickly flipped channels, eventually finding a 1940s romance to get lost in. Tom reappeared.

'Twenty-four million, eight hundred thousand entries, I'm afraid, mum. We'll need to narrow it down a bit. I'm going to try Russia, shareholding, stuff from that article from earlier.'

'Fine.' Kate was glad to be able to keep him occupied. Almost immediately she fell asleep. She slept for a full two hours, waking with a start. The television was still talking softly in front of her, though now seemed to be a gardening programme. Her half-drunk cup of tea stood on the table beside her. She forced herself to stand up, holding the padded arm of the sofa until she felt steady.

In the downstairs cloakroom she splashed her face with water. She could hear Tom tapping away upstairs.

She called up, 'Any luck?'

'Not really, Mum. I've given up for now, to be honest. Really need another clue.'

Kate paced around the ground floor of the house. She felt as if she should be doing something, getting on with sorting all of this out but nothing occurred. She longed for Muddle to come home. He would know what to do. If he was coming home.

She decided to clean the kitchen. The intruders had worn

gloves so there was no danger of erasing valuable evidence. Evidence. Should she call the police? It had not occurred to her until that moment. Surely they could track these people down. Then she thought of the questions, about Boris, about their relationship, about the incident in Sheffield, perhaps. And they would want to go all over the house.

No, she couldn't take all that. Not just now. Muddle would know what to do.

By five thirty, the kitchen was scrubbed clean. Kate looked around. It was the first time she had cleaned a kitchen for at least ten years and she felt very satisfied with her work. Surfaces gleamed, the floor shone.

Exhausted, she sat again in the living room. The early evening news was coming on. Unlike her mother, who insisted on total silence while she watched the news at least twice a day, Kate had little interest the events of the outside world. She rummaged in the sofa cushions for the remote and was about to change channels when she heard the words 'Fire at Bournemouth hotel.'

She stopped, transfixed. But this had just been the headline and she had to sit through stories about bombs in Karachi and a sacked cricket coach before the story came up in detail.

'A fire raged early this morning through one of Bournemouth's most prestigious hotels. The Royal Spa, a hundred year old hotel that has, in its past, played host to royalty of many countries, was badly damaged in the early hours of this morning by a fire that is believed to have started in the kitchens but quickly spread to the guest accommodation. Over to our reporter at the scene, Richard Hannington.'

A boyish figure stood in front of a scene of fire engines and hoses. 'Yes, Sarah, it was mass evacuation instead of the usually more sedate ballroom dancing here at one of this coast's most premier locations. So far there is no report of any serious casualties, though some guests were treated for smoke inhalation.' The shot changed to a night time scene of people filing out of the hotel. Kate looked closely. Among the figures, a large shape seemed to veer off away from the cameras, push past some firemen and disappear from view. Had that been Boris? The shot changed again to a brief interview with a senior fire officer, who simply repeated in a very self-important manner what had already been said and the programme moved on to an item about gerbils.

Kate rushed upstairs and into Tom's room. Tom quickly clicked off what he was looking at and went bright red. Kate decided to ask no questions.

'Tom, can you get news stories on there?'

'Yes, no problem.' He was unnaturally pleased to help. 'What did you want?'

'There was an item on the news just now about a fire at a hotel in Bournemouth. I thought I saw Boris.'

Tom went onto the BBC site and quickly found the story. Embedded in it was the film she had just seen.

'There. Can you run that?'

She studied the images. 'Stop, there.' The picture froze as the large man started down the stairs. 'Him, there. Is that Boris? Can you enlarge it?'

'No, sorry. That's all I can get. You'd need a much more powerful machine to get it bigger,' he added wistfully.

'Dream on.' Miranda had arrived at the door from her room to see what the fuss was about.

'Miranda, look,' called Kate urgently. 'There. Is that Boris?'

Miranda peered. 'Could be,' she muttered doubtfully. 'Run a bit more.'

The film continued but none of them could say with any certainty that they had been looking at the man they had shared a house with for a week. Kate slumped back onto Tom's bed.

Just at that moment, they heard the front door open. They all froze. Kate crept out onto the landing. She heard first the kitchen door then the living room door open and close.

'Anyone at home?' The clipped tones of Muddle wafted up the stairs. To Kate they felt like pure oxygen. She ran downstairs.

'Oh, Muddle, you cannot believe how pleased we are to

see you.' Before she knew it, tears were running down her cheeks and dripping onto her shirt front.

'Why, madam,' cried Muddle, forgetting their earlier agreement about names. 'Such distress. Come, tell me all.' He took her by the arm and guided her to the living room, calling behind him, 'Thomas, Miranda, tea for your mother, I think.'

Kate shook her head. 'Any more tea and I shall turn into a teapot.' She turned back to the others. 'Why don't you two get on with the supper? You'll find stuff in the Tesco bags and in the fridge. Should be self-evident but yell if you get stuck.'

She sat down opposite Muddle in the sitting room. He leaned forward and encased her hands in his.

'Oh, God, Muddle, I don't know where to start.'

'I have always found that the beginning is a good place, then proceed through to the conclusion, then stop.'

Relieved at last of having to protect her children's feelings, she told him of the terror she had felt. She felt her whole body shake as she spoke but Muddle held her hands firmly. Kate sensed a kind of strength passing through from his hands to hers. He listened, nodding at frequent intervals as Kate spoke about the two intruders, everything they had found on the internet, the bedrooms, right up to the news item. His eyebrows went up and down as each part of the story unfolded. Finally, she stopped, unable to say more, deeply tired.

Muddle continued nodding.

'Well, here's a how d'you do. Tell me, when do the children go back to school?'

'What? What's that got to do with it all?'

Muddle waited.

'Ten days, Wednesday of next week, I think.'

'Then can I suggest a brief camping holiday?'

'Can you what?'

'Madam, sorry, Kate. Would you like, in view of the events of the day, to vacate this house for a few days?'

'Well, yes, to be honest. I think I would.'

'And do you think it would be a good idea to be somewhere where we cannot be traced?'

'Yes. I can see that. But how does camping…'

'I know a location in the New Forest, unknown to all but a few, a leafy glade where sunlight dapples gently. If you have not sat there with the birds singing as you fry bacon and eggs on a hand-made fire then, I would venture to suggest, your life is not complete.'

Kate grimaced. 'Muddle, while I understand that you find that sort of thing lovely, I have to tell you, I'm more of a cappuccino and croissant kind of a girl. Camping, as in cold, wet, uncomfortable and, well, hearty, is not really what I was put on this earth for. Sweet offer and thank you but no.'

Chapter 22
SATURDAY EVENING

And so it was that half an hour later they were all planning their camping trip. Tom was discussing with Muddle the possibility of building a rope bridge; Miranda and Kate were debating the best brand of instant cappuccino.

Eventually, Muddle brought the discussion to a halt. 'Now, we need to pack. May I suggest that we dispense with anything that may veer more to the decorative, less to the practical.'

'That leaves me with two pairs of jeans, some t-shirts and an old school jumper,' muttered Miranda.

'An ample sufficiency, if I may say so.'

'But what if I meet the man of my dreams?'

'He will be a poor man indeed if he cannot see beyond the falderals, young Miranda.'

God, Kate thought, and here's me, who's spent most of my life relying on the falderals, and look what I ended up with; Stephen the Bastard. She was about to agree with Muddle's analysis but stopped herself in time. While a teenager may take advice from one adult, she is certainly not going to take it from two, especially when one is her mother. After all, thought Kate, I still don't; how could I expect Miranda to be any wiser? Hell, does that mean I'm no better than my mother?

Kate felt it was time to tune back into the conversation before she came to a conclusion that she didn't like.

'So, we set off,' Muddle was saying, 'oh eight hundred hours sharp tomorrow morning.'

'Just one problem,' Kate cut in, still hoping that somehow this dangerously jolly expedition could be avoided. 'We don't actually have the one essential ingredient here; a tent.'

'No problem. I have several at my disposal.'

'Yes, I was rather afraid you would.'

'We will collect them on the way. Now, action stations.

Pack enough for three, no four days and we will see how it goes.'

'Three or four days?' wailed Kate.

'Well, Mum,' grinned Tom, 'you could always come back here on your own if you don't like it.'

'Tom, you are a horrible child and I don't know where you came from.'

The flippant response was easy, but the prospect of being alone was simply too frightening to consider.

Just then, the doorbell rang. Muddle immediately jumped up. 'Stay here. I will go.'

'Be careful,' whispered Kate.

Muddle disappeared into the hall and Kate soon heard the high-pitched voice of Miss Davies from the bank. She went through.

'Hello. Look, I'm sorry, we have had rather an eventful day and it had slipped my mind that you were coming. Do come in, though I'm afraid that there is a bit of a problem with the bedroom.' A bit of a problem? Kate was impressed with her own very English understatement.

'Oh, has it gone?' Miss Davis's face dropped in disappointment.

'No, no, far from it, it's just that … I tell you what, why don't you come up and have a look?'

Muddle disappeared discreetly into the kitchen as Kate led the way upstairs. The young woman gasped as they went into the bedroom.

'Who did this to you?'

Kate hesitated. Where to start? She opted for the simplest version.

'It was while I was with you this morning. I came back and found this.'

'Vandals, I suppose. There's so much of that around at the moment. So, I suppose that rather scuppers any chance of a room.'

'Sadly, yes. I'm sorry, you've come on a wasted journey.'

'That's OK, I suppose. I had nothing else to do. Oh, and

I've got some papers for you to sign and some interesting news.'

'Good news, I hope. I've had more than enough of the other.'

'Interesting, certainly. Good, maybe.'

'I'm intrigued. Let's go downstairs.'

Kate poured two glasses of wine and they settled themselves at the dining table.

'Well,' Miss Davies took a drink before continuing, clearly enjoying the dramatic pause. Come on, thought Kate, get on with it. 'When someone defaults on payment, as your husband has, we put an automatic check onto their account to see if it's still live. Did you say your husband was working abroad?'

'Yes, China.'

'Are you sure?'

'My parents have had postcards from him.'

'And that's all the evidence you have?'

'Well, yes. I suppose so. Why?'

'It seems that someone, whether your husband or someone else we don't know, has been withdrawing funds from the account at cashpoints, here in the UK.'

Kate stared at the girl as the implications sank in. 'You mean, he could be here, in this country?' She felt the anger soar through her. 'The little shit.'

Miss Davies sat quickly back, eyebrows soaring. 'Well, we can't be certain. You know, it could be someone else.'

'Who? No-one else is going to have his cards and numbers.' Kate spluttered with rage. 'No, it must be him. The toad. The nasty slimy reptilian…' Kate growled with frustration as she failed to find insults rich enough. 'How much does he have in this account?'

'Well, we're not supposed to divulge the information. In a way, I've already told you more…'

'How much? Is it regular income? Is it paid in pounds or Chinese whatevers?'

'Let's just say it's regular and substantial. And would imply that he is based here.'

'So, can we track him down?'

'I'm afraid not. We do know where the withdrawals have come from, of course, mainly on the south coast, Southampton area, but that doesn't really narrow it down much, does it?'

Kate stared back silently.

'Anyway,' continued Miss Davies hurriedly. 'I'd better be off.' She quickly drained her wine and stood. 'Well, it's been … yes, well, goodbye.' She held out her hand. After a long pause, Kate shook it briefly and silently. 'I'll let myself out, then.'

Kate shook herself. 'Sorry, I'm being horribly rude. It's not your fault that my ex-husband has the moral values of frogspawn.' She rose and accompanied the younger woman to the door. 'And sorry about the room.'

'Oh, no, I mean, quite understandable. I hope, you know, that you get it put right soon.'

'Sure. Look, if, when we get it fixed, I'll give you a call and check if you're still looking.'

Kate opened the door and Miss Davies dived for freedom.

Chapter 23
SUNDAY MORNING

Kate stood in her bathroom, saying a fond farewell to the row of Clinique facial creams that had been her life support for so long.

'Oh, well,' she sighed, 'they're going to run out soon anyway. This way they can last a bit longer.'

She didn't really have any old clothes but gathered up jeans, jumpers and a leather jacket and piled them on her bed. All her suitcases seemed more fitting to five star hotels than a damp clearing in the forest – Kate was determined that it would be damp, even though the day had dawned clear and bright. She went downstairs and rummaged in the understairs cupboard, finally finding, among the old tennis racquets, piles of plastic bags and bits of bicycle, a backpack that had been a free gift from some hotel they had stayed in. As she stuffed as much as she could into the pack, the smell of bacon and eggs wafted up the stairs.

Muddle was busy at the hob as she walked into the kitchen. 'Start the day well and it is yours to command,' he declared as he sliced tomatoes and added them.

Tom came sleepwalking into the room wearing only a crumpled pair of boxers, arms out in front of him. 'Food. Good. Me want food,' he intoned.

They sat down, soon joined by Miranda, hair scraped back and held with a band.

'God, Mum. You're not going to wear those shoes, are you?'

Kate looked down at the studded white trainers.

'Well, I thought, you know…'

'If I may venture a suggestion, Kate, something with a greater waterproof facility may be wiser, in the unlikely event of inclement weather.'

'Well, I have wellies.'

'Oh, yeah,' chimed in Tom, 'I can just see you marching miles in wellies without complaining.'

'Who said anything about miles?'

'The site I have selected has vehicular access to within about a quarter of a mile, after which we will need to walk, carrying our equipment.'

'Any more nice surprises, Muddle?'

Muddle just smiled and continued cooking, leaving Kate certain that there was more to come.

Within an hour they were ready to go, Kate now wearing some gardening shoes, that had been bought many years ago for a farm holiday in Devon that had promised much but had rained persistently, making the passage from the house to the car, some fifty feet, a challenge equal to the Somme on a bad day. Not a good omen, really.

Everything was dropped into the capacious boot of the Rolls.

'Muddle, I see no tents or food or any of the really important stuff.'

'Never fear, Kate. All is arranged.'

'Do you know,' announced Kate, 'I would like to drive. This is, after all, supposed to be my car and I haven't yet had a go.'

After a moment's hesitation, Muddle passed over the keys. 'As you wish. We will be stopping en route but I shall navigate for you.'

Kate checked twice that the house was locked and the alarm on then climbed in behind the wheel.

'All aboard for fun and jollity,' she called to her children in the back seat.

'Yeah, whatever, Mum,' Miranda replied.

'I propose that we start out on the M3, madam. Are you familiar with the way to it?'

Kate looked steadily at Muddle. 'I have lived here for fifteen years, Muddle. And remember, I do maps. It's like the cards, I can remember the detail.'

Her thoughts were suddenly filled by Boris and Anastasia.

A great sense of loneliness washed over her.

Muddle spotted her sudden frown. 'Yes, I wonder where they are,' he murmured, 'And how they are getting on.'

'Mm. I wonder whether we'll ever know.'

'Who knows the future? It rolls out on its diurnal course as the waves crashing in on the shore.'

The car rolled sedately through the centre of Teddington and out towards the motorway. They had just passed Kempton Park racecourse and were about to reach the junction with the M3, when Muddle pointed to a narrow turning on the left. 'Just turn down there, if you would, Kate.'

'Why?'

'It is here that we are to pick up the missing essentials.'

Kate obediently turned onto a small service road that led to some factory buildings.

'Just over there. That first shed on the right. Pull in behind it, if you please.'

Kate pulled in. The only other vehicle was a black, long wheelbase Land Rover. A man stepped out as they approached. Muddle jumped out and went to talk to him as the others looked on, intrigued. After a moment, he returned. He leaned in through the window.

'Do come and met Mr Jones.'

Kate stepped out cautiously. The others scrambled out and ran over. Mr Jones was standing by the open back of the Land Rover. 'Tents, four, sleeping bags, four,' he pointed to each in turn, 'Stoves, two, rations and provisions for five days.'

'Five days?' Kate asked sharply.

'One can never be too careful,' muttered Muddle, staring into the distance.

Kate sighed. 'Right, kids, let's get this lot into the car.'

'One moment, if I may,' Muddle interrupted. 'I am proposing a slight change of plan.'

Kate's heart sank. What new depths of heartiness would Muddle propose now?

'Given the unfortunate visitation yesterday, I suggest that we allow Mr Jones here, an expert driver in my experience, to take the Rolls while we proceed to our destination in this Land Rover. That way, if our unwelcome friends are looking out for us, they will not find us.'

Kate nodded firmly. 'Fine. Let's do that. If I never see those two again it will be too soon. A Land Rover is much more suitable for this kind of stuff anyway.'

They quickly transferred everything from the Rolls. Kate walked over to where Mr Jones was discreetly standing back.

'Where will you put the Rolls?'

'Oh, we'll find somewhere safe for you, madam, and return it to you when you are back home.'

Muddle walked over. 'Everything seems shipshape and Bristol fashion. Shall we be on our way?'

'Certainly,' nodded Kate. 'I'm almost looking forward to it.'

Muddle turned to the other man. 'Thank you for your assistance. We will contact you when we know our ETA.'

'No problem, sir. We'll be ready.'

They were soon on the motorway. Kate allowed Muddle to drive and settled back, enjoying the hum of the tyres on the road surface as they drove further away from the events of the last twenty-four hours. But something did not fit. She leaned over to Muddle.

'Why did that Mr Jones call you sir?'

Muddle glanced awkwardly across. 'A well brought-up young man with fine manners, I thought.'

'Uh, huh. And who are 'we'?'

'Sorry?'

'As in, "We'll be ready".'

'Ah.'

'Yes, Muddle, ah. Is there something you would like to tell me?'

'Not really.'

'Muddle, you have always been scrupulously honest. Indeed, you were shocked that time in the casino when I suggested otherwise. Now, come on. There's something fishy going on here and I want to know.'

'Kate, if I have ever or indeed am now concealing any matter, then it is because it is better for you not to know.'

Kate felt her heartbeat abruptly quicken. 'OK, now you're really spooking me. Muddle, you have a choice. Either you leave me to imagine all sorts of terrible scenarios that all end in the mutilation and death of me and my children or you tell me what the hell is happening.'

'Tell her about the spying stuff, Muddle,' Tom's voice came excitedly from the back seat.

Kate swung round. 'Spying stuff? What spying stuff. What have you been keeping from me, Tom?'

Tom grinned smugly back. 'Only the stuff that you wouldn't let me tell you.'

'Yeah, mum,' Miranda butted in, 'You really should listen to us sometimes. Just because we are younger doesn't mean we're stupid and stuff, you know.'

Kate opened her mouth to explain that this was exactly what being young meant then, remembering her own behaviour over the last few days, thought better of it. She turned back to Muddle.

'Well?'

Muddle dipped his head and gave a wry grin. 'Yes, thank you.'

'Muddle, no-one likes a smartarse. I'm sure your mother explained that to you.'

'Not in those exact words, no.'

'Explain yourself.'

Muddle sighed. 'Well, firstly, I need to correct young Thomas. I am not a spy.'

'But…'

'No, Thomas, it is important to be aware that not everything that appears on the internet is accurate. Sadly, the democratisation of information that that innovative medium represents has led to certain parties, either out of stupidity, mendacity or sheer bloody-mindedness, to treat rumour as fact, lies as truth and conspiracy theory as proven reportage. In my view, many people today do not have enough excitement in their lives and feel the need to fabricate. They should, as the expression goes, get out more, go hiking or climb a mountain.'

Kate was already feeling lost. 'So, what did it say, this internet thing?'

'Oh, it was the random and rather fevered jottings of a junior member of the security forces, desperate for a publishing contract after he was sacked for incompetence. I suspect he just pulled a list of names out of some filing cabinet that should have been better secured.'

'But he had your name,' Kate cut in. 'What was your name doing in the filing cabinet in the first place?'

'I have, occasionally, done a couple of small tasks for HMG, in a purely advisory manner.'

'HMG?'

'Her Majesty's Government.'

'What sort of small tasks?'

'I can't really say. Let us say just that there are times when certain discussions or meetings might be embarrassing for a person in an official position.'

'How did you get into that sort of thing?'

'A gentleman approached me one day, in the bar of the Continental Hotel in Nairobi, as I recall, where I was working as a barman. It was there that I invented the Nairobi Knuckleduster, one part gin, one part brandy, guava juice, fresh, of course…'

'Muddle.'

'I'm sorry. Anyway, after some polite preliminaries, he suggested that I might be able to serve my country.'

'But not as a spy?'

'As a travelling occasional supernumerary member of the Foreign Office. An odd job man, if you wish. But no, not as a spy.'

Kate stared across at Muddle as he sat, calmly, behind the wheel and realised just how little she knew of this man. Behind him, the English countryside flashed by, the familiar mix of lush and dusty greens of late summer. She felt completely disorientated, as if someone had rearranged all her furniture without telling her.

'So what on earth brought you to Teddington?'

'Last year my dear mother became most unwell, so I felt the need to return. I had spent so little time in Britain that I had forgotten what a verdant paradise it was. So, when she passed, I decided to spend some time here.'

'But how did that bring you to be working as a doorman in a brothel?'

'Brothel?' Two excited voices from the back seat chimed in together as two bodies leant suddenly forward.

'Never you mind,' commanded Kate.

'Come on, Mum,' Miranda wailed. 'You can't drop a word like brothel into the conversation and expect us not to be just a little bit interested. What were you up to?'

As Kate was desperately searching for an answer, her phone rang. Thankfully she grabbed it from her jacket pocket waving a finger at the kids that, she hoped, conveyed 'I have the perfect answer to that but you'll have to wait'. 'Home' showed on her phone's display. God, The Mother. Good timing, for once. Taking a deep breath, she answered.

'Hello.'

'Hello, poppet. It's your Dad.'

Kate breathed a sigh of relief. 'Hello, Daddy.'

'How are you?'

'Oh, fine. Just off for a camping trip, actually.'

'Camping? You?' Her father could not have sounded more astonished. 'You do know that there's no room service when you're camping, don't you? No en suite. No a la carte…'

'Alright, Daddy. Enough. It'll be, well, an experience.'

Her father's laughter boomed down the phone. 'I hope you have Muddle with you.'

'Well, actually, yes, though…'

'Thank God. Then there's a chance of seeing you again.' His laughter died quickly as he realised what he had said. 'Actually, that's partly why I'm calling.'

'Yes?' Kate waited, not sure what to say.

'I thought I'd just give you a call, you know, see how you

are.'

'Fine. Really. It's been … eventful but I'm OK.'

'How's Boris?'

'I don't know, Daddy. I haven't seen him since Sheffield.'

'Oh. I'm sorry.'

'Well, yes. We all make mistakes.'

Silence hung between them. Finally, Kate spoke.

'What's up, Daddy? Is it Mum?'

'Well, in a way.'

'Is she OK?'

'Oh, yes.' Did Kate hear a tinge of regret? 'She's out, at one of her committees, I suppose.'

'Oh, Daddy. Look, why don't you come and stay for a while?'

'Well, yes, thank you, poppet. I think I might. I mean, the garden doesn't need so much work now.'

'I'd like that. So, what's the matter with Mum, as if I need to ask.'

'Oh, well.' A dry laugh. 'Yes, that, but there's something else. She had a call the other night. From Stephen.'

Kate jerked forward in her seat, startling the others. 'What did he say?'

'I don't know, I'm afraid. Your mother wouldn't say, said it was none of my business. But, you know, I answered the call and it was strange.'

'Strange? In what way?'

'Well, you'd expect if someone was calling from China that the line might be a bit fuzzy. But, you know, it was as clear as a bell. I mean, I don't know much about modern phones but it does seem a bit odd. As if he was just around the corner. I just thought you ought to know.'

Kate stared out of the window, watching the cars on the other carriageway flash by. What had been a suspicion now seemed a certainty. She surprised herself by feeling very calm.

'Did you dial 1471.'

'Did I what?'

'1471. It tells you the number that called.'

'Oh. No, sorry. Didn't know about that.'

'Never mind. Daddy, I think he may be in this country.'

'Really. But he's supposed to be … I mean, how do you know?'

'I don't. I'm just putting two and two together.'

'Oh.' Silence again. 'Well, I'll listen out for him. If he calls again, I'll do that … what was the number again?'

'1471.'

'OK, I'll write it down. Whoops, I can hear your mother coming back. I'd better go.'

'OK, Daddy, thanks for the call. I'll call you when we're back and we can arrange your visit.'

But he had already rung off.

She slipped the phone back into her pocket and sat, staring at her feet. Muddle glanced across.

'Developments?'

'Yes. Something's up. Stephen, it seems he's definitely around. Here, in England, as Miss, um, Davies implied. He phoned my mother.'

Muddle's eyebrows shot up. 'Miss Davies?'

'Sorry, I didn't have time to tell you.' Kate started to explain the conversation with Miss Davies.

Tom interrupted from the back seat. 'Mum, are you saying that Dad's in the country?'

'Well, maybe. I'm not sure.'

Tom thought for a moment. 'Well, I suppose he'll get in touch if he is around.' He shrugged dismissively. 'Now, what about this brothel stuff? More. More.'

Muddle leaned back. 'Your mother exaggerates for effect. She and I held perfectly respectable positions of some authority and responsibility in a club, catering for a broad range of requirements including an excellent restaurant and some gambling tables. Nothing untoward was going on. Indeed, a police inspection confirmed that it was run in accordance with its licence.'

Kate was once again impressed at Muddle's ability to present the truth in such a positive way.

Tom gave a disappointed frown. 'Doesn't sound nearly as interesting now,' he muttered. 'I mean, "my mum works in a brothel" would be a great opening line for the school debating challenge.'

'Tom, don't even think it, not if you want to grow up with all your limbs. Now, Muddle, I haven't forgotten what we are talking about. Back to my question, why Teddington?'

'At this juncture, I would prefer not to go into too much detail about that.'

Kate thought for a moment. 'It's about Boris, or whatever his name really is, isn't it?'

'Well, as you already know, Mr Boris is something of a well-known character, what with him being a billionaire.' I wish people wouldn't keep reminding me, thought Kate. I must be one of the very few girls in this world who's told a billionaire to sod off. Some kind of distinction, I suppose. 'As you also know only too well,' Muddle continued, 'there are certain people who wish to, let us say, have a forceful discussion with him about whether this money rightly belongs elsewhere.'

'So, that's why he can't go back to Russia.'

'Exactly.'

'And..?'

Muddle shrugged. 'People want to ensure that no harm comes to him while he's here.'

'People?'

A nod, no more.

'That was nice of them.'

'Self interest, to be honest. To them, he means business opportunities, tax revenue, and similar pecuniary benefits.'

'Oh, I see. Yes, I suppose no one does something for nothing at that level. Oh, and IDG, the letters on the bedroom wall; how do they fit in?'

'They are the initials of his company's name in Russian. Tom would not have found them on the internet – Russians do not see any great value in sharing information.'

'Service station, one mile. Need a pee,' Tom announced from the back.

'OK,' sighed Kate, doing away with the 'you should have gone before we left' speech. 'I need a strong coffee anyway.'

The car pulled in and stopped. Kate swung out of the door then had to steady herself. Her legs felt as firm as liquorice. She leaned against the Land Rover, pretending to tidy her hair. She had felt surprisingly calm during the conversation. In a way, it had not really come as a great shock. The air of mystery that had always hung round Muddle allowed anything to be possible and being a whatever he was, one of the security force's little helpers, seemed as naturally appropriate for him as someone else announcing that they were a plumber.

Clearly, her body did not agree with her brain. After the last 24 hours, it had had enough shocks and was announcing the fact forcefully by not letting her put one leg in front of the other.

She turned to the others. 'You go ahead and get me a cappuccino with an extra shot. I just want to get some fresh air.'

'OK, mum, got any money?' Tom asked.

Armed with a ten pound note, her two children ran off.

Muddle hung back. 'May I be of assistance?'

'No, thank you, Muddle. I'll be fine. All just a bit too much.'

'As you wish. Well, if you'll excuse me, nature calls. I'll leave the keys with you. Lock up if you decide to come in.'

Kate leaned back and looked up at the clear sky, breathing deeply. 'I'm Kate Bradshaw, née Bostock from Sheffield. I live in Teddington,' she muttered. 'I go to the gym. I meet my friends for coffee. This sort of stuff doesn't happen to me. Can I have my life back, please?'

But, even as she was saying it, she knew that she didn't want to go back, would never go back to the old life. She scanned the dreary, litter-strewn car park and even here felt excited. She remembered as a child her first visit to a fun fair. Holding tight to her father's hand, she had felt her heart pounding, feeling the whirling noise and flashing lights cascade over and through her. She couldn't remember ever being as excited since. Until now. Even yesterday's terrible experience was bearable, almost, because it was part of this new life.

A large black car had pulled in just after them and was parked some distance away. Kate imagined it to be full of enemy spies. She giggled, took a deep breath and carefully pushed herself away from the car. She didn't fall. Head down, she walked towards the service station, remote locking the Land Rover as she went.

A double strength cappuccino and Kate was ready to get back on the road. They sat in companionable silence. The kids plugged themselves into their iPods and Kate was glad of the opportunity to absorb everything she had heard. She forced herself to think back over the time she had known Muddle. Images paraded before her. He stood in his bright red doorman's uniform, condemning her car to the rear car park, quietly threatening the drunk who had waylaid her. None of it seemed to be planned infiltration. But what about his sudden appearance in the car park during the raid, just as she and Anastasia were about to drive off? Certainly not chance. If this man was supposed to be looking after Boris, why was he at the club with his sister? If she was his sister. And what was he here for now, with them? The more she thought about what Muddle had told her, the more she realised how little he had revealed.

Her mind spun; it was all too difficult to work out. Had this man just been manipulating her all the time? But then she thought of all the kindness and consideration he had shown her.

So many questions, but she did not feel up to re-opening the conversation with him. She closed her eyes and let it all drift away for a while.

She was awakened by a change in the steady rhythm of the engine. They were pulling off the motorway onto a side road.

'Where are we?'

'Four miles north of Lyndhurst, some twelve miles from our destination.'

'What's the plan?'

'Well, an army marches on its stomach so I suggest that that we ensure that lunch occurs in the very near future.'

'Sounds good. Will we stop somewhere?'

'I propose that we stop in Lyndhurst for some extra comestibles, then continue to our destination, since it is so close. I was able to arrange with Mr Jones for appropriate provisions but I noticed that the supply was rather short of fresh fruit and veg. One must have one's five a day.'

'Good. I need to freshen up anyway. There's bound to be a public loo or a local pub I can use.'

They pulled into the car park in Lymington. Miranda and Tom were sent off to find bread. Muddle and Kate found a stall in the High Street that provided all the fruit and veg they needed, Muddle carefully checking each piece and its origin. Kate spotted a half-timbered pub across the road.

'I'm just popping in over there to use the loo. Do you want to join me? I mean, well, you know what I mean.'

Muddle smiled. 'Well, I suppose it would be impolite to use their services and not purchase their wares.'

The pub was dark as they stepped in out of the sunshine. Muddle pointed out the Ladies and Kate, after placing an order for a small white wine, headed off. She emerged a few minutes later. Muddle was seated at the bar. She started to walk across to him, then froze. The world seemed to stop, sounds echoed in her head. She was aware of Muddle jumping from the bar stool and heading over to her. One sound, one voice resonated over and over again. Muddle was beside her, his arm supporting her elbow.

'What is it, Kate?'

She held up her hand. 'Wait.'

She turned back, focusing on the voice. There it was again. Unmistakable. Signalling to Muddle to stay where he was, she walked towards it. She arrived beside a table at the back of the pub. Two men faced each other.

'So, as you'd imagine, dealing with old Johnny Chinaman was … Oh fuck.' The man looked up, open-mouthed.

'Hello, Stephen,' Kate said quietly. 'It's been a while.'

'Kate.' He made no attempt to stand up. Kate looked across at the other man, hair dragged over a balding pate, stomach oozing over his belt.

'And George. I'm beginning to understand why you didn't return my calls.'

'Kate, my dear, this is not what it seems.'

'Really? Let's have a look at how it seems. It seems like my ex-husband and my now ex-lawyer, I'd say, are sitting in a pub in Southern England together when he is supposed to be in China and you are supposed to be chasing him for my money. Tell me, which bit of this am I getting wrong?' Kate's voice had risen from its earlier quiet tone to something close to a shout. The other conversations had died away, discreet Home Counties eyes turned towards them.

'Kate, please,' Stephen whispered. 'There's no need to make a scene.'

'You think so?' she spat back. 'Do you know, I think this is the one supreme moment in my life where making a scene is really, really the right thing to do. Or you can start talking.'

Stephen held his hands up. 'OK, OK. Look, why don't you sit down?'

Aware that, for the second time today, her legs felt like giving way, Kate was tempted. But she had to keep the upper hand.

'I'll stand.'

George half rose from his seat. 'I think I'll just...'

'Sit.'

He subsided.

She turned back to Stephen. 'Well?'

He spread his hands. 'Kate, it's complicated.'

'Simplify it for me,' she said with a tight smile. 'You know how thick I am.'

'Yes. I mean, Kate, you've changed, you're more...' He looked past Kate, to her right. 'Excuse me, can I help you? This is a private conversation, you know.'

Kate turned. 'Stephen, this is Muddle. Muddle, this is the poisonous, goat-faced blowfish that I used to be married to.'

Muddle kept a straight face and bowed slightly. 'How do you do?'

'Well,' said Kate, 'Now that we have the formalities out of the way, I'm waiting.'

'OK. Look, in a nutshell, I'm broke. About the time of the divorce, I lost my job. I couldn't pay the alimony so I just decided the best answer was to disappear.'

'Oh, I see.' Kate stood, nonplussed, not sure what to say next. Muddle leaned forward and whispered in her ear. Kate nodded.

'Sounds possible and I would believe it, if it were not for a couple of things.'

'What are those?' Stephen asked cautiously.

'One, my banker tells me you have plenty of money in your account on a regular basis.' Kate liked the sound of 'my banker'; she would use it again somewhere. 'And two, you are sitting down with Lardarse here and I know his hourly rate. He wouldn't even bugger his office boy without being paid for it.'

'I say...' George's rich tones butted in.

Kate glared at him. 'Quiet, George. You're in enough trouble already.'

Muddle leaned forward and whispered again.

'And another thing. The way you manipulated my mother. I don't know exactly what the plan is, Stephen, but I know there is one.'

Stephen glared at her from under his eyebrows. A long silence. He leaned over the table.

'If I wasn't broke, I certainly would have been, paying you that much.'

'Stephen...' George tried to interrupt. 'Careful.'

Stephen waved him away.

'She can't do anything about it. She's got neither the wits nor the money. Frankly, Kate, I didn't see why you should get the money that I worked hard for, while you sat around having a twenty-year lunch with your poisonous friends. George, as you say, has his price but was more than happy to ensure that you never found me and never got the money.'

'Do you know, I think I will sit down. Muddle, would you be kind enough to get my drink?'

As Muddle walked away, Stephen leaned in. 'What is that, exactly? I mean, he's surely not your significant other.'

Kate smiled broadly at Stephen. 'Oh, yes, and I have to say,' she raised her voice, 'It's wonderful at last to understand what really good sex is after so many years of your amateur fumblings.' Kate was happy to hear a murmur run round the bar. 'How is your new toy, by the way? Tiger Lily, wasn't it? Poor girl.'

'Lin Sen,' Stephen replied through gritted teeth.

"Ah, so that's how the postcards got sent from China. Tiger Lily's family, no doubt.'

'OK, you've had your little moment, Kate. Why don't you just run along now and let me get on with my life?'

'No, I don't think so. Not just yet.'

Muddle returned with the drinks and sat by George, blocking his escape. Stephen turned back to Kate.

'Look, I mean it, you're getting nothing. So, just wiggle your middle aged arse out of here and out of my life.'

Kate's eyes widened. 'You know, up till that last little comment, I was starting to feel sorry for you. You're right; I did make a career out of spending your money. But I have to remind you, Stephen, that's what you wanted. You wanted a little wifey who'd scrub up and look good when needed and be at home when you got back from work so you could be treated as the big beast in the jungle. Well, medium-sized beast anyway. There's nothing big about you, Stephen, and I mean that very sincerely.'

Stephen glared back. 'You're still not getting anything.'

Muddle leaned forward. 'Perhaps I should, at this juncture, introduce myself more fully. My full nomenclature is Alfred Bertrand Alderton-Muddle.'

'So?' Stephen shrugged.

'Chief Inspector Alfred Bertrand Alderton-Muddle.' He reached into his top pocket and drew out a small leather wallet. He flicked it open to show a very official badge.

The two men looked at him in horror-struck silence. Kate struggled to fix an expression on her face that looked as if this was not a surprise to her too.

'Oh, fuck,' muttered Stephen for the second time in five minutes.

'Yes,' nodded Muddle with apparent sympathy, 'an apposite response in the circumstances. Those circumstances being, of course, ones that can be repeated fully and verbatim in a court of law.'

Kate took a swig of her wine. She put her glass back down carefully, trying hard to disguise the shaking of her hand.

George grasped Stephen's arm. 'I would advise you to say nothing further.'

'Bit late for that, I think,' muttered Stephen.

Kate realised that she had not breathed for some time and took a very deep breath. She turned to her ex-husband.

'So, shall we make a deal?'

'What do you want?'

'Stephen, what I want right now is to see you hung from that rather nice old oak beam up there by your balls. However, given that that would cause this pub a major health and safety problem, let's talk money.'

'Go on.'

'You do understand that I could take you to the cleaners now, don't you?'

Stephen gave a short nod.

'And that I would be fully justified to do so.'

He stared back at her, motionless. Kate raised an eyebrow and waited. He gave a conceding shrug.

'OK. Here's the deal. You pay the backlog of the last two months. You pay the interest charges on my credit card. You pay all the house bills and you get the car people off my back. After that, I'm going to sell the house, move somewhere smaller and we will split the difference. Then I'm going to get a qualification and a job and pay for myself.' Stephen's eyebrows shot up. 'And if you laugh at this point the price will double.' He instantly reset his face to interested listening. 'Until then, you pay as agreed. You see, Stephen, I'm bored with the idea of doing nothing. And I'm worth more than you will ever pay me. You'll keep paying for the kids, of course, and the odd extra whenever I say. That way, at least, you can keep Tiger Lily in all the Chop Suey she wants.'

Stephen glanced over at George, who sat studying his fingernails. He sighed.

'I don't seem to have any choice.'

'Oh, you have a choice, but it would be much, much more expensive.' She turned to George. 'And as for you,' she saw with pleasure that sweat was running down his forehead. 'You will ensure that his payments arrive on time, every time, a service that you will not charge me a penny for. One day late and you will be shopped, defrocked or whatever happens to you parasites.'

George nodded vigorously.

Kate turned to Muddle. 'Well, I think our work here is done. Shall we?'

Muddle nodded and stood up. Kate followed, rather shakily. On the table next to them, two older men were sitting over their pints, gazing admiringly at her. Kate leaned over them.

'Excuse me, I wonder if I might....'

She took a nearly full pint glass, turned back and threw its contents in Stephen's face.

'Yes,' she hissed, 'your children are both well. Thanks for asking.'

She replaced the glass on the table.

'Thank you,' she murmured to the older man and headed for the door as Muddle discretely pressed a five pound note into the astonished man's hand.

The profound silence in the pub was suddenly broken by the sound of clapping as a woman who had been sitting with friends nearby rose to her feet. She was joined by more and more. Kate swept out on a wave of applause, turning at the door to take a deep bow.

Once outside, she threw her arms into the air and let out a

loud whoop.

'God, that felt good.' She turned to Muddle, dropping her arms. 'Now, I feel sick.' He caught her as she stumbled forward and eased her onto a nearby bench.

'Deep breaths. Head between your legs,' he commanded. Kate obeyed and, after a few minutes, felt better. They slowly made their way back to the car.

Muddle walked beside her, his hand under her arm. 'I suggest that we refrain from sharing this with the children at this time.'

'Yes, I suppose you're right. I don't think they'd want to see their father in his present state and I dare say he won't want to see them. But I'll make sure he does see them. He needs to be part of their world whether he likes it or not.'

'If I may be so bold, I thought you were quite magnificent in there.'

'Well, thanks, Muddle. That's kind but a lot of it is down to you. Well, you and Boris, I suppose.'

'Well, one does what one can but flowers only bloom in fertile soil.'

'Thank you, Muddle. I don't think I've ever been called compost in such a complementary way before.'

Muddle gave a little bow. 'My pleasure, my dear.'

'By the way, Chief Inspector? I thought you stuck to the truth.'

'Kenyan Police Force, honorary position. Always carry it with me. Something of a talisman. And people are so lazy about actually reading badges; I didn't feel it necessary to elucidate. Oh, and I'd be grateful if you did not divulge my Christian names to the children.'

Kate grinned back. 'Your secret is safe with me. I have already forgotten that you are called Alfred Bertrand.'

Muddle winced and walked on.

'By the way, Muddle, I don't suppose you had anything to do with that chance encounter.'

The small man smiled. 'The world is full of wonders and mysteries."

Kate knew that was all she was going to get on that subject.

They reached the car. Tom and Miranda were standing by, each gnawing at the end of a baguette.

'You've taken your time. We're starving.'

'Me too,' grinned Kate. 'Let's go and find that camping spot.'

Chapter 24
SUNDAY LUNCHTIME

Muddle's choice was inspired, a small glade off the main road. A stream ran through it and there were views beyond the trees over the gently rolling countryside. Kate lay back on the grass chewing happily on a ham baguette. She felt freer than she had for many years. More important, she felt herself, a real person rather than someone's wife or someone's mum. Or someone's daughter.

The kids wandered off to look at some ponies nearby. Muddle walked over and sat down by her.

'Did you have a plan for the eventuality of meeting your former spouse or was that spontaneous?'

'Bit of both, I think, really. What with everything that's been happening recently, I've sort of changed my expectations. I don't want to be sitting around any more waiting for someone else to pick up the bill. And that reminds me, I can pay you back soon.'

'No need. I'll put it on expenses. The government can afford it.'

'OK, won't argue with that. Thank you.' Kate reached over and put her hand on his arm. 'And thanks for everything.'

'I can genuinely say it's been my pleasure.'

'You know, I'm really looking forward to actually doing something.'

'What will you do?'

'Don't know. Something to do with kids, I think.'

'Kids? As in children?'

'Yes, I know. Sounds a bit weird, coming from me. But when I think back to when Miranda and Tom were small, I really enjoyed that time. Maybe it's because I'm on their intellectual level.'

'You do persist in underestimating yourself. What about the retentive memory?'

'Oh, no more cards, that's for sure. If I never see the

inside of a casino again, that's fine by me.'

A silence fell between them. They both sat looking out at the view.

'And what about Mr Boris?'

'Ah, yes, Boris. I suppose life as a billionaire's bit of stuff would have been fun. But it's not going to happen, is it? And not very dignified for a girl of my age.'

Muddle looked at her, raising his eyebrows.

'Yes, Muddle, I'm finally admitting that I'm not twenty-five. Bit of a breakthrough, wouldn't you say?'

He nodded slowly. 'Would you like to see him again?'

'It does feel like unfinished business. I mean, there's no chance of anything, you know, happening now, not after what I said to him, but I'd like to wish him luck and so on.'

Muddle sprang up. 'Let's get those tents up. Then we can relax.'

'I thought we were relaxed.'

'Carpe diem, Kate.' He reached out a hand and pulled her up.

Kate called the children back and they all helped to unload the Land Rover. It seemed to Kate that Muddle had to give each tent just one tug and they leapt into their shape.

'How do you do that?'

'A new design. Held under tension, release the tension and you have a tent. Invented by a Frenchman, I believe. The French are always expert, I have found, at creating the elegant labour-saving device. I find the Moulinex mixer a thing of beauty as well as of great functionality.'

Kate, who could not remember ever using a mixer, nodded solemnly and carried on unpacking the provisions. To her immense surprise, she was enjoying herself here, miles away from her civilisation. Even the sight of the instant cappuccino packs peeping out from the top of the box of provisions did not make her yearn for home.

Within half an hour, four tents were erected in a circle, bedding laid out for the night in each one and the spare provisions stored back in the Land Rover. Muddle surveyed the scene.

'Excellent. Well done, team. Now, wood foraging party. I suggest young Tom and I.'

'Excuse me,' Miranda chipped in. 'Sexist or what? Where does it say that a girl can't collect wood? Are you scared I'll tear my crinolines, whatever they are?'

Muddle bowed deeply. 'My apologies. I'm afraid that the subtleties of the role of the female in Western contemporary society have rather passed me by. For me, time is indeed out of joint.'

'Well,' responded Miranda cheerfully, 'better than your joints being out of time.' And with that she led the party away.

Kate watched them disappear. She walked away from them, to the stream, and knelt down letting the cool water run over her hands. She pictured herself coming home to a small house, a cottage, perhaps, after a day working with the children in the local school. She liked what she saw. She felt an excitement building, expanding in her chest, and it was as if she herself expanded with it. She smiled as she recognised the beginnings of a long-lost sensation of self-worth. Her reflection, broken up by the ripples of the stream, smiled back.

So did a face behind her.

CHAPTER 25
LATER THAT SUNDAY

A black-gloved hand clamped over her mouth. She was jerked backwards and flattened onto the ground. She felt stones and sticks press sharply into her back. Above her, the face of the smooth-talking Englishwomen, a face she had hoped never to see again.

'We meet again, Mrs Bradshaw,' she whispered.

Kate's eyes, wide with terror, stared back at her.

'You weren't quite honest with us, were you?'

Kate nodded desperately.

'Where is he, Mrs Bradshaw?'

The figure of the man came into Kate's view. He nodded in the direction that Muddle and the kids had taken, then reached down and grabbed her arm.

'Time we took a little ride, Mrs Bradshaw.'

He dragged her to her feet and the two of them, one either side of her, set off at a run out of the glade and towards the road, pulling her along, her feet barely touching the ground.

Ahead of them, a black car stood. Kate realised that she had seen it before, in the service station car park.

They threw her into the back seat. The man jumped in beside her, with the Englishwoman behind the wheel in an instant. The car leapt forward along the path towards the main road. Kate desperately looked behind her but there was no one.

The main road came rapidly closer and with it the loss of any hope. Kate closed her eyes. Suddenly, she was thrown forward as the car braked hard. Her eyes flew open. She grabbed the back of the seat in front of her. Ahead, two police cars had appeared, blocking the way to the main road. The Englishwoman swore and threw the car into reverse. It shot backwards up the path. Kate spun round to look out of the rear window. There, coming down the path, was Muddle's Land

Rover. She felt a sense of elation overwhelm the terror.

The big car slewed to a halt.

'Come.' The man beside her grabbed her and dragged her out. He stood, holding her as her feet scrabbled for purchase on the leafy ground. Police were piling out of their cars. Kate recognised the mysterious Mr Jones from earlier. Then she felt cold metal against the side of her head.

The man shouted. 'Stay where you are.' Everyone froze.

The Englishwoman slowly came round from the other side of the car.

'Dimitri. Forget it. It's over. Just put down the gun.'

'No.' Kate felt Dimitri's arm tighten around her neck as he dragged her backwards.

Straight into Muddle, who had noiselessly come up behind them. A sharp chop to the back of the neck and Dimitri was a heap on the ground. The tall English woman nodded her approval. 'Neat.' She turned towards the policeman. 'Well, gentlemen, shall we?'

Kate clung onto Muddle as the other men led their captives away. She took great gasps of breath, aware now that she had barely breathed for the last five minutes.

'Kate, I'm so sorry. I dropped my guard,' Muddle whispered.

'Yes, you bloody did,' she sobbed. 'How did they find us? What did they want?'

'A couple of freelancers, didn't fall for the car swap. It seems they wanted the reward for delivering Mr Boris.'

'Reward?'

'Yes, it was not only the Russian government that wanted to talk with our friend about his shareholding in one of their most profitable businesses. Unfortunately, several other, even less salubrious organisations saw an opportunity to make a lot of money and were more than willing to pay for that.'

'And you knew they were coming?' Kate's voice rose up the octaves and decibels. She felt indignation soar through her at being used as a lure.

'I knew that they had pursued us but my understanding

was that our friends in the local constabulary, ably abetted by our Mr Jones, would pre-empt their arrival. It seems that police are not to be relied on for punctuality nowadays. Most vexing.'

'Most vexing? Most bloody vexing? I am grabbed, half strangled, threatened with a gun and the best you can come up with is "most vexing"?'

'My apologies. An inappropriate understatement. But I assure you that such a thing will never happen again.'

'And how exactly can you assure me of that?'

'Because Mr Boris has already done the deal on IDG with the Russian government. Our friends here were rather behind the game. That is what leads me to believe that they are freelancers, out to sell Mr Boris to the highest bidder.'

'That's horrible.'

'Indeed. It is sadly true that there are many in this fine world who would sell their grandmother for a day old lamb and a bag of sugar, as the Albanians put it. I fear that they were never taught the correct way to behave. Though I am surprised by the English lady. I detect the Cockney accent to be fake and note some signs of breeding. Her tie was, I believe, of old Etonian designation. Clearly well-connected.'

'The bastard Stephen is the product of a good school. Doesn't guarantee anything, I'm afraid, other than knowing how to choose wine and total emotional constipation. But look, Muddle, there may be other freelancers, as you call them. How do we, or rather you, stop these others from getting to us?'

'The deal on the shares will be in the papers tonight. After that, the hunt is off.'

'And what about Boris? Will he be safe?'

'He'll have to be careful, a sad necessity for any rich man nowadays. But no more than any other.'

'So, still rich, then,' Kate sighed.

'Oh, yes. Not perhaps a billionaire any more. But enough for a sheep in the shed and a wall against the East wind.'

'Albanian again?'

'Hungarian.'

Kate took a deep breath. 'I must be getting used to this. I

feel really quite calm. Though I'm not sure about sleeping in a tent… Oh, God, the kids. Where are they?'

'Never fear. Mr Jones and his team have them quite safe. They have told them everything is all right.'

'And is it, really?'

Muddle turned to face Kate. 'My dear, I promise you, it's over. Your life goes on as you wish it to.'

Kate looked hard at him. She had every reason to trust him but not enough reasons to be sure that he was always right.

'You know, Muddle, I don't think I will ever quite be able to lead the life I wish, as you put it, whatever that may be. I feel like I'll always be looking over my shoulder, especially without you around. But, the funny thing is, well, funny peculiar, is that I wouldn't have changed any of it. Maybe rather less of the total terror bits but I am really so glad that my life has changed. Just before those men arrived, I was feeling so, I don't know, free. I guess what I'm getting to is that a bit of looking over the shoulder is a price worth paying, I suppose. Does that make sense?'

Muddle nodded. 'A very balanced and mature view. I don't suppose you would consider a career with the rather specialised part of the police with whom I tend to work, would you? They could use someone like you.'

Kate laughed out loud. 'Now that's just…' She was interrupted by her phone ringing in the back pocket of her jeans. She pulled it out. Number withheld.

'Hello.'

'Kate, it's Boris.'

'Oh.' She could not think what to say and stood, holding the phone tightly.

'Hello, are you there?'

'Yes, sorry, Boris, I'm here. Just a bit of a shock.' At Boris's name, Muddle stepped discreetly away.

'Are you OK?'

'Yes, I'm fine. Been a bit of a bumpy ride but I'm, yeah, I'm fine.'

'That's very good.'

Kate felt the silence press in on her. 'Um, how about you. We thought we saw you on the television, coming out of that hotel.'

'Oh, that. Yes, that was me. Damn TV cameras just when I didn't want them. Look, did Muddle tell you what's been happening?'

'About you selling the shares? Yes.'

'That's why I was down there. No-one's going to think that international deals are going on in Bournemouth.'

'I suppose not. Hey, how's Miss Ferguson?'

'Oh, she and her friend are having a lovely time, taking hearty walks. Their part of the hotel wasn't even damaged. I've paid for them to stay until the end of next week.'

'And you, Boris.' Kate felt her mouth go dry. 'What are you going to do?'

'I'm off to the States tonight to sort everything out. The paperwork is all over there. On my way to Heathrow now.'

'Oh.'

'Yes, it seems that people are rather impatient. Odd for a nation that is used to change taking centuries.'

'Yes, I suppose. What about Anastasia?'

'She'll come too. I can't leave her here on her own. Even Aunt Irena has had enough of her.'

'Maybe what's his name, Curly Manciati can help.'

'Not from high security jail.'

'You never did tell me the rest of that story.'

'No. Look, Kate, I'm sorry I put you through all this. It was not my intention.'

'It's OK, really.'

'I mean, another time, another place, you know.'

'Yes, I know.'

'Maybe, when everything has settled down, I could come back. We could meet up.' She heard a smile build in his voice. 'I could tell you the rest of the Curly Manciatti story then. And maybe a chance for that 'whatever' that we never got round to.'

'Don't count your chickens.'

'Sorry?'

'Old Albanian phrase,' Kate laughed. There was a puzzled silence at the other end. 'Never mind, I think I've just spent too long with Muddle. No, that would be nice.'

'Good. He's a good man, Muddle.'

'Yes, I know. Boris, listen, about Anastasia. Is she really your sister?'

'What? Yes, of course. There are times I wish she wasn't but, yes, I seem to be stuck with her. Why do you ask?'

'Oh, just something someone said. Made me wonder.'

'Look, Kate, I really am sorry. We, I haven't been fair to you. I will try to make it up to you.'

'Oh, you know…'

'Listen, we're arriving. We'll be in the tunnel in a minute. Look after yourself.'

'You too, Boris. You too.' Kate responded, hearing her voice shake.

'Bye.'

'Yes, bye.'

She lowered the phone. Took two deep breaths. Muddle was watching her carefully.

'Is all well?'

Kate rubbed her eyes. 'Oh, yes. All is well. Let's go back to the camp site.'

'We can return to London immediately, if you wish.'

Kate looked around her, taking in the view, smelling the clean air. 'No, I think we will stay. The kids will want to. Though I suspect that I will not sleep too soundly.'

'I will sleep across the door of your tent, my dear. I shall, as the Masai say, sleep the sleep of the desert rabbit.' Seeing Kate's blank expression, he explained, 'Asleep but aware of every sound and movement.'

'Oh, right. Thank you, Muddle.'

Later that evening, replete from one of the best dinners that Kate could remember, they sat, staring into the embers of the fire. For the first couple of hours, the kids had stayed very close to Kate, as if protecting her and themselves from any further attacks. Now, reassured by the calm setting, they had wandered off with their torches to look for badgers. Kate looked up.

'And what about you, Muddle? What will you do now? Any more odd jobs, saving the world?'

'No. I think I shall return to Kenya.'

Kate reached over and squeezed his hand.

'I shall miss you.'

'Oh, I shall return but, fine as this green and pleasant land may be, Kenya is home.'

'I'm glad you have somewhere you feel settled.'

'Well, I have a base there.'

'A base?'

'Yes. I have my family over there.'

Kate sat up suddenly. 'Muddle, you have a wife?'

'Wives, actually, and seven children, so far.'

Kate threw her head back and laughed out loud, her voice echoing through the woods.

'And I thought I had stopped underestimating you.'

'Well, life would be dull if there were no more surprises.'

'Wouldn't it just, Muddle? Wouldn't it just?'

ACKNOWLEDGEMENTS

When I look back on the gestation of this novel, so many people have helped along the way through the six drafts that have brought us to today. Because I've been able to share the story as it's evolved, it has not felt like the usual clichéd lonely journey.

Thank you to Siobhan Curham, who edited the book with great insight and gentle candour, right down to the last missing question mark. Thank you to every one at the writing groups, who listened and read with unwarranted attention and fed back really valuable observations. And, of course, eternal thanks to the ever-patient Jeannine.

I am grateful to all, even the 'if I was writing this, I'd ...' ones and the 'sorry but ...' and the 'shouldn't that be a semi-colon?' and the 'is that meant to be funny?' ones. They all made me think again, sometimes re-write, sometimes stick to my version, but always valuable.

RESPONSE

If you have enjoyed this book, do please post a review on Amazon. Indeed, if there's something you haven't enjoyed, let me know. It's all learning.

Do visit my website phillawderwriter.co.uk for more information about me, and the chance for us to have a direct conversation.

34327077R00190

Printed in Great Britain
by Amazon